DOORS OF DARKNESS II
TRICK OR TREAT

EDITED BY
CALEB J. PECUE

INTRODUCTION BY
BRIANA MORGAN

TERRORCORE
PUBLISHING

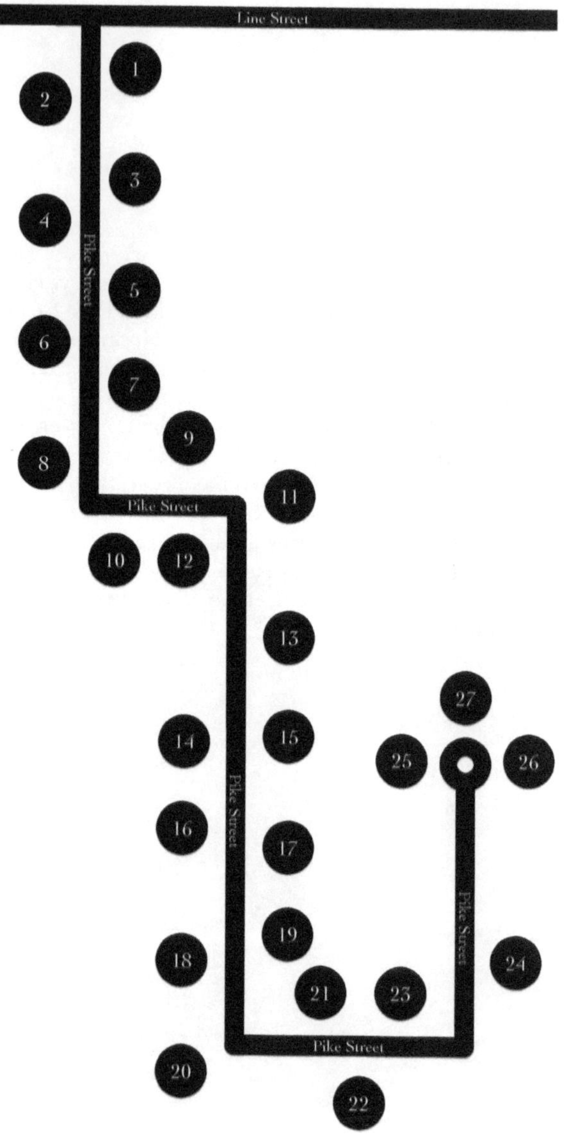

Line Street
Pike Street
Pike Street
Pike Street
Pike Street
Pike Street

Contents

WHAT FEELINGS DOES HALLOWEEN conjure for you? For some people, it brings visions of demons, fear, and superstition. For others, it represents comfort. It's flickering candles, children in costumes, haunted houses, and pumpkin spice. Since you've picked up this book, I'll assume you fall into the latter category. That's where I fall, too.

Every year since I was a child, I've waited eagerly for autumn. There's nothing like opening the windows to let a crisp breeze in, watching the leaves change colors, and spending hours watching horror movies on TV or carving jack-o'-lanterns with my family. The night before the main event, we always attended our church's fall festival. Everyone dressed in church-appropriate costumes, and we'd bob for apples and go from activity to activity collecting candy. This was far from the main event, but it helped set the tone for the magic to come.

On Halloween itself, my mom helped my brother and me dress up, and then she'd take us trick-or-treating through the neighborhood. Some of my fondest memories involve going door to door dressed as a cartoon character (Bubbles from *The Powerpuff Girls*, complete with a heinous plastic mask) or Disney princess (Sleeping Beauty). Once we got home, Mom and Dad checked our candy. They threw away anything unwrapped out of an abundance of caution. We only got to eat a little before bedtime, but I always went for my favorites — Tootsie Rolls, candy corn, and Blow Pops. In the lead-up to the main event, I also remember watching a lot of Halloween-themed family movies, including *Casper*, as well as Disney Channel movies like *Halloweentown*, *Hocus Pocus*, and *Don't Look Under the Bed*. As I got older, my tastes moved toward more traditional horror fare like *A Nightmare on Elm Street*, *Pet Sematary*, and *IT* (that TV miniseries haunted me).

When I was younger, Halloween felt endless. I felt something similar reading this anthology.

Beyond this introduction, you'll discover tales of terror that capture that quintessential Halloween spirit.

Perpetually locked in the 1980s, the characters in each loosely interconnected story face, fall victim to, and sometimes overcome the antics of All Hallow's Eve. From fighting back against bullies to playing a cursed computer game and more, each of these pieces provides the chance to step into spooky season and invites you to stay awhile. As unique as they are, they also do a phenomenal job of distilling whatever wicked elixir makes Halloween so special. This anthology has something for almost everyone — whatever your favorite flavor of horror, you're sure to find it here.

My love for horror fiction should surprise no one. I write, read, and devour as much of it as I can. Put simply, I like being scared. I like testing my limits in a safe environment where I have total control. My first spooky book was *Scary Stories to Tell in the Dark*. Shortly after that came *Goosebumps* and *Fear Street*. I had night terrors, but I couldn't stop. I just couldn't. I think it's in my blood.

At thirteen, I discovered *Cujo* by Stephen King. Since then, I've read much of King's work, but I've expanded to more diverse creators. Now, I read a lot of indie horror such as *The Worm and His Kings*, *We Need to Do Something*, and *To Be Devoured*. With reading, if you get too scared, you can put the book down — though, with this book, you won't want to.

So, sit back, relax, and get out that candy. Turn out the lights and get comfortable. You're in for a scary good time.

Briana Morgan
July 25th, 2024

GHASTLY NEIGHBOR
Caleb J. Pecue

THE CHILDGHOST JUMPED JOYFULLY AS the stair finally gave way to a very slight, audible creak. So slight, in fact, that no one but the childghost heard it. Not the elderly man who took residence there some time ago; not the other two specters across the room. Of course, their hearing wasn't what his was. They were old when they died and their ears didn't function quite the same. He heard it and that's all that mattered.

He jumped again, more determined. The stair creaked louder and one of the specters who was looking out the door frame's window turned her head, giving the childghost a side-eyed glance before returning to her nightly ritual.

The elderly man across the house coughed and wheezed. He had come down with something nasty, thought the childghost. Mother would have kept him in bed all day if it had been he instead of the elderly man. He wondered where his mother was now. She couldn't stay after he died.

Too hard.

Then the elderly man came, alone. Hardly a good replacement for his mother, he knew. But it was better than the house being constantly in the dark. No matter if he wasn't that interesting and kept to his humdrum routine. The childghost knew he'd be watching the news right about now with a pipe hanging from his mouth. A few cookie crumbs nestled in his long, white beard.

As he jumped for a third time, the male specter, who up until that point had been sitting in the corner smoking a phantom pipe of his own, grabbed his translucent arm, snatching him from midair, and hoisted him up higher. He snarled, exposing a patchwork of gnarled and decayed teeth. Dentistry must have been awfully expensive in his time, thought the childghost. And for a moment, the childghost felt a pain in his arm.

The male specter hissed, and he *heard* it.

He never heard them before.

They had always silently gone about their business and no matter how hard he had tried, he had never been able to make an audible sound. That was until tonight.

"S-S-S-Stop!" he cried out. Like the volume knob of a TV being turned up, it wasn't there and then it was, full and crescendoing. "Let me go!"

The male specter let go and the childghost hung there momentarily before coming down with a *thud*. He had seen the older ghosts hover before but he had never been able to. He had seen them pass through walls too but he didn't have that kind of power either. For all intents and purposes, he was only a boy: a very, very dead one, but a boy nonetheless.

"Brat!" shouted the female specter at the door. "You little pest! Why'd you have to go and die here?" Her voice was a tinny shrill, almost like a character from one of the childghost's favorite morning cartoons.

Before he had a moment to collect himself and realize what she was saying, the male specter slammed his fist on the banister. "Silence! Not more of your complaints this year! I won't have them!" The female moved her hand to her mouth and shifted back a few steps.

"I-I-I don't understand . . . " said the childghost, backing away from the staircase, away from the male specter. "How can —"

"It's all rather compli—" started the female.

"It's not that complicated. The veil between our worlds . . . that is the living and dead . . . is at its thinnest during Halloween."

"Is it really that time already?" the female questioned, returning to peer out the window. Had she really been looking carefully, she would have noticed the brown and umber colored leaves which lay here and there, but she wasn't looking at anything in particular. Just staring out, as she typically did, thought the childghost.

"What veil?" the childghost asked.

"Just our world and theirs, I suppose," the male said and the childghost didn't need to ask who *they* were in this, as the old man let out another hacking cough.

"Are we really going to have to listen to that everyday until that old bastard croaks?" the female said, matter-of-factly.

"So, is that why I can make sounds now?" asked the childghost.

"Sort of," the male specter said. "*We* could any day if we wanted but we aren't exactly new like you are. And after all these years, what do we really have left to say? But we are more accustomed to our way—"

"*Pfft*, if that's what you call it!" the female interjected.

"—to our way of life," the male continued, crossing the room from where he had come. He puffed on his translucent pipe and the childghost coughed as he breathed it in.

I really can smell again, thought the childghost and he wrinkled his nose in disgust.

The house didn't smell like it did when his mother was there and he was alive. Like freshly baked cookies and potpourri. Instead, it had the smell of an elderly home, which, if he could've placed it, was also the smell of death. He wasn't sure of the last time the old man left the house or opened a window.

Then came a sudden *knock* at the door which caused the childghost to jump. The female looked through the glass. "It's a child," she said.

"I'm not home! Go away!" shouted the elderly man

from across the house. "I don't have any candy, thank you very much! Ate it all myself!"

He laughed and a fresh bout of coughing commenced.

The knocking continued and while the elderly man was content to ignore it, the childghost couldn't help but attempt to turn the knob.

"Stop it," the male specter said from his chair. "We must stay unseen."

"Why?" asked the childghost, feeling the cold brass on his fingers.

"There are those that wish to do us harm if they knew we existed."

"It's just a child. I want to have fun. Isn't that the point of *trick* 'r treating?"

"No! Stop it!" screamed the female who stuck her hand through his to grab the knob.

From the other side of the door, the childghost could hear a kid scream through at the elderly man, "Fuck off, you old codger! You'll get your trick for sure, now!"

"What foul language these children have nowadays!" The female specter pulled her arm back, aghast.

"It's a shame the old fart didn't hear him," laughed the male specter.

"We need to stop him!" the childghost pleaded as he pulled on the knob. The female's hand remained in his and the childghost felt a coldness across his palm. He felt his fingers loosen and suddenly the female was holding onto his hand and neither were attached to the knob any longer.

"While it is possible for us to leave on Halloween, I must insist that we stay inside," said the female specter, patting his hand with her free hand.

"Quite right you are, deary," said the male who let out a translucent puff of smoke. "Best to stay inside." He pulled the childghost by the shirt away from the door just as a shattering of glass flew across the room, showering the female, followed by a loud *thud*.

"Haha! I told you, you old bat! I told you!" laughed the kid outside.

"What in the Sam Hill was that?!" shouted the elderly man from across the house.

The childghost saw the brick hit the wooden newel cap at the end of the staircase before ricocheting across the wall. The kid's laughter became farther and farther away as the creaky floorboards filled the room and the elderly man hobbled his way down the hall. With each step, the childghost could hear the *clank* as the cane hit the floor.

"Disperse," the male specter said, disappearing through the wall. "He cannot see us," said the female, sinking through the floorboards.

The childghost stood dumbfounded as the clanks grew closer.

"What twat is wrecking *my* home?!" shouted the old man. "If I catch you!"

Suddenly, the childghost felt a tug on his shoulder. He turned and caught an arm protruding through the yellowed wallpaper. It pulled him toward the wall. "Wait!" yelled the childghost, "I cannot . . . " He closed his eyes as the wall rushed up toward him and prepared for an impact that did not come.

A second later he opened his eyes just as a dusty cobweb phased through him and a spider skittered disturbed by his unexpected appearance. The studs and backside of the drywall greeted him before he popped out the other side. Like the rush of waking up while falling in a dream, he collected himself, pinching his arms and face, ensuring that he was in one piece.

They were in the formal parlor, which had little use nowadays. The male continued to pull him by the shoulder toward the old grandfather clock that had always been in the corner of the room — at least for as long as the childghost had lived there. The elderly man had little tenacity to change how the house had come. The clock's face greeted his and through it they went. The cogs and inner-workings all ticked away, despite the fact that the time was wildly off. The childghost blinked and when he opened his eyes, they were in the dining room.

"I hear you, you fuckin' twat!" the elderly man

screamed as the cane clicked with determined furiosity. "When I catch you, you'll pay for that fuckin' window! And the wall too!"

"Quick, down," the female's voice came from below. The childghost looked down, only to be greeted by the female's face looking up through the linoleum tile. He jumped, a little startled. It was not a sight he'd have ever seen at such an angle. She pulled his leg and down he fell, like a balloon that had lost its buoyancy. As the floor enveloped his vision, he caught the sight of the male specter as he floated upward into the ceiling. And just as he popped out underneath, in some dusty crawlspace, he heard the clanking of the elderly man's cane above.

"Get back here!" he shouted, followed by quick successive raps of his cane on the floor. Dust and dirt fell on them through the cracks of the termite-infested floorboards which lay under the linoleum.

Due to his incorporeal inexperience, the childghost caught a few bugs in the mouth momentarily before they fell through him. If he could've, he would've vomited. Then he had a happy thought that his body didn't go solid when he was halfway between the walls or floor. Instead, he hunched down; the crawlspace barely allowed him to stand straight even at its deepest. The female would have had to be bent in half to fit, if it weren't for her ability to phase herself into the dirt floor below. Her midsection viewable due to the sunlight that speckled the dirt here and there, parted by the lattice of the porch.

"Why didn't he follow us?" whispered the childghost to the female.

"Well, I suspect it is rather hard for him to go between the floors," she smirked.

"Not the old man, the other . . . Uh, what do you call yourselves? Ghosts?"

"I suspect we would. Spirits, perhaps? He doesn't like the ground."

"What does —"

"Never you mind," the female said before phasing back up through the floor, leaving the childghost alone in the crawlspace.

"Wait I cannot . . . " started the childghost before reaching up to see if he could get his hand through. Yet, all he was able to do was feel the sliminess of the wet and cold boards.

He walked and then crawled as the dirt sloped up, narrowing as he reached the underside of the porch. Lucky for him, he knew that his old dog, Chuckwagon, had dug a pretty sizable hole on that far side, much to his mother's dismay. *Maybe, just maybe, I can squeeze through*, the childghost thought.

He underestimated how narrow it was, though, and struggled to wriggle himself through and toward the hole. If only he were a more advanced ghost, he thought to himself. As he pulled himself through the hole after several minutes, he froze in place as he heard, "Boy, whatcha doin' down there?"

The voice was familiar. He looked up to see Old Man Kitterwall who lived across town and had taught him math in the third grade. What was he doing in his neck of the woods, the childghost wondered.

"I said, whatcha doin' down there. Yer mother's gunna have a bird with you. You gone and mussed up your fine clothes!" He chuckled as the childghost pulled himself free.

"I don't think she will," the childghost said with an air of sadness as he dusted himself off.

"Why's that?" Old Man Kitterwall asked, smiling, exposing his coffee-stained teeth. He wore the same old brown cardigan that the childghost always knew him to wear. "Where's she at? She may want to know that her kid's traipsing around under her house and *look whatcha've done to her begonias!*"

The childghost circled around him and caught a glimpse of the female specter through the window. She ushered him with her hand, waving to come. The childghost ignored her. He hadn't been outside in such a long time. The breeze felt nice, despite the air having the same coldness of death.

"Yer mother's gunna have a bird," Old Man Kitterwall repeated. "*Tsk tsk*, Mr. Brayward."

Brayward, thought the childghost. *Yes. Brayward.*

If there were a guidebook for the newly christened ghost, the childghost would have appreciated having been told that memories after weren't easy to explain. He knew who his mother was, yes, but couldn't quite picture her. He knew that this was his house, but ask him to plot it on a map and he couldn't. He knew who Old Man Kitterwall was but couldn't tell you of a single lesson he had taught him, aside from the fact that it was math. But even still, he wasn't able to conjure up his own name. Such a simple thing, a name, but until that moment he hadn't given it much of a thought.

He supposed some things stuck when you died and other stuff didn't.

"Or should I tell yer gramps?"

"Sorry?" the childghost asked.

"For the love of Jesus, who the fuck are you and why are you standing in my flowers?" asked the elderly man. He peered through the bug netting that adorned the wraparound porch.

Taken aback, the childghost almost sank into the ground. The elderly man looked right at him. The male and female specters would be displeased with him, thought the childghost. Then, out came the shotgun, poking through a hole in the screen. Not at him, the childghost thought. *Through* him. The elderly man was looking through him and right at Old Man Kitterwall.

"Wait, I know you —"

"I mean no harm," said Old Man Kitterwall, backing away, his hands held up. "I was just talking with yer grandson."

"I ain't got no goddamn grandson! You've got five seconds to get off my lawn, you fuckin' woman stealing son of a bitch!"

The childghost felt the chill on his hand.

"Is that so?" Old Man Kitterwall exclaimed. "Then who's that?" He lifted his hand to point toward the childghost just as the childghost felt pulled back through the sidewall of the house.

Inside, the male specter paced in the study, as the woman straightened her dress.

"I hate the outside!" she shouted.

Through the window, the childghost could see Old Man Kitterwall backing away until he disappeared into the wooded area behind the house.

"How come he couldn't see me?"

The male specter continued to pace back and forth, muttering something to himself. The female attempted to comfort him, whispering too. She tried to stop his pacing by placing her hand on his shoulder but he phased through her without breaking his concentration.

"How come he couldn't see me?" repeated the childghost.

The fire lit itself in the fireplace, which was a wonder given that the logs had been there. So long in fact that a caked layer of dust covered the topside. The flames grew higher and reflected a red light across the male specter's translucent face.

"Careful," the female specter stated and the flames dwindled.

"HOW COME HE COULDN'T SEE ME?!"

"What?" the male specter asked, stopping and glaring at the childghost. "We have bigger issues to figure out than why the old cataract couldn't see you. He's half-blind as is, you know that. But the man!"

"Oh, lordy. That man!" the female said, staring out the window to see where he had gone.

"Mr. Kitterwall?" the childghost asked.

"Perhaps, to you," the female stated.

The front door slammed and the childghost heard the crunching sound of broken glass as the raps from the old man's cane grew near again.

"God damn fucking crazy man! Breakin' my windows! Traipsing in my petunias!"

Begonias, the childghost thought, annoyed, knowing that his mother was the one who planted them. They had withered long before Old Man Kitterwall had stepped foot in them.

"I'll fuckin' teach him! Wasn't loaded the first time. Will be this time."

The childghost heard the familiar sound of a gun loading and a memory of his father came flooding back to him. It was a nice memory of the pair hunting in those woods behind the house. Thinking about it, the childghost wasn't sure that was even legal. Now, he couldn't remember what happened to his father. *Stupid memories.*

Click.

"Old coot! Thought that bastard was dead or at least in some joint for the nearly dead . . . "

Click. Click.

"Mr. Carlyle has been fucking up my life too fuckin' long!"

Mr. Carlyle?

The childghost listened with his ear pressed toward the long hall that separated the kitchen from the study. He didn't hear the door open a second time. He didn't hear the knife slide across the elderly man's throat. But what he did hear was a last "YOU BASTARD!" and the gurgling that came afterward, as well as the thumps as his cane bashed around, knocking dishes and pans off the counter in a chiming cacophony.

"Attic!" the two specters said in unison before disappearing into the ceiling. Then, after a moment, the female stuck her head through the ceiling, followed by her arm, grabbing the childghost and yanking him upward.

From below, he heard the sound of Mr. Kitterwall calling up, "Oh Mr. Brayward, how you've been a naughty boy! But, I must thank ya!" The childghost heard the creak of the stair.

For the childghost, what had just transpired was not processable. He remained in a daze as the two specters flew between the first and second floors, finally landing in the attic.

"M-M-Mr. Kitterwall k-killed—"

"That's not Mr. Kitterwall," said the male who resumed

his pacing, mirroring his earlier movement. "And we are absolutely fucked!"

"Who—"

"Please, child, let us think. This is really bad."

"What should we do?" asked the female, but the male continued his pacing.

"Old Man Kitterwall—"

"CHILD, IT IS NOT THIS KITTERWALL!" shouted the male specter.

"Listen, that man is not a man. He's a demon. A demon who feeds on souls of humans and ghosts! Why do you think we asked you to stay unseen? He lurks in those woods. It's bad enough that the elderly man enticed him closer. They can smell death as it approaches. Normally, he is bound to those woods, but during Halloween . . . "

"But he knows my name," the childghost said.

"Yes, child. They are very good at knowing who is in front of them and they make you see who you hate the most. They feed off that pain," the female said, placing her cold hand on his shoulder.

"Oh, Mr. Brayward, yer bein' a right naughty twat! Come down here and get yer punishment!"

"Don't listen," the female specter said. "He wants in your head."

"Why are we just sitting here? Shouldn't we get out of here. We are sitting ducks!"

The hunting memory flooded his mind once again. *Aim!* shouted his father. *But, dad, I cannot kill an innocent duck!* His father became annoyed, yanked the gun from his hands, and shot the animal. That night, he made him clean and cook it.

"I can smell your freshness, Mr. Brayward. All the sweeter!"

"He doesn't know about us," said the male specter. "Maybe we just give him the boy?"

"Honestly? You cannot be serious," the female said, stepping between the male who was giving the boy a squinted-eye glare, like a starving wolf in front of a wounded animal.

The male phased through the female and grabbed for the childghost. He closed his eyes, felt himself rise. The childghost knew the male had him in his clutches. Yet, the female's screams came from farther and farther away. Opening his eyes, he saw the ceiling just as it disappeared and tasted shingle as he clipped through the roof. Suddenly, he was standing on top of the house, looking out on Pike Street where it met Line Street.

He had flown by himself.

Trick-or-treaters dotted the sidewalks, weaving around cars, as darkness started to set in. Some rang doorbells; others threw toilet paper into neighboring trees. Several started for the first house, on top of which he stood. One trick-or-treater dressed in a ballerina costume screamed as she noticed the childghost as another strolled by dressed as a mummy. Pointing, the ballerina got the attention of the two others standing next her. The childghost heard them say, "Nice decorations!" before proceeding.

The childghost felt a tug on his feet and noticed the female's hands protruding from the shingles, latched around his ankles.

"No!" shouted the childghost. He flew higher and higher, pulling the female out of the attic. The male was attached to her. As he strained, the woman's grip began to falter. The male became stuck between the roof and attic.

"Oh, Mr. Brayward! What a lovely surprise! Not two souls, but four?!" the demon shouted. The childghost wasn't sure exactly how he heard, but it seemed as though the demon's voice came from within. "I won't need to eat for a few years at least after this buffet?"

Just then, he heard the familiar chime from the doorbell.

"Oh, and just in time for the children too! What a splendid night!"

The childghost watched as the female was sucked down. Her scream became muffled as her head disappeared. There was a slight *pop* and then silence. "Tasty, Mr. Brayward. I tell you what. Come down here and I'll show you my ways. Then, you won't need to remain in hiding." All hints of Old Man Kitterwall's accent were gone. "We can share the children. I'm not that hungry anymore, anyhow."

"Or . . ." the demon continued, "you can come down here and I will eat your soul and then the souls of every trick-or-treater on this godless street."

The doorbell rang once again.

Reluctantly, the childghost descended and just as his feet touched the roof, he was pulled through so quickly that the phantom air from his lungs spilled out. Inside the attic, he saw no trace of the male or female specters.

"What happened to their bodies?" asked the childghost.

"You see, it is much easier for me to eat the souls of ghosts. You don't leave any trace once your soul is gone. It's so much easier than humans and their bodies. In fact, that's why I need you, Mr. Brayward. You're going to clean up that old bastard after I get his soul. Then, you'll do the same to each child. But you see, I'm not that hungry and I think it would be best if we store these children for later consumption. Don't you think?"

"I, uh, guess?"

The plan was set much to the childghost's chagrin. He was only to try and capture the souls of the parentless children or teenagers. The ones who knocked alone. He couldn't understand why someone —*something*—would willingly kill innocent children. Then it dawned on him. He never contemplated his own death. Watching as the first loner was brought into the house, unaware, he understood how he died.

His father and he were hunting.

A flash from the gun.

A pain in his gut.

The cries of his father.

Left in the woods.

"That's right, Mr. Brayward," the demon started as he hunched over the innocent girl, who had already passed out upon seeing the two of them. She looked about thirteen and wore a t-shirt that said "Get your tricks!"

on it. The demon still looked like Old Man Kitterwall to him, but the childghost presumed that the girl saw something else. "If it weren't for your dad pulling your lifeless body out from those woods, I could have had your soul months ago. Lucky for me, they abandoned you here and I just had to bide my time for Halloween. It does get terribly lonely in those woods, though. For that, I'm thankful that this old codger bought the house after your parents divorced and left. Happenstance that there were already two others here. Didn't know about them."

"But why this house?"

"That, I've never really contemplated, Mr. Brayward. I suppose I'm bound to these woods, and this house has always had a bit of bad luck. It's always offered me what I need and I haven't needed to venture off anywhere else. I do, from time to time, get lucky with a stray runaway, every now and again. Now get over here and help me with this child!"

"No!" shouted the childghost.

The demon shifted. He changed from Old Man Kitterwall to a leather-skinned entity that looked like a creature from the pits of Hell. His animalistic features included pointed teeth. He snarled. "What did you say?"

"I-I-I," the childghost stuttered as he backed away. As he did so, he tripped over the brick laying in the entryway.

The demon's voice became gruff and deep. "You dare defy me! Then you can die like all the rest!" The demon raised his clawed hand. His elongated fingers capped equally sharp talons.

"GET THE FUCK AWAY FROM HIM, DEMON!" a man shouted from the entryway.

Through the broken glass, the childghost could make out two shapes: a male and a female. For a moment, he thought the two specters had returned. A smile came across his face just as the two blasted the door with a shotgun and entered.

Instantly, the pit of his stomach turned as he realized who the two figures were.

His parents stood side-by-side in the doorway. The two looked like a pair of trick-or-treaters, loaded with holstered weapons.

"Mom? Dad?" the childghost asked while the demon laughed a guttural laugh.

"Oh! How much sweeter this will be for me. To watch your boy die, again? That'll make your souls that much more tastier!"

"The Father and the Son and the Holy—" the childghost's mother flung the liquid at the demon, cut off by its cries. It retreated slightly from the childghost.

"I command thee, demon, retreat from this house!"

"Never!" shouted the demon as the little girl began to stir. "I'll eat all of your souls!"

The demon hissed.

From behind him came the voice of the elderly man, "Kill me in my own house, you bastard!" The elderly specter came to be. He appeared behind the demon and wrapped his translucent cane around him.

"I killed you!" said the demon wriggling behind the cane, pressed to the elderly specter.

"But you didn't get my soul yet! Ha!"

The childghost's parents fully entered and stood between him and the demon. The childghost's father held up a gun and the demon laughed. "What do you think that'll do? You'll just be punching more holes into the walls!"

"Is that so?" the father said and pulled the trigger. He shot at the demon and a deathly cry poured out. "These bullets have been blessed by the Diocese!"

The demon wriggled out from the grip of the elderly specter's clutches, turned, grabbed him and jumped through the window. The elderly specter screamed as he was pulled down the yard and the two disappeared into the woods.

"Dad!" shouted the childghost's mother.

"Mom! Dad!" the childghost exclaimed.

"Baxter!" the mother said, turning to her boy.

"We're so sorry!" the father continued.

"I thought you two were gone forever."

"No, my boy. We tried—oh how we tried to get back sooner! The travel from Italy was plagued, as if the devil himself were protecting his minion. We just needed the right training to deal with that ghastly neighbor. Your mother was desperate to stop the curse on this house. Your grandfather—"

"Grandfather?" the childghost asked, peering up as he sat on the creaky stair.

"Who'd you think that old man was? We've come to learn that a new ghost takes awhile to remember its past, especially the faces of their loved ones. He came here after we left to protect you. We couldn't let you know that we could see you. You wouldn't have accepted it when we left."

"Your grandfather," the mother continued, "made sure that if the entity appeared, he'd protect you. We knew it was only a matter of time before he'd reach the house. What with Halloween and all."

"Now, we are prepared," the father said. Together they sat on the staircase, looking out the blown apart doorway, as the little girl looked up.

"This is a really fucked up house," she said before she passed out once again.

A DISAPPOINTING HARVEST
Elisabeth Tuttle

*O*NE . . . *TWO* . . . *THREE* . . . *FOUR* . . .

Four sets of footsteps coming up the path. Didn't it only need four more?

It quickly checked on the prey it had already captured. They'd been lured inside by a puppet that promised a party. Some of the little things were moving throughout the cavities of its body, though it much preferred the ones that chose to stay still. It had created places for them to rest for a reason, after all. Some of them understood. Five of them were sitting on the couches. A light pressure poked at it from the inside where they sat. There was almost a tickle each time they shifted on the floral cushions, turning to engage with another of them or getting more comfortable. It decided that those ones would go quick. That was the least it could do to thank them for being well-behaved food.

The other three nuisances, however, weren't going to be so lucky. Insects that they were, they scurried over its teal-carpeted insides. Shrieking and giggling, they seemed to believe this actually *was* a party. They tugged at knobs on the stereo, yanking on its flesh and forcing it to keep making more and more music. One of them even tried pulling it open while grumbling about wanting to play some cassette that it had picked up down the street earlier that night. Why were they always so greedy? Was the echo of the holiday songs it had collected through the years not enough? And the way they stomped up and down the stairs to explore more and more rooms that it had to scramble to form was maddening. One thumping blow to its bones after another. It could barely keep a thought together with how it had to focus on keeping from wincing. If its body began shifting, they might notice. Already, some of the party decorations, which it had been very proud of creating earlier in the day, were faltering. There was a hanging cutout on the wall of a . . .

It thought for a moment. Not a dog. Dogs were larger than . . . rats? Bats? *Cats!* It remembered that they were called *cats*. Dogs didn't seem to scare them the way that cats did, though the little beasts hardly seemed like anything to be concerned with. Some years, it awoke to find that a scraggly one of them had found its way inside. None of them stuck around the second things began shifting. They always seemed to know just when to run, just when to be afraid.

It had gathered that was what this day was about — scaring the things that crowded the surface of this world. And yet, it was a day when they flooded the streets. They willingly went to each door with their guards down and their arms open with the apparent expectation of receiving something. In the decades it had been lurking at the edges of Pike Street, a more suitable day to feed had yet to present itself. There was no need to hunt. Prey presented itself willingly. Before it had discovered this new way of feeding and taken this form, when it had still had to move and hunt and take a meal with every moon cycle, it had once heard one of them say *work smarter, not harder.* A single night of feeding to sustain a year of rest seemed to be doing just that.

So, it concentrated on fixing the picture of the *cat* on the wall when the new group got close enough to ring the doorbell. Somewhere inside of it, near to where one of its many limbs had ended up, a heavy curtain twitched in response to the small finger poking its skin.

It rang in response. At least, it tried to ring. It was doing its best with everything going on. It hummed a mimicked amalgamation of the other rings it had heard in the neighborhood, but it panicked when it realized that the sound seemed to make the four small figures uncomfortable. The one who'd poked it stepped back. Though it couldn't see the expression on its face through the mask it wore, a horrible thing with features that were too exaggerated and too sharp and topped with molded yellow hair that it was not looking forward to tasting later, it saw the young thing freeze. A grating squeak that made it want to tear the thing's entire head off came from the mask as it looked over to one of its companions. Before it could get a word out though, before the smaller one in a white robe with its hair twisted into lumps on the side of its head that it looked toward could say anything either, the tallest one pushed it forward again.

"Take a chill pill. Either stop being a baby, or we'll make you get candy from the freak in the window," the tallest of them snapped.

But was that one not a baby as well? Was the entire group not made up of their young? That seemed like a silly thing to say, considering. They were nowhere near as large as the ones already inside. Even the bold one in the green and red striped sweater, the one who'd spoken up like it held authority over the group, couldn't have been that old. It didn't love the idea of a decent portion of its meal being comprised of such small pieces, but who was it to argue with what it had been presented with? It had to take whatever came to it, even if that meant having to endure the taste of all that awful plastic to get to the soft, tasty bits underneath.

Choosing a few decorations far enough from the already doomed prey, it pushed them from the walls. By the time they fell to the floor, one wet thump after the other, they'd reverted back to formless pieces of flesh. A misshapen pumpkin at the base of the stairs lost its integrity. Holes opened across its orange surface, strings of tissue stretching until they snapped and the thing fell open in a blossom of meat that draped over the first step. It willed the pieces to pull themselves together. There was no grace in the way the bits dragged across the carpet. Slugs leaving mucus in their wake had more finesse, but it had speed on its side. It created this form year after year. This wasn't like when it had to modify its entire body to keep up with the changes in the neighborhood, to shift its skin so the windows looked correct or pull its insides this way and that until there were pieces of furniture that they might see in other houses.

Houses that *were* houses. Houses that weren't alive.

The process of molding the pile of flesh still paused though, when the striped one pushed the masked one forward and that small hand jabbed at the doorbell again.

"Trick or treat!" they called in unison.

Could they not give it a second or two? It was busy and had to remind itself to make that exact same hum again while entertaining the ones inside and changing its shape *again.* Briefly, it wondered if all of the effort was worth it. A gentle breeze ran through the halls as it sighed and reminded itself that it was, that it needed to grow in both size and power before it would be ready to join the others. Much to the creature's relief, the quick rush of air went unnoticed. Everything was fine. There was nothing to get worked up about. This would all be over soon.

Its attention returned to the partially formed lump of meat sitting on its side of the door. The last few wouldn't stay for much longer. The younger ones always seemed to be the most eager to move on. Did some competition between them exist? Could it use that to —

Stop.

That was a question for another time, another harvest. It could already see them glancing toward the next house. Opportunities didn't last forever. The beast hiding in plain sight on Pike Street had lost enough of them to learn that. So, it began twisting its insides once more, confident that it could replicate its puppet the way that it had so many times before even without enough time to pay attention to the details. The mass it had gathered bubbled and stretched. Shifting from one color to another like a rapidly rotting steak until it settled on something vaguely similar to the wood cabinets it had mimicked for the kitchen, invisible hands sculpted it like clay. They pushed it upward until a tumor of a head grew from the stump and strings of black grew from the tumor. It teetered on a too-thin neck, but some bits were pushed around, and the right balance to keep it in place was eventually found.

The face on the tumor was a rush job. Bulbous lips sat beneath a crooked nose. They didn't close properly. The misaligned jaw didn't even allow them to close at all. And it couldn't get one of the eyes right. That damned clump of cells just wouldn't settle into the socket it had gouged into itself. It gouged deeper. It tore frantically at its own flesh and flung pieces of it here and there for the walls or floors to absorb. Too many pieces. Now less of a socket and more of a gaping hole, the eye rolled back down to the floor and unceremoniously melted into the carpet. There was no time to make another one. There was no time to start sculpting again. The lights flickered throughout the house as it panicked. Music began to skip. Its walls expanded and contracted with quick, shallow breaths.

Someone inside looked around in confusion. The two little ones closest to the door stepped back again, much to the chagrin of their companions. Both of the larger ones began to sneer at them. The striped one pushed past them to bang on the door. Unable to stop itself this time, it winced at the feeling of pounding on its exterior while the ones inside got restless and started to stir.

"Do you see that? I think that wall just moved," the one with hair like an overgrown shrub asked.

"And I think you're al . . . you're alr-ready drunk," a horned individual slurred in response. That one was the drunk one. It was going to taste sour. Rotten. It nearly moved again, this time from barely holding back gagging at the thought of having to digest something so foul. "It's not even eight. *Pathhhhhhhetic,* dude, We just got here."

"No, the—" that hair finally wobbled as it shook its head violently and pointed to where the cat on the wall that had been repaired only a few minutes earlier was beginning to melt. Other decorations followed suit as the seasoned hunter tried to hold too many things, too many thoughts, too many sensations together at once. It turned the lights back on, but the music stopped entirely. Then it started the music again, but the flowers in the wallpaper expanded until the walls were once again the wet pink of flesh. Even the skeleton that was sitting on a chair in the corner, one that it was particularly proud of the accuracy, shuddered in place before collapsing in on itself. The chair followed suit, then the other furniture that the prey occupied and began to sink into. In moments, the carefully crafted environment was falling back to shapeless masses of meat.

It scrambled to scrape its insides back into place as though everything would be fine and the courses of its meal weren't already shrieking in horror as they slipped around on its wet innards. This was all wrong. It wasn't how the night was supposed to go. The threat of failure tasted nearly as bitter as the drunken one would.

Feeding had always come so naturally to it. It had been doing this particular routine for years, waking up this night and taking this form to capture twelve of them then shrinking down to the shell of a house to slumber until it needed to feed again. The neighborhood would remember their missing, sure. They always did. Sometimes, it even saw pictures of the ones it took during the previous harvests, still hanging on the bare trees that were threaded together along the street. Faded and peeling, they still served as reminders of those it made a meal out of, but they never seemed to look in the right place. On the contrary, those in the neighborhood seemed eager to point the finger elsewhere. 2 Pike St. simply faded into the background. In its place sat a building lost to time and the elements. Sometimes it could feel them running around inside when they got bored of antagonizing and throwing stones at the abandoned house farther down the street. The chill of snow blew in through open windows from time to time. Minor disturbances. When it was sated, when it consumed enough of them, it had no trouble just going back to sleep.

A low whine rumbled through the chambers of its body. Only the sheer size of the creature whining made the young outside able to hear the strange keening over the screaming of those already inside, the ones who were being trapped in rooms that were rapidly packed with flesh as more of the illusion fell apart. The eight of them weren't going to be enough. It was going to be hungry. It was going to *starve*. Walls shuddered with a hiccup as it wept at the thought of having to stay hungry for another four months. Did they think it had enough power to create the entire illusion more than once a year? It didn't. It had been sent here to feed and grow until it was strong enough to be useful, but how was it supposed to do that when it wasn't going to get enough food? *Gods*, it was almost as much of a baby as the ones who were now fleeing from it.

Except for the striped one.

The striped one remained frozen on what remained of the doorstep. Wide eyes were glued to one of the few remaining windows and watched as a neighbor was shoved against it by a wall of flesh, face compressed and unrecognizable. Thick mucus dripped down from the top of the window. The little thing could see it foaming where its neighbor's mouth gaped for breath like snot bubbling from a clogged nostril. It couldn't look away.

Not when its neighbor's face began to blister. Not when its neighbor's eyeballs and tongue sizzled and popped and smeared across the glass of the window in a vomitous mixture of blood and melted sinew. Not when the face that it couldn't even put a name to started to fall in wet clumps away from the skull. Not when those clumps liquefied until there was nothing left but bone that was already going spongy. Not when its friends called for it a few times before giving up and choosing to save themselves. Not when they made it to the sidewalk and suddenly couldn't remember where it had run off to.

This wasn't ideal—eating a less than complete meal and having to consume them all so quickly instead of savoring each course. What choice did the predator have though? It was either some prey or none, either be a little hungry or waste away, either swallow them all down at once or risk the disguise completely falling apart before it could shrink back into the derelict building that everyone passed without a thought. They would be so mad at it if it was discovered before the time was right. They would never come back for it. They would leave it to rot away with nothing but pests to eat while they consumed entire galaxies in one gulp. It would never get the chance to taste the suffering of countless lives being snuffed out all at once. That wasn't fair. One shameful harvest wasn't going to stop it, neither were a few months of hunger. So, it forced its way through the eight of them.

The horned one came with the burnt taste of plastic and the bitter edge of alcohol. Clumps of chemical coated hair coming off of its friend caused the house to heave with a gag. Surprisingly, one of the nuisances tasted sweet. That one must've been gorging itself on those tiny bits of treasure that everyone was after that night. At least something good came out of its behavior. Hardly the biggest surprise of the night, but maybe the most pleasant one.

Eight bodies didn't last long in the face of the beast's stomach acid. They melted into nothing but nutrients that would sustain it for the coming months and were done with much too soon for its taste. Usually it would feed slowly throughout the night once it had ensnared enough, but there was always next year to get back on track. One year older, one year wiser, one year stronger.

And it realized that there was one last treat to be had. The striped one still stood at the door. Its face was red and mottled, a mix of tears and snot smudged across its skin. A damp stain ran down the front of its pants, something acrid pooling at its feet. Though it had postured itself as the leader earlier, it couldn't have looked more pathetic now. Barely able to tremble in place, there didn't seem to be much hope of it turning and following the ones who'd escaped. Mumbling something about "mommy, mommy" was the only other movement it appeared to be capable of anymore. That was perfect.

Because three months going hungry was better than four.

Just as the façade of the house began to fall, the door flung open to make way for a single appendage to shoot out, coil around the striped one, and drag it inside before it even had the chance to scream. It had half a mind to save this one as a snack for later as it unburdened itself and settled into Pike Street's forgotten little corner the way it had so many years before that. Burrowing the lion's share of its true, grotesque form into the earth again, the creature was eager to sleep again after it had exhausted itself for such a poor showing. That was more than enough excitement for one year. The cool autumn soil was calming against its oozing skin as it rooted deeper into the ground, and it felt right at home in the quiet dark of it all. Though the one it was holding wouldn't stop with its unfortunate, muffled shrieking as that soil filled its mouth and nostrils.

But it would soon enough.

N<u>º</u> 3

WANNA TRADE?
Louie Sullivan

THE HOUSE OF CANDY APPEARED overnight between the 30th and 31st of October. Before that morning, 3 Pike St. had been an empty lot, left open for reasons the neighbors didn't bother to ask (or even particularly care about). But they certainly cared about this. It was like something out of a fairy tale, a glamorous manor decked out from bottom to top with all sorts of appetizing treats. There were strands of licorice inlaid into the railings, bars of chocolate intricately placed along the steps. The windows shone with frosted sugar, the sunlight catching perfectly in their butterscotch haze. Like a gingerbread house, the whole thing seemed to be held together with icing (and in some spots, bubblegum!) finely laid with expert craftsmanship, not a single gumdrop out of place. Even the landscaping seemed edible: what looked at first glance to be a small reflecting pond on the front lawn was upon closer inspection filled with bubbling soda, the "rocks" placed symmetrically along its border actually gigantic jellybeans. The grass seemed to be made of cotton candy, light and green and wispy, smelling strongly of sour apple, and the flowers that stuck up from the ground at odd intervals were no more than ornate lollipops. It was a masterpiece, and a mystery.

Where had this strange place come from, and how did it emerge so quickly? The adults of Pike Street wondered this as they first noticed it, but ultimately they gave it little thought beyond the initial consideration. For some of them, it was a brief curiosity to ponder on their way to work, before other muddling miseries and mundanities took over. There is little room for wonder in the hearts and minds of such people, for whom the flickering jack-o'-lantern flame of belief in the otherworldly has long since gone out, in favor of stark fluorescent lighting and clean orderly lines. For the rest, well, they were busy enough with their own Halloween plans to worry about some upstart showing them up with a very fancy display. And so the only ones left to truly acknowledge the house of candy were the children.

The news passed between them in rumbling rumors, as such things often travel among the young. Little of the curiosity focused on where the place had come from; this was Halloween, after all, and for children and the youthful-of-spirit it's a time where magic is allowed to more readily intrude across the veil and into our average world. No, what the kids cared about was whether or not the place was cursed. Plenty of debate sprung up about what would happen to someone if they ate any of the candy it was made of: some swore it would fill you up forever so you'd never want to eat anything else ever again; others, that you'd be cursed and drop dead on the spot immediately after your first bite. Some even insisted that you couldn't eat the candy at all, and that it was just foam and rocks and plywood all painted up to look delicious, but that if you went to eat any, all you'd end up with was a mouthful of construction supplies. There was even a rumor that if you tried to eat the candy house, the house would eat you instead. That one didn't make it far, though—some headstrong girl in a cat costume shut it down as outright ridiculous, and pretty soon anybody who suggested this option just got laughed at. But regardless of what the children believed or didn't believe, whether blessing or curse, carnivorous dwelling or Home Depot concoction, none of the gawkers that came to stare at the house of candy had dared a taste.

Then little Sally Schulz toddled out onto the scene, bedecked innocently in a witch costume that was several sizes too big for her. ("She'll grow into it," said her mom when she inadvertently chose the wrong size at the department store). Her over-large hat tipped over her eyes as she bent to reach some of the flossy, sugary grass, and a crowd of onlookers held their breath as she raised a handful to her lips. They leaned forward to watch as she carefully chewed it, expecting maybe for her head to explode or her teeth to fall out, or maybe for her to dissolve into a Sally-sized puddle of goo. But nothing happened. She was safe (for now)!

So more of them chose to eat the candy, and did not die—not immediately, at least, and certainly not as a direct result of this choice. One, a boy named Mark, pried some chocolate from the doorway and was flattened years later in a ghastly incident at a petting zoo. Jessica Barker, who took some lollipops from the lawn, later suffered from a rare tongue disease (ironically, there was no discernible link between the lollipops and the disease) and then was bitten by a venomous snake (not from the petting zoo) while on vacation in Bora Bora. And as for the little girl in the witch costume . . . well, you'll find out more about her later.

With the debate about the house of candy's edibility aside (for the most part), the kids' attention turned to another facet of the place: a large sign on the lawn that appeared to advertise some upcoming festivity that evening. "Halloween Candy Exchange," it read, "Tonight at Midnight." I don't know what sort of trick-or-treater you were as a child, but in my experience it's one of the great joys of Halloween: to dump out your candy at the end of the night and trade out your least favorites to hopefully make a fairly decent pile of sugar you actually like. So it was a nearly-unanimous decision among the Pike Street kids to give this exchange a shot. Mark and Jessica, of course, were impatient enough that by midnight gorged themselves on other candy — from the house and otherwise — so they and a few others didn't attend. But for the most part, as the night drew on, the consensus up and down the block was generally in favor of the meetup. It was no surprise, then, that by 11:59 a large crowd of costumes assembled in front of the now-infamous house.

A few kids anxiously checked their watches as the seconds ticked down. Less than a minute until midnight. Ten seconds now . . . three . . . two . . . one . . . nothing. Nothing at all, save for a wave of confused glances between the expectant trick-or-treaters and a growing hum as they muttered their uncertainties. Maybe the owner of the place fell asleep early by accident, some suggested, or the whole thing was some kind of *Candid Camera* situation — a good-natured prank they were about to be let in on. But they would soon discover that the house of candy's owner was very much awake. And if this were any sort of joke, it would be far from a harmless one.

With a groan that seemed thunderous in the midnight air, the doors of the house slowly opened, and the owner emerged. He was an ugly little imp of a man, scarcely taller than a child himself. Most of his face was hidden by a large flowing mustache, which bristled out in every direction from under a red and warty nose. The man's eyes were small and bright, and seemed to glow with a cunning edge as he proceeded toward the mass of children, scanning the crowd as he went. Behind him, he dragged two enormous sacks, one in each hand — how he managed to carry these, and how they even were able to fit out of the front door in the first place, seemed a mystery. They had to be at least double his size each, and filled to the brim. He set them both down, and from the one in his right hand, he removed a small card table and folding chair. Then he set both bags behind it, sat down at the table, and grinned. Staring out at the crowd, he spoke only two words, in a creaky voice that sounded like it had not spoken for years: "Wanna trade?"

The kids were shocked and confused. Some of the more

easily-outraged older kids in the back almost turned on their heels right then and left—but deadly curiosity kept them all rooted in place. Then, from somewhere in the first couple rows of trick-or-treaters, a pair of little arms pushed their way forward, clad in witch-sleeves that would have been better suited for an older girl. It was Sally. She approached the candy-man's table, and as he peered over the edge to get a look at her, they shared a glance. He tilted his head inquisitively: "Wanna trade?"

She nodded, stretched up onto her tiptoes, and put her bucket of candy onto the table. The crowd held their breath. None of them knew what could come next, but they all felt the deep significance of it—this felt primal, like a ritual they could innately sense the sanctity of, even though they'd never been a part of something quite like this. The candy-man reached behind him into one of the cavernous sacks, delving so deep it looked like he was about to fall in, and after a great struggle, bent back upright. Clutched tightly in both arms he held an enormous jack-o'-lantern, overflowing with candy of all sorts. And he presented it directly to Sally.

Somehow, even though the pumpkin was almost as big as her whole body, Sally seemed to carry it effortlessly as she walked away from the table, smiling ear to ear and gleefully chewing the spoils of her victory. The flood-gates opened—in an instant the kids of Pike Street had descended upon the candy-man's table in an overzealous throng—and yet in all the chaos, he maintained calm. Always grinning, always ready for the next deal, always repeating to each child in their turn: "Wanna Trade?"

I could not tell you how long it took, but it felt like a flash. Soon all of the trades were completed, and the bartered candy littered the lawn. And every last trick-or-treater that had come to the Midnight Candy Exchange had gotten their reward. Then, somewhere in the late dark hours, as the children feasted on their spoils and Halloween faded back into memory like a crumbling orange leaf, the house of candy vanished, returning to whatever unseen corner of the earth had spawned it in the first place.

The next morning, every single child that traded candy at the midnight exchange was nowhere to be found. Missing posters went up, and stayed up, unanswered and fading, a grim backdrop to daily life on Pike Street.

Seventeen Octobers have passed since then, with no sign of the children. Not even the slightest trace of them has been seen, or heard, or remembered. They simply vanished into the November dawn, and were banished to legend. In most places, the disappearance of an entire generation would cause quite a stir — chaos in the streets, frantic parents, calls to police and private detectives and the local news — but Pike Street is not most places. Here, people are more willing to move on with their lives, to accept things unquestioningly as they are. To forget. Such is the way when you're faced with the otherworldly as often as the people of Pike Street are. It's much easier to lock yourself inside, physically *and* mentally, than it is to face the horrors that lurk outside on your porch, peering back in through the peephole to see if anyone's home.

In that way, seventeen Halloweens have come and gone with little fanfare on Pike Street. For a few years there was barely any trick-or-treating at all (how could there have been, with so few children to do it?) and yet, time pressed on all the same. New families moved to the street, doubtless unaware of the monstrosities that pervaded it, and brought new kids along with them. New babies were born, fresh life in spite of the stale death that hangs about this place like a putrid fog. And this morning, something else new (or perhaps older than any of us could know) appeared as well. A house at 3 Pike St. A house constructed ornately, and built entirely of candy. Some of the old-timers felt a strange shudder when beholding it, nearly shaken from their decade-plus trance. But by and large it was met with the same indifference it received the last time . . . from the adults at least. Once again, the children of Pike Street were enthralled, and those who could read translated the sign out front to the younger and dumber among them:

"Halloween Candy Exchange. Tonight at Midnight." And so, a cycle continues.

~

Now, long after the sun has set over this cursed block, after the sky has faded from candy corn orange and yellow to the stark and somber blue-black of night, a crowd gathers in front of the whimsical house at 3 Pike St. A chatter of excitement thrums through the throng, as they excitedly show off the treasures they've managed to gather already. Trick-or-treating is serious business here, especially when word gets out of a mysterious exchange happening at the house of candy. And as the light of the full moon filters down through the newly-bare branches, there is a faint creaking from the house, as the long-untouched front doors slowly open. The crowd falls silent, waiting breathlessly to see what the inhabitants of this place could possibly look like.

At first, they can hardly see the scant form that appears at the entryway, its shape only just tall enough to avoid being mistaken for a child as well. But as it steps forward into the moonlight, gigantic orange and black trick-or-treat bags trailing in its wake, they are soon able to see much more clearly. "It's just like in the fairytales," a few of them think, "a witch living in a candy house!"

For some of the kids, it's nearly enough to scare them away, some primal trigger set off by the fabled archetype. But they remain captivated for a moment longer, watching her make her way down the winding pathway and across the lawn. Then she stops, evaluating her place, and nods contentedly. She snaps her fingers and by some magic there appears before her a small ornate wooden table and chair, and the bags arrange themselves perfectly behind her seat, so the ritual can begin. She takes her place, and stares up at the children from the brim of her perfectly-fitted hat (I suppose after all these years, her mother finally was right about growing into it). Her weary face betrays a hint of a wry smile, the slightest twinkle behind her faded eyes, as she whispers into the silence: "Wanna trade?"

CANDY INSIDE
Nick Krenn

S O WHAT DO YOU GUYS THINK?" asked the vampire with bloody, protruding fangs.

"I don't think we should. It's a stranger's house," said the green-faced witch with the pointy hat.

"We've been taking candy from strangers all night," argued the red-nosed clown. "This wouldn't be any different. The candy's just inside. Probably in the hallway in a bowl or something."

"But why don't they just hand it out like everyone else?" asked the witch.

"Maybe it's a lil' old grandma that doesn't move very well and can't get her crotchety ass off the couch," said the clown, snickering at his comment.

Quiet among the group was the alien in its shiny costume and the springy antennas. He stood back listening intently; secretly wishing that the group would just move further down Pike Street past the stone house with its flickering porch light, a moldy looking jack-o'-lantern, and a seated scarecrow holding a sign that read, "CANDY INSIDE."

The alien, twelve-year-old Josh Rencher, watched with anticipatory dread as his fellow classmates Pete Stokely (the clown), Emily Steen (the witch), and Glen

Sharp (the vampire) debated on their course of action. It was going on 7 p.m. according to Josh's Timex, which meant the group only had an hour left before they had to march back to Line Street where Glen's older sister was supposed to pick them up at the corner streetlight where she dropped them off.

Josh and Pete were excited about trick-or-treating with Glen because they knew his sister would just leave them be instead of insisting on going with them. Glen's parents obviously thought their daughter Stacey was more responsible than she actually was. Stacey said she was going to stop off at a friend's costume party while Glen and his friends went door-to-door. Emily, who was tagging along with the group because she secretly liked Glen, was the only one surprised when Stacey dumped the group off at the street light.

"She's not coming with us?" she asked with a tremble of fear.

"No, it's cool," said Glen with a Fonzie-like confidence. "You got us to protect you," he said while flexing his arm underneath his white shirt, his dark cape hanging off his shoulders.

Apparently that noodle-armed flexing was enough to ease Emily's mind, and the group made their way into the neighborhood on Pike Street. Several other kids could be seen trick-or-treating. Some little ones with their parents. Then there were some older kids, not even in costume—probably because they were plenty ugly with their red pockmarked faces—that were also going door to door.

Josh and his group had already picked up a nice share of candy from other neighborhoods before Stacey dropped them off. The original plan was to stay on Line Street, but the group collectively smelled a sweetness perfuming Pike Street, especially in this particular area. It was hard to pinpoint the scent. *Licorice, Sweet Tarts, frosting?* It gave them hope that Pike's bounty would be better than what they were carrying so far.

They had amassed a decent stash of the cheap stuff—

generic suckers, Tootsie Rolls, Pixie Stix. They also got a few fun-sized candy bars but no king-sized bars yet. The king-sized bars were the white whales of trick-or-treating. For past Halloweens, some kids would show up at school the next day brandishing the rare treasure. It was a trophy, a badge of honor among the other kids. Josh and his friends were determined to get one this year no matter how many houses they had to go to or what they had to do to get one. But it was here at 4 Pike St. that tested their resolve.

The sign promising "CANDY INSIDE," written in fast scribbled Sharpie ink on a piece of brown cardboard, was both inviting and intimidating. Josh wondered if anyone else had actually gone inside and claimed any of this promised candy. The older teen group they saw earlier had probably gone inside already and cleaned out whatever candy was being offered.

Glen pulled his latex mask up and let it rest on the top of his head. His face glistened with a little sweat. "Maybe the sign is decoration. Like it's meant to be spooky or something. The door's probably locked, and as soon as we try to open it, that scarecrow is going to pop up and scare the shit out of us," he said.

Pete snickered at this. "If that's what happens, then we can collect the shit and put it in a brown bag, light it on fire, and leave it for them later," he said with a smile.

"That's gross, Pete!" said Emily.

"I don't think we'd have time to do that," said Josh. "It's already a little past seven, and we're supposed to be back on Line Street at eight."

"Glen, there's still plenty of houses left that we haven't gone to," said Emily. "We don't have to go here. I don't want a scarecrow jumping at me!"

"I don't think there's anyone in that scarecrow," Glen said. "Plus, this place at least looks better than that house next door. I wouldn't snatch candy out of that bowl with Pete's hand."

Suddenly, the stone house's door banged open with a bigger kid in a mummy costume stumbling out with a heavy dark bag over their shoulder. The mummy dragged their left foot while carrying the bag. Josh and the others watched with great interest as the mummy got closer, the kid's enormity becoming more apparent as they approached the group. The four kids parted, Glen and Emily on the one side and Josh and Pete on the other, making way for the mummy. As the mummy started to move up the sidewalk, Pete called out to them.

"Hey! Is there really any candy in there?" he asked.

The mummy, hearing this question, stopped in their tracks and slowly turned around. Pete looked to the others, smirking a little because of the bigger kid's absurd commitment to their costumed persona. The mummy stood there staring a hole through the four kids. Josh felt himself getting a little nervous as he now noticed that there didn't really seem to be other trick-or-treaters in the area with them. It was deathly quiet other than the hum of a streetlight. The wind picked up just a little, sending a chill through Josh. He noticed Emily gripping Glen's forearm.

The mummy's wrappings weren't as stark white as you'd expect if you purchased the costume in a department store. These wrappings were dingy, nasty looking. As the mummy stared at Josh and his friends, Josh couldn't really find the mummy's eyes. A dark shadow seemingly fell over where they would be. An uncomfortable silence grew, yet no one seemed gutsy enough to break the silence except the group's clown.

"Well!" Pete continued. "Is there any candy in there or what?" he asked.

The kid in the mummy costume shifted just a tad. Then, they slowly nodded their head, an up and down motion three times. The mummy pulled the bag off their shoulder, letting it fall to the ground with a heavy *thud*, and dipped their hand inside. Their hand dug around for a few seconds as the kids watched. The mummy's hand returned with a king-sized Snickers and a king-sized Baby Ruth. Josh noticed a reddish tinge to the Baby Ruth's wrapper that reflected the bandages covering the mummy's hand.

The mummy shook the bars in their hand at Josh and his friends. To Josh, the action felt more menacing than playful. After this response, the mummy pulled its bag back up over their shoulder, turned around, and resumed walking, still dragging their left foot. The scraping on the pavement was unpleasantly loud in the absence of any other trick-or-treaters. The sound grew progressively quieter as the mummy moved down Pike Street, leaving an opening for Pete to exclaim.

"That settles it!" said Pete. "There's candy inside. Great candy! So what are we waiting for?"

Josh's antennas nearly flew off his head as he turned in Pete's direction at this response. He looked to Emily, who no longer appeared to be a painted-up witch, just a frightened child. Glen, always cool as a cucumber, was smiling.

"Come on, Em! That kid was just messing with us. Trying to spook us! He's just an asshole," said Glen.

"More like a dried up turd wrapped in toilet paper. Who even dresses up like a mummy? Mummies aren't scary," said Pete.

"Speak for yourself. That kid was creepy, and that costume was nasty!" said Emily.

Pete gave Glen a look that seemed to say *work your magic.* No one apparently was concerned with how Josh felt. But at the end of the day, Glen and Pete were the decision makers on most things, so Josh was resigned to go along with whatever they wanted to do. Even if it meant entering a stranger's property offering candy.

Glen flexed at Emily like he was Hulk Hogan. She seemingly melted into a puddle at Glen's feet. Glen shifted his mask back down over his face. Pete looked at Josh excitedly. At that reaction, Josh knew they were going into the spooky house.

The door to the house opened easily enough with no creepy creaking to make the kids second guess their decision. Glen entered first with Emily following, then Pete and Josh. Josh closed the door as the three ahead of him stopped in the entrance. A small lamp on a table provided light in the area. Glen led the way moving the group out of the entryway into a den. Natural cobwebs decorated the room in the corners of the walls where they met the ceiling. A fireplace glowed with dying embers. Josh found it strange that the den had no place to sit. There were no couches or chairs. The only furniture in the room was an old oak table with a big empty bowl.

"Son of a bitch!" Pete yelled. "That turd wrapper cleaned out the bowl."

"What a piece of shit," Glen said, chuckling.

"Good! That means we can leave then," said Emily as Pete walked closer to the bowl. He stopped at the table looking at something.

"What are you looking at?" asked Josh.

Pete held up another cardboard sign that read "MORE CANDY THIS WAY" with an arrow pointing in the direction of another room of the house. Josh could make out what looked like linoleum flooring in the other room from the den. Likely the kitchen. Emily broke the silence by asking the obvious.

"Why wouldn't they just sit more candy out here instead of making us walk deeper into the house? This doesn't feel right."

Pete clapped his hands together with an excited expression on his face. "Oh! I bet I know what this is. This person turned their house into a haunted maze. We probably have to walk through rooms of crappy decorations, and it ends with us getting some king-sized candy bars!"

"And what would make you think that?" asked Emily.

"Probably because whoever's house this is belongs to an old lonely person who just wants to see some kids have some fun and then reward them for providing a little company."

Everyone, even Glen, looked at Pete with his stupid red clown nose skeptically.

"I guarantee you when we go into that other room that looks like a kitchen, there's going to be another sign pointing us somewhere else. We'll walk a little farther and some spider or something is going to dangle down from the ceiling. Emily will piss her panties, but we'll push on and finally we'll get to the owner, and they'll thank us for coming with some big ass candy bars!"

"That mummy seemed to say so," said Glen. "I'm willing to find out."

Emily looked annoyed but willing to go along with what Glen was doing. Josh didn't have a good feeling about any of it, but he didn't want to rock the boat with Glen or Pete and risk a teasing later from either of the boys. *Are you supposed to be an alien? Because you look more like a sissy . . .* Josh swallowed his worry and followed the other three into the connecting room that was indeed a kitchen. Inside was another table off to the side. Sitting on top of it was another bowl. Instead of being empty, there were a few crumpled wrappers inside. Little flecks of chocolate also rested in the bottom of the bowl.

The room was sparsely decorated with black and orange streamers hanging from the ceiling. To the right of the kitchen was a hallway. The kids couldn't see it from the den as it was blocked by a wall in the den's entryway. Here, the kids could see jack-o'-lanterns lit on the ground as a guiding path. Doors could be seen on each side, but the carved pumpkin faces seemed to be guiding the children to a black-painted door. The ghoulish visages silently beckoned the kids to come this way. *We have something to show you.*

"That seems dangerous," said Josh referring to the lit jack-o'-lanterns in the house.

"How'd that mummy kid make it through here without catching himself on fire?" Glen questioned.

"Candy's that way, my friends," said Pete while showing the others another cardboard sign with an arrow pointing down the pumpkin-lit hallway. "We doin' this or what?"

Glen just shrugged. "We've already gone this far."

The kids began their trek down the hall single-file. Josh glanced at each jack-o'-lantern as he passed. The first couple were goofy with single-toothed grins and triangle eyes. But the next pumpkins took a frightening turn with jagged fangs. The pumpkins that followed appeared even more aggressive; threatening to bite anyone attempting to blow out their candles.

The last two pumpkins were not goofy or scary. Instead, their faces wore a mask of despair–their mouths carved in big O's. Glen put his hand on the doorknob. Josh continued to stare at the anguished pumpkins, a feeling creeping up his neck. Glen began turning the knob. Josh recognized that feeling on his neck of great terror. His face shot up from staring at the pumpkins to his friends.

"Stop!"

But the door opened inside to a green-lit room. The color was spooky, yet mesmerizing. The kids became swallowed by a glow, and before he could even discern how it happened, Josh was standing in the room with his friends. The door shut behind them with a *BANG*. The kids jumped and snapped out of their temporary trance.

"Welcome," said a voice stepping out of the room's shadows. The person's identity was hidden under a hooded cloak, but Josh could tell it was a woman, *an old woman.* Stepping more into the green glow, Josh could see her face was as wrinkled as a burlap sack. Wispy, white strands of hair poured out from under her hood down over her shoulders. Her stature was short and non-threatening, but the ghostly light gave her a frightening presence. Her eyes betrayed her withered appearance with an excited glee for the children that stepped inside her room. She was the real-life embodiment of what Emily dressed as for Halloween.

Pete stammered with fear, "The . . . the . . . sign," he swallowed. It was a dry swallow, making his next words come out with more difficulty. "It said there was candy inside."

The woman smiled at this. She quick-stepped to Pete and blew something out of her palm into Pete's face as the other kids watched horrified. Pete screamed. Glen turned back to the door with Emily hanging on his arm.

He jerked on the door knob, not able to turn it. Josh stood off to the side of the chaos in shock. Pete fell to his knees. His screams died as his face froze with a crystalline shine—the room's green glow shimmering across it. His hands beckoned to Josh to do something. All Josh could do was watch.

Glen and Emily fought with the door, but it stubbornly refused to cooperate. Consumed by their panic, the pair remained oblivious to the witch's stealthy approach. The witch traced her fingers across the backs of their necks. Both kids trembled under her touch. Emily's face contorted in horror as she began to cry. The sound assaulted Josh's nerves.

The witch thrived on the kids' fear like a spider playing with its food. She leaned in close and whispered into their ears. Josh heard her tongue clicking, but the words were unintelligible. Glen and Emily's posture shot straight with their arms falling to their sides. The witch slightly pulled them both by their shoulders, and they fell straight down with a *thud* next to Pete and his shiny, grimacing face. Josh was trapped in his mind, horrified by what he was seeing, and terrified as the witch turned her attention to him. He fell backward into a wooden chair.

"You can watch for now," she said with a chilling grin. Some teeth were missing, and her gums were black. It looked as if she had spent her life eating too much candy. Indulging in too many sweet delights. The kids just wanted candy too, but the house's promise of *candy inside* was a lie–*a trap.* But the mummy kid, Josh thought. The mummy came out of the house unscathed. Then, Josh remembered the mummy's appearance. The dingy rags. The shadow over its eyes. *Was that blood on the candy bar and its hand? Just what the hell is happening? Is this real? This can't be real!*

The witch stood in front of Pete holding something in her hand. Josh realized that it was a hammer. The witch clapped the side of the hammer against her left hand. *Pop, pop, pop.* Pete's hands went from touching his face to pantomiming a beggar. *PLEASE!!!* He was looking for mercy, yet the witch leaned in close to his face.

"You're the candy," she said laughing, an eruption of insane giddiness. Her body leaned back with laughter. Then, she swung forward in a fluid motion, hitting Pete square in the face with the hammer. Pete's face broke apart like peanut brittle, falling in shards of colorful hard pieces. *Like candy.*

The witch laughed and hit Pete in the face some more. He continued to shed pieces like a burst piñata and the witch danced around him, swinging and swinging until Pete's face was gone. Emily and Glen made no sound as they lay like boards next to the carnage. Glen's face was covered by his latex vampire mask, showing zero emotion. Emily's eyes were pooling in terror, leaking down the side of her face.

The witch gathered up the pieces of Pete's face. *Peteces.* She dropped them into a bowl. They clattered with a tinkling sound. She dug more out of Pete's hollow husk of a head and dropped them in the bowl. *Plink plink plink.* She sat the bowl over on a table. Moving on from Pete, the witch looked to Glen and Emily.

"You," she said to Glen. "You will make a friend of mine very happy." She turned her attention to Emily in her witch costume. "You . . . *a mockery.* Why must they continue to mock? I'll tell you why. To forget. To soften. Make us a joke. Make us a costume. Then, we're just a myth, *a story.*" The witch lowered down next to Emily's face looking into her eyes. She was trying to intimidate Emily, though Josh was sure that smashing in their friend's face already did an effective job of that. The witch looked at Josh.

"I am *real.* We are *real.* And you should be scared." She grinned her black-gummed, toothless mouth and said, "I know you are!"

The witch's hand disappeared inside her cloak and returned holding a blade. The handle looked old and weathered. From a different time, a more frightening time. Josh shook his head. Now, without speaking, he was begging, the way Pete was begging before his face turned into hard candy. *Don't hurt her. Don't hurt me. Don't hurt any of us!*

The witch's arm flashed in an extraordinary motion. Emily's stomach opened with a vertical slash like a roll ready to be buttered. The witch dug her hands inside the bloody mess and began tugging out her intestines.

"Licorice rope!" she yelled excitedly while pulling and pulling and *pulling.* Josh's vision was trying to shutter closed. His head felt woozy. A coppery-shit smell permeated inside the room. If Josh felt like he had more control over his body, he would vomit all over himself. Probably across the room. The room's green glow would give it a slime-like appearance. But Josh's body wouldn't allow him to. *She* wouldn't allow him to.

Just then the door creaked open. A tall figure entered the room. It was a man stylishly-dressed, oozing charisma. He was a presence you couldn't ignore. The witch finished gathering Emily's intestines and addressed the stranger. "Special one for you there," she said, motioning to Glen's stiff body.

The man smiled. Josh noticed his canines were particularly longer, *sharper* than any normal adult's. He leaned down and picked Glen up one-handed by Glen's vampire costume. He appeared to admire Glen's latex mask at first. Then, he slowly pulled it off Glen's terrified face.

"Mmmm . . . I bet this candy's sweet," he said while winking at Josh, still frozen in his seat watching a nightmare come to life.

The man turned Glen so that the left side of his neck was exposed. The man leaned in gently, sniffing Glen's neck. His head reared back and then bit into the boy's neck with his fangs. Then, he JERKED BACK! Blood and skin slung across the back of the wall and on the stranger. He laughed and then sunk back into Glen's neck, chugging ferociously. The stranger's throat swallowed as his lips sucked and slurped like a baby to a teat. A real vampire consuming a fake vampire. Swallowing him down like a sweet, bloody soda.

The vampire stopped sucking and dropped Glen's

body to the floor. It landed with a dull *thud*. Glen's corpse was pale, almost translucent. Every bit of his life force was now in the vampire that was speaking to the witch.

"Sorry about the mess. This holiday always puts me in a fun mood." The vampire turned to look at Josh. "So much to TASTE!"

"Well, plenty more still out there tonight. You're always welcome here, Osric, especially on Halloween. I always keep plenty of candy for my friends."

The vampire Osric acknowledged his departure with a nod to the witch and left. Josh knew that his time was almost up *(his LIFE was almost up!)*. The witch was currently busy with arranging the candy bowls of Pete's *Peteces* and Emily's *licorice rope* on a table near the back wall.

She returned to Josh holding a jar. With an impassive gaze, she twisted off its lid and threw pinches of its contents in his face. It was grainy, sandy. The sand tickling his face was a morbid contrast to his paralyzing fear. Some touched his lips, his tongue. It tasted sweet like . . . sugar. She was sprinkling him with sugar.

Terror crawled up Josh's spine. In the air, he could feel a change. It was an energy, another presence of something remarkable, a story, a nightmare come to life. It was all of these things, and Josh knew it was coming for him. He was sugar-coated. He was the dessert. He was the *candy inside*. A growl rumbled down the hall. The floor underneath Josh's planted feet vibrated in a soft rhythm. Before Josh saw the door open, he knew what was coming, but he didn't want to believe it.

The door swung open to confirm his dread. There stood a werewolf. The beast walked on its hind legs, wearing ripped dress pants and a torn button shirt. The movies got the appearance right. But what you don't get from the movies is the smell of the wolf's drool, the heat from the wolf's exhaled breath, and the taste of the dirt clinging to the wolf's fur.

The witch stepped aside and motioned to Josh in the chair. The wolfman snapped his head in Josh's direction and moved closer. *Closer.* Inches from Josh's face. The wolfman's maw opened — enough to fit Josh's entire head in.

The witch observed the scene with grotesque fascination.

Josh's mind tried to leave his body, escape to anywhere but this moment. Then, he remembered their debate at the house's entrance on whether to enter. The promise of those king-sized candy bars they were so desperately after. And now this. *Does the wolfman consider me king-sized or fun-sized?*

INVASION OF THE BAG SNATCHERS
Ryan Peña

As Halloween night was slowly coming to an end, the self-proclaimed "King of the Streets" stood atop the neighborhood surveying his kingdom. Tony, who was already eighteen years old, had given up trick-or-treating years ago. Why go to all those houses when you can just wait for one of the weaklings to do it for you? Knock on twenty to thirty doors or knock over one dweeb? It's simple math. The self-proclaimed King felt strongly that this was the type of knowledge that needed to be shared with his juvenile band of impressionable misfits that surrounded him on this chilly evening, hanging on to every word.

Tony took his hand out of his brown flight jacket pocket, pulled his aviators down to the tip of his nose and peered over them as he had seen his heroes do on television. His eyes darted back and forth from trick-or-treater to trick-or-treater searching for his prey as he thought an alpha wolf would, sniffing out the weakest of the herd for his pack to prey upon in the darkness.

"Bingo," he said with a sinister grin as he found their intended target.

All alone in front of 5 Pike St., was a ghost: a young girl covered in a plain white (almost clean) bed sheet with two crooked eye holes cut out that failed to hide the large bifocals underneath. She stood motionless and was seemingly staring off into space, paying no attention to the wolf and his pack. In one hand she held a pillowcase colored with a marker to resemble a jack-o'-lantern, presumably full of the night's spoils. In the other, she gripped a flashlight.

Behind her was her own home, a hollow shadow of its former self. What was once considered one of the most pristine residences in the neighborhood now sits what used to be a copper-painted home, faded and peeling to a dull and sick, sandy color, uneven and thin. The former white and neat, wooden picket fence with a gate now sat unevenly, missing posts, broken latch, leaning to one side or the other as if the ground beneath the house protested at the fence's existence in the earth. The once beautiful garden, so full of life, colors, and scents of the seasons, now stood dormant, dry, and dark. It smelled only of moldy things, things once living that had died long ago. The lawn was overgrown with triffid-like weeds and termite-infested pieces of siding dangled off the sides of the house like broken limbs. The property was completely dark except for the strange, flashing multicolored lights that were shining out from a small basement window which has been the subject of much discussion by the townsfolk, and determined by popular opinion to be the scientist's own private laboratory where unspeakable experiments were conducted deep into the night.

"Hello Mary Lou, it's Halloween night two," Tony said chuckling to himself.

"Oh my God! Is she really wearing the exact same costume she wore last year? What a loser," laughed Paulie, "A ghost again? How creative!" Paulie, one of Tony's three little droogies, was dressed up as a very uninspired vampire. Yet the irony eluded him. "I thought that a little know-it-all brainiac like her would be able to come up with something better than that.

"Right, Tony?" he nodded to his fearless leader, in a transparent gesture seeking approval.

"It's not creativity, it's poverty," Tony said matter-of-factly.

"Yeah . . . wait, what?" asked Paulie.

"Tell 'em, Margo," Tony said, nodding over to the only girl in the posse.

Calling her a Tom Boy would have been an understatement. Margarete went by the nickname "Margo" with her friends and family. The neighborhood kids affectionately called her Large Marge, but NEVER to her face.

She was built like a linebacker, which she used to her advantage as she played football with the boys. She didn't play for the love of the game or sport in general for that matter, but for the pure love of sheer physical violence. She relished the fear in their eyes, the snap of bones and pops of sinews in limbs as she twisted, snapped, and drove the boys into the ground. For those who did not know her personally, they would assume that her costume was that of a simple farmer. The overalls, pitchfork, and pigtails looked innocent enough, however to the horror movie aficionado, they would see that she was indeed something else far darker and very specific to the blackness inside her.

Margo was, in fact, Ida Smith, sister to the notorious Farmer Vincent from the film *Motel Hell.* Her resemblance to the screen-killer was uncanny. Margo liked to warm up before inflicting physical torture by starting with emotional pain, gradually drawing others in. Her smile, curling at the edges would grow wider and beyond the edges of her face, stretching outward, yellowed teeth, that looked like jagged bits of old china, jutting out from thin and bloodless lips. Wearing the costume always gave her that chance to tell the story — *her story* — the tale of woe that had befallen young Mary Lou and her family, the little ghost, who stood shaking in front of the ramshackle house that barely still stood at 5 Pike St.

"Story goes," she began, "that Mary's mom was a bit of a floozie and a boozy. Everybody in town knew it too except for Mary Lou's dad. He was way too busy with his scientist job at NASA to notice that his old lady wasn't happy at home. He worked long hours, and she soon grew tired of being left at home alone with their creepy little kid. So one day, Mary Lou's dad caught a red-eye home early to surprise his wife, but he was the one that ended up surprised. He found her in bed with another man!" she said excitedly.

"Who was it?" Paulie asked.

"It was Coach Schneider, the P.E. teacher!" she exclaimed.

"But I thought that Coach Schneider liked boys and not girls," Paulie said with a bewildered look on his face.

"WILL YOU SHUT UP!?" Tony interjected. "Just let her finish the story so we can get on with our night . . . and for the record, I saw Coach Schneider coming out of a bar one night dressed in all leather like the lead singer of Judas Priest. No one that dresses like that would have the hots for other dudes!" he shouted.

"That's right, Tony," Margo continued. "So, the coach and Mary Lou's mom ran off together leaving her dad crazy broken hearted. They say he had a complete mental breakdown. He lost his wife. Then he lost his high-paying job, and finally he lost his sanity. He spends all his time down in his basement laboratory doing all sorts of strange experiments at all hours of the day and night. He never leaves the house at all anymore. Without his job he can't even pay someone to cut his grass. That's why the house looks the way that it does now," Margo explained.

"Yeah," Tommy chimed in, grinning, I bet that anytime Mary Lou watches an episode of *Silver Spoons,* she starts crying."

In fact, Mary Lou was not crying, her shaking hands suddenly became still but Margo and the others were far too invested in the story to notice. Being a ghost has its advantages after all, even if the eye holes weren't cut very evenly at all.

Paulie grabbed his own stomach and forced out a fake laugh.

"Good one, Tony! That's why you are the *Top Gun!*" Tony turned to face Paulie. His smile had vanished, replaced with an angry scowl.

"Do I look like Maverick or Goose to you, Moron? I told you that I'm the pilot of Airwolf!" Tony shouted as he raised a fist to strike the younger hooligan.

Paulie immediately recoiled in fear, wincing as he shielded his face with both hands. "I'm sorry, I'm sorry!" he pleaded. "I forgot."

Tony's wicked smile returned. "I wasn't going to hit you, *but* . . . now you do have to get two for flinching."

"*Awww,* come on Tony, please don't hit me!" he pleaded.

"I told you that I wasn't going to hit you and I meant it." A look of relief came over Paulie's face.

"Gee, thanks Tony. For a minute I thought you were serious about the two shots."

"Oh, I'm dead serious about that. I'm not going to give them to you, but Margo is."

She laid the pitchfork on the ground and began to crack each one of her knuckles, savoring Paulie's fearful anticipation. He offered his upper right arm to her knowing that if he flinched again, the consequences would be much worse. She landed two quick punches. The force of the blows made him rock back on one foot, almost falling over. He rubbed his arm with his other hand and mouthed the word *ouch.* He dared not say it aloud and show weakness.

"Okay guys, I definitely deserved that! Good two!" Both Tony and Margo's blank expressions were enough of a sign to Paulie that his joke did not land so he quickly tried to change the subject.

"How about I go ahead and snatch that little loser's bag and let you guys have first dibs on her candy?" he asked hopefully.

Tony turned his attention back in the direction of Mary Lou. "No. I think Tommy should do this one. Right Tommy boy?" he asked.

His question was met with silence. The trio looked all around for their newest would-be member. "Where is he?" Tony demanded. "Is that him across the street?" Is that Tommy knocking on the old witch's door?"

Tommy was the newest and youngest recruit of the crew that Tony had named the "Ravens." He had come up with the name one day in English class. It had nothing to do with the work of Edgar Allen Poe. In fact, Tony couldn't understand most of the words in any of the author's works. The idea actually came from a lesson the teacher was giving on the different names given to groups of animals. As the teacher was giving examples like a smack of jellyfish or a flamboyance of flamingos, it was the term for a group of ravens that caught his attention. The teacher went on to say that a group of ravens is known as an "unkindness." Some would think this particular name was chosen because of the crew's antics and activities, like stuffing kids' heads in toilets or shoving them into their lockers. However, the irony would be lost on Tony as he chose the name simply because it sounded cool.

Tommy himself was not unkind by nature. He did not take pleasure in bullying like the other members of the crew. While Tony was of the "survival of the fittest mentality," little Tommy was more in the camp of *"if you can't beat them, join them."* He knew that it was much safer behind the Ravens than in front of them. He was a bit brighter than the others so he regularly offered to do their homework, which kept him in their good graces and out of the nurse's office. It also didn't hurt that his father owned the local arcade and gave the group unlimited plays on *Galaga* and *Pac-Man.*

"Ay-Yo Tommy! Get ova here!" Tony shouted. Tommy came running back across the street. "What the hell are you doing man?" Tony demanded.

"I was trick-or-treating real quick," he replied through the plastic Superman mask. It was the kind you got in the Halloween aisle at the local five and dime.

"WHAT?" the three Ravens asked in unison.

"Yeah guys check it out." He extended his bag of candy out in front of the others and opened it for inspection.

"She's giving out full-sized candy bars! I told her you all may want some too and she said she had more inside."

Tony looked in the bag and then shot Tommy a confused look. "You do know what we are doing out here tonight, right? You remember the mission?"

While Tommy was book smart, it sometimes took him a little while to pick up on certain cues. "Of course I do. I just figured it wouldn't hurt to get a little bit more. I mean, it's a full-sized candy bar after all."

Tony's confusion and anger were battling inside his brain trying to see which one would come out of his mouth first.

"Are you kidding me right now?" he finally managed to exclaim.

Instinctively, Margo the Muscle snatched the full-sized candy bar from Tommy's bag. She crushed it in the palm of her hand with chocolate oozing out between her fingers like a cocoa Play-Doh factory.

"You were saying?" she asked menacingly.

He wisely stopped talking. Tony once again turned back around toward the little ghost girl.

"All of us have done this many times tonight and now it is finally your turn, Tommy. You do this and you are officially a member of the Ravens. And just to show you that I'm a nice guy, I've hand-picked your very first mark," he said, gesturing grandly toward Mary Lou, the little ghost, who had not moved from where they found her. She was still clutching her hand-colored jack-o'-lantern treat bag.

Once Tommy saw who it was, he was conflicted. He knew her from class and felt sorry for her. She never spoke unless she absolutely was forced to do so by a teacher. She walked the halls alone, head perpetually down, glasses always smeared, clothes rumpled and a waft of sadness followed her wherever she went as did the "unkindness" of others, taunting, laughing, and whispering about little Mary Lou. He searched for the words to protest without a harmful repercussion.

"Didn't you guys get her last year? Didn't you guys

say that she had nasty stuff in her bag? Shouldn't we get someone new? I mean, what's the fun in that?" Tommy asked in rapid succession.

Tony pulled down his aviators to glare at Tommy. "I thought you wanted to be a Raven? I thought you would be happy with me picking such an easy target for your first one. But . . . if you don't want to, you don't have to."

"Really!?" Tommy replied optimistically.

"Sure." Tony said with that familiar grin on his face. "We'll just take your candy instead. Then we'll beat you down and leave you lying here in a bloody heap on the ground. Now, sweep the bag, Mr. Lawrence. Do you have a problem with that?"

Tommy gulped audibly before back peddling. "No, no. I'll do it. I was just thinking that since you all got her last year that she may be expecting it again and could scream."

Tony was unfazed by this potential situation.

"Look around you, Tommy. Everyone is dressed up like ghouls and goblins. There's spooky music being played on numerous stereo systems across town like a satanic symphony. People are jumping out of the bushes trying to make people jump out of their skin. Everyone is trying to scare everyone. It's Halloween. Nobody pays attention to screams."

Tommy started to make his way down the street toward Mary Lou's house with the three others not far behind. He mustered more of his courage with each step, weaving through trick-or-treaters like a skier on a slalom course. Beads of sweat began to form above his brow. His stomach felt like it was doing somersaults. Nevertheless, this was a code-red, life-or-death mission.

He reached his hand underneath his mask and wiped away the salty sweat before it could run down into his eyes. As he drew closer and closer to his objective, he noticed she hadn't moved at all. It was as if she was waiting for something. He picked up the pace and widened his stride. The wind blowing against his plastic costume made him believe he was almost flying, so he pretended to really be Superman. *Just a few more feet and this will be all over,* he thought to himself. He reached out with outstretched fingers for the prize.

He grabbed the top of the bag and turned to make a break for it when the unimaginable happened. He could not pry it away from her grasp and it felt like he was yanked back like a ship leaving a dock, moored. As his body whipped back around he found himself face to face with the young girl, their eyes now locked together. His eyes were the ones wide with panic and hers were void of any recognizable emotion. He just stood there staring at her for what felt like a lifetime to him. Then the laughing began. Followed by clapping.

"Wow! That was amazing! I wonder if we'll see that on *Ripley's Believe it or Not!,*" joked Tony as he and the others circled the interlocked pair.

"What happened?" Paulie asked.

"Yeah, what happened Tommy? It was literally taking candy away from a baby and you couldn't even get that right. *Sheesh!*"

"She's a lot stronger than she looks guys," Tommy said.

Margo was the next to get in on the fun. "Oh yeah? Is she freakishly strong? Are you freakishly strong, you little freak? Did your dad Dr. Freakenstein, make you freakishly strong in his lab like the Incredible Hulk?" Margo asked, spitting as the words passed over the jagged teeth and cracked, stretched lips.

"Shut up!" Mary Lou shouted.

"So, she can talk after all!" laughed Paulie. The Ravens began circling the two like sharks catching the scent of blood before the frenzy.

"I don't think her dad made her strong, Margo," Tony began, "I think the only thing that her dad made, was her mother disappear."

"Ooooh burn!" added Paulie. "Tell us four-eyes, did your dad kill her, your whore momma, and her boyfriend? Did he bury them in the backyard or in the basement?"

"PISS OFF!" Mary Lou yelled, now shaking with rage.

"Piss off, huh? Now that's not a bad idea," Tony said as he stopped directly behind Mary Lou.

What came next surprised everyone. First was the unmistakable sound of a zipper being pulled down. Then the undeniable look of horror in Mary Lou's eyes. She felt hot liquid hit her back and then run down her legs. Frozen in fear and shame, she released her hold on the bag of candy, leaving it in Tommy's grasp.

"Dang, Tony! Now she's a yellow ghost! Casper the cowardly ghost!" Margo said. The three Ravens cackled with cruel laughter.

Suddenly, something inside Mary Lou's candy bag shook violently, jerking the bag from Tommy's hand and falling onto the ground. Tommy let out a shriek and jumped back.

"What's wrong with you?" Tony demanded.

"Something in the bag moved!" Tommy said, eyes wide, his hand trembling as he pointed at the jack-o'-lantern sack now lying on the dead lawn.

Tony zipped up his Jordache jeans and gave Mary Lou a shove. "What's in the bag, you little weirdo? You put something in there that's gonna bite my hand when I stick it in Flash Gordon style?"

Mary Lou stayed silent.

"Check it out, Margo." Tony ordered.

Margo picked up the bag and peered in. She looked back at Tony with a very confused expression.

"It's just a bunch of candy and a . . . " She reached in and pulled out a cool whip container.

"Go on . . . open it," he said.

Margo pulled the lid off, revealing a green ooze.

"Oh cool, it's slime! Like from *Ghostbusters*," Paulie exclaimed.

Margo grabbed a handful and let it drip down her arm. She then passed it over to Tony who did the same thing.

"Is this part of your costume? Did your dad make this for you?" Tony asked in a mocking tone.

Mary Lou nodded yes.

"What an idiot. Slimer is green you twit, and your

cheap costume is white," Tony chuckled.

"Yellow now," Margo corrected.

"Don't hog it all you guys, I want some," Paulie whined.

"Here ya go," Tony said as he half-slapped, half-smeared some across Paulie's face.

Tony and Margo shared a hearty laugh at the vampire's expense. A few seconds later, though, the laughter stopped.

"It feels like it's moving, doesn't it?" Margo asked with a bit of worry now in her tone as she stared down at her hand, wide eyed, clearly spooked but still trying to chuckle weakly, her smile now reduced to only half as wide.

"That's because it is," Mary Lou stated simply.

"It's also getting hotter," Paulie added. "I can see it moving! It's like crawling underneath my fingernails!"

Tony howled. "It's burning me like the blood from those Aliens in the movies!"

Mary Lou removed the sheet that was still dripping piss from her small frame. She stared at her three bullies as they started writhing in excruciating pain, rushing to wipe the green ooze from their hands, arms, and face on the grass, their clothes, and each other.

Mary Lou smiled. Tommy had never seen her smile. Then she took a deep breath as if it was a bore to try to explain complex scientific concepts to a group of complete imbecilic idiots.

"Alien blood is more like acid that burns from the outside. This particular substance does the opposite. It burns you from the inside out," she said, rolling her eyes as if this was common knowledge to the general public and it was a chore to have to explain the difference.

The Ravens watched and saw the green, slimy gel begin to burrow and push its way into every pore, through the nail bed, into the right side of Phillip's eye, crawling, digging, finding its way to the tender filling within. Their skin rippled as if their veins had come to life and decided to revolt, shifting and ripping away from the bones like maggots moving through the body of a dead rat. It made it's way deeper, entered, and then began flowing through their veins, causing them to swell and pulsate, with each pulse causing sharp nuclear levels of pain. Paulie was shrieking and clawing at his eyes, nose and mouth, his screams soon becoming gurgles as the ooze consumed and devoured his tongue and vocal cords.

Paulie dropped to his knees, gurgling and clawing at his throat then suddenly he stopped, looked up, and a flood of blood, bile, ooze, and pieces of vital organs spewed from what used to be his mouth onto the other Ravens.

Mary Lou calmly took a couple of steps backward as Tony and Margo's veins began to blister and pop like the grease in a pan cooking bacon. Tommy was the only one of the group that did not get any of the stuff on his person. The fluid he felt in his pants and streaming down his leg was his own urine, losing control due to sheer terror of what he was witnessing—three humans simultaneously exploding and melting into the lawn.

The other two howled and screamed in absolute pain until their throats swelled like bullfrogs. What used to be Paulie was lying in a puddle of twitching goo that no longer looked human.

When the gurgles and hisses had ceased, the jerking movements stopped, and the damage was done, what remained was only three green heaps on the ground.

Finally, Tommy's terror had subsided to a level where running home as quickly as possible seemed like the best and smartest decision of his young life, he smashed through the dilapidated gate and ran faster than the Flash ever did, away from 5 Pike St.

Mary Lou calmly picked up her bag of candy, brushing the dust off the jack-o'-lantern she had hastily colored on its side, turned, and without a sound, drifted to the door and into the dark of the once happy home. As the green ooze liquefied and seeped into the ground, as if the earth craved sustenance, the last of the trick-or-treaters scampered by, parents calling out to children, laughter, and screams.

Not a single soul gave a second look toward 5 Pike St.

On Halloween, your screams go unheard.

THE BOWL ON THE STOOP
Kevin Higgins

H E PUT THE BOWL OUT on the stoop, even though he knew they wouldn't come.

They never did. Never had for as long as he'd lived on Pike Street—twenty years now, maybe more. *(Really, who could keep track?)*

Still, he did it anyway.

Old habits die hard.

He knew that better than anybody.

From the top step of his wraparound porch, he surveyed the neighborhood. There were no kids out yet, but it was early. Up and down the block, he could see lights ticking on in windows, fighting the fast-fading sun. He knew without seeing what was going on behind them: hurried dinners and homework, frantic fixes to costumes damaged at the various school parades and parties. The witching hour was yet to come, but it would be here soon.

He looked at the bowl, full as it was, and wondered if maybe, just maybe, this might be the year.

Hope springs eternal.

He had seen that somewhere once and liked it. The world was so full of nastiness these days; a little optimism was good for the soul.

He inhaled deeply. Somewhere not so far away, someone was burning leaves, spicing the autumn air with an intoxicating, earthy sweetness. Halloween had arrived, a mangy black cat on a fencepost, here only briefly and then surely gone again, onto its next dark appointment. The holiday was unique in that way, he thought. The night felt both precious and endless, in a way few other nights of the year do.

He never cared much for the spectacle of the day, with all the hocus pocus talk of spooks and spirits and specters. Everybody wanted their boogeymen to have green skin or a disfigured face or claws for hands, but in his opinion, there were far worse things in the real world to be afraid of. The real boogeymen looked just like your next door neighbor, or your mailman, or the cashier at the town grocery. Some people were just born bad—but he knew that bad without bluster didn't sell. Still, he could appreciate Halloween for its Celtic roots, the festival of Samhain (he never quite knew how to pronounce that), a time to mark the end of one season and the birth of the next. That kind of reset was healthy, he thought.

Sometimes, a fresh start is needed.

And of course, there were appearances to keep up. He knew what happened to the homes that kept their doorsteps darkened on Halloween, and he didn't particularly feel like cleaning eggs off the siding; it looked bad enough as it was. So he put the bowl out every year, because that was what tradition dictated. Halloween was a holiday with rules, a social contract between child and homeowner. He would honor his end of the deal. And he hoped that this year, they would finally honor theirs.

~

He saw the flag on his mailbox was up, so he stepped out onto the walk and headed toward the street. When he opened it, he was pleasantly surprised; no bills today, and his package had come. He put the padded envelope under his arm, closed the mailbox, and looked back at his home from the sidewalk.

He knew what the kids said about Pike Street, and

his house in particular. Dead ends in small towns were like that; there was simply no way around it. It was all nonsense, of course . . . the urban legend greatest hits, played on repeat. But kids trafficked in nonsense, especially bored kids living sheltered lives. It was the essential currency of youth.

He supposed it might be the condition of the house that brought on all the rumors. He knew it was an eyesore, but as he looked at it now, in the darkening amber of the day, he was struck by just how off-putting it was, its features obscured and distorted in the failing light, the aging woodwork and trim drawing jagged and harsh with shadow. Even the number was missing, the faint outline of a "6" visible on the façade only as the sun-burnished silhouette of proper iron numbers long since rusted and removed.

It was no prize when he purchased it, all those years ago. He remembered overhearing a young couple at the open house deride the property as a "money pit." But the price and location were right, and he had bought it anyway: a large, lonely Victorian with ample privacy, surrounded by mature oaks and hydrangea and other lush flora beyond his scope of botanical knowledge. At the time, he had been very busy with his work, and wanted a place where he would be left alone. In so many ways, 6 Pike St. felt like *him,* only in house form; set far back from the street, shy and mysterious, its secrets held tightly within. When he saw the house, it had been love at first sight (despite all its flaws), and he had learned very early in life that he was powerless to ignore his impulses when they were that strong.

From the moment he had moved in, the issues were legion: there were busted pipes in the walls, the roof leaked like a motherfucker, and the subfloor had settled comically in spots, giving his living room carpet the undulating appearance of a putting green. He tackled things when he could, as time and money and energy would allow, but he wasn't very handy, and old houses are stubborn, and it was never enough. He had given up on the lawn several years back, when his knees could no longer take the push and pull of the old crank-start mower. He knew how it looked, knew that it probably drove his neighbors crazy, but that was okay. If they were talking, it was in whispers; nobody had once dared to approach him about it. And so the house remained, decrepit as it was, for young imaginations to run wild about its secrets, and those of the man inside. And that was fine, he supposed. If people wanted to think of 6 Pike St. as some kind of haunted house overrun with ghouls and goblins, he couldn't stop them.

There are no monsters like that in here, he thought, chuckling to himself. *Just little old me.*

~

He went back inside, put on the radio, and found himself shuffling across the kitchen to the tail end of "Monster Mash." He was in a good mood today, better than most days. He knew it was because of the bowl. A silly little thing to most, but to him, it was a big deal. He wanted to give something back to the neighborhood that had for so long afforded him the quiet lifestyle he lived. And this just might be the year, he convinced himself *(hope springs eternal, hope springs eternal)*, when the trick-or-treaters would finally come.

The song ended and he made himself some dinner. When he was finished, he put his dishes in the sink, went upstairs, and looked out the large picture window in his bedroom. He was immediately encouraged; the neighborhood was alive with activity. Up and down the block, groups of kids ping-ponged back and forth across the street in all kinds of costumes, carrying bags and pails and pillow sacks of every variety. He saw monsters and princesses in colorful abundance. The breeze of the day had picked up considerably; across the street, an older girl draped her coat around the shoulders of a younger boy dressed head to toe like a cat, a tussle of fallen leaves dancing spasmodically at their feet. Through the single-pane glass he heard the sounds of the season, coming from all directions: giggling and shrieks and sneakers pounding pavement, exasperated parents yelling *"slow down!"* and *"look both ways before you cross!"*. All Hallow's Eve had begun in earnest.

He watched as a group of younger children raced past his house without a sideways glance. Moments later, a gaggle of toddlers skipped by the opposite way, hustled along by a set of stroller-wielding parents. He saw one of the moms steal a look at his porch as she passed. He knew she was rendering some silent judgment on his home, on the uneven walk or the failing condition of the porch stairs, deeming whatever was inside the bowl not worth the risk of possible tears. He wondered if she had seen him up here, watching her from the window.

He felt anger, then shame, then sadness, in that order. Here he was, fixating again. The house was what it was; he couldn't change that now. If they were going to come, they would come. Standing there at the window wasn't helping anything. Sitting out on the porch would be even worse. He had a good idea about what people whispered about him behind his back; his presence would only scare people away.

After a few minutes at the window, he went downstairs to search for something to occupy his mind. He settled on the ragged paperback on the coffee table, a dimestore thriller he had picked up at a garage sale many years ago. It was a police procedural, a well-worn tale about one detective's dogged efforts to track down a wily serial killer, highly unrealistic but nonetheless entertaining. He found the dog-eared page that marked his place and began to read. Minutes later he was asleep.

~

It was some time later when he woke up on the couch, the book still open on his chest. It was much darker now, inside and out. Only a dim dusting of light, ugly and yellow, floated in from the streetlamps outside. He wondered groggily how long he'd been out.

Then he heard kids outside, lots of them, a few houses down. Not that long, then; Halloween was still in full swing. He suddenly felt a live-wire energy running through his whole body like an overloaded circuit, as if at any moment he might spark and catch fire.

Maybe someone had come and taken a treat from the bowl!

He rose quickly and shuffled to the front door. The frosted glass panels on either side returned only darkness, so he opened the door and went out on the porch.

The bowl, unfortunately, appeared undisturbed.

He poked around the contents, just to be sure, counting the wax treat bags inside and arriving at the same number he had started with. He thought about bringing the bowl in for the night, but realized he was just being petulant. Instead, he watched quietly as a clown, an alien, a witch, and a vampire approached the house next door. Maybe they would come here next. *Good things come to those who wait,* he reminded himself. Another saying he had seen somewhere once and liked.

He left the bowl where it was and went back inside.

His energy was coming back to him quickly now. He'd been on edge for weeks, mentally preparing for this day. He knew that wasn't normal, but his brain was his brain. He'd had a lifelong tendency to overthink every detail, overplay every anxiety. It was both a blessing and a curse. His line of work required him to be very detail-oriented, almost impeccably so, and he had been wildly successful at it, for decades on end. There was no room for error in the work he did, and he had made none. Now though, sitting here at home, his micro-obsessions were more of a nuisance than anything else. He was fixated on the bowl, and the incessant checking was only making things worse.

He went into the back room and put on some TV as a distraction, clicking around until he found an old science fiction picture he remembered from his childhood. The soundtrack was harsh and loud and would've drowned out any trick-or-treaters on his doorstep, but that was fine; he didn't have a working doorbell anyway. That's what the bowl was for. He needed to just sit here and let it happen.

Once, several years ago, he had thought about bringing the bowl out to the end of the walk and putting it down on the pavers there, where it would get more foot traffic, but he was worried about animals getting into it and ruining it, and so he nixed that idea. *And that's not how it works,* he thought. *Approach the house. Get the treat.* Those were the rules. They needed to come to it naturally; that was the deal on the table. He found himself growing indignant. He wasn't going to spoon-feed it to them; they had to work for it.

He felt himself getting groggy again, so he turned off the movie and went to do some busy work in the basement. When he came back up again, fifteen or twenty minutes later, he couldn't help himself; he went out onto the porch once more to check the bowl.

Still nothing.

He could feel his frustration building.

It was full dark now, and colder too, the breeze from earlier escalating to brash, uncoordinated bursts, like an out-of-breath giant. From his spot on the porch, he could feel the wind race down his neck and back, icy witch fingers probing ever deeper. *Very spooky weather,* he thought, *perfect for the occasion.* He scanned the sky and saw a thick cloud cover had blown in, bringing a heavy blanket of black over the new night. Even the shadows felt darker now, the negative space between the branches and bramble that lined his property an inky soup through which his eyes could not penetrate. He shivered, and realized it was not exclusively from the cold.

Impulsively, he decided to go for a drive, if for no other reason than to tamp down the urge to keep checking the bowl *(they must come to it themselves)*. He eased the old, champagne-colored sedan carefully out of his driveway and down the street, going extra slow on account of the increased foot traffic for the holiday. As he crawled down Pilke Street, he was encouraged by the number of kids still out and about. Maybe if they saw him leaving, the quiet man in the creepy house, they would have less trepidation about paying his bowl a visit.

At the end of the road, he made a right onto the busier

Line Street, accelerating up to speed with the other traffic. He continued on for a while, past the dog park and jungle gym and town pool, all popular spots in the summer, all empty now. When he passed the police station, he noticed there was only one cruiser in the lot. *Halloween must keep them pretty busy,* he thought, especially when the younger kids returned home for bathtubs and bedtimes and the older kids hit the streets, harboring darker aspirations than filling plastic pumpkins with processed sugar.

He drove to the town line, then turned off the main drag and worked his way through back roads until he came to an abandoned commercial building with a large, overgrown parking lot. It had been empty for years, the victim of some unresolved tax or ownership dispute, left to rot long ago by the more spiteful of the parties.

He pulled in and wound slowly around the building to the back, watching the crickets jump this way and that in the beams of his headlights, clearing a quiet path for his car as he crossed the heavily weeded macadam. He had been here many times before. It was as close to a black hole as anything else you might find on Earth, which made it a perfect spot for lots of things, thinking among them.

He parked the car — not in a spot, there were no spots anymore — and killed his engine and lights. Then he cranked down his window, letting the fall chill wash over him and his racing thoughts. From the surrounding darkness and woods beyond, he heard noises of all types, but he was not afraid. Halloween or not, no cursed doll would be emerging from the treeline, no mummy or monster hungry for flesh. Those things weren't real, he knew. The scariest things in life were human, and there were no humans around.

Except him.

~

When the cold became too much to bear, he cranked up his window, turned on the engine and headlights, and headed back. The illuminated clock on his instrument panel showed that it was getting late. Halloween was mostly over now, he figured. There were unwritten rules about when the doorbell ringing stopped; he didn't know if there was a grace period for bowls, but if there was, they were probably past that too.

Maybe somebody came while I was out.

The thought gave him a charge, small as it was, and he began to negotiate with himself; he would check the bowl one more time, then call it a night. Yes, that seemed fair. One more look, and then another Halloween would be in the books.

He smiled the entire ride home.

~

It was almost ten when he arrived back at the house. He navigated the winding driveway around back and parked. Before he got out, he reminded himself of the deal he had struck.

One last check, and that's it.

He went up the back access steps to the wraparound porch and followed it around to the front. He paused about ten feet away from the bowl, wanting to know but not wanting to know at the same time, hoping for the best but expecting the worst.

He stood still and squinted, trying to interpret what he could see from this distance. Was anything missing? The interplay of light and shadow made it impossible to tell. Slowly, he approached the bowl, counting his steps, holding his breath, and looked inside. The wax treat bags with their dancing skeletons and smiling pumpkins were still intact, all their tops still neatly folded over and stapled, his handiwork on display.

His heart sank like a stone.

Nobody had touched one, lifted one, made any effort whatsoever to remove it from the bowl and take it home.

Another year that nobody had come.

He was angry now.

Kids these days.

He was aware of how old he sounded. *But it's true!* Where was the curiosity? The sense of adventure? The embrace of the unknown, the unfamiliar, the unusual? Halloween was dying, of that he was instantly sure, replaced by video games and cable TV and every other kind of brain rot that had captured this lazy, self-centered generation. It was all a damned shame.

He carried the bowl inside and set it on the console table in the foyer. He swung the heavy oak door shut, leaned against it to turn the deadbolt, and flicked off the porch light. That was it, he decided. No more Halloween. Not in this house. Definitely for tonight, maybe forever.

He selected one of the wax bags from the bowl and opened it by tearing away the top. From it, he pulled out a clear zipper-lock bag, about the size of a sandwich, and held it up to the foyer light.

Teeth.

Scraps of clothing.

A lock of hair pinned together with a cheap barrette.

And something else in there too; something wettish, something heavier, something that slid into the corner of the bag as he turned it this way and that. It was a dark red color, brownish in places, wrinkled and moist.

The tongue, he thought.

I always like to include the tongue.

Everything the police needed to stop his reign of terror, served up on a literal platter *(close enough, anyway)*. All the evidence they needed to end the impulses that he could not, to bring peace to the dozens of families from whom he had taken so much, to halt the decades of destruction wrought by his broken brain.

He wanted so badly to be caught, but they had to play the game.

Approach the house.

Take the treat.

End the madness.

Set me free.

He placed the zipper-lock bag back in the bowl and carried everything down into the basement. He took the steps gingerly, bracing himself with the rail, and crossed the floor to the large freezer on the far wall. There was no need to turn on a light; the only dangerous thing down here was him.

He opened the freezer and slid the bowl back onto the top shelf. Briefly, he looked at the other jars on the other shelves, each one labeled by victim and date, a catalog of a lifetime of flawless work. He didn't keep much, just a few souvenirs; a finger here, an eyeball there. The rest of the bodies were in the woods behind the abandoned office building, where he knew they would never be found.

He considered the treat bags one last time. Eventually he would have to swap the tongues out for something else; the thawing and refreezing every year was hell on the soft tissue, and he'd noticed earlier in the day that they were starting to smell. He closed the freezer. That was a problem for next year.

He went back upstairs and tore open the package he had received in the mail earlier that day. He was glad the clown suit had made it here on time. It was a little large, which didn't shock him. He wondered if he was shrinking in his old age. Still, it would do. It would do just fine.

As he stood in front of the bathroom mirror, applying his face paint, he felt his mood thawing. This Halloween was over, but he'd put the bowl out again next year. He was sure of it.

As many times as it takes, until they figured out what I've done.

He grabbed the butcher's knife from where he kept it between outings. The impulse was very strong again, and he knew it could not be ignored. He went outside and down the back steps, his knees creaking in the cold. He was getting too old for this, but some things are non-negotiable.

One year the trick-or-treaters will come, he thought.

Then I can rest.

As he stepped off into the night, he remembered something his father used to say to assuage disappointment:

There's always next year.

№ 7
HOUSE LIGHTS
David E. Kruegger

CARA WAS SWEET TO GIVE him her coat even though it hid most of the costume. That's what big sisters were for, though, right? To give you a coat or a little encouragement when you needed it? Justin thought so. The wind cut right through the spandex-like material of the catsuit, only held at bay at the shoulders or other parts where a tuft of fur blocked it.

"You still cold?" Cara asked.

"No," Justin said, pulling the oversized coat around his shoulders.

"There's a light on at 11, let's go on up!"

Justin showed his big sister a lips-only smile. He was old enough to know there had to be something she would rather be doing on Halloween than taking her nine-year-old brother trick-or-treating. She was a lot older than him. At eighteen, Cara was a grown-up. He could hardly remember the last year she trick or treated alongside him. Here she was, handing over her coat, never complaining. It was, he thought, calling up the notes at the back of his throat, resisting the urge to hum them out loud, *Loverly*.

"Yeah, okay," he said.

The bell rang, deep and luxuriously inside the house. Only a few moments later, a woman in a floppy black hat pulled the door open. The material was cheap: the light in the hall shined through the top of it, but the rest of the outfit was superb. It was a hip-hugging black number. Her hair was pinned up in gorgeous brown waves. Justin loved costumes. He loved them because they transformed the ordinary into the extraordinary. If that was an obvious reason, it was still good enough for Justin. He believed things should be loved in ways that were obvious.

He loved Cara because she was his big sister, and she talked to him and bought him records and told their dad there was nothing wrong with him listening to them. He loved his mom because she was warm and kind and made the best back-to-school cookies anyone had ever had. He loved his dad because — well, fathers had to be loved in their own way. Everyone knew that.

"Trick or treat!" he shouted.

The woman, who with a costume had transformed from a plain housewife to an alluring and playful witch, glanced at the ears on top of his head. Her smile was gracious, wide, and warm. "Oh! A kitty? How sweet!"

"Actually, I —"

"He's Rum Tum Tugger!" Cara said. She wrapped an arm around his shoulders. "You know? From *Cats?*"

The woman's smile twisted in confusion before righting itself. Justin's face grew red, burned under the skin. It was kind of Cara to interject, but he realized now that this woman had probably been hit with a parade of obscure cartoon ghouls and movie goblins. Here was something she thought she could grab onto, a cat to go with her witch, and it turned out to be one more mirage.

"I haven't seen it, I'm afraid. Is it good?" she smiled down at Justin, but the illusion was broken. He saw the strings that held it all up. The light through the hat had been only one break in the chain. Now he spotted the wrinkles at the center of her forehead, worry lines. He caught the nicotine stains on her fingers as they passed a handful of candies into his pillowcase. A witch for a day, and then back to life.

"It's the best," Cara said, winking. "Have a good night, ma'am."

They made their way back to Pike Street. "I wish he'd let me wear the makeup or the collar. I just look like a cat."

"I know, kiddo. Count it as a win that he let you go out as something other than an executioner or a commando."

"Why does he care anyway? It's just one night, and it's just for fun."

"I probably shouldn't do this, but do you want a little High School Knowledge? Hell, this is practically College Knowledge."

Justin nodded. Every once in a while, when Cara was in the right mood, he would ask a question and she would give him an answer from the future, an answer based on what she was learning a block away from him at the high school. Well, before she graduated last May. He didn't always understand it, but sometimes he would write it down to review later, to see if he got it.

"Dad belongs to a generation that was raised on stories of tough men fighting hard wars. The toughest thing Dad has ever had to fight is an unruly Xerox machine, or someone mad that they can't get a refund on a ball they damaged. Even then, he has guys to fix the machine, and the store policy comes from corporate. He was raised to think men fight, they build, they conquer, and then he got stuck managing a small town sporting goods store. His own distress at not measuring up as a man comes out as his fear that you're gay."

"I'm not gay," Justin said.

"It doesn't matter if you're gay—"

"I'm not."

"—It matters that he's afraid you are. You don't like guns or sports. You like musicals."

"But there's lots of straight guys in musicals," he said.

"And there's probably lots of gay guys in sports. There definitely is in war. Wait until you read *The Thin Red Line.*"

Justin looked down at his shoes as they walked. They skipped a house with the lights off and came to another one with the porchlight illuminating a bowl of candy. He liked being with Cara. Most of the time, he liked it when she shared High School Knowledge. Sometimes, like now, it left him more confused than ever. He liked musicals. He got chills when the songs built up, when the high point of a ballad came, when a high-energy number broke into tap-dancing. He loved the stories, both on stage and off, the actors and directors who collaborated, who originated this or that role, who defined it. He had no idea why that had to mean anything at all more than it did.

"You want to go up?" Cara asked. She was looking at her watch. The last few houses, she'd looked more and more, though only a few minutes had passed at most.

"I don't know," he said, lifting the bag. "I think I'm done."

"You sure? Kiddo, we have time for a few more houses, and I don't want you to have any regrets after tonight."

The uncertainty and confusion that swirled in Justin's chest clarified themselves when he stopped walking. He was angry.

"What aren't you telling me?" he asked.

"Come on, let's go get more candy."

"No, Cara. I know something is going on. Dad's been making those weird calls. Mom's been crying. Don't think I haven't noticed you getting mopey too. You look sick. But whenever I come into the room, everyone acts like it's all normal." He took in a breath, shocked to find his nose clogged with snot, tears burning at the back of his eyes. "Are they getting a divorce?"

"Oh honey, no. They're not getting a divorce. It has to do with me. I really can't tell you more. I want to say I wish I could, but I don't want you to know either."

"Is it High School Knowledge?"

"No, kid. It's bigger than that. It's temple stuff."

The breath left his body. He'd never heard anyone say anything about the temple outside the house. He didn't know where it was or what happened there. One time, a couple of years ago, Cara told him about a ceremony she witnessed. She was allowed to go because she was older than fifteen, and they got a babysitter, and the next morning, she was covered in scratches and bruises. The only thing she told him was that a guy swallowed a snake.

He repeated it during dinner; the spaghetti made him think of it. The next thing he knew, his face stung with a slap from his father's hand. The hand wasn't too big, but the rings on it were thick and heavy. He didn't have time to cry out before Cara was dragged away by the hair. The meaty sound of her punishment carried through the closed door to her room.

"Eat your dinner, sweetie. She knows the rules." His mom pointed at the plate, and took a bite of salad, her eyes swimming with tears.

"No, no no no," he said to Cara. She knelt in front of him.

"I really can't tell you more. We gotta get back soon. I'm sorry, but things change and move on. Next year, I'll be at college, I hope."

"Why did they make you take a year in between?" he asked. She pinched his cheek with her thumb and forefinger.

"Don't worry about it." Her smile was thin and getting thinner. "Two more?"

"Two more," he said. He didn't correct anyone on the nature of his costume. He was just a cat.

Cara was holding the bag by the time they got back to 7 Pike St. He dragged it behind him for a short distance before she offered. Her asking if she could carry and him nodding was the most they talked on the way back. As they passed 8 Pike St., they both stopped to take in the state of the house. They exchanged a glance, if not a word, and continued on their way.

"Hit the porchlight, will ya?" Dad said as Cara pulled the door shut. He had things laid out on the table, but he stood between them and Justin. All he saw was a glint from something long, the dark curve of a cup, and a bolt of black cloth. These things slid from view, blocked as his father came closer.

Cara flipped the lightswitch to turn off the porchlight and dissuade candy seekers, and went into the kitchen, where the sink ran and dishes clattered.

Dad put a hand on Justin's shoulder, the thin fingers gripping firm but soft. He felt the metal of Dad's ring through the jacket material. Justin looked up, caught the thin light of the entryway lamp as it shined through thinning hair, making each careful strand stand out. Face cast in shadow, the light made an artificial halo behind the man. He was still wearing a tie. He stunk like brandy.

"Kid, you should head downstairs. I got the turntable down there, and some books for you. Now, you play whatever you want, and you can turn it up to the little mark I made near the volume dial. Do you want me to lug a TV down? For video games?"

Justin shook his head. The cat ears were coming loose.

"Last chance. No? Okay then. And you remember what we talked about?"

"I'll change into jammies and stay down there, in the basement."

"Until when?"

"Until you get me."

"What else?"

"Go right to bed after."

"And?"

"And don't ask about anything," Justin said. He slipped the jacket off, the cold air washed over his shoulder. The costume material was so light. The actors could only stand it because of the hot lights, he guessed. "If I go right to bed, how will I brush my teeth?"

"Brush them now."

"But if I eat candy downstairs, it would make brushing them pointless." Justin said it more to himself than to his father. After he slipped off the jacket, the hand had not returned to his shoulder. Would he have felt it tighten at what might be seen as backtalk?

"Then don't worry about it. Brush more tomorrow morning. It's a special night."

"Dad, is Cara going away?"

"What did I say about questions?"

"I thought that was for after —" The hand rose, catching a sparkle on the ring. With the light behind his head, Justin couldn't make out his father's expression. The blow never came.

"Cara won't be going away. That was your one slip. Say goodnight to your mom and sister and go downstairs."

Justin walked into the kitchen, dragging his bag of candy behind him. The yellow light washed out the earth-tone tiles, the brown stove. The two women stood next to each other, Mom washing, and Cara drying and putting away. Standing behind her, with her coat off, Justin could see the way Cara's body had changed, even in the last couple of months. She was wider, with small rolls of fat on her sides and back, but her neck looked thinner than before. Whatever weight she gained wasn't even. It was hard to avoid the idea that she had swelled in a way that had nothing to do with fat. Justin hadn't seen many pregnant women, but was that possible? Wouldn't he know if Cara was pregnant? Even if they tried to keep it from him, the fight would have been nuclear. They would have heard it two towns over.

They spoke in hushed tones until he made a noise, and then they stopped to exchange a glance before turning to him. Mom's eyes were red, but she smiled wide and showed teeth, slightly yellow and in a neat row above her lip.

"Did you get lots of candy?" she asked.

"Yeah," he said.

"Don't eat it all tonight, you'll get a bellyache!"

"Dad said to say goodnight. I'm going to the basement."

He kissed his mom on the cheek and hugged her.

"Goodnight sweetie. Set aside anything not wrapped, I'll toss it in the morning."

"Night kiddo," Cara said. "I love you."

Justin looked at his feet when the warm sting appeared at the back of his eyes. Tears welling for what? Dad said Cara would be here.

He went into the basement without saying anything

else.

~

The candy was sorted and he had just flipped the first disc of *Into the Woods*. The Prince was seducing the Baker's Wife and Justin liked this one because so much of the story was in the songs. Someday, he would see the show, but he would already know it, because it was all on the disc.

The candy mounded up in neat piles. He was never sure if he should sort by type, or color, or what, but it didn't matter too much in the end. Before the night was done, he'd have to pack it all back in the bag to take upstairs. Still, this gave him a sense of what he was working with and helped distract from what was going on above him. The volume knob was right up to the little line marked by Dad, but even at full blast, he wouldn't have been able to drown out the footsteps above, the creak of the floorboards as people traipsed across the entryway.

A few times, he had thought to go to the window and try to see if he could catch an arrival. The problem was, they were coming right in, no doorbell. That meant he'd have to catch them at just the right time, and what if they spotted him? Justin was too young for the temple, but he wasn't stupid. The temple was the only thing grown ups got this cagey about. The only thing that his dad would dole out a smack over was temple business. Snake swallowing. Or being questioned, but especially being questioned *about* temple business.

Something rolled on the hardwood above him before going silent on the living room carpet. Justin tried to count the footsteps. To get a good count, he'd have to turn down the music, and if he did that, they might think he was eavesdropping. To make matters worse, of course, he was. Besides, the number of feet might not tell him anything at all. People stepping on and off the living room carpet would ruin his count, and people standing near each other might be hard to track.

The big area on the wall looked so empty and blank, and Justin wished he said "yes" to the TV and video game console. Way too late now, of course. He popped a Tootsie Roll in his mouth. Eat through the least favorite, save the best for last.

Feet above him began to move in one direction. The floorboards creaked and groaned. Over the music, he could still chart the movement of men's hard shoes, of women's heels. The first made a light clomp. The heels clicked in a one-two rhythm on tile and wood. One by one, the footsteps quieted in the living room. Justin strained so hard to hear that when something fell, something small but heavy and made of metal, he jumped.

"Fuck!" a husky voice cried from above.

There may have been more chatter, but between the carpeted floor and the sound of the stereo, he had no access to it.

His hand popped something else into his mouth, something medicinal and slightly sweet. Looking at the wrapper with an involuntary grimace, Justin saw that he was distracted enough to eat a licorice-flavored candy. No garbage down here to spit it out. He dutifully chewed, swallowed, and then grabbed a sucker from the favorites pile to wash out the taste.

"Let's go over it." he whispered to himself. It helped to speak out loud, to take the tangle of thoughts and put them into sentences that could be spoken only one at a time. The problem was that *Into the Woods* was bad thinking music. With careful movements, he popped it off the turntable and set *Anything Goes* on in its place. Nice songs, but Cole Porter wouldn't distract him with something like a plot to be followed. Well, he could take a break during "It's De-lovely."

"First," he counted on a finger, "Cara was being cagey and sad tonight. She seemed like she had something on her mind. She wouldn't tell me. Second," another finger, "Mom and Dad made me come downstairs, so I wouldn't see what's happening upstairs. Cara didn't have to come down, and there's weird people. Third, Dad got mad when I mentioned the temple, so it's gotta be a temple thing."

He racked his brain for more clues. What did he do last year for Halloween? He went out with some kids from school and their dad. The dad made a couple of jokes about Justin's Danny Zuko costume, but when he didn't respond the jokes fell off. He was annoyed because he had to go home with that guy and his kid, Robbie, who was in Justin's homeroom and who was a little dull. That was because Mom and Dad and Cara were going to be out. When he got picked up by Mom that evening, she didn't say anything the whole ride home, and Cara didn't leave her room for days, even to go to school. He'd tried to give her some Dots, her favorite, but she only took them on the third day.

So they were probably at the temple that night and something odd happened. Did it have anything to do with tonight? If so, why weren't they at the temple?

He gulped, because he knew what had to happen. If he was going to get any answers at all, he'd have to eavesdrop for real. A tiny amount of the living room was visible through the kitchen if he used that crack under the door. If Cara was sad, if she was going to be in her room for three days, if she was in danger, he had to at least know. If only to make sure he still had Dots for her three days from now.

He kept the music up to make sure. He'd thought right through "It's De-Lovely" and missed "Heaven Hop." That meant he had to be back down before the end of side one to avoid suspicion. Two tracks, about six minutes. *Okay.*

He tip-toed to the bottom of the stairs, stepping lightly on the thin rug his mother spread over the cold concrete. The first step was silent, but when he put weight on the second one, it protested with a loud *creak*. When he tried again, turning his foot sideways like he'd seen on a show about ninjas, it still cried out. So he skipped it. He stepped on the third step, which also groaned, but was quieter. Whatever was happening in the living room, he had to hope it commanded enough attention.

"I Get A Kick Out of You" was halfway done by the

time he got to the top, skipping known creaky stairs and stretching his little legs as far as they would go. Settling in, he held his head in position to be able to angle into the living room from the kitchen.

It was dark, so he couldn't make anyone out unless they were holding candles. The music was clear to him, but they seemed to take no notice. Maybe the door blocked it out? In the sliver of the room he could see, people shuffled, lips moving in the flickering light before disappearing. Light glinted off something raised in the air. In one small corona of light, a shaved leg lifted up as though the owner was laying on their back. Cara's leg. In the passing candlelight, he almost made out the chipped color on her toenails.

If he saw little, he heard less. Without anything to block the sound from the stereo, he had no way to hear what the people with the candles were saying. A deep voice murmured from the living room, the way that the sound in a movie theater bled through to those outside, all tone, no content.

The track ended, he held his breath. It was quiet enough for him to hear, ". . . what was planted a year ago has now borne fruit, the bir —" and then the opening notes of the song, "Anything Goes."

The voice, it was Dad. It was a deeper version of Dad's voice, the voice Dad put on when he dragged the whole family to high school football games and vigorously shook hands with the other men there. A good look was hard to come by, but if he strained, the angle began to reveal itself.

The music went out with one more burst of sound. Had he really spent more than three minutes trying to get the angle right? But now he was in trouble. The steps would creak if he moved down them too fast. He hovered at the top of the steps, holding in his breath.

One of the candlelit faces, moving in the circle, cast a glance at the basement door. They were the dour, concerned eyes of his mother. They passed by, but how long would they tolerate the quiet?

That question never got an answer, because in the next moment, Cara shrieked like she was being torn apart, like she was trying to scream the house to pieces, and Justin sprung from the top of the stairs.

Like a commando launching an ambush, he burst out of the basement door. The coordination he showed, standing, turning the knob, and pushing forward all in one motion, might have made his dad proud in another context.

As it was, the darkness in the living room rippled. Cloaks and capes writhed and spun, candles were lifted to avoid accidentally setting anyone ablaze. Mutters of "What the hell?" or "Hey, watch it!" soon interrupted the soft chanting, but were overwhelmed by another scream.

Bare feet gripped the tile floor and launched Justin forward. No one moved toward him as he entered the threshold of the living room, a doorless passage with an arch at the top, and flung his hand along the wall. The popcorn scraped against his skin. His hand found and turned the plastic dimmer wheel, and he spun it all the way as bright as it would go.

The light burst on, and then dimmed. In that flash of light, Justin made everything out. About twelve people stood around a stainless steel table on wheels. They wore black cloaks and held candles and other, weirder, stuff. Mirrors, cups, bowls. Temple stuff, he knew. They were confused, agitated, and terrified of what was in their midst.

On the table, his sister writhed. Cara shrieked, her legs kicked. Fingers, white from gripping anything they could, lanced out, opening and closing on the thin sheet that covered the table. He saw her shirt and a sea of skin underneath, and he had only a moment to be embarrassed that his sister wasn't wearing pants.

The thing that wriggled between her legs was a matte black color. A mouth like clay twisted and groaned, empty sockets searched the room. The top half which arced out from between her thighs was the size of a full grown man. The light from the lamp was dim. The filament in the bulb was visible. One shapeless hand reached toward it.

"Hit the fucking light! It'll absorb too much!" His dad's voice called over the fray.

"Keep chanting you idiots! It's not bound! *It's not bound!*" another voice yelled.

A cloak approached, one of the people holding a bowl. It was a fancy bowl, black and inlaid with silver, weird shapes set in it. A hand with long nails and lots of rings emerged from the sleeve. Justin peered up, hoping to catch the face, when he heard his father shout, "Beth! Don't turn your back!"

Too late.

The black flesh of the creature was hard to make out against the cloak she wore, but Justin watched as massive fingers gripped the cloaked head from behind. Those long nails clawed at the hand, but a sickening crunch spat hot liquid in Justin's face and when he opened his eyes, the hood was empty, save for the thick red stuff oozing out from it. The thick fingers swam in the dark cloth, and the body slumped to the ground.

"Turn out that light! It's too strong!" Dad screamed. The hand released the cloak and swung for someone else. A dagger plunged into the black wrist, but that didn't stop the fingers from curling around the face of the man Justin recognized as the family dentist. The fingers pulsed, more than closed, but it was enough to bulge the man's eyes. Justin watched the hand go limp and fall off the hilt of the ceremonial dagger, as a glob of red with little white teeth dripped from the thing's hand.

He still couldn't see his sister, the monster's body blocked her in a way that he couldn't fathom. Where was it standing? Why was she there? Was it coming out of her, somehow? The misshapen face writhed, black, clay-like lips wriggled, forming words and unforming them just as fast. The sockets were empty, but Justin knew they were on him. He might have expected a chill on his back or a racing heart. Instead, he felt like his guts would fall out of him. It took all his focus not to release his aching bladder in fear.

"Justin!" Mom called, "Sweetie! The light! Flip it off!"

A lump with the shape of a hand slapped the carpet and pulled forward, bringing another scream from Cara.

"It'll kill her!" someone screamed. Another cloak approached Justin, frozen at the switch. It held a chalice full of some white fluid that sloshed from the brim. The hand of the creature whipped around the leg of the runner and yanked it down. The cup flew through the air, flinging the liquid against the wall. A balled fist slammed the back of the head of the person who was now on the ground, crushing it like a rotted pumpkin. Who was that? His teacher? His doctor? Why were these people here?

A wet *slumph* brought an end to Cara's screams. She sat up whimpering, and the thing's malformed legs hit the ground and made all the Precious Moments figurines jump and clatter. The hand pulled the mass closer. It rose in front of Justin, until all he could see was the massive field of black clay, something like clay, something molding itself into something else.

He wondered if it would be painful, if the feeling of the thing crushing his skull would be like anything at all. If it would be so fast the pain wouldn't even register. Would he know it had happened? Heavy, cold fingers wrapped around his shoulder. Some sound on the other side of the creature told him there was a struggle. People yelled, stuff bumped around. Justin closed his eyes, ready to die. Cold, damp lips pressed on his forehead. They felt like Play-Doh, crackling gently at the edges, soft and yielding underneath.

Another yell, another clatter, some footsteps, and then an arm ripping him away from the thing. The cold fingers lifted from his shoulder and warm and slender fingers pulled him through the kitchen and entryway and out the front door.

"Pick up your feet, Justin, come on!" the voice said. Urgent, but soft.

"Cara?"

"Come on!"

A cool breeze on his face told him that he was crying. His cheeks were cold where the tears dried. When he opened his eyes, Cara was there, tears streaking her own face.

"Why did you come up?" she asked.

"I heard you scream," he said.

"Over the music?"

"It was a scream, Cara. And I was at the top of the stairs."

"They should have sent you somewhere else." He grabbed her hand and she didn't pull away, but he sensed frustration, anger.

"Cara, what was that?"

"Temple stuff."

"But the temple, I mean, everyone in it, Mom and Dad—"

"Yeah, I guess you're right. No temple anymore." She sighed. "This was a stupid idea, I don't think they knew what they'd do with him once he got here. The lights—I mean, what a fucking waste."

She pulled her hand out of his to bury her face. He noticed for the first time that she was wearing a white gown, like a big baptism dress, and that the black cloth from the table was around her waist.

A car drove past. Most trick-or-treaters were off the streets by now, and the porchlights winked out one by one. From this area, they could see the lights turn off all down Pike Street.

"Cara?"

"Yeah kiddo."

"I'm sorry." He laid a head on her shoulder.

"Don't be," she said, standing up. "You're kind of an uncle. Let's go in, see what's become of the temple."

"He won't hurt us?"

Cara shook her head.

She held his hand as they stepped across the threshold, into the silence of the new temple.

triktreat.exe
Christopher Robertson

IN THE DYING HOURS OF THE NIGHT, in a basement beneath a broken-down bungalow on Pike Street, he dies. The paper faces of muscle-bound heroes and humanoid creatures watch from torn-out video game advertisements taped to cinder block walls, staring in anticipation as a gangly, pale kid leans ever closer to a CRT monitor. He smirks, flashing raw, red gums.

On-screen: a cave with a small pool, a skeleton resting somewhere near the back. There's a menu to the right and a list of commands below, replaced by a text prompt:

>>The waters of this subterranean lake are as still as a corpse.

The kid clicks MOVE and then on the water.

>>As you swim toward the skeleton, you feel the jaws of a shark
>>grab you and pull you under.

"Dammit!" The kid slams his fist down next to his keyboard, making an empty can of Diet Pepsi Free bounce off the table.

>>You curse yourself for using your body as bait.

"No shit," the kid scowls.

>>Even before the life has left your body-

"Shove it." He pushes the power button on the monitor and plunges the basement bedroom into near-pitch darkness. Only slivers of light filter through the high, letterbox windows from street lamps, casting long shadows through the shrubs. He sits and sulks in the gloom for a minute, then grunts as he turns the monitor back on.

Just as he's about to start a new game and venture once more through the *Shadowgate*, the front door to the house above him crashes open. He spins in his chair, eyes darting to the crutch leaning against the nearest wall. Before he can reach for it, he hears laughter. Drunk, raucous, *we don't care that it's the middle of the night* laughter.

He recognizes his mother's slurred, throaty chortle, but the man, gruff like a chain-smoking bull chewing barbed wire, is new. No surprise there.

"No, stop it," his mother giggles, offering no real resistance. "We can't, no, ohmygod, not h-here." Her insincere protests fade into gasping moans, punctuated by thrusting *thuds* and the slapping of flesh on flesh.

Dust stirs from bare supports above as what has to be the living room sofa scrapes and bangs against the floor. It's over in a matter of seconds. The man's grunts, in between his mother's racing gasps, grow more forceful with each *thud*, ending in a groan like a dying boar.

Hoping that's it, the kid listens to the silence that follows, eventually broken by the clump of his mother's heels on the floor as she heads toward the back of the house. After a few steps, they switch to heavy, dull *thuds*, followed by the slamming of a fridge door and clanking of glass bottles. He sighs; it's not over after all, and to save himself from having to listen to his mom and whoever this guy is for the rest of the night, the kid grabs his Walkman. He cranks the volume to the max and throws himself on his bed.

~

The front door slams, jerking the kid awake. He limps to the window over his bed without his crutch, dragging his braced right leg behind. A man makes his way down their weed-cracked path, some heavy-set biker dude with a protruding beer gut stretching his torn Motörhead t-shirt to its limit. He stops to drain the last of a beer, tosses the empty into the jungle of an overgrown lawn, and brushes back long, greasy gray hair.

He glances back at a porch unladen with decorations, no jack-o'-lantern smiles waiting for a candle, and yet in its abandonment, it's the most haunted of all. It makes the house next door look like the Ritz. A pretty dogwood tree lives in that yard, while the only thing growing in this dump's grass is a mountain of dry dog shit.

A younger kid on a bike approaches, sagging messenger bag stuffed with newspapers and magazines. She skids to a halt near the biker dude and hands him a rolled-up, elastic-banded wad. The biker dude snorts, sneers, and slaps it out of her hand.

"Shit ain't mine," he growls and watches as the girl rides off quicker than she arrived, a smirk and raised eyebrow on the creep's face. "Not bad."

As the biker douche leaves, the kid in the basement turns his attention to the discarded delivery. The local paper, a home magazine, and . . .

"Shit."

The newest issue of *Computer Gaming World*. A car drives past fast enough to catch the magazine in an updraft, and the kid watches as it drifts to a halt in the middle of the road.

"No, no, no," he says as he shakes his head and hurries away from the window. He makes it two steps, clumping his braced leg in rigid hobbles before the dizziness sets in. The floor rushes to meet his eyes, the room somehow stuttering in blurred half-rotations while also staying impossibly static.

"Parker?" he hears a voice echoing from miles away. "Parker, sweetheart, are you okay?"

The swirling basement coalesces as three images of a round-faced, middle-aged, redheaded woman wearing a loose bathrobe merge into one.

"Mom?" Parker smacks dry lips, gums itching. "My—"

"It's here, honey," Parker's mom draws his attention to the new issue of *Computer Gaming World*. A gray and red spread promises interviews with Pete Rose and Michael Jordan, alongside over 100 reviews, with Lucasfilm's

Zak McKraken and the Alien Mindbenders taking the main focus. It sits on his bedside table next to a freshly made breakfast smoothie.

"Hope I didn't wake you up last night." She pats Parker's floppy red curls. "You need your rest."

"Just a dizzy spell, Mom." Parker makes no mention of being up most of the night with her antics. "That's all." She continues to pat his hair, almost robotically repeating the same strokes. "Really, Mom, I'm—"

She grunts, expelling all the air from her lungs as she goes completely rigid.

"Mom!" Parker grimaces as her hand tightens into a fist, ensnaring his hair. He can't do anything but bite down and bear it till she releases him a few seconds later. "Mom, it's okay," Parker tries to reassure her as she unfastens her robe, exposing herself without shame or even awareness, then closes it precisely as it was. He continues to reassure her till some semblance of sentience returns to her glazed, faraway stare. "You're okay, Mom. You're okay."

She nods, trying to make her lips form words, and produces only spit-heavy smacks.

"P-Parker?"

"It's okay, Mom." Parker pats her hand. "You just had another seizure."

"Oh," her face turns red. "I'm sorry, you shouldn't have to see that."

"Don't, Mom. But they're happening more often. Maybe you should—"

"I'm fine, honey," she insists, ruffling his hair. "You're such a good boy, looking after me." She pulls him into a hug.

"Okay, Mom."

"Oh, I'm going out tonight so I'll make you some extra smoothies."

Again, Parker adds to himself. *She's been out almost every night since Dad left.*

"I thought we could watch a movie? You know, 'cause it's Halloween."

"Parker," she screws her face up, "you're too big to be spending Halloween with your mom. I'll leave some candy by the door outside," she says as she stands. "So the trick-or-treaters don't bother you."

Somehow, Parker doubts they'll be seeing a lot of those tonight. He looks down, hiding a pang of sadness twinging at the corner of his mouth, forgetting something his mother hasn't. She lingers, cheek offered to him, and when Parker notices, he plants a kiss on it.

"Love you," she chirps as she bounds back up the stairs.

"Love you too, Mom," Parker drones as he picks up his magazine. He begins to flip through the pages, casually drinking his smoothie, even the touch of the straw and fresh chillness a little too much for his overly sensitive gums.

Something falls to the floor as he turns another page, and Parker looks down to see a floppy disk sitting on the floor. He picks it up, turning to check the label. Handwritten in red ink made to look like blood, it reads TrikTreat.

"Huh?"

~

From: Parker <shadowwalker>
Newsgroup: adventure_games
Subject: trick or treat simulator?
Date: 31 Oct 1988 14:05:43 +0200

SHADOWWALKER: You guys ever heard of a game called TrikTreat? I got a floppy for it with my CGW.
NERFHERDER: Never heard of it.
DLIGHTMAN: Maybe it's a demo copy meant for CGW writers?
JOUSTKING: What if it's got Brain on it? You could wreck your computer.
SPARROWHAWKE: SW is a liar. There is no such game. It's just a stupid Halloween prank. Ood, you guys are such LOSERS!

Parker snorts at the on-screen Usenet chat, playing with the disk in one hand. "Screw you, Sparrowdork." He flips open the catch on his disk drive, ejects *Shadowgate*, and slots the mysterious new floppy in.

For a few moments, Parker holds his breath, waiting for the screen to freeze or be taken over as some malicious virus infects his computer. But then a folder opens, offering a single file for him to click on: triktreat.exe.

"Here goes." Parker double-clicks.

The MS-DOS prompts load, and then the screen turns to black as the game launches. A single text prompt reads:

>>TERRORCORE GAMES PRESENTS...

Spooky, low fidelity chiptune music pipes through his speakers as a static image of a grinning 8-bit, two-tone jack-o'-lantern fills his screen. A rhyme appears, line by line, as the jack-o'-lantern's mouth rotates through a simple animation.

>>Trick or Treat,

>>An Offering of the Sweet,

>>A bribe, an Entreat,

>>To Stave off Hoofen Feet

The words fade as the shape of a suburban neighborhood appears within the jack-o-lantern's eyes and grin.

Parker hits ENTER to start a new game, and a prompt appears:

>>Where do you live...

Parker types [Pike Street] and hits ENTER.

The jack-o'-lantern steadily fades away, exposing more of the dark, small town skyline. Parker squints; it almost matches where he lives.

>>It's Halloween on [Pike Street].

>>The Children are out trick-or-treating.

The image of the town fades to black.

>>And they are not alone...

>>DO NOT run out of candy...

>>DO NOT open the door for HIM...

"The heck?" Parker narrows his eyes and jumps as something flashes on the screen. It was only there for a fraction of a second, but in that brief glimpse, it looked almost like a devil.

The game screen loads — the top half a dot-matrix suburban front door from inside the house rendered in black and orange CGA graphics.

"That's so weird," Parker laughs. "Kinda looks just like—"

KNOCK-KNOCK appears on the screen as a similar sound comes through Parker's speakers. Only it sounds way more realistic than his soundcard should be able to produce.

>>KNOCK-KNOCK.

Parker jumps, realizing that it's not just coming from his speakers. Someone's at the door upstairs.

His throat goes dry. "No freaking way." He turns back to his screen and reads a new prompt as it appears.

>>THEY GO AROUND THE SIDE.

Parker's eyes go wide as he hears someone outside walking through the grass. They rap on the glass of the living room window. At the same time, a low-quality matching sound punches from the speakers, loud enough to be heard outside.

"Shit-shit-shit!" Parker spins his speakers to mute, but it's too late. He glances to the open window to see a pale, lifeless face, lips leaking a trail of fresh blood, dropping to peer inside.

Parker screams. So does the guy at the window.

"Jesus, kid, the hell is wrong with you!" The guy might look like a Wallachian count, but his accent's more Hoboken than high-brow.

"Me! You—"

"Look, kid," the guy dressed like a vampire holds up a pharmacy bag and a clipboard, "you're the last delivery, and I've got a party to get to. Mind signing for it?"

Parker recognizes it. His mother's Tegretol.

"Sure," he sighs and spins his chair around to let the delivery guy see the brace. "But unless you wanna wait a week for me to get up the stairs, can you hand it through the window?"

"Whatever gets me outta here fastest, kid." As Parker uses his crutch to hobble to the window, the guy takes a look around. "So, uh, where's Splinter and the rest of the gang?"

Parker rolls his eyes.

"Seriously, kid, it ain't good for you."

"I got anemia," Parker says as he tosses the clipboard back and snags the medication. "Get tired all the time. Easier to day-sleep down here."

"Yeah?" The delivery guy nods to Parker's brace. "You get that fightin' with Shredder?"

"That's new. I . . . fell down the stairs."

"Uh-huh." He takes the clipboard back. "Well, tell you what, kid, thanks for that. Happy Halloween. Oh, and if you see April O'Neil, put in a word for me," he finishes with a wink.

"Yeah, Happy Halloween." Waving him off, Parker waits till he's gone and adds, "Douchebag."

Leaving the medication on his nightstand, Parker goes to return to his computer, but after a few steps, the dizziness hits again. He comes over all woozy, and figuring it was the rush of the fright, he allows himself to stagger back, falling asleep a fraction of a second after his head hits the pillow.

~

Parker dreams in CGA, in slowly refreshing orange and black. His hand moves before his eyes in three static images, a pixelated 8-bit approximation of the appendage. He stands in his hallway, or maybe it's the game's. Both are interchangeable to him, and it's been over a month since he's been up there anyway.

>>KNOCK-KNOCK.

Text scrawls before his eyes in lieu of words, the only sound coming from his mouth indistinct MIDI gibberish.

>>PARKER: Who's there . . .

He steps closer to the door, an empty candy bowl beside it. The hallway mirror reflects something that's not there, black words bleeding on the wall —*don't open the door for* . . .

>>KNOCK . . .

Parker hesitates.

>>KNOCKKNOCKKNOCKKNOCK!

>>PARKER: Go away!

It stops, and a moment of silence follows.

THUD!
Something like the smear of an egg appears on the window beside the door.

THUD!
And another, and—

~

THUD!
Parker jerks awake to an egg smashing outside. He rises, shaking off the nightmare, and watches through runny yolk as two brats in dime store masks run away, discarding an empty egg carton. They're gone before he can get a clue as to who they are, lost in a parade of princesses and pirates marching through twilight streets strewn with flickering jack-o'-lanterns and toilet paper confetti.

He watches his mom walk down the path in heels she can't walk in, stopping to fix her run tights, and as she leans over, she spills out of a too-tight corset. A tacked-on tail and cat-ear headband complete what passes for a costume.

Parker sighs; it's another night alone, though that doesn't usually bother him.

Three costumed kids watch his mom go, a Luke Sky-walker and a Karate Kid with cartoonishly slack jaws. The third, an older Risky Business Tom Cruise wannabe, keeps his cool, but his Wayfarers follow Parker's mom all the same. They start spouting shit about her, but Parker's in no mood to listen. He closes the window and climbs down, sitting on the edge of his bed.

There's a fresh smoothie waiting for him, but he always feels like sleeping after he eats, and considering that dream, Parker doesn't exactly feel like loading that save file.

He grabs a Diet Pepsi Free from his mini-fridge and flicks on his portable, carefully sipping as he watches a *Movie Macabre* re-run—some lame old British movie called *The Devil Within Her.* Something about a possessed baby. It has that Loomis guy in it, but it does nothing for Parker, so he switches it off. In the silence that follows, he can hear the distant trill of mischief and the hum from his computer. The latter niggles at him, an indistinct taunt.

It clicks then what's bugging him, and it's not just the nightmare. That game got under his skin enough to creep him out, and he's been avoiding booting it back up. It's beating him, and while the entire world seems hellbent on breaking every part of Parker, in the virtual one, he's a badass. No game's going to get the better of him.

"Screw this." Parker pushes up and uses his crutch to get to his computer. A few minutes later, he's back on the bootleg game.

~

>>KNOCK-KNOCK!

Parker has several options in his command box: OPEN DOOR, CLOSE DOOR, GIVE CANDY, QUESTION, LOOK, LOCK DOOR, RUN.

He clicks OPEN DOOR.

The pixelated door doesn't so much open as it disappears, revealing a boy and a girl, dressed as a robot soldier and ninja, respectively, on the step. Behind them, the 8-bit street is frozen in motion, Across the road, a black SUV fades in, depositing a bedsheet ghost kid in front of a smart suited kid with a used-car-salesman-serial-killer smile, a hockey-masked maniac, and two identical skeletons before fading out.

"Reusing character models?" Parker scoffs, "Lame," and turns his attention to the kids on his digital doorstep.

>>BOY: Trick or treat!

Curious, Parker clicks QUESTION.

>>PLAYER: Who are you supposed to be?

>>GIRL: We're Cowboy and Silver, duh! Trick or treat!

Parker snorts; he knows those characters from a Saturday morning cartoon and tragically bad console game; how did this game from a nobody developer he's never heard of get those rights? He clicks: GIVE CANDY.

>>BOY AND GIRL: Yay! Thank you!

>>YOUR CANDY BOWL IS 95% FULL.

So that's how it works; Parker nods. He guesses if he runs out of candy too early, it's game over—which means he's going to have to conserve. It shouldn't be too hard.

Parker clicks CLOSE DOOR and waits.

>>KNOCK-KNOCK!

Parker clicks OPEN DOOR to find not a child but a full-grown man wearing an emotionless, plastic mask, something sharp in his hand dripping red pixels. The Plastic Man doesn't say anything, but Parker doesn't give him a chance—he clicks CLOSE DOOR as fast as he can.

>>YOU HEAR SOMETHING SCRATCH AGAINST THE DOOR AND

>>THEN FOOTSTEPS LEAVING.

"Yeah, get lost." Parker heads to the fridge and pops another Diet Pepsi Free. By the time he hobbles back to the computer, he has another visitor at his digital door. He clicks OPEN DOOR as he's sitting down, and as he sips, Parker notices that though the background changes each time, a single kid dressed like a dime store devil with pixelated horns seems to never move from the same spot, just on the edge of the scene.

>>PRINCESS: Trick or treat!

There's just one kid this time, a parent with them. Parker clicks GIVE CANDY.

>>YOUR CANDY BOWL IS 93% FULL.

>>PRINCESS' MOM: What do you say?

>>PRINCESS: Thank you!

>>PRINCESS' MOM: Somebody carved something into your door.

Parker clicks QUESTION.

>>PRINCESS' MOM: It says ... CALL HIM ... how odd.

>>Say, what's up with those creepy showtunes next door?

Parker notices that his soundcard's doing its best to produce a light, jazzy showtune without it sounding like garbled chips. In fact, it's oddly high quality and familiar, too. Trying to place it, Parker fills in notes ahead of time mentally, and when it comes together, he clicks—the big band song from *Temple of Doom*. But that's not why it's familiar and, again, it sounds too clean. Suspicious, Parker turns his volume down and strains his ears. Over the sound of a street swarming with trick-or-treaters, Parker only manages to catch faint, singular notes. Putting it down to his imagination, he turns back to the game.

The Princess and her mother leave. Parker clicks

CLOSE DOOR.

>>KNOCK-KNOCK.

He clicks OPEN DOOR and lets out a sharp, "Huh?" Two pixelated children stand on the doorstep, one of them in a generic white karate outfit and the other almost the same, but holding a blue lightsaber. A third stands in the back, hands in his pockets. A low-budget cartoon is one thing, but no way Lucasfilm licensed this, and weren't those kids outside dressed just like . . .

>>KARATE KID: Trick or treat.

Parker is too creeped out to do anything other than click GIVE CANDY.

>>YOUR CANDY BOWL IS 89% FULL.

>>STARWARS KID: Hey man, thanks! Glad you're normal.

Parker squints and clicks QUESTION.

>>KARATE KID: Dude, your neighbors are fuh-reaky.

Parker clicks CLOSE DOOR, unease gnawing at him. Laughter interrupts his thoughts, and Parker glances to the window to see the kids, dressed like the trio from the game, making their way from his house. They're putting away fresh candy gains, and Parker tells himself it has to be from the bowl his mom left out.

>>KNOCK-KNOCK.

Parker clicks OPEN DOOR to find two girl clowns, one with green hair and the other with a giant bow on her head.

>>CLOWN GIRL 1: Trick or trick! Hehehe!

"Huh?" Parker squints.

>>CLOWN GIRL 2: Hey mister, who's that behind you?

"Shit," Parker panics and clicks LOOK.

>>YOU LOOK BEHIND YOU, BUT THERE'S NO ONE THERE.

>>YOU TURN BACK AROUND TO FIND YOUR CANDY BOWL GONE.

"No!" Parker slaps his desk, but there's nothing he can do. The two clown girls make off with his entire stash of digital candy, and they even stop on the way to kick over his in-game mailbox.

Something crashes and clangs outside; Parker drags his braced leg to the window to see his actual mailbox lying in the street.

"No way . . ."

And then he notices something else. Standing stock still in the middle of the road, trick-or-treaters move around him as though he's not even there, a kid dressed like a red devil, just like in the game.

"This is too weird." Parker hurries back to his computer to find another costumed kid waiting at his in-game door with their parent. He clicks GIVE CANDY just to see what happens.

>>YOU HAVE NO CANDY LEFT TO GIVE…

>>SCARECROW KID: *CRIES*

>>SCARECROW PARENT: What kind of jerk does that to a kid on Halloween?

"It's not my fault," Parker finds himself trying to explain to the game. As the disgruntled parent leaves with their child, Parker notices the screen refreshes and the devil kid is slightly closer now.

It goes on like this, with Parker opening the door only to be berated by parents and kids for having no candy. He gets egged, toilet papered, and eventually stops answering the door as his frustration grows.

"This is bullshit!" He expects this kind of instant fail-state bullshit from something like *Shadowgate*, but not some lame Halloween Night simulator.

He clicks OPEN DOOR, then CLOSE DOOR almost instantly, hoping to push the game to an ending—too worked up to pay any attention to the devil kid creeping statically closer with each failed interaction. Not till he clicks OPEN DOOR, and Parker finds no one there but the devil kid, the neighborhood behind him now gone, just an endless black void. Up close, he can see that the legs sticking out from under the red cape don't belong to a child. They're narrow, buckled, and end in cloven hoofs. Parker's hand shakes as he clicks CLOSE DOOR.

>>BANG-BANG!

In time with the game, Parker hears someone slam their fists against the front door above his head.

"Shit." He pushes away from his desk and limps hurriedly to the window. It's gotten late, real late; where did the time go? Pike Street is dark, lights inside pumpkins burning low if it all with no sign of anyone.

Above, he can hear angry slaps against the door and someone rattling the handle violently. Parker glances at his monitor.

>>BANG-BANG!

"Screw this!" He lumbers toward the wall and, with spindly, weak arms, puts everything he has into moving his computer desk enough to get to the socket. Sweating, floppy hair plastered to his forehead, Parker reaches down and yanks the cord out.

"Try getting in now!" he yells at the dark monitor, a half-smirk of triumph spreading across his face before it twists into harrowing fear. The door above him crashes open.

Heavy footsteps pound along the hall toward the basement door.

"Shit-shit-shit." Parker looks around in desperation and finds the only thing he has to defend himself with is his crutch. Grabbing it, Parker holds the crutch like he's stepping up to the plate and drags his braced leg behind as he approaches the stairs. He gulps, dry swallowing as he watches the door begin to open.

"Come get — Mom?"

"Parker honey," his mom giggles, "What you doin' with that?"

She takes the first step, and on the second, she misses, sliding down the rest on her backside so fast her two sizes too small for her skirt rides up into a belt.

"I thought someone was breaking in." Parker lowers his crutch and uses it to get to his mother's side. She seems none the worse for her fall down the stairs. Before he reaches her, Parker's assaulted by a powerful aroma of box wine and cheap beer.

"Mommy's brave little soldier," she giggles as she gets to her feet and puts a hand on Parker's cheek. "It's late, honey; you should be asleep."

"I'm not tired," Parker says and surprises himself with the realization. This is the longest he's stayed awake in a while.

"Mommy will fix that," she says and staggers over to

Parker's mini-fridge without bothering to fix her skirt. Her tights are torn, and her underwear is half-pulled between her exposed cheeks. Parker looks away, not wanting to see that, as she takes one of his cans. She sits down on the bed, the can hissing as she pops it then reaches for the bag of medication.

"You're not supposed to drink with your meds, Mom," Parker says with his back to her.

"I'm not drunk," she insists with a laugh as she cracks the lid of a Tegretol bottle and tips some into the Pepsi. "Come have a drink, sweetheart; Mommy will tuck you in."

Parker sighs and does what he's told, limping over and sitting on the bed beside her. She hands him the Pepsi, and as Parker takes it, her hand falls to his thigh.

"That's a good boy." She giggles. "You're always such a good boy. Defending the house, more of a man than your limp-dicked deadbeat dad." Her hand moves up Parker's thigh, moving inward as she bites her lip.

Parker's hand shakes as he holds the can. He looks down through the popped tab, watching the medication dissolve. He's not surprised, not really. After the accident, why should he? He closes his eyes and downs the spiked Pepsi in one gulp, hoping it gets to him faster that way.

"Not telling those nosey doctors what really happened to your leg." She leans in and kisses Parker on the cheek, letting her tongue linger and trace a line up to his ear. She whispers with a breathy promise, "You're always Mommy's good boy."

~

After, Parker lies awake. The dose is not enough to knock him out. His mother lies face down, naked on his bed, snoring as drool pools around her mouth. The sheet covers her back, leaving her rear exposed. Parker stares at her cellulite folds, slightly scabbed razor bumps, and palm-sized fresh bruising, forcing the bile back down his throat.

He hears the words she spoke the first time. It started with a hug, she needed to hold him. Mommy's sad, she moaned into his ear as her hand found its way to his fly. *Help Mommy feel good again. Be Mommy's good boy.*

She promised it wouldn't happen again. But it did.

He makes his way to the computer she bought for him the very next day.

They never spoke of what happened, and in time, Parker convinced himself it didn't happen. Too delighted with a whole new world of games to realize she'd made for him a prison of fun and frivolity he'd never want to leave. And then it happened again. And again. Each time, nothing would be discussed; the closest to any acknowledgment would be the appearance of a new game—a new reality to escape into.

Parker clambers down and reaches for the plug, jamming it back into the socket. The computer turns back on, and the game is right where Parker left it. The impossibility of that doesn't matter right now. It's what he expected, what he hoped for.

>>BANG-BANG!

Parker glances at his snoring mother and wishes he had the strength to say no, to stand up and leave. But he doesn't and so, without hesitation, he clicks OPEN DOOR.

N⁰ 9

TAKE ONE
Alex Crandall

I REMEMBER THE GREAT SUGAR CRASH like it was yesterday.

You see, I was the greatest trick-or-treater this town had ever seen. Ever since I was little, I had planned each Halloween down to the doorstep. My schemes included building a fake little brother from wire hangers and cardboard to collect extra candy per house (the aptly named Operation Fun-Size) and crafting spare costumes so I could hit houses multiple times (Operation Gobstopper, on account of the many layers). You know when you see a bowl of candy left out that says *Take One* and you just empty the whole bowl? I actually invented that. So, it goes without saying that every Halloween I came home with a veritable candy mountain. The day after Halloween was when James came in.

James was descended from Wall Street sharks, and cutthroat negotiation was in his blood. I once watched him turn a handful of Smarties into five packs of gummy worms, and that was just during recess. In a couple of days, James could nearly triple what we started with, but he never ate his share. Eleven months of the year, neither of us had any other friends, but when November came around and the kids at school saw our king-sized hoard, everybody wanted a piece. James convinced smart kids to do our homework for bubblegum and got older kids to protect us from bullies for candy cigarettes. He even supplied our gym teacher, whose wife had him on a strict sugar-free diet, in exchange for hall passes and excused absences from square dancing. If you ask me, I think he got more joy out of making deals than from whatever he got out of them.

The only thing that kept our business in check was James's violent peanut allergy. He couldn't even touch contaminated wrappers without instantly breaking out in furious red blotches, so peanut-based goods were out of the question. This included a large portion of what our end users considered premium sweets: Snickers, Reese's, and Baby Ruths, just to name a few. Of course, and I trust you'll keep this to yourself, I had a small Butterfingers operation going on the side. Always best to have a safety net in this line of work.

We were halfway through seventh grade, teetering on the edge of that age where people started wondering if you were a little too old to play dress-up. The second I got home from school, I put on my nicest shirt and slacks, threw one of my dad's black ties around my neck, and donned a rubber mask, the kind that covers your whole head and smells like you've been sealed inside a well-worn pencil case, of President Reagan. Now *there* was a man who knew the value of a jelly bean. My mother kissed me on my floppy, oversized head as I dashed out the door faster than you could say, "Tear down this wall." I hopped on my bike and tore down the street as fast as my presidentially-inhibited vision allowed.

When I arrived at the meeting point across from Pike Street, Charlotte was sporting a green jacket and blood-spattered hockey mask, replacing the batteries in Walkie Talkies, while Ross and Lewis bickered nearby. They both wore bright blue outfits with purple hoods and identical yellow skulls over their faces, and I wasn't entirely sure who was who.

"You said you were gonna be He-Man!" Ross or Lewis

said.

"My mom wouldn't let me. Said he's too whorish." I was pretty sure this was Lewis.

"You could've been Beast Man," Ross (probably) retorted.

"Who the hell wants to be Beast Man?"

"Your mom called me Beast Man last night."

"What does that even mean?"

I tossed my bike under a bush and sprang out from behind them, wiggling my fingers in the air and shouting, in my best impression of the president, "I'm from the government, and I'm here to help!" I didn't understand how this was meant to be frightening, but my dad sure seemed to think so, especially around tax season.

Ross and Lewis jolted, and Charlotte raised her mask to reveal her freckle-spotted face. "That is the creepiest mask I've ever seen, man. You look like my grandpa right before he didn't come back from the hospital."

"Where's James?" I asked. As if summoned, a black SUV veered off the main road and pulled up onto the curb. The passenger door slammed open, and out stepped James in what I can only describe as the lamest costume I had seen in all my years of Halloweening.

"Dude," I said. "Did you just pull that thing off your bed?"

Ronald Reagan, Jason Voorhees, and two Skeletors watched as the richest kid in school, a guy whose parents could probably afford custom-made costumes from those companies that do makeup for scary movies, climbed out of the car in an honest-to-god white bedsheet, a costume so cliché that I had until this point assumed it to be reserved solely for Charlie Brown strips and Scooby-Doo villains. I mean, if you sold Halloween in a can, a sheet ghost would be on the front. James's costumes were historically lazy at best, but this was another level entirely. Needless to say, there was not an unraised eyebrow among us.

The height of James's eyebrows, however, was not visible through the lopsided eye holes cut crudely into his costume, so it was impossible to say how plussed he was by our reactions. He slapped the back of the car, which pulled off the curb and sped away, sounding a farewell with a friendly honk of its horn. James's bed sheet flapped gallantly in the breeze as he rubbed his hands together beneath his costume.

"Are you gonna stand there gawking all night? We've got work to do."

I had drawn out our plan more than a month in advance to avoid the failures of the previous Halloween. In the weeks leading up to the end of October, I always conducted thorough market research, trying to find the perfect balance of wealth without stinginess; too poor, you'll end up breaking your teeth on year-old Tootsie Rolls, and too rich, you risk coming home with a pillowcase brimming with toothbrushes and church pamphlets. It's a delicate equation. The year before, my phone polling had indicated that Jackson Boulevard would be our greatest score yet, but last Halloween's bottom line had been an all-time low. It took James months to get over it.

This time I was sure that I'd found the ideal candidate. Pike Street had been on my radar for years already. It possessed an air of latent spookiness that is difficult to describe to someone outside of the industry, so I won't. Just know that I could feel in my bones that Pike Street was where the sugar was. It had been a tough sell to James, who pushed hard for his own wealthy neighborhood, but I presented a chart highlighting the high concentration of dentists in his community, a damning rebuttal.

James reluctantly conceded, on the condition that we expand our group. It was a small compromise, but also a subtle sign that James had lost faith in me. After several rounds of auditions, we settled on our three most capable classmates: Charlotte, Ross, and Lewis. I elected for one of my simpler plans, though one of the most effective: James and I would take the most promising side of the street, while the others took the "B" side. We would all rendezvous at the cul-de-sac that marked the end of the road and report on which houses had been the most generous (and which were better off skipped) so that on the way back to the meeting point, we would only double-dip the best doorsteps. If all went according to plan, we could even have some time to hit a couple more streets before the knocks of beggars were no longer heeded. Once I had run through Operation Kit-Kat with the group a third time, we split up (get it?) and our mission was underway.

The sun dipped low behind the trees as we got to work, and a pleasant chill quickly fell over Pike Street. I lifted my mask enough to inhale deeply, enjoying the invigorating sharpness of the autumn evening. I could taste the distant yet certain promise of winter in the air. Lively characters filed from house to house; vampires and princesses and Thundercats and robots and witches all marching to their sweet tooth's tune. The worst costume of the lot walked conspicuously beside me. I was grateful my face was covered.

When James and I reached the end of the cul-de-sac our recruits were nowhere to be found. I passed the time by memorizing the notes I took along our route. The house with the party inside seemed like it was trying too hard, presumably overcompensating for mediocre loot. No need to stop there. The house with the red dogwood tree was generous and friendly, definitely worth another visit. I tried to ignore the frustration radiating from beneath James's sheet.

I pulled out my Walkie Talkie and held down the button for the fourth time. "This is the Great Pumpkin. Team Linus, do you copy? Where are you? Over."

The Walkie finally buzzed in reply. "Sorry guys, we're done trick-or-treating," Charlotte said. "Lewis and Ross ran into two He-Mans, or He-Men, and now they're doing a tag team poetry slam at the park. They're doing the voices and everything. It's terrible. You should come watch!"

James kicked the nearest mailbox, hard.

I hesitated, then pressed the button again. "Negative,

we're still below quota. Do you at least have a report on optimal houses? Over."

"Somebody left a motherload of candy on the porch of some abandoned house. I think it was 9 Pike St.? It's probably picked clean by now."

"You mean you didn't take it all? Over."

"We had enough already. Besides, that's just selfish."

Static continued to stream out of the Walkie, and I heard snippets of muffled conversation. Her button must have stuck. I distinctly made out the words "quota," "bossy," and "lame" followed by the sound of a group laughing. In the background, somebody asked if there was anything that rhymes with Grayskull. I felt my face flush.

James crushed our map into a tight ball. "Amateurs," he muttered. "If we hadn't been waiting here this whole time, we'd have hit that house an hour ago!"

I reached into my pillowcase and slid a Heath bar out of its sleeve. James slapped it out of my hand.

"Put that toffee down. Toffee's for closers only. We're running to that house."

"Maybe we should go catch up with the others," I said. "It sounds like they're having a good time."

James jabbed a finger into my chest. "I'm sorry, are you not having a *good time?* Have you forgotten that it was your idea to sit here waiting in this shitty neighborhood when we could have been collecting more capital? Screw your plan. Screw the others. Screw you."

"You're taking this way too seriously, man," I said. "And that's coming from me. We've got plenty of candy to trade, and your folks are gonna buy you a bunch more anyway." I paused, and a sudden big boy realization struck me. "I think we're getting a little old for this, James. Trick-or-treating is almost over, and this could be our last one. Maybe we should just enjoy it while it lasts."

I struggled to meet his gaze. Mostly because his eye holes were abysmal. Eventually, he spoke. "We're just a couple of nobodies, only good for shoving in lockers when the mood strikes. But as long as the sugar is flowing, everyone's lining up to be our friend. So if you want to walk away and go back to being a loser, feel free. I'm getting my just desserts, with or without you." He bolted off in the direction of the house.

"James, wait," I started, but he was already out of earshot. I think. The mask really made it hard to see. Either way, there was no reply. Guilt bubbled in my stomach like a witch's cauldron, so I swallowed my misgivings and chased after him.

By that point, most trick-or-treaters had returned to their homes, and Pike Street was eerily silent. Wind whistled through bare branches, and somewhere an owl called solemnly. By the time I caught up to James, he was already on the porch of an ancient house at the end of a patchy, yellowing lawn. The paneling was soft and rotten, and I wasn't sure if its pale black color was aging paint or mold. The roof had collapsed in two places, and the whole thing sagged like it was sodden, as though it had been recently dragged out of a lake. James was flipping and shaking crumbs out of empty orange bowls, turning the toothy jack-o'-lantern smiles printed on them into frowns. The shiny plastic was out of place beside the decrepit structure. James threw the last of them off the porch into cobweb-covered bushes, looking for all the world like the worst poltergeist of all time.

"Idiots! It's all gone! You're all useless!" he shouted at no one in particular.

When I began to cross the dying lawn, a groaning creak, like some immense weight shifting inside the house, froze my feet in place. Ice crawled up my spine. Suddenly, I was certain that if I took another step toward that house, I would never leave. Don't ask me why. Instead, I bravely called from the sidewalk, "James, let's go. This place is freaking me out."

Another creaking of wood like a dying animal. A frigid gust buffeted the house, bringing with it a horrid stench. The front door floated open with the breeze. Suspended from the ceiling by a silver thread just beyond the doorway was another bowl, overflowing with all the best candy you could imagine. There was enough sugar in that bowl to kill a diabetic who looked at it for too long. It was like the pot at the end of the obesity rainbow. The bowl's toothy grin mocked me, as though it could see me salivating. James spotted it too, and he peered in to get a closer look. The interior of the house was immaculately dark, but even from my place at the edge of the sidewalk I could make out two words scratched onto the inside of the door:

TAKE ONE

It occurred to me how late it was. It was well past the point where scary felt inviting and magical. Truly frightening night had set in, the kind of night where kids without supervision went missing and were never seen again. At some point, Halloween had ended. Now it was just November and well past our curfew. James glanced back at me once, then approached the door. Behind his eyes I saw his sense of self-preservation fighting his avarice in a losing battle.

James stepped up to the doormat.

He reached through the doorway and grabbed the dangling bowl of candy.

Eleven spindly, jagged appendages, glistening with ooze or moisture or who knows what, enfolded him like the legs of a colossal spider. I know there were eleven because that night and every night after for a long time, I could count them whenever I closed my eyes.

Before he could make a sound, James was yanked inside.

The door slammed shut.

I pissed myself a little.

Okay, a lot.

If I screamed, I couldn't hear it over my own heart, loudly pummeling me from within as if trying to escape. For what felt like hours I just stood there, searching for any signs of life behind the clouded windows. I braced myself to catch a glimpse of James being peeled open and devoured like a chocolate bar or pulled apart like taffy, but I saw nothing. The house, the street, the whole world was still and serene. Somehow that was worse.

Before you criticize my next actions, consider for a moment what you would do in my shoes. Be honest, are you going anywhere near that house? Of course not. So, I did what you and anyone else with half a brain would do: I ran home and lived to fight another day.

The police would remember that night as the fastest missing person search in our town's history because they found James right where I left him, standing on the sidewalk with a massive bowl of candy under his arm, his lips coated with chocolate. His ghost sheet was nowhere to be seen. From the back of my dad's squad car, I could see that he seemed unharmed, if a bit pale. James said nothing as he got in the car with us; he just smiled and offered me a Twizzler.

Things were different after that. At school the next day, James gave away candy to anyone who asked. As you may have guessed, this market oversaturation caused the 100 Grand Standard to plummet, sending the confectionary economy into an unprecedented depression that has since been dubbed by experts as the Great Sugar Crash. He didn't seem to mind, though. Whatever people didn't want, he scarfed down himself, but he saved me all his Almond Joys because he knew they were my favorite.

Ross, Lewis, and Charlotte started sitting with us at lunch, and James ate all his desserts instead of trading them for baseball cards. In fact, whenever I saw him he was eating something. He was always ravenous, though he never seemed to gain any weight. Maybe it was some trauma-induced coping mechanism. Or it could have been a growth spurt; after all, he did seem a bit taller than I remembered. I regarded James with suspicion for a while, waiting for the day he would finally break into tears and confess how he escaped the house on Pike Street, but that day never came. Life went on, and James seemed fine, happier even, so I assumed he had filed that night away for his therapist to unpack someday. Eventually, I figured it was best that I did the same. The year went by swiftly after that, and before I knew it,

October was upon us again. When I approached James about our strategy for the coming holiday, he waved his hand dismissively.

"We can go wherever you want, man. I'm just happy to be included!"

When Halloween night finally came around and we met up at Carpenter Lane, there were no maps, Walkies, or call signs, just the setting sun and quiet anticipation. Charlotte waved a prop chainsaw wildly in greeting when I arrived. She wore a bloodstained butcher's apron and an extremely convincing human skin mask. Ross and Lewis showed up soon after, both dressed in gray outfits with cowled capes and pointed ears.

"You cannot be serious," Lewis grumbled. "You said you were gonna be Robin!" Charlotte and I laughed as Ross tackled Lewis to the ground, and the pair scuffled in the grass.

"Nice suit," Charlotte said to me. "But I didn't vote for you."

"Thank James's folks. Speaking of, where is he?" As if summoned, a black SUV veered off the main road and pulled up onto the curb. The passenger door slammed open, and out stepped James in what I can only describe as the greatest costume I had seen in all my years of Halloweening.

"Read my lips," I said, in my best impression of the president. "Did somebody just pull you out of a tomb?"

George Bush, Leatherface, and two Batmans (Batmen?) watched as the nicest kid in school, a guy who convinced his parents to buy us custom-made costumes, climbed out of the car wrapped in the scariest mummy outfit I've ever seen. Every exposed piece of skin was painted like decaying flesh. He raised both arms in front of him and moaned menacingly at the group, though it was impossible to miss his beaming smile behind his wrappings.

"It's Payday, gang! What's the plan?"

A strange but not unwelcome sensation washed over me, an electric uncertainty in my chest, as I realized for the first time that I didn't have one.

We didn't bother knocking on many doors, content to spend most of the night goofing off. Ross and Lewis made plans to wear matching costumes again next year. We all watched as Charlotte hid behind shrubs for a while and leaped out at passersby. James ate almost as much candy as he collected, and by the time we called it a night, his pillowcase was practically empty.

"Who are you, and what did you do with the real James?" I joked. Everyone else laughed, but James stopped in his tracks. His eyes bulged, and fear squeezed my throat as he slowly blinked, one eye at a time, and his mouth stretched wide, exposing his teeth. His head jerked abruptly to one side. After an agonizing moment his face twitched, and I realized with horror that he was laughing.

"Dude, you should've seen the look on your face. I had you going, man!"

I didn't want to seem like a bad sport in front of our friends, so I forced a chuckle. "Yeah, you got me. Scary stuff." He slapped me on the shoulder good-naturedly, but every detail of that night crawled around the corners of my mind. I had to know for sure.

"Hey, you want a bite of this?" I pulled a piece of chocolate out of my bag, peeled away the wrapper, and offered the end to him.

James grinned. "You know I do, scaredy-puss." He took an exaggerated chomp and licked his lips. I watched him carefully as he swallowed the Snickers bar, peanuts and all.

"Thanks, man. I'm glad I have a friend like you."

It wore James's smile so sweetly, daring me to reach for more of the truth. I decided that more than one piece might be bad for my health.

"Don't mention it," I said. And I never did.

№ 10

APPOINTED GUARDIAN
Lennox Rex

Saturday, October 11th

MANDY LAURENT INSISTED THERE was a way to contact your guardian angel.

She'd heard some of the older kids whispering about it at reception just the other Sunday. The group had been huddled so closely together at the farthest, loneliest edge of the courtyard that Mandy's brother hadn't noticed her walking up with a Dixie cup of lemonade and half a glazed donut. She'd been able to get the full story out of him later that evening, but there was no knowing if he'd told her the truth or had changed up details just to scare her.

When they heard about the blood required, Sarah felt just as skeptical as Mandy. It all sounded a bit more like spirit communication and a lot less like prayer, and when Sarah really thought about it, their father's disapproving grumble echoed in their head: *Sounds like witchcraft and Satan to me.*

Sarah sent the letter all the same, so they could know for sure.

Pricking their finger with a sewing needle was surprisingly scary, but Sarah managed. They made sure to puncture deep enough to get two bright crimson beads dropped down right onto the paper before popping their finger into their mouth and mindlessly pressing their tongue against it until it stopped hurting. Once the blood dried, they folded the letter up, placed it in a plain, unstamped, unaddressed envelope and waited. Setting their alarm clock was an impossibility. With the shrill racket it made, the entire household would stir. It was easier for Sarah to feign sleep for the in-between hours.

Midnight came sooner than anticipated, and anxious excitement buzzed just under their skin, pimpling the flesh, as they slipped out from under their covers. Quiet as their mother always expected them to be whenever the *men* were talking, they crept out of the house. An abrupt door slam made them cringe and they glanced to their left. As expected, belligerent shouts and answering shrieks immediately carried out into the street. Sarah shoved their hands into their windbreaker pockets, careful not to crumple the letter, and hurried past number 8, silently praying the neighbors would have moved on to making up by the time they returned. *Dad would be way too embarrassed to call the police over that kind of noise.* They turned right onto Line Street and walked until they reached the public mailbox over by the Laurent house, where they dropped the letter inside before heading back home.

Sarah had written a simple message: *Please, I need a friend. Love, Tom.*

Thursday, October 30th

Sarah huddled into themself, propping their elbows up on the ceramic tile counter of the cutout that separated the kitchen from the living room, and lowered their voice. "You know I can't—"

There was a pointed cough from their father, and Sarah immediately corrected themself with a frown.

"You know I don't go trick-or-treating." Sarah wanted to add that they appreciated the offer, but quickly thought better of it. "You really should stop asking me," they said instead, making sure their voice carried clearly. Listening to their friend's response, they tugged anxiously at the telephone cord. "Yeah, alright. See you in English." They stole a quick glance toward their parents at the dining room table. "Bye, Nolan."

Their father huffed disapprovingly as Sarah came back to their spot at the table. "I think you should stop associating with that boy." He leveled a stern look at them, and Sarah was able to hold his gaze only briefly before they shifted to look down at the table. "He wants to lead you astray."

Sarah's mother responded in a meek, conciliatory tone. "Rob, honey. Let's not get carried away now. He's just a lost boy. He's not *trying* to cause any harm." She reached out to grab a pamphlet from the neat, orderly stacks of 3" x 5" gospel comics she'd gotten through Pastor Jones, and slipped the Chick Tract into a goody bag with a couple of Dum Dums as she thought about what she wanted to say next.

Before she could figure it out, Robert took back control of the conversation. "I tell you one thing, Deborah. There's something wrong with that boy." He shook his head as he shoved a completed bag away from himself, toward the far end of the table, and grabbed an empty one. "How long have we allowed him to be friends with our Sarah? And he's not shown any interest? A healthy boy should be looking for a girlfriend at his age." He spared a glance in Sarah's direction and snorted. "He must be one of those *queers!*" His face flushed and he sat taller in his chair, knocking his fist against the tabletop indignantly. "Only to be expected," he pushed on in a tone not unlike their pastor during a particularly impassioned sermon. "When a boy is raised without a father." He thrust his pointer finger up in the air, shaking it at his wife and daughter in turn. "Single mothers make soft little boys, not strong, respectable men."

Sarah kept their body loose and their expression blank as they avoided their father's gaze and mechanically grabbed a Chick Tract.

Deborah reached out and patted his leg. She left her hand there and began to rub his outer thigh soothingly.

"We are a good influence for him, Robert," she asserted in a hushed, slow voice. She moved her hand up, to stroke the back of Robert's neck—a move she'd discovered never failed to even his temper whenever he started to work himself up. Sure enough, Robert's shoulders began to relax, and the ruddiness left his cheeks.

"A good girl like Sarah is just the kind of friend he needs." Deborah turned a proud maternal smile over to them and winked. "And if a romance blooms, think of what a glorious testimony it will be!"

Robert sighed deeply and closed his eyes, taking one more moment of comfort from his wife's touch before he shrugged, cueing her to take her hand away and go back to filling trick-or-treat bags. "You're right. Of course you're right." He blinked his eyes open and gave Sarah a sheepish smile. "I'm sorry, baby girl." He reached out and put his hand atop theirs, patting it briefly. "It's just all this." He gestured to the loosely sorted piles on the dining table: twist ties and empty goody bags, opened bags of cheap candy, and the Chick Tracts. "It puts me in such a sour mood."

They could understand that, at least. Halloween always made Sarah especially anxious. Things had improved once Deborah finally succeeded in convincing Robert that concessions had to be made to secularism. Sarah no longer had to help him get toilet paper out of the tree outside their bedroom window or clean all the egg and shell off the garage door, but they paid in the way he needed to be treated with kid gloves all throughout October.

"You catch more flies with honey," Deborah reminded in the placating sing-song voice she often used when pointing things out to her husband. She smiled to herself as she put down another perfectly assembled treat bag.

"It just feels too much like paying a blackmailer," Robert grumbled, "or negotiating with terrorists. It's a damned shame we have to give any kind of acknowledgement to such a satanic holiday!" He gave a violent, huffing snort and shook his head again. "This country is really going to Hell in a handbasket, the way Halloween is getting to be such a big deal."

Sarah quickly bore down on their lower lip with their right canine, to hold back the heavy sigh that wanted to escape, and to fight the impulse to apologize for something that wasn't their fault.

Just when it seemed he was done, Robert forced out one final, exasperated huff. "I tell you what, Sarah." He shot them a pointed look, to make sure he had their attention. "You should be grateful we care enough to forbid this nonsense." He shook his head. "You don't want to be the next Lindsey Turner."

Deborah shook her head sadly. "There's pure evil out there."

"Amen."

The three of them continued prepping what Deborah preferred to call *Gospel Bags* in silence. *At least it'll be over and done with tomorrow,* Sarah reassured themself. Not for the first time that day, they wondered if their brother celebrated Halloween, out in the world and free from parental scrutiny, and felt a bitter pang of jealousy knowing they'd never be allowed to go to college. They had to hold in another sigh.

~

Eamon paused for a moment, reading the house. 10 Pike St. — a single story craftsman — sat unassumingly behind immaculate flower beds and a perfectly maintained yard graced by a Dogwood tree sporting glorious, fiery red leaves. Its modest taupe exterior, remarkably clean white accents and trim, and well-swept welcome mat seemed to broadcast a message of peace and familial harmony. *A den of deceit,* Eamon surmised. They turned their attention back to the imploring tug of blood that had led them here. The pull was strongest near the first bedroom, the one that looked out onto the street. As desperately as it called to them, Eamon kept moving — down the foyer past the second bedroom that emanated no signs of life, past a dining table and through the living room, into the master suite. They were curious about the other humans that lived here.

Robert and Deborah slept, oblivious to the late night visitation. Robert's snores filled the room with a harsh, discordant sort of music. He lay starfished across the bed, a thin line of drool escaping out the side of his open mouth. Eamon could stand to look at him only so long, and threw their attention to Deborah. A sense of tragedy overtook them as they considered her, crammed along the edge of the bed, her face as blank as the feeling that came from her. Having sensed all they needed to know, Eamon turned back to the rest of the house and finally made their way to Sarah's room.

They paused at the bedside, taking in everything they could as Sarah slept with a soft, peaceful expression on their face and their hands tucked up under their cheek, as if in prayer. Sarah's lips were loose and relaxed, letting out soft breaths that shifted the stray strands of ashy brown hair that had fallen over their face. A band of light freckles scattered from one cheek to the other, and their lashes fanned out across their fair skin like little dark ribbons of silk. The moonlight filtering in through the slanted blinds bathed them in a gentle light that only enhanced Sarah's innocence, and Eamon decided their mission was to protect this human child with all their strength. They fashioned themself a corporeal form so that they could sweetly brush the hair from Sarah's face and rest a hand on their forehead. "I have come, child."

Sarah stirred slightly as they began to dream under Eamon's watchful eye.

～

Tom found himself drenched in darkness, clutching at his own elbows, and shivering in the unnatural chill. He blinked twice, to clear the haze from his brain, and waited for his eyes to adjust. "*If* they adjust," he huffed. To his relief, things began to take shape within his field of vision, and he soon realized that he stood in the shadows of an empty alleyway. "Okay, so obviously, I'm dreaming," he mused. He confirmed by patting his chest and noting the absence of developing breasts. His dreams were the only place he knew where he didn't have to force himself to fit the pinching, biting confines of being Sarah. "Well, this is new. Where on Earth am I?" Not fully trusting what little he could see, he groped about until his hand met brick, and used that to guide himself along. "Thank God," he muttered when the alley suddenly opened up. The silvery light of the moon and stars exposed an empty cityscape. He turned right onto the cobbled street and walked on, ignoring the cheap, cardboard look of the buildings. The air seemed to heat up as he moved, just enough to keep him from dropping to the ground so he could huddle into himself for warmth.

"Hello," he called out after walking for what felt like miles. "Where is everybody? I know someone's here!" An involuntary shiver wracked his body. "I can feel you watching me!" The staged buildings had disappeared some time ago, replaced by a gaping, infinite nothing on either side of the cobblestones under his feet. "This has gotta be the most bogu—" Tom stopped short, nearly tripping over himself, when he spotted what looked like a child at the side of the road, just a little way ahead. The curiosity and concerned confusion written all over his face morphed into terror the closer Tom got. *Totally heinous*, he thought as he took in tattered rags hanging loose on a pale, scabby and scared, emaciated little body. One corner of his lip was curling up in a disturbed grimace when the stranger abruptly turned their head to face him. The scream that wanted to claw its way up his larynx and explode out from his mouth was stuck, sitting in his chest like heartburn. His legs trembled, but firmly refused to carry Tom away as the sightless ghoul approached, its void-like eye sockets trained on his face. Once it was close enough to reach out and touch Tom, it stopped and raised its withered face.

"Lend me your light," it suggested in an ambiguously genderless voice far too old for its child-like stature.

That overrode every command Tom's brain had been trying to send to his body, and he found himself slowly lowering into a squat, his left hand resting on his left knee and his right hand splaying out against the cold ground, to help him retain his balance. His pulse quickened, rushing through his veins and booming in his head like cannon fire. Droplets of sweat formed at his temples and his throat constricted in panic as the creature's hands reached up and those skeletal fingers came closer and closer to Tom's eyes. He tried frantically to slam his eyelids shut, but to no avail. He could only stare, wide-eyed, as fingertips began to press against him.

To his utter astonishment, it did not hurt. There was simply an odd, slightly uncomfortable pressure as those fingers forced their way in under his lower lid and scooped under his eyeballs. Then came more insistent pressure, this time in the other direction and, along with the disquieting sound of tearing and popping, two short, sharp tugs that were over before his brain could decide he was in pain.

"You will not want these," stated his grotesque little guide. "Not to talk to the Angel."

"Th-The angel?" Tom was interrupted by a soft squelch, and somehow, he knew that the creature had just popped his eyeballs into its own empty sockets.

"I will keep them safe. Now stand and take my hand, child."

Tom did as commanded, sensing how the thing he'd assumed was a child had suddenly grown tall enough to reach down for his hand and gently pull him forward. As they moved along, the air continued to warm, until Tom felt the pleasant drowsiness of a perfect day on the cusp of Summer. The freshly mutilated sockets that previously housed his eyes still felt the searing brightness of a mighty light, and he was glad to have been shielded from it. An energizing sense of awe tugged at the deepest parts of his soul, and he felt uplifted. *This must be what Church is supposed to feel like.*

There was the rustling of wings, and then a voice came creeping toward him from all sides, its multiple layers of young and old, gendered and genderless, human and inhuman like waves lapping at the shore. "Tom, my child." The voices all met together and settled into one eerily quasi-human tone as it continued. "I have followed your blood. I am Eamon, and I will enact retribution on the non-believers."

Tom shivered in a mix of fear and instinctive reverence. Then, Eamon's words fully registered and he staggered back a step. "Retribution? Non-believers?" He shook his head in bewilderment. "You mean my parents? But they're—they *are* believers!"

Eamon *tsked*. "The woman is emptied, mindless. She is a doll manipulated willingly and seeks only to produce more of her ilk. The man overflows with greed and malice. He lusts after control and defames the Lord."

Tom wanted to protest. He desperately wanted to be able to argue, but he simply couldn't counter the truth. Instead, he tried to appeal to Eamon's sense of mercy.

"But retribution? You really mean—You'll *kill* them?"

A blast of white-hot heat burst forth, leaving him feeling singed, though a quick pat down of his arms and torso assured him his body had been unharmed.

"They will be judged for their mockeries," Eamon roared, their voice separating once again, into myriad layers of rage.

Tom's knees nearly buckled as he was engulfed by the fervent desire to drop to the ground and beg forgiveness, but a bony hand on his shoulder stilled him.

"Strength," advised his creature guide in a soothing whisper. "The angel will do no harm to the innocent."

A new thought struck him, and Tom stammered as he collected his nerve. "B-but Eamon. I-I'm just a kid. I can't be left alone. It's not—It's against the law. I need a guardian!" He chewed nervously on his lower lip and offered his vulnerability. "Also, I don't want to be left alone. Please, Eamon. Please, don't do this and leave me all alone."

A cool, refreshing breeze caressed his face, and the brightness stinging Tom's eye sockets seemed to lessen for a moment, putting him at ease. "Fear not, my son. You will not be abandoned."

The cozy heat radiating out alongside Eamon's light began to dissipate and Tom felt himself being guided downward.

"Rest now." The cold enveloped him like an icy cocoon as his back flattened against the ground. "I will return and all will be just."

~

As Tom succumbed to the chill, Eamon vanished and Sarah fell into a deep, dreamless sleep.

Friday, Halloween Night

Robert paced irritably as Deborah and Sarah worked together to clear the table, then wash, dry, and put away the dishes. "It's almost time," he snapped. "Any time now, those little heathens will start ringing our bell, demanding candy." He paused to breathe in deeply and let the breath back out loudly. "And we'll have to smile and tell them what little sweethearts they are in their little costumes." He stopped again, sneering at no-one in particular, though he was facing his wife and daughter. "Those older kids these days, dressing up as pop stars. Idolatry," he spat. "Idolatry right on my doorstep!"

Deborah handed Sarah the last dish to dry and flocked over to her husband, stroking his neck and shoulders. "Now now, honey." She went up onto the balls of her stocking feet and kissed his cheek. "Let's not get ourselves into a knot over this. It'll be over soon." She ran her fingers along his jaw and down the side of his throat, melting the lines of tension in his face. Sarah tried not to sigh as they finished up in the kitchen and started looking through the cabinets for the biggest bowl they could find.

"This is important work we do," Deborah cooed, "witnessing with the Gospel Bags. What better night to spread God's message than . . . "

She trailed off, her fingers going limp and her hands dropping away from Robert.

"Deborah?" His body tensed in concern and his heart seized, sending a jolt of pain and raw, frigid dread through his body. Cold sweat dotted his hairline as he caught his wife in his arms just before she crumpled to the floor. "Debbie!" He whipped his head up, toward the kitchen. "Sarah," he barked, "your mother! Call 9-1-1!"

He didn't bother to make sure they'd followed his direction, too busy reading Deborah's face for clues. Her mouth dropped open, as if her jaw had unhinged, and she emitted a shrill shriek. Unwilling to let go of his wife, Robert clenched his jaw and squirmed in agony, waiting for his eardrums to burst. Just as quickly as she had begun, Deborah stopped screeching. Her mouth snapped violently shut with a loud *clap*, followed by a sickening *crunch*.

"Debbie?" Robert blinked away tears and cautiously caressed her brow, brushing hair out of her face as he continued to hold her. "Sweetheart?"

In the kitchen, Sarah struggled to see through their hot, frantic tears and act despite the wild panic brewing in their gut. They picked the phone back up from where they'd dropped it to cover their ears, and blinked to see the numbers more clearly. Their left pointer finger was poised to dial when a surge of voices filled the back of their mind. *Fear not, my son. I am here. Come and bear witness.* An uncanny sense of calm overtook their brain and seeped slowly down their spine as they placed the phone back in its cradle and came out from the kitchen, to observe the unfolding scene.

Focused intently on Deborah, Robert didn't notice that he'd become a spectacle. "My wife," he worried in a tiny, petrified whimper, "my beautiful wife. What's happening?"

His eyes bulged and he let out a terrified grunt as Deborah's eyelids stretched open impossibly wide and her green-flecked hazel irises seemed to fracture and expand. "What in God's name," he mumbled. His pulse slammed in his ears, and the sweat trickled down until it soaked the collar of his shirt. Before his own wide, horrified eyes, Deborah's sclerae seemed to bubble and boil, until they hissed and popped like a foil of Jiffy Pop on the stove. Finally, with one last gut-churning *pop* that reverberated in Robert's head, her eyes exploded, sending wet chunks of organ meat though the air. He shouted in disgust and threw her body to the floor. The back of her head made a horrific *crack* against the vinyl flooring of the dining room. Blood began to seep out from underneath her like searching fingers.

"No!" Robert dropped down, not even noticing the sharp pain of his knees slamming against the floor. He crawled to straddle his wife's still body, sobbing openly as he reached up and cradled her face in his shaking, sweaty hands. "What have I done," he wailed pitifully. He came down and pressed his tear-soaked, snotty lips to hers. "Please, " he whispered against them. "Please, God. I'm sorry, just please. My wife." He repeated himself, turning the words into a prayer as he closed his eyes and willed God to notice his torment.

Deborah's mangled eye sockets began to glow with a blinding brightness that Sarah had to close their eyes to. They continued to bear witness through the sounds of struggle and the smell of blood and burnt flesh.

Deborah's mouth twitched, lips separating and broken teeth making an unsettling sound as they ground together. Robert sprang back, kneeling astride her, and sucked in a few shallow, wavering breaths. "Deborah?"

She tilted her head, directing her blistering gaze right at his face. The air punched out of his lungs in a harsh, painful gasp as he felt his own eyes begin to sizzle.

"Charlatan!" A bone-chilling fury leapt from Deborah's mouth in a voice not her own as she whipped up her hand and caught Robert by the throat hard enough to make his eyes bulge again. He found himself held up in the air, dangling helplessly and struggling for breath in his wife's viselike grip. She herself was somehow suspended several feet off the ground, her mouth an angry slash of ruined teeth, and blood-matted hair clinging to the sides of her face. Those blinding shallows that once held eyes continued to bore into his, making them cook and burn faster, until they turned to ash and Robert wheezed in misery. His mouth flopped open and shut stupidly as he attempted to breathe and struggled to form sounds other than his labored breaths.

"You butcher the Divine and defile the love of Christ," Deborah accused in an animalistic growl. His windpipe crushed and his spine snapped as she tightened the grip on his purpling neck, yet he did not die. Every neuron in his brain pleaded for the mercy of death, but something kept him alive and conscious. The only grace he could enjoy was his inability to see the ghastly beast his wife had become. Relying only on the feel of her and the sound of this voice that had never belonged to her before, he could almost convince himself it was not her doing these ghoulish things to him.

An abrupt pain made his heart clench, and he wished he could cry out. A molten heat plunged into his gut and shot up through his esophagus, down through his intestines, and all through his veins. His brain now howled for death, but it still didn't come.

"Your kind preaches often about a lake of fire," Deborah hissed, "so I shall let you burn even beyond the end of days."

～

Outside the humble little Craftsman, with its clean trim and spectacular red-leaved tree, Halloween was finally underway. The first, early groups of eager trick-or-treaters were beginning to stream down Pike Street.

It was just as a gaggle of little ghosts, fairies and clowns, and some teenaged Madonnas and Boy Georges started up the walkway to 10 Pike St. that the house seemed to explode into an almost blinding pillar of unearthly fire that reached up to the Heavens, all with an unnerving, unnatural silence. Parents that had fallen behind raced up to grab their children and yank them away, the teenagers stood rooted to the spot, unable to look away as everyone screamed in shocked disbelief. It took less than a minute for the trick-or-treaters to realize that the flames were not spreading beyond the house and that no blazing, burning heat came rushing out to lick at their feet and sear their skin. As the crowd gathered back around and gawked at the fire with gaping mouths and candy-filled pillowcases slack at their sides, a form emerged from the flames.

Tom stepped out from his home, holding his mother's largest mixing bowl out in front of him. Goody bags were piled high, threatening to spill out over the sides of the bowl. His mother followed shortly after, moving in awkward jerks as if she had somehow forgotten how to move and needed to reacclimate to her own body. As she came to a stop on the last porch step, the soundless inferno behind her extinguished, as if it had never been, and the house stood exactly as it had before. Tom continued down the walk, to meet the crowd where they stood, and greeted them all with a welcoming, toothy grin. He squatted down, to be at eye level with the smallest trick-or-treaters, and held out the bowl encouragingly.

"What do you say," he asked in a bright, cheerful voice.

THE SCENT OF HALLOWEEN
Brady Tiel

THERE WAS A SMELL IN THE AIR that could only be attributed to the buzz of another Halloween night. It was a combination of many scents drifting in on the October winds; the decaying leaves of an autumn giving way to winter, the aroma of coffee breweries and their fall crowd baring down en masse, or simply the electric energy of a neighborhood brimming with excited children.

Halloween seemed to create its own atmosphere on Pike Street.

A lone jack-o'-lantern rested on the wooden porch, a small yellow flame burning in the triangular cutouts of its eyes. It was signal enough—someone was home. Nobody would be so irresponsible as to leave a flame unattended, much less on a night when unruly kids surely did things only acceptable on an evening seemingly dedicated to the macabre.

The jack-o'-lantern, however, was not the source of the smell emanating from the property. The neighborhood's garbage day had come a day early, a proactive decision to avoid burning dumpster fires and excessive litter. It was just another step to keep said unruly kids at bay. If the smell could not be connected to the lonely jack-o'-lantern or the lack of garbage then it must have been the only other decoration making up House 11's lackluster display.

A white skeleton, cobbled together with old H/VAC pipe and a cheap second hand mask, was seated in a reclined beach chair. It leaned all the way back with a slick pair of black sunglasses resting over empty eye sockets. It was rather uninspiring in a neighborhood that seemed to grow only more attached to the final day of October each passing year. The arrangement did not strike anyone with the fear of ghosts and ghouls, much less a chill on the back of their neck. The skeleton was almost inviting the way it casually sat watching over the neighborhood.

The skeleton was wide. The bones comprising its arm swelled into white bulbs, almost translucent from how far the rubber-like material stretched. They appeared to be filled with nothing but stagnant air. The skeleton's head seemed disproportionate to the rest of its rounded caricature, and even the sunglasses did little to detract from how grotesque the display looked for anyone who gave it more than a passing glance. The head, where it should have been emaciated and gaunt, was round like a balloon. The facial features; deep set eyes, a hard brow ridge, and thin cheeks, were seemingly painted onto the base of a flexible sheet that was supposed to be its face. The display was almost cute from a distance, the telltale sign of a newly moved-in family that did not want to be too excessive in their dedication.

The smell, however, could surely be attributed to the swollen amalgamation of painted bones and the swelled torso.

Jonsi thought it smelled especially rank, but it was alluring in its own kind of way. Things were supposed to smell bad on Halloween. That was part of the fun, part of the thrill.

What was in the bucket? What was that goo coming out of the zombie's eye? What did the silk feel like that oozed out of the spider's abdomen? It was one of many questions that only Halloween, of all things, could spur in a thirteen-year-old's mind.

Jonsi stood at the end of the cobblestone path that meandered up to the steps of number 11. His eyes had not left the inflated skeleton sitting in the lawn chair. What an odd choice of decoration, he thought. Sunglasses were not scary. And a lawn chair? It was October. The beach was nowhere close. The odd choice of decoration, combined with the pungent smell wafting from the property, made Jonsi more eager to race up to the front steps.

Micah and Lori were behind, still a couple houses away. They were so slow. *Too slow,* Jonsi thought. They were going to miss all the good candy. Number 11 seemed wealthy, if Jonsi's definition of wealthy as a thirteen-year-old boy was anything close to accurate. Sure, the lawn looked like it needed a trim and the roof did look fairly tattered in some places, but they had a skeleton sitting on a lawn chair! That was unusual and unusual things were usually expensive. In his thirteen years of life he had learned if it was unfamiliar it must cost a lot of money.

Jonsi's friends, Micah and Lori included, had a lot of the same things Jonsi did. The same backpack, the same lunch kit, even the same costumes. This year, they were all firefighters. Jonsi was not rich. His parents told him so. That meant Micah and Lori were not rich either. Between the three of them, none of their houses had a skeleton sitting in a lawn chair. So, number 11 must have been rich. It was the only possible reasoning for such strange decor.

Tim would have loved the skeleton.

Tim had been Jonsi's best friend up until two weeks ago. That's when he went missing. How did kids go missing? Jonsi barely understood it, but he had not let it bother him. Adults could go missing, that happened all the time. They got old and sick. It happened to Jonsi's grandpa. It even happened to one of the teachers at his school, Mr. Bartley. He had been the shop teacher and after one silly accident, he was gone, too. That made sense, that was the way the world worked. But kids?

No. That did not make sense.

Tim had a rich family, or at least Tim had always told Jonsi so. Tim said his family had a cottage on a lake only an hour from the neighborhood and had a timeshare in Mexico, whatever that meant. It sounded rich to Jonsi. Mexico sounded rich. He had never been before and wondered if he ever would. He imagined that was where Tim was now, lounging in Mexico looking no different than the skeleton sitting on the beach chair in front of number 11.

Micah and Lori were taking too long. Jonsi saw them from where he stood, his black boots barely touching the cracked stone path. He was itching to go. The only saving grace of having waited around for so long was that across the street, the woman handing out candy had a costume Jonsi could not get enough of. Everytime the door opened and the scantily dressed nurse stepped out, Jonsi stole a look, careful not to let his eyes linger too long. It would be too embarrassing if either Micah or Lori saw him do it.

Micah and Lori were still two houses down, ensnared in aimless conversation with whatever crank lived in that house. The neighborhood was starting to get busy. Halloween was in full swing. Sooner or later Jonsi and his companions would be swimming in an ocean of costumed kids, racing for the goods before they were all taken by face-painted monsters and homemade abominations.

The smell was too much now, maybe even more alluring than the nurse across the street. Number 11 smelled *scary*. Was that possible? Jonsi started up the path. He held his candy bucket in hand, feeling the weight of the candy inside press against his thigh. His eyes were trained on the vacationing skeleton the whole while he walked. The smell grew. It was pungent. It made Jonsi's eyes squint and his nose sting, like something had crawled up his nostrils and bit him on the soft skin inside. Jonsi sniffled, disturbed by the smell but excited at the prospect of whatever it was. There must have been a hidden decoration somewhere, waiting to pop out at him. He would not be scared. He never was. Micah and Lori would be though. They jumped at everything.

Jonsi paced up the few steps that landed him on the porch in front of the white door. Resting beside the welcome mat was a jack-o'-lantern, expertly cut out and glowing with ember breath. Jonsi's dad always cut out their pumpkins. He did it the best, or at least he thought so until he saw the one that belonged to number 11. This pumpkin looked like one straight out of a catalog, so perfect it resembled something Jonsi saw in a movie.

Tim would have gotten a kick out of that, too. Tim's dad always carved pumpkins with Jonsi's dad while the boys sat in the living room playing Nintendo. Tim's dad was bad at it. *Really* bad at it. Jonsi thought the jagged cuts and broken slices gave the pumpkin more personality. Now there was a story there, a gruesome tale of how a pumpkin had become so disfigured. It was a shame Tim was not here to see the jack-o'-lantern in its perfect glory.

Jonsi took a deep breath. The jack-o'-lantern was surely not the cause of the smell. The odor was not as strong by the front door. He looked over his shoulder to the backside of the vacationing skeleton staring out at the street.

The front door opened. It startled Jonsi. He took a step back, feeling his heart flutter for only half a second before he remembered he was standing in front of a stranger's house. He was not scared. No. He never was. That was Micah and Lori's job. Where were they anyway?

"I love your costume!" The woman in the doorway exclaimed. She clasped both her hands together, the same way Jonsi's aunt did every Thanksgiving when he went over to her place and she excitedly pointed out how much he had grown when he had, in fact, not grown at all. "You're the first firefighter I've seen all night," the woman said.

Jonsi wanted to say thanks. His mind had loaded the acknowledgement, put it in the chamber of his mouth, but failed to fire. He still could not figure out where the smell was coming from and now that the door was open, he realized it was not from inside either.

"Trick or treat," Jonsi said. It came out a lot less enthusiastic than he wanted, but it was tradition. Without the magic word there would be no candy and without candy? Then there would be no Halloween and that would surely mark the end of his world.

The woman beamed. Her smile was larger than some of the clown smiles Jonsi had seen on the masks at the local dollar store. It weirded Jonsi out, but his mother raised him right, telling him not to say anything if he had nothing nice to say at all. She surely was no half-dressed nurse though, that was for sure.

The woman moved out of the way for a moment, just long enough for Jonsi to get a quick glimpse inside. It looked like any other house Jonsi had seen. The walls were painted a cream white, a small potted plant was tucked in next to the railing where a set of stairs began and whimsical art lined the walls. Jonsi's family did not hang art. Instead, they hung family photos. Jonsi's mom said that, in its own way, was art. Jonsi did not agree, but then again, he did not have his own house to understand such things.

What caught his eye, however, right before the woman reappeared with a fist full of Kit Kats and Skittles, was a distant dining room table dripping with red paint. He saw it trickling down the legs, onto the floor in a crimson puddle. The image was blocked as the woman shoved her hands into Jonsi's bucket, smiling her creepily long smile the whole while.

Jonsi blinked. It had been paint. What was she painting, he wondered. What was she painting that she needed that much, that it required so much it had gotten all over the table and floor?

"Did you make the pictures on your walls?" Jonsi asked. The words came out of his mouth before he could really process what he was saying. He had not meant to ask it. That was supposed to be a thought only for the inside of his head to hear.

"Oh, those?" The woman asked, she stepped to the

side, still blocking the red-soaked table, but enough that Jonsi once again had a view of the art hanging on her white walls. "I wish, but I'm no artist," she said, waving a hand through the air passively as if it was one of the nicest things she had ever heard.

"Are you making more Halloween decorations?" Jonsi asked. He had already asked one question, something he would mentally scold himself for the rest of the night. He might as well keep going.

"I'm really not that into Halloween," the woman replied. "All this fuss of decorating for one day of the year. It's really not my thing. But kids like you deserve some candy now and again, so I can't help myself."

Now, Jonsi was even more confused. If that was not an art project or a Halloween decoration then why did this woman have a table soaked in red paint? The question was there, forming on Jonsi's tongue when —

"It smells like horse shit here, holy cow," Micah said, pinching his fingers against his nose and running up the steps to stand beside Jonsi. Lori was not far behind him. Her face was scrunched into all kinds of discomfort, too. "Trick or treat," Micah said, his nose plugged, sounding like he was speaking underwater.

The woman in front of Jonsi did little to change her demeanor in the face of Micah's inappropriate language. Jonsi did not understand swearing, but Micah did it a lot. He thought it was embarrassing, but Micah thought it made him sound cooler because adults swore.

Tim never swore. Tim's family went to church and prayed and read the Bible and always dropped a big bill into the offering basket. Jonsi had never seen it. His family did not go to church, but Tim had told him so. Jonsi believed him. Tim never lied. His family went to church. It was against the rules to lie. At least, Jonsi believed all this to be true. He wished Tim was here now to scold Micah for upsetting God and maybe getting some extra candy to go along with the gesture.

The woman dipped off to the side, grabbing a handful of candy for Micah. Jonsi saw the table again only for a split second, but just long enough to see a thick glob of red ooze snake down to the floor. The woman dropped the candy in Micah's bucket and then once again leaned over for yet another handful, this time for Lori. One final time, Jonsi saw the table, gleaming in the yellow light of the kitchen. The candy fell into Lori's bucket.

"Thank you so much," Lori said.

The woman beamed. The smile made Jonsi uncomfortable. Or maybe it was simply the smell of her property finally getting to him. Micah still had not pulled his fingers away from his face as he stood there, his eyes excitedly watching as the candy pile in his bucket grew.

"You three have a good night. I'll make sure to give you a call if there's any fires," the woman said, laughing and locking eyes with all three kids for an uncomfortably long several seconds. She closed the door.

"Did you see that?" Jonsi asked as soon as the latch clicked close.

"What? Did she have a pile of cow shit in there?" Micah asked. He had moved to pulling the neck of his shirt up and over his nose. Lori looked no more impressed, but she was sucking it up. She always did. Jonsi always admired Lori's willingness.

"There was a table covered in something. I think it might've been blood," Jonsi said. The disturbing guess had not come to his mind until moments ago.

"Oh, shut up. Probably just some other lousy Halloween decoration. Look how shitty that one is." Micah pointed to where the lounging skeleton was, soaking in what little light remained from the sunset.

"I didn't see anything," Lori chimed in, innocently.

Jonsi did not know what blood looked like, at least in quantities like that. There had been so much of whatever it was. It looked like some kind of spill or leak, but coming from where? He had not been able to see long enough.

Tim would have known what it was. Tim was smart like that. Tim liked crossword puzzles and word searches. Tim had spent weekend mornings watching old VHS tapes of monkeys and lions and learning how they ate, slept, and interacted with each other. Jonsi had thought it weird at first, but after Tim told Lori a cool fact about lions, and she seemed to like it, Jonsi got jealous. He started spending weekends at Tim's just to be able to do the same thing. Surely Tim would have been able to deduce what was inside. Or furthermore, what the awful smell was.

"Can we get out of here, fast this time? You guys are going so slow," Jonsi said.

Micah nodded approvingly. Lori said nothing. She would follow them around at whatever pace they decided on. The trio hopped down the steps and began passing the overblown skeleton once again when they slowed, much to Jonsi's disapproval. The smell was the worst here, in the center of the pathway leading up to the door.

"Come on," Jonsi groaned. He was a few steps past Micah. Lori had stopped beside him. That made Jonsi jealous, too. Why did she follow him? He swore and was rude. He was the type of boy Jonsi's parents always said not to be friends with, yet here he was.

"I kind of want to touch it," Micah said. He took a step off the beaten stone path and onto the weed-filled lawn. This time Lori did not follow. She remained in place on the path, simply watching Micah as he approached the lounging skeleton.

Jonsi wanted to protest, but said nothing, letting his own curiosity get the better of him. Tim would have probably said something. Tim was the type who would stand up for something. Jonsi assumed it was just because it was another rule in their church or something like that.

Micah approached the skeleton. His bucket of candy swayed side to side next to his legs. Next to the decoration, Jonsi realized how large it actually was. It was roughly the same height as the boys, but larger, a lot wider than Micah's thin frame even with the added size of his costume. The skeleton's arms were puffy and it looked even more bloated than before now that there was someone beside it for comparison.

"Holy shit! It smells even worse up close!" Micah said.

His shirt and hand were covering his nose as he laid a hand on the skeleton. "It feels so weird. Dude, check this out!" he called.

Jonsi found himself retracing his steps back to Micah. It was a bad idea, he knew, but the allure of the decoration was too tempting. This was a rich person's house. He may never get to experience something like it again. Lori did not move. She watched both boys as they stood next to the skeleton.

The skeleton looked even more deformed up close. Its head looked leathery, as if the inside had been filled with a water balloon that had slowly been leaking over time. It looked soft and wet, barely able to retain its shape. The body itself had indeed ballooned just as much as Jonsi had surmised from the end of the property. Its arms were tube like, painted over with the decal of bones and anatomy. The legs were the same way, tubular and soft and rubbery. There was no mechanical whir of a generator or hum of a blower that was keeping the decoration in place. Jonsi's parents had a generator and he knew the noise well from the sound it made in the winter when it got particularly cold outside. Whatever this was, it was not being powered that way.

"Why does it smell like that?" Jonsi asked. It burned his eyes, stinging the corners. He sucked in a deep breath, almost tasting the foul odor on the tip of his tongue. He swallowed the smell-taste down once, twice, and then spat on the lawn. He should not have done that. His parents would have disapproved, but he could not help it. The smell was overpowering.

"Touch it, man," Micah said, prodding the inflated arms with a single finger, gently poking the skeleton enough that it bobbed back and forth in the beach chair.

Jonsi touched the skeleton. It was not his to touch, but just as the smell had lured him in, so did the urge of wanting to know what such a strange thing must feel like. It was soft and, in fact, rubbery. It curved around his finger when he pushed in and then stretched back to its original shape when he pulled away. It was cold, so cold it almost felt wet. The smell clung to his skin when he pulled his hand away. He smelled it on himself.

Tim would have gotten a kick out of this. Tim liked gross things, too. He had a doctor VHS he once showed Jonsi where a man had to get surgery done after getting in a bad car accident. Jonsi had asked where he got it from and Tim had been quiet about his response. It made Jonsi uncomfortable. Tim was never one to shy away, but he had not been entirely forthcoming about where the tape had come from. Still, the boys watched it, and to this day, Jonsi wished he never had. There had been so much blood, the same color as the liquid he saw inside, except maybe even more. It covered everything. Thinking about it now was enough to make his stomach twist into knots. That, combined with the stench of the skeleton, made him queasy.

"Should I set it on fire?" Micah asked.

The question caught Jonsi off guard. He looked at his friend. "It's not ours," he replied.

That fact did not seem to bother Micah who revealed a small green lighter from his pocket. This surprised Jonsi even more. His parents would never approve of something like this. Tim would have never approved of something like this either. Jonsi, however, had no protest as Micah lit the lighter with a strike of his thumb and held the small flickering flame up to the edge of the skeleton. Jonsi watched with nervous anticipation as the flame licked the side of the skeleton, turning the soft tube-like arm into a bubbling foam that popped the same way a zit did.

In an instant, the smell amplified itself into something much worse. Micah jumped back, startled as the flame spread over the skeleton, melting away its meshy skin. The material clumped together, forming a thick sludge that oozed down the frame and onto dead grass. Jonsi pulled his shirt up over his nose and gagged. His nose burned. His eyes burned and watered. He saw Lori backing away, too, clearly disgusted by whatever awful thing Micah had just unleashed beneath the rubber skin of the skeleton.

Jonsi returned his attention to the mess Micah made. By now, several other groups of kids had been alerted by the smell of smoke and whatever the rotten scent was. The curb was lined with several curious children, all of them with faces twisted into disgust.

The white bubbling sludge continued to slide off the skeleton until all that remained in the beach chair was a barely recognizable clump of what Jonsi could only assume was a person. Their arms and legs were bent together, as if they had been shoved into whatever casing the skeleton had been constructed from. Their limbs were twisted and clearly broken. No person could feasibly bend in ways like that without breaking their bones.

It was, however, a person. That much was clear to Jonsi. And they were in fact not far off in size from himself and Micah. They were lounging inside the skeleton, their limbs tangled up, but their head knocked back looking into the darkening sky of October 31st. Resting on their head, unmistakable to Jonsi, was thick glasses. He took a step forward, the smell, unaware it was burnt flesh, had a way of pulling Jonsi closer.

The black-framed glasses resting atop the bulbous head and short squat body jumped out at Jonsi. It must have jumped out at Micah too because he dropped his lighter and ran away, back to Lori, his face something of utter horror. Micah never cried but he sure looked like he was going to now.

It all clicked then, as the front door opened and the woman from before stepped out onto the front porch, her hands the same blood-red that had been dripping down her table. She stood there, looking stunned at the trio standing on her property as her single Halloween decoration smoldered and popped.

Jonsi knew it then. Tim was not in Mexico at his family's timeshare or at his cabin only an hour outside the neighborhood. He was lounging, yes, but not on a beach listening to the sound of the ocean and birds.

Tim was lounging in front of number 11, a burned and

smoldering corpse that stood as the house's only decoration next to the lonely jack-o'-lantern that flickered in the growing dark of the night.

DECONSTRUCTING ARTHUR
Vanessa Leonardo

"YOU AREN'T TAKING MY VCR apart again, are you?" Arthur's mother asked in a grating voice.

"I'm not taking it apart. I'm enhancing it . . . " Arthur refused to explain further. She wouldn't understand. It was way beyond the comprehension of a simple diner waitress. He tried to explain it once by using the burger as an analogy: "A burger is still a burger without the pickle and the lettuce. So take those out. What do you get?" She had given him a hard stare and a deep sigh. Arthur surmised that it was just too complex for her to understand.

His mother scoffed. "Every time you *enhance* one of my appliances, it stops working. Not much of an enhancement." While looking at her reflection in the scratched up mirror, she manually lifted her breasts so that they peaked above the top of the uniform. An unlit cigarette hung limply from her bottom lip as she tied her overly dyed blond hair up into a messy bun. She was dressed as a nurse in a white leather uniform, entirely too tight for a woman who never exercised. Arthur could see her stretch marks outlined in the fabric. "Why can't you go out with kids your own age? It's Halloween night! You should be at a party."

It was now Arthur's turn to scoff. Party? Friends? His mother didn't know him at all. Arthur hated Halloween, and by extension, anyone who participated in it. He curled his lip at black bats dangling in windows, rolled his eyes at the decorated gourds perched on front lawns, and choked back acid at the gluttonous pillow cases full of candy swinging from chubby germ-ridden hands. What a ridiculous holiday. What were people even celebrating? Ghosts and monsters weren't real. That was a fact.

Arthur preferred facts and machines over emotions and people, and dedicated his time to taking machines apart and putting them back together with some augmentation.

Arthur liked to see how something functioned without all of its parts. He felt akin to a surgeon removing an appendix. Would it work? Could it work? If so, how well? How important was the part, *really?* Arthur kept copious notes on his experiments, as any great scientist does. He was to be the next Nikola Tesla.

"Hey," his mother said, sitting across from him at the dining room table where his experiment lay strewn from one end to the other. "I'm serious. After everything with Mr. Bartley." Arthur cringed. "I know it's been hard."

"It hasn't been hard."

"He was the only friend you had."

"He wasn't a friend. He was a teacher."

"A mentor then."

Arthur responded with a scowl.

"I just don't want you to go back to the way you were before . . . " his mother said, gently caressing a strand of greasy black hair away from his eye. Arthur flinched. He told himself it was because her fingers smelled like menthol. Because he hadn't showered in days and didn't want to be touched. Because he was concentrating and needn't be interrupted.

Not because of Mr. Bartley.

"I'm fine," Arthur said, inching away. "Accidents happen all the time in woodshops." Arthur spoke softly, as if more to himself than to his mother, who looked at him with pitying sadness, the same look his teachers now gave him. He let his greasy hair fall back onto his face.

Poor Arthur. His only friend, a teacher nonetheless, bled to death in his own classroom. And Arthur had been the one to find him . . . "There's nothing you could have done," the EMT said when they packed Mr. Bartley's body in a thin black bag.

What would poor little Arthur do now?

Arthur was fine. After all, he was fine before Mr. Bartley, wasn't he? Nothing had changed. Not a single thing. Well, not for Arthur. Mr. Bartley had lost three fingers and 4 pints of blood. Arthur shuddered. He didn't like to think about that. He had other things to focus on at the moment.

"Well, don't forget to give out some candy tonight. You could afford to eat a few pieces yourself, too." His mother was using her coddling voice as if Arthur were a little child having a bad dream. Without waiting for him to respond, she left.

Arthur dumped two bags of candy into the Halloween bowl and set it out on the front porch. This way, no one would interrupt him as he reassembled the VCR. No poorly-dressed middle schoolers would knock repeatedly on the door. No stumbling toddlers in oversized bee suits would spit "Trick or treat!" at him while grabbing for fistfuls of sugar. No neighbors could judge him for being home on Halloween night dressed in the same holey 7-UP t-shirt and sweatpants he had been wearing for days. And most importantly, no one could give him that pitying look.

He was finally alone.

~

The pinch roller, along with its screws, was the only part left on the dining room table when Arthur finished reassembling the VCR. The manual said that the VCR could work without the pinch roller. Naturally, Arthur tested the idea. Most mechanisms didn't need all the parts and safety features that were added. It was just a way to drive up costs and to keep idiots from hurting themselves. Why thwart Survival of the Fittest?

Arthur hooked up the VCR to the 27" TV in the living room and slipped in a cassette of the *Ray Bradbury Theatre* show. The machine sputtered as it started, as if clearing its throat. Then, the TV screen began to show the first episode with Leslie Nielsen's smooth voice crackling from the stereo: "People ask where do you get your ideas . . ."

"Yes!" Arthur exclaimed! "I knew it!"

Just as Arthur was celebrating, there was a knock at the door.

It was faint at first. A small rapping.

Knock knock knock.

Then it was louder.

Arthur waited, hoping the trick-or-treater would just leave.

They knocked again. Louder this time.

KNOCK KNOCK KNOCK.

Pausing the cassette, Arthur yelled, "There's no candy left! Go to another house!"

For a moment, there was stillness as Arthur waited to hear the child's footsteps retreating from the door. Nothing. "Go away!" Arthur added for good measure.

DING DONG DING DONG DING DONG, the doorbell chimed incessantly.

Furious, Arthur stomped toward the door and swung it open yelling, "There's no candy left you fat losers! Go away!"

He was greeted by the crisp October night. The porch was empty. The street was quiet. The few candy bars left stared up at him from the bottom of the bowl. As Arthur went to grab it, he noticed something on his hand.

His palm, thumb, and pointer finger were dripping red.

The door knob was covered in red paint.

"Seriously?" Arthur ran out to the street, certain he'd find a couple of strays from the Dullahan house. "Come out you cowards! I'll teach you to vandalize my house!" From down the street, a dog barked in return. The moon, perched high in the cloudless sky, looked down on him with its giant white eye. But no one came forward. Still, his chest heaved and his fists were rolled up and ready to swing.

Arthur was relieved no one was there since he had never won in a fight, had never even fought back. He was too uncoordinated to throw a punch and too scrawny to intimidate anyone. One good shove knocked the wind out of him and could keep him on the ground.

Arthur wiped his hand furiously against his pants.

The paint crusted and dried into the crevices of his palm.

Again he thought of Mr. Bartley. *All that blood*...

Though most of the paint came off, his hand was still dyed red. Paint splattered the worn wooden planks of his porch. *Great.* He would have to spend the night cleaning this up. So much for enjoying the fruits of his labor! He grabbed a bucket of water and a sponge from under the sink and turned on the porch light.

But the porch wasn't just splattered in paint.

It was covered in prints.

Palm prints with a thumb and a pointer. The symbol his classmates made at him when they stuck their tongues out and called him *"Loser!"*

"Creative," Arthur said. What a terrible prank. But what should he have expected? His schoolmates were crude and dumb and impulsive.

Scrubbing the paint from the wooden chips only darkened it. The yellow sponge turned red, the water inside the bucket a dark maroon, his own hands pink. And the handprints remained.

"Ugh, forget it!" Arthur said to himself. His mom would just have to deal with it until he had time to paint over them tomorrow. That should do the trick. She probably wouldn't even notice. It was already dark out, and she'd be drunk. Arthur was intent on having a relaxing rest of the night, in spite of the last turn of events. Some candy and his favorite TV show would do the trick.

But something in the living room made Arthur freeze in the doorway.

The room was covered in handprints—the floor, the

walls, even the ceiling! As though someone had stamped every inch of the room with the loser symbol while he was cleaning the deck. But that was impossible! He would have *heard* something, *seen* something.

Then he did see something: Someone was sitting in the living room.

~

The room smelled like sawdust and cheap cologne. The episode of the *Ray Bradbury Theatre* that Arthur was sure he had turned off was playing at a loud volume. Fuzzy black hair poked up from behind the La-Z-Boy recliner.

"How's it hanging, kiddo?" a male voice said without turning around. His voice was warm and cheery. And familiar.

No, this wasn't happening.

"Mr. Bartley?" Arthur stepped forward, just enough to get a look at the man's profile. He looked just like Mr. Bartley, from the unkempt hair peppered with dandruff to the irritated skin from cheap shaving blades. But Arthur couldn't get any closer. He knew it wasn't real. It couldn't be. People didn't come back from the dead. But it *felt* real. Maybe he was dreaming. Maybe he had fallen asleep . . . Arthur pinched himself. The annoying twinge of pain confirmed that he was awake.

"You always say that," Mr. Bartley continued. "No, I haven't read that book. Is it good?" Then Mr. Bartley chuckled. It was his patient, oh-Arthur-you'll-never-learn laugh that even made Arthur smirk. But Arthur wasn't saying anything. "Before we talk about the summer internship I want you to do, you wanted me to show you the bandsaw again, right?"

Arthur suddenly recognized this was the last conversation he had had with Mr. Bartley.

"You're n-n-not here . . . You're dead," Arthur stammered, his voice meeker than he'd liked. With his eyes closed, Arthur recited all the facts he knew to be true: "Mr. Bartley died on May 1st from blunt force trauma after experiencing a bandsaw accident at 4:47 p.m. in the afternoon at Morris High School —"

The old wooden floors creaked and moaned underneath Mr. Bartley's weight. Each heavy footstep caused the floor to rumble. His heavy breathing sounded strained and desperate.

"Why are you so interested in the bandsaw suddenly?" Mr. Bartley asked.

When Arthur opened his eyes, he found Mr. Bartley standing in front of him, in the same outfit he had worn that day: a red and green flannel shirt with a coffee stain near the pocket and faded Levi jeans whose edges were white and worn. The gash where he had hit his head was angry and red. Dried blood caked the left side of his face, so thickly it looked fake. Like paint. And he held his hand where the pinky, ring, and middle fingers were missing.

"Let's turn this bad boy on . . . " Mr. Bartley said.

"No, *no, no, no,*" Arthur finally managed to say while backing away from Mr. Bartley. "You're dead! They told me you died!" Arthur yelled, hoping his mother would magically come through the door. She would know how to fix this. She could fix anything! Even Arthur.

Arthur ran to the phone to call 9-1-1.

But the phone had no dial tone.

Shit!

Arthur ran for the front door.

But the door had no knob.

There was no exit.

"What the fuck?!"

The whir of a bandsaw made Arthur turn around. Suddenly, he was in the woodshop room with Mr. Bartley. It looked the same as it had that day: woodchips peppered the floor, sawdust floated in the air, tables of worn blades sat in neat rows. And Mr. Bartley was next to the center table.

"Don't touch the bandsaw, Mr. Bartley!" Arthur yelled. "Don't touch it!" Mr. Bartley stared at the bandsaw, holding his bloody stump of a hand.

"It was an accident . . . " Arthur said, sobbing now, horrified to remember the true events of that day. Not what he told people. Not what people believed. But what really happened. The facts of it all.

Mr. Bartley's hand had slipped while he was showing Arthur how to use the bandsaw. His fingers had flown off across the room. Like a rabid dog, the blade had sunk into his skin and had chomped down on the bone. "Call 9-1-1!"

"Wait!" Arthur had said.

"Wait for what? I need an ambulance!" Mr. Bartley had made a run for the door, but Arthur had stopped him. "What are you doing? Get out of the way!" He had never spoken to Arthur that way—exasperated, annoyed, incredulous. Like everyone else did. Mr. Bartley had always understood Arthur, listened to him, encouraged him. Surely he would understand . . . "Just give me 5 minutes! And then you can call an ambulance!" Arthur had insisted. He had just needed to get the bandsaw tires back on. That morning, Arthur had taken out the bandsaw tires without Mr. Bartley knowing, certain the machine could work without them.

If anyone found out this was his fault . . .

Then Mr. Bartley had run forward and, by instinct — and it *had been* instinct, the lizard part of his brain that no man had control over — Arthur had pushed him backward. It wasn't even Arthur's fault really because no one could blame a man for what he did because of years of evolutionary conditioning. It was just a survival instinct.

But Mr. Bartley had fallen backward and hit his head on the sanding table.

He had stopped moving. He had stopped trying to run.

"Please . . . " Mr. Bartley's voice had sounded like it was partially underwater, muffling the cries as blood sputtered and pooled in his mouth.

"Just let me focus!" Arthur's hands had been shaking. The blood on his fingers — *Where had that come from?* — were making everything slippery. But the second he had finished, he had run for the nurse.

"It couldn't have been more than 10 minutes, Mr. Bartley . . . " Arthur insisted. "It would have been quicker if you had just listened to me. Maybe then you'd be alive."

When Mr. Bartley turned around, his eyes were gray and lifeless. The pupils were fixed and dilated. He didn't blink. "What would happen . . . " Mr. Bartley said, while walking toward Arthur, "If we took your parts out, Arthur? Would you still work? Surely, you don't need every part of your body . . . "

Arthur sprinted toward the door but Mr. Bartley was in his way. No matter where Arthur turned, Mr. Bartley was there. There was no escape. And despite his screams, all Arthur could hear was the deafening whir of bandsaw blades.

CHILLING, THRILLING SOUNDS
Matt Hickey

Halloween on Pike Street was the same as it was anywhere. And the same as it had been for hundreds of years and under many different names. Crops turned golden for the harvest. Sun and summer died to make way for winter. All acted accordingly as a hand in the crouching darkness turned the wheel of the year forward another spin. And it all depended on two boys who were riding their bikes side-by-side down Pike Street carrying a coffin between them. Inside the coffin was a third.

"I love this holiday," said Patrick, who wore a raven mask. "The only day of the year people refuse to believe their eyes."

"Look at us, carrying this in broad daylight and no one's looking twice," said Tom, who wore a crow mask.

Inside the coffin, Felix was silent.

There were many ways for children to make extra money on Pike Street if they wanted to. Some children sold lemonade, some walked dogs or babysat. But Patrick and Tom helped their neighbor, Mister Dullahan, make Halloween. They liked the job. They'd found it on a flier.

Making Halloween was a year-long task and required many hands. Mister Dullahan spent twelve months preparing like a farmer for harvest. Patrick collected cardboard boxes for his front yard haunted maze. Tom carved sticks and tied them into cross-shaped things called parshells, though he didn't know what that word meant. And both boys wandered the streets with recorders in hopes of finding the sounds of Halloween.

"Get any good tape today, Tom?"

"Nah. Just crickets, again."

"Hey, crickets are better than nothing! What else is on the list?" asked Patrick, who liked to lead but not to memorize.

"Slow down so I can spare a hand to check," said Tom, whose right hand was preoccupied with a bike handle while the left was busy pallbearing. They slowed their cycling and Tom pulled the errand list from his pocket. "Let's see . . . 'Leave an offering at the Hawthorn tree,' check. 'Tie apples to the evergreens,' check. 'Avoid oak trees and pick up chicken from Hooper's grocery,' check. That's it! Done and dusted."

"That's Halloween then. Time to head to Mister Dullahan's for the last delivery." Patrick tapped the coffin shaped box. "Sound good to you, Felix??"

Inside the coffin Felix knocked once.

Felix had been on his way to the library when the two boys jumped him. Looking forward to a night of weird tales and controlled terrors. John Bellairs, Caroline B. Cooney, and Mary Downing Hahn were his planned company for the night. It wasn't because of Halloween that he seeked them out. In fact, he was probably the only kid on Pike Street who wasn't dressing up for the Halloween Parade or attending the candy exchange at midnight. It was because of the fear. The constant knotted stress in his stomach he'd felt since his mom got sick. And "sick" was all the adults were prepared to tell him since her hospitalization. If he had an inkling of what was going on there wasn't a book he wouldn't read to understand. So here he was. If he couldn't stop the fear, terror would do. At least terror fit between two covers.

He'd almost made it to the library when he saw Patrick and Tom and they saw him.

"Felix, my boy!" Patrick shouted, "Just the man we were hoping to see!"

It was the moment Felix had dreaded. He knew it was a matter of time before he'd encounter his two classroom bullies outside school, outside the library, away from any world that made sense, and this was it. They'd long been making a cruel game of inviting Felix to "join the gang." But in Felix's experience you were only safe with a bully as long as they weren't bored. Felix wasn't sure why they sought him out, but it seemed that the sheer oppositeness of their personalities made Patrick and Tom want to grind him under their heels. Especially since they started working for Mister Dullahan, which brought out a strange side of them. He'd overheard them bragging at school that they'd learned tricks from the man like "how to make leaves turn orange." Felix didn't want to find out what they meant.

He darted down an alley to the rear parking lot of Halloway's Funeral Home. He ducked behind the dumpster for cover and found something completely unexpected: a delivery box. Made from cardboard. Covered in stamps. But unmistakably shaped like a coffin. He stared for a moment in fascination before remembering where he was. He opened it and climbed in, pulling the lid back over him.

For a moment he thought he was safe, but only a moment.

"Patrick! Look!" said the voice of Tom. "It's straight out of *The Addams Family!*"

"What do you know," said the voice that made Felix's skin crawl, "I guess everything gets mailed from somewhere. Do you think this is how the post office sends their dead mail-persons to the afterlife?"

Patrick lifted one end of the box up and down, jostling Felix. "This will make the perfect gift for Goth Uncle Mark. I bet he'll give us a good tip too."

"Open it up and see if there's a body in there!"

They lifted the lid and, without thinking, Felix reached his hand out to pull it back down.

"Well, well, well! Another surprise! It's Felix, the missing member of our trio, overdue for his induction."

"And he's packaged himself up like a present!"

"Which gives me an idea," said Patrick, lifting his end. "If we play our cards right we can make this delivery box into a Trojan Horse."

It was as unimaginative a plan as Felix expected. Patrick and Tom were on their way to make their final delivery to Mister Dullahan. And the old man did Halloween up big. He was known in the neighborhood for the scale of his yard decorations. Gifting him an ersatz coffin would be an easy sell, but if they could keep him talking and from noticing how heavy the box was, they could deliver Felix inside the house without him being the wiser.

"Think of it as procuring our holiday bonus," Patrick said loudly to the boy in the box, "just one the old man won't know he's giving. He's got loads of cool stuff in that house. Microphones, records, instruments. Did you know he was a musician before he moved here? It's true! We saw a gold record in his office. Me and Tom are thinking of starting a band ourselves now that we'll have some free time, aren't we Tom?"

"We're gonna be rock stars, Felix."

"That's right."

"The old man taught us songs you've never heard."

"Says he learned them from the fairies."

"Now we just need to learn how to play them."

"That's where you come in. Why don't you get us something we can pawn so we can buy ourselves some nice instruments. Something like that pretty gold record. Or anything that looks expensive, really. I'm not strict."

"I can't wait for you to join the gang, Felix. Mister Dullahan has taught us all kinds of cool stuff."

"Like how to make pumpkins last all year."

"And old words like *psychopomp*."

"That's why we're wearing these masks, see?"

"Yeah, we're supposed to be guides to the afterlife, or something."

"Right, or something. So is it a plan? Tap once for yes and twice for no."

Felix tapped once unenthusiastically.

They arrived at 13 Pike St. —a tall, gaunt manor with a growth of moss ascending its first floor. And if there was a Halloween tradition forgotten there you couldn't tell. Apples hung from branches, tied twigs hung from every entryway, and sad-faced turnip heads were lit by burning coals. The boys walked past a bowl of candy set out by the gate and entered into a towering maze of stacked cardboard boxes.

"This might take a minute, Felix." Patrick apologized to the box.

"I wish we'd never built this stupid maze," grumbled Tom.

"It's not a maze, idiot! Mister Dullahan called it a labyrinth. It's meant to symbolize, um . . ."

"A descent and return from the underworld, or something?"

"Yeah, something like that."

They made it to the other end of the labyrinth and stepped onto the porch. Another bowl was left out for the trick-or-treaters, this one full of tapes labeled *Chilling, Thrilling Sounds*.

"Tom! Grab one. This is what we've been recording, Felix!" Patrick whispered to the box as he rang the doorbell.

"Mister Dullahan! It's Patrick and Tom. We're ready for our severance package!"

"Still remember the plan, Felix?" asked Tom.

Felix knocked once.

"Just stick to the plan and everything will work out just fine," said Patrick. "As easy as taking candy from a bowl."

"And if it doesn't," whispered Tom, "the poor bug isn't going to leave here alive."

~

A long time passed before Felix climbed out of the box. Inside, he could only hear the muffled tones of the boys being greeted and brought upstairs. Once he was set down, he waited to make sure they had gone. He didn't care about being caught by Mister Dullahan. Was he worried about being discovered trespassing in a stranger's house? Of course. But how bad could any adult be compared to the hoodlums who'd just ruined his night? He'd made up his mind to tell Mister Dullahan the whole truth five speed bumps ago. Snitching be damned.

Felix peeked out of the coffin.

"Hello? Mister Dullahan?" He looked around and saw that he was in some kind of trophy room. Patrick and Tom were right. There was endless paraphernalia that told the story of Dullahan's career. A hand-drawn, punk-style flier for a band called The Croms. A framed poster promoting the release of their single, "Hey! We! To the Otherworld Go!" produced by Mark Dullahan. An award for "best soundtrack" from *Computer Gaming World* among other trophies.

There was a poster for a movie Felix recognized, "The Gate of the Firebringer," and Dullahan was credited with music and sound design. Felix remembered watching it when he was younger. One of those Amblin-esque productions that sat uncomfortably between wondrous and traumatizing. It was one of the few tapes he and his mother owned, so he watched it endlessly and made her fast forward through every scene where the titular Firebringer appeared. Which was most of the movie. He could still remember the sound of the Firebringer's footsteps. Heavy. Sizzling. And he'd never forget the song the creature sang to lull its victims to sleep. In fact, he heard it now.

Through an adjoining door he heard a voice lilting its peculiar notes. A melody that felt as if it came from somewhere long ago and yet to come. But another sound interrupted it. A thick scratching. And screams. It repeated and got louder with each effort.

Scratch. Crunch. Scratch.

Felix found himself walking closer to the source, a doorway opened just-so-much. He drew the handle open to peek inside. The sight stunned him.

A huge man was hunched over a tarpaulin with his back to the door. A single lamp lit him from behind making him mostly silhouette. His arm swung again and again. His singing of the tune grew heavier and breathier as the hacking became pulpier and wetter.

But the most disturbing part was what he was swinging. It just didn't make sense. It moved like a whip but crunched with impact. Like it had angles. Like a human spine. Felix looked closer, not believing his eyes. He drew the door farther open, not realizing that as he did so a loose frame was hung on the other side of the door. It slid and fell to the floor with a *crash*.

The man stopped his progress.

"Who's there?" he asked in a voice that flanged and delayed. Felix scrambled backward but was too shocked to stand.

"No one was expected at this hour. Were the offerings outside not enough?"

The man stood and Felix saw that he was wearing an apron covered in viscera. His posture was so poor that for just a moment he didn't seem to have a head. Then his posture straightened.

"A child?" the man said, "Why have you come here? On this of all nights?" Felix couldn't speak. The man's scornful eyes were clear in the dark. They darted from him to whatever mess was on the tarpaulin. He seemed to be doing quick math. Then his gaze fell onto the cardboard coffin. His eyes smiled as any hint of panic left them.

"I see. They snuck you in. I thought that box had more heft than it should." He glanced at Felix.

"I apologize. Did the screams scare you? That's perfectly understandable. We scream to warn the herd after all. Good survival instincts. But the body hates the sound of it." He bundled up the tarpaulin, dragging the huge mass of detritus across the floor behind the light of the lamp.

"But there's no reason to be frightened here. Excuse

the viscera. These are chicken carcasses I was hacking for sound effect. And the screams you heard?" He produced a remote control from his apron pocket. "Simply a recording."

With a press of a button the screams repeated. And the man was right. Felix hated it just as much the second time.

With the press of another button a few wall sconces lit softly and revealed various microphones, mixers, and sound dampening panels.

"Welcome to my studio," the man said, now a little better lit. Yet even in the light the man looked dark. Incredibly dark. His beard and hair were a deeper black than any Felix had ever seen. His skin, meanwhile, looked starved for sunlight and cracked like stale bread. And the instrument Felix had thought was a spine now looked like a regular riding crop.

"You interrupted my session. State your business."

"Um, my name is Felix, and I . . . shouldn't be here! I'm sorry!"

"Why the deceit? Devil's Night was yesterday." A sly smile formed under his beard and threaded his voice. "Did those two boys put you up to steal from me?"

"Yes — I mean, that's why they put me in there, but — "

"Those boys always had itchy fingers," he sighed, "but good help is so hard to find. This is a busy season for me. Summer's end brings many travelers. I hired the boys to run errands and help with field recording for my next record. Crows, leaves, etcetera. But I knew they'd be more trouble than they were worth."

"But I wasn't going to take anything!"

"Not if you weren't caught, you mean."

Felix turned red. He wasn't used to adults not taking him at his word.

"No! Those two stuffed me in that box and dragged me here. I didn't want to come."

Dullahan considered the boy. He tapped the crop against his palm.

"You're in an unenviable position, Felix. You're asking

me to trust you. You, an intruder in my home, with your fingerprints all over my gold record."

For the first time Felix looked down at the busted frame he'd knocked off the door. A gold record, sure enough. But the title made Felix gasp.

Chilling, Thrilling Sounds of the Otherworld. Produced by M. Dullahan. The cover art was unforgettable. A misty landscape of wraith-like figures carrying lanterns up a hill to attend a bonfire. He knew it well. There wasn't a yard sale, second hand store, or estate sale on Pike Street that didn't have a copy.

"Wait . . . you're Mark Dullahan? *The* Mark Dullahan? The one who made this record?"

Dullahan smiled. "Have you listened to it?"

"Only every Halloween." It was true. At first the record had terrified him. The whistling winds, wailing women, and creepy descriptions of druidic sacrifices were way too intense for a boy his age. But once his mom explained that the sounds weren't real he became curious. And Felix's mother, never missing a chance for an educational moment, took him to the library. She checked out every book available on foley and sound effects. And he read them all. He was probably one of the few boys who could tell you that foley was named after a person, a silent film director, stuntman, and cartoonist named Jack Donovan Foley, but that was besides the point. Once he knew how the sounds were made he played the album non-stop, with each listen explaining to his patient mother which sound was *actually* a piece of lettuce snapping, or cellophane crackling, or metal sheet thundering.

"Every Halloween, you say? Then why not tonight?"

"I usually listen to it with my mom. But she can't this year. She's . . . sick."

Dullahan stared at Felix like he was weighing his soul. Then he saw it. The fear.

"Poor boy." Dullahan said neutrally. "This way."

Felix followed him into a traditional study that felt lifted from another time. Two chairs sat opposite a vintage victrola. Wrapped around them were walls of bookshelves whose only modern touch was that they contained records as well as books. And while the previous room might have told the story of Dullahan's accomplishments, the titles of this collection told the story of a man obsessed with pre-Christian history and pagan rituals.

Dullahan changed out of his apron and slipped into a flowing black robe.

"Sit," he said as he grabbed a glass from a sidecar and poured from a bottle of something rare and old.

"Your story has a ring of truth to it," he left the room with his glass and returned with a vinyl record, "but sounds can be deceptive."

"Does that mean you believe me?"

"No. It means we're going to play a game." Dullahan pulled an LP from its sleeve and placed it on the turntable.

"I'm going to play you an album. It's new. Just finished it tonight. We'll listen and you're going to guess what sound you're hearing."

"What happens if I guess right?" Felix gulped.

"A treat," he smiled, "of course. If you guess all of the sounds correctly you get to go home."

"You mean you won't press charges?"

"I'll be honest, Felix. If you guess wrong, the consequences will be much worse than that."

Felix's blood went cold as Dullahan's heavy hand patted his shoulder. "Relax. This will be fun! And you'll find the odds more fair in here than out there in that street tonight, believe me. Well? Shall we?"

"Sure . . . sounds good," Felix said unconvincingly. It was the second time that night he felt like a bad choice had been made for him.

"Dandy," said Dullahan as he applied the stylus. The black lacquer crackled and gave life to thunder. It was gigantic. It surrounded Felix. Louder than any speakers he had ever heard. It was so full it shook his chest. A sharp scratchy narrator spoke from the record:

"Tonight is the night of Hallowe'en. When dreadful sights are sure to be seen. Listen? Do you hear the sound of music?

Sad, mournful airs? That is how you know the Otherworld is near. The veil is thin. The Good People about. And the call of the Otherworld rises to a shout!"

Dullahan snorted. "A bit of scene setting. Ignore the theatrics. It's the *sounds* that I want you to listen to."

Felix was distracted by the voice, which he recognized from the radio. "That can't be who I think it is, is it?"

Dullahan nodded, "I booked a session through her tour manager." Felix wondered how long before her accident it was recorded. The record continued playing eerie sounds of nocturnal life.

"Tell me what you hear," said Dullahan.

Hoot. Hoot. Rustle.

"Sounds like an owl."

He nodded, "Raised myself in my rookery. A cliché way to start a record of thrills and chills, don't you think? But you must tell the listener it's nighttime quickly. If they imagine daylight for even a second the tension is completely destroyed. What else do you hear?"

Felix shrugged, "I don't know. Autumn stuff."

Dullahan huffed.

"Specify. And Listen. What kind of *autumn stuff?*"

The boy squinted as he attempted to listen past the distracting voice of the narrator.

"Follow me to a Halloween night long ago! The High King Tigernmas has gathered his people around the bonfire to pay tribute to the God of the harvest. Watch. Their firstborn children approach an executioner's sword to offer their heads in sacrifice. Hear them cry! All hail Crom Cruach! All hail the crooked dark!"

Felix shivered as he struggled to focus on the sounds of the record instead of the pictures the words conjured.

"I hear . . . fire crackling. And leaves blowing. Do I have to be more specific than that?"

Dullahan looked disappointed. "Felix, it hurts me to say this but I believe you are taking your incredible gifts for granted." He set his drink down and leaned toward the boy. "You seem to me a boy of common health and sensory development. Did you know that your ears can recognize frequencies of up to seventeen thousand hertz? But soon presbycusis will set in and the human ear degrades at an alarming rate. Soon you'll only be able to hear sixteen. Then fourteen by age forty, and by fifty less than twelve. But right now you have a mind and an exceptional pair of ears. Use them."

Felix flushed and felt like he was back at school. He looked down at his feet to avert his gaze and to try listening closer.

"The wind sounds like it's whistling."

"Yes?"

"And there's something else. A bell ringing so low it's hardly there. There's only one place in town with a bell tower. Ten, eleven, that makes . . . twelve chimes. It's Rose Hill Cemetery at midnight."

"Spot on," Dullahan clapped his hands and leaned back in his chair, "Two for two, Felix! Well done. But the record's not over yet . . . ignore this next bit." The chanting voice of the narrator returned:

"The Christians came and the tributes ceased, but Crom Cruach did not fade. For Crom Cruach is the land itself demanding forever the tithe be paid. And so Crom sent his foul dark man to collect men's heads in debt for the land. Warn everywhere you dare to stand, beware of the name—"

Dullahan coughed up his drink and slammed the glass onto the table, causing the record to skip. "Excuse me, strong stuff. Oh, listen! This is the good part."

It was that sound again. The slicing and the screams. Two, three times the cut repeated with the weighty drop of a melon.

Scratch. Crunch. Scratch.

"Well?" asked Dullahan.

Felix felt queasy. He'd seen the chicken and the riding crop, but he didn't see how they could produce what he heard. The sound unsettled him completely. He reminded himself it wasn't real, just like when he was younger. But it didn't work.

"Traditionally stabbing sounds are recorded with fruit. Like a watermelon. Sometimes with pieces of wood inside."

"Is that your guess?" Felix was alarmed by Dullahan's smug smile. It telegraphed without subtlety that his guess was wrong.

"No . . . " he stalled, "Knowing you it wouldn't just be a melon . . . It would be something to do with the season. I've seen your garden. You grow winter fruits. Yes, that's my guess. An ash gourd."

"Well done!" Dullahan slapped his knee and looked genuinely pleased. But Felix's heart sank when he saw the self-satisfaction return to his face. "I'm tempted to give that to you based on deductive skills alone. But no. That was not a fruit. Not at all."

Felix's heart sank. It didn't make sense. "A vegetable then? Cabbage? Is it cabbage?" But Dullahan shook his head.

"More chicken carcasses?" Felix asked hopelessly.

Dullahan grinned and moved the stylus, "Shall I replay it for you?"

The screams repeated. And the slicing.

Scratch. Crunch. Scratch.

Felix tried to think of what it could be, but the closer he listened to it, the more queasy it made him feel. He covered his ears.

"Listen, Felix," Dullahan commanded. "You're so close, and you've guessed them all correctly so far." Felix realized the whip from the recording room was resting on the table.

"I can't. That sound is making me sick."

"Is it?"

Scratch. Crunch. Scratch.

"Yes!"

"Then it's doing what it's supposed to. Listen closer."

The room was getting darker. Felix couldn't see Dullahan's face anymore. Just his great silhouetted shoulders rising to stretch the whip. It twisted and became more skeletal in the creeping shadows.

Felix had to guess. He thought about everything he'd heard. Everything Dullahan had told him to listen to. Then he remembered what Dullahan had told him not to listen to.

"I know what the sound is," Felix said.

"Do you?"

"Yes. It's like you said. Survival instincts. Sounds the body hates to hear." Dullahan raised the grotesque weapon. "It's murder."

Dullahan froze. Thunder struck. Felix couldn't tell if it was real or from the record anymore.

"Murder?"

"Yes." Felix still clenched his eyes shut. He could barely force himself to think it, much less say it. "I've heard loads of scary records but I've never heard anything like those . . . *things* I heard in your recording studio earlier. When you said that I interrupted your recording session you were telling the truth. But I also interrupted something else. I think you're playing me a recording of what you did before I climbed out of that coffin."

"You think I killed someone in that room?"

"I do."

"And I think that's not specific enough, Felix. Who did I kill?" Felix met his heavy, sizzling gaze.

"Patrick and Tom. You killed them with that . . . thing you have in your hands." And now he could see exactly what the whip was made of.

"Why would I do that?"

"Like you said. They had itchy fingers. But sneaking me in to steal from you wasn't enough. It was a double blind. They wanted me to distract you while they broke in from somewhere else to steal that gold record. Only you caught them. And you killed them."

The voice on the record player returned:

"I hope you enjoyed your visit to the Otherworld! If you survived, please turn the record over to enjoy side B."

Dullahan set the whip down. He switched off the turntable as it ran off into dead wax.

"Side B is mostly crickets," he sighed. He turned to Felix and offered out his hand.

"Happy Halloween, Felix. A deal is a deal."

They walked down the hall past the spot where Felix

now knew his bullies had died. To the studio where a master tape reel was running a duplicator to dozens of cassettes. They all finished at once as if standing at attention to Dullahan.

"I love Halloween," he said, collecting the tapes. "The only time of year that people refuse to believe their ears." He led him downstairs and through the cardboard labyrinth. There were no turns and yet the spiral passage led them away from the house and to the front gate.

"You're not afraid that I'll tell someone about this?" asked Felix.

"No one would believe you. And if enough people came looking they would never find me here again. But one thing, Felix," Dullahan held open the gate that would deliver him to Pike Street. "Even if they weren't thieves I would have taken their heads. They were promised. Even if man has forgotten. The blood of the firstborn is owed for the land." Felix could see shadows moving behind Dullahan in the labyrinth. Other things were traveling to Pike Street tonight.

"Here, take a tape. And listen closely while you still have those good ears. You might be able to hear Patrick and Tom calling from the Otherworld."

Felix took the tape and stepped from a world far away to a place slightly closer to our own named Pike Street. Where the skulls were still plastic, and the tombstones still made of foam, but the dead leaves had regained some of their color. And the screams heard on any album recorded at 13 Pike St. were real.

Nº 14
____

BLOOD IN THE DARK
Tucker Joneson

As the flames in jack-o'-lanterns flickered, children roamed along the sidewalks of a dead-end road. The scent of sweets lingered in the cool night air. A boy dressed as Dracula, with slicked back hair, fake blood dripping from his lips, and a flowing black cape, made his way down the street. The boy carried an old pillowcase filled with candy; the wrappers and small candy boxes crinkled and rattled as he walked along the sidewalk. The boy's two friends were also dressed as classic monsters; The Invisible Man and Frankenstein's Monster. The vampire boy, named Edgar, was currently searching for these two monstrous friends. He'd lost them in the crowd of costumed children earlier that night.

Laughter and screams echoed through the fog-filled streets. As Edgar turned the corner, he was overcome with an odd feeling. There was something different about this street. The boy had no idea of the tricks that were in store for him this Halloween night.

Edgar and the two missing boys, Steve and Joe, were the only ones left in their group of friends that wanted to dress up and celebrate this night. Everyone else their age was either going to parties or out on dates. None of the others were filled with the same passion for horror films and haunted houses that these three shared. It's what bonded them together since the beginning. Despite that, Edgar believed that this would be their last Halloween together. He couldn't ignore the fact that they were all growing up. Eventually, they would have to leave behind their beloved childhood like everyone else. For now, Edgar was going to enjoy this night filled with candy, costumes, and creeps.

Aside from collecting sweets, the three thirteen-year-old boys were planning to visit a haunted house. Children would whisper tales of an evil house tucked away on a dead-end road. That week at school, Steve and Joe told Edgar the stories of this creepy place. This house had been standing for nearly a century, and in all that time, the owners had never been seen. There were never any cars seen sitting in the driveway or any lights on inside. The curtains were always drawn and the doors were all locked. No mailmen ever stopped at this house and no gardeners ever mowed its lawn—yet the house always stayed in pristine condition. However, the legend claims that over the years, anyone who dared visit this home would disappear without a trace. Children who knocked at the door never left the front porch, and any animals that went to relieve themselves on the lawn were never seen again. Edgar wasn't sure if he believed in any of this, but he was still curious enough to go investigate with his friends.

Unfortunately, they forgot to mention the address of this deadly home. *If this haunted house was even real in the first place,* Edgar thought. The only thing he could remember hearing was that it was the fourteenth house in the middle cul-de-sac. Somehow, Edgar had never heard of the horros of Pike Street, but Joe and Steve claimed they were all true. They swore they were told by a group of high schoolers, who heard it from some other kid, whose friend went missing last year.

Edgar continued trick-or-treating as he searched for the missing monsters. Children ran past him dressed as cowboys, demons, wrestlers, and princesses. Some wore the classic plastic masks while others were covered in makeup. Tired parents struggled to keep up with their sugar-rushed kiddies in the shadows. Unwrapping a chocolate bar from out of his candy bag, Edgar took a bite.

Might as well keep collecting candy, he thought.

The vampire boy turned and made his way across another home's walkway and up onto the front porch. This older wooden structure was a colonial style clapboard house. The two-story house was a ghostly white, with dark burgundy shutters and white columns along its semicircular front porch. The porch was dark and Edgar couldn't see any lights on inside either. *Why not give it a shot?* He thought as he knocked his fist against the dark red door. The boy's eyes glanced down at his feet to see his friend's plastic Frankenstein mask beside the doormat.

"Steve?" he whispered as he bent down to pick up the monster mask. On the inside of this mask, Edgar spotted a spider sticker stuck along the forehead, confirming that this was his friend's mask. Steve had a booklet of creepy-crawly stickers which he had been applying to his lunchbox and school supplies this month. As Edgar inspected the mask in his hand, the front door of the large house slowly creaked open.

Had to be a breeze, he told himself. Beyond the red door was nothing but darkness. Edgar wanted nothing more than to turn around and run. Although his gut told him not to step inside, he knew that he needed to find his friends. Edgar reached down into his candy sack and pulled out a small flashlight. For once, he was thankful for his overbearing parents and their nagging. They made sure that he and his friends took flashlights with them when going out that night.

The small burst of light broke through the wall of darkness before him. The house was empty. His eyes scanned the room, noticing that there were no picture frames hung on the walls, no couches, tables, or any other furniture in sight. There was nothing. There wasn't even a hardwood floor. Edgar took his first step, which was farther down than he expected, and stomped down onto a dirt floor. Using his light, he examined the ground, searching for any kind of explanation for this strange place. It felt as if the home was a façade, like the fake structures they build in Hollywood for filmmaking. Edgar had taken a tour of one of those studios on a summer road trip with his family last year. As he thought back to those happy days, his eyes grew wide and his arm froze still. The metal flashlight trembled in his hand. The light was directed at the center of the dirt floor. A large opening in the earth loomed before him, like a cavity in a rotten tooth. The bright summer time memories faded away. Now, there was only moonlight on a gloomy October night.

Edgar slowly walked up to the dark pit, flashlight still gripped in his hand. His knuckles grew white as panic started to seep in. *What is this? What's going on here?* Before he could think, Edgar spotted Joe's faded blue pillowcase hanging limp along the edge of the crater. *This gap in the floor must be, at least, five or six feet wide across,* Edgar thought to himself as he struggled to make out any visuals amongst the dark descent. Breaking the deafening silence, he called out for his friends. His throat was dry as he whispered, "Steve? Joe? Are you guys down there?"

No response.

He looked around the house once more, realizing that it was getting darker. Edgar turned back to see the front door was now closed. Before he could move, he began hearing a squeaking noise coming from below. Edgar peered into the darkness. His small light did almost nothing to help, until something small appeared. It was fast and jittery as it flew up toward Edgar's face. They flew up and around the boy's head, wings flapping and grazing the boy's skin. Edgar panicked and flung his arms around in the air. As the boy danced, he hoped they wouldn't bite him. He turned to run for the door, but the winged creatures flew back at his face, causing him to fall backward. At that moment, Edgar realized what he had done. The vampire boy fell into the abyss. Bats shimmered in the moonlight above, for only a moment, before everything went black.

Edgar hit the ground hard.

He choked and gasped as the wind was knocked out of him. Clouds of dust filled the air and coated the boy's lungs as he struggled to inhale. His skull rattled and vision blurred. Rolling over, he continued wheezing and coughing, fighting for air. His body ached as he slowly rose to his knees and then to his feet. His left arm and shoulder had taken most of the impact. Tears began to glisten at the corners of his eyes, but he held them back as best as he could. He cautiously raised his arm, bending it and clenching his fist. Weary tendons strained under his pale skin. *At least nothing was broken*, he told himself as his breathing settled.

The flashlight blinded him as it rolled back and forth along the cold floor. He clutched the light in his trembling hand. The empty cavern walls stretched out into infinite darkness — much farther than his weak light could reach. As his eyes adjusted to the vast space, he began to see strange rock formations peeking out from the dark.

The air was crisp. The rocky floor was harsh and lifeless. The sound of bat wings fluttered in the distance. His staggering footsteps moved across the dusty floor. Every little sound echoed off the dark stone walls. He could even hear his own heart beat. Edgar had descended into another world. He was alone in an ancient cavern hidden just below Pike Street.

Beads of water dripped from stalactites above and into puddles around him. *Or were those stalagmites?* He never remembered which was which, but he did learn how long they took to form in his science class. Based on the size of these formations, he estimated that this cave had to be close to a million years old.

Staring back up at the large gap in the earth, Edgar realized that he had fallen close to eight feet. The boy shambled in circles, searching for something — *anything* — he could use to climb out of this pit. There was no ladder, no rope, no way back up that he could find.

Why on Earth is a fake house built over this? Who built this house? What is it hiding?

A chill ran up Edgar's spine as he pondered that last question. The boy was covered in goosebumps and his teeth began to chatter. Edgar could see his breath in the air as he limped forward, shivering. The sound of water droplets falling from above echoed throughout the cave along with the sound of his shoe dragging across the rubble. Having taken more of the impact than he initially thought, Edgar dragged his left foot across the earth.

Edgar winced as he rubbed his aching arm and glared up at the empty house above. "Someone help me!" he called out. "Anyone out there? We fell into this hole! We need hel—" Edgar froze. He was sure he had heard it. A faint, yet audible scream, replaced by silence. He squinted ahead, sure that the scream had come from within the cave and not from above.

"Joe! Steven!" He shouted, "This isn't funny anymore! Where are you?"

Nothing.

He pressed forward, limping away from the cave's entrance above. "Guys! I'm hurt! Are you okay?" His voice began to tremble. It faintly echoed along the cavern walls before returning to silence. As Edgar stepped forward, his flashlight began to highlight the outline of a tunnel entrance. The tunnel floor was littered with Halloween candy. *Like Hansel and Gretel,* Edgar scoffed as he followed the trail of sweets to find his lost friends. He rubbed his sore left arm as he made his way down the dark corridor. Descending deeper into the earth, Edgar watched as the candy trail grew thinner, until finally there was no more. A sharp pain etched across his right arm. "Son of a . . . " Edgar groaned. Holding the flashlight toward himself, he watched as something trickled down his arm. A jagged rock protruding from the cave wall glistened as his blood met the flashlight's beam. His sleeve was cut, with fabric dangling along his bleeding forearm. He wrapped the material around his arm and applied pressure to stop the bleeding. The short time he spent as a boy scout had taught him a thing or two. *Let's see if they taught me any other skills to survive a creepy bat cave.*

Traveling farther, the caverns would both expand and constrict. At times, the rock ceilings would stretch far beyond his reach, endlessly leading into more dark mysteries. Other times, the boy was practically crawling his way through. His Halloween costume was soon covered in layers of dust and mud. He didn't want to go much farther, scared of getting lost himself. He remembered times of exploring historic caves, like Ruby Falls and Carlsbad Caverns, on road trips growing up. However, those were lit and guided.

"Guys! Call out to me, please! We gotta get outta here!"

Dust and rubble fell around the boy, reminding him that this was not the safest place to shout. *What am I doing? This is crazy!*

The rock walls were beginning to close in on him. He could feel them scraping against his shoulders. He stumbled and tripped as his shoes became caught on crevices along the path. He had to pivot sideways and squeeze his way forward. He kept his flashlight raised to shine ahead, while his other hand gently glided along the rocks behind him. Chilling water droplets rolled down his skin.

This tight path began to bend and turn, not allowing Edgar to see far ahead anymore. Taking his time with his steps, he continued moving forward. The rock walls were beginning to push up against his chest and back as the path became narrower and narrower. Squeezing himself through, he had to keep his head turned to his right, looking ahead. Soon the walls were too close together to move at all. He had to stop, feeling his foot caught between the rocks. He tried to pull at it, but his limbs were now locked in place as well. His chest had begun to burn.

Now knowing that he was stuck, a sense of dread overcame him. His heart raced as beads of sweat dripped down his face.

He struggled to breathe. The walls were crushing his lungs. The darkness was closing in. He yanked at his limbs, trying everything he could to break free. His breathing was short and heavy. "Someone help me! I'm stuck! I'm scared! Please! I—I can't do this!" He yanked his right arm back, loosening it, but cutting the back of his wrist. Pain struck his hand like lightning. His hand twitched and lost hold of his light. The flashlight bounced off the walls, blinding him like a strobe light, before hitting the dirt floor. It rested before him, just out of reach.

"Oh God! No!" Edgar cried as his body shuffled and pulled, desperately trying to free himself. *Calm down! Get it together, Edgar! You are not dying down here! Your friends are not dying down here! They need you! Your family needs you! You will make it home!*

Edgar attempted to slow his breathing. *In and out.* Closing his eyes, he listened as his heartbeat slowed. The boy clenched his fists and began pushing his way forward. The sharp edges of the cave walls scratched his chest and back. A tear ran down his face as he pushed along. Finally, his chest began to feel some relief. His lungs could breathe again. His head was soon able to turn. He smiled and whispered to himself that he was making it out of here.

Edgar struggled to reach for his fallen light. Trapped between sharp ridges, there wasn't space to kick at it. With no success, he continued forward, watching as the light behind him grew smaller in the distance. It began to flicker and would soon be dead, leaving the boy in total darkness. He had to find his friends before they were all lost in the dark forever. The smile faded and Edgar gasped. His eyes panned up from the flashlight to see two glowing dots in the dark. Like cat eyes staring back at him from within the shadows.

At that moment Edgar began to feel weightless. The ground had vanished from beneath him as he fell backward into the night. The boy flipped and tumbled down a steep hill, hitting rocks and rough formations. He clenched his jaw as his bones rattled, until finally rolling to a stop along the cavern floor. He grabbed his side as he rose to his feet, praying he wouldn't crack his skull on any stalactites or stone walls.

Blind as a bat, Edgar shuffled forward. His arms were outstretched, searching for anything that he could take hold of. His left arm, now covered in dark bruises, ached and quivered. Warm blood ran down his right arm. He imagined the terror and sadness that would overwhelm his parents when he never came home. As well as the pain that the families of his friends would endure. He knew they—and the police—would spend days, weeks, maybe even years, hopelessly searching for them. No one would ever think to explore the secret, never-ending basement of this cursed house.

We are all making it out of this place, he told himself, unsure if he believed it, but knowing he couldn't afford to give up now.

His bloody hand clasped a chilling round object before him. He stopped and stood in the dark as he tried to make out what it was. It didn't feel like the earth of the cavern. His fingers ran along its unique curves and texture before feeling smaller rounded pieces. *Teeth*. His heart stopped the moment he discovered he was touching a human skull. Edgar leapt back, ready to scream, and crashed into something—someone—who wrapped their arms around him. Before he could shout, a hand clasped his jaw shut. Edgar panicked and fought to get loose.

"Edgar, stop! It's me! Steve!" The voice hissed in his ear. Edgar's heart fluttered as he turned around to see the dark silhouette of his friend.

"Thank God, I finally found one of you! Where's Jo—" he started. Steve cut him off and turned his flashlight on, casting devilish shadows across his face.

"*Shh!* We're not alone in here!"

Now his heart sank. His friend's eyes were wide, his skin was dirty and drenched in sweat. Dark blood ran down his face and arms. The boy in the shredded Frankenstein costume raised his arm and pointed ahead.

Edgar noticed that his hand was trembling. He turned around to see that Steve was pointing at the skeletal remains of what looked like an old miner. The bones protruded from mangy black overalls. Beside the body laid a metal helmet and a rusty pickaxe. The corpse sat on the ground with its back against the wall, staring back at Edgar and Steve with empty black eyes.

Steve turned his light, pointing right to reveal another miner's body, along with old bags, buckets, and crates. He brought the flashlight back and held it under his frightened face.

"There's more bodies in here. Some older and others more recent . . . We need to find a way out!"

"Where's Joe? We can't leave him!"

Steve shook his head, "Something got him."

"There's another person down here? WHERE?"

"*Shhh!* Not a person," Steve whispered. "Something else." His eyes swelled as he slowly exhaled. "When we were exploring one of these caverns—this thing—came out of nowhere and got him. It carried him off into the dark. I tried chasing after them, but at some point I slipped and tumbled down into this pit, hitting my head . . . "

"What are you talking about? What was this thing?" Edgar pleaded.

Steve rubbed his eyes, almost like he was questioning his own vision. "A vampire. I think. It was huge. Not like anything I've ever seen before!" He answered coldly. *You really did hit your head,* Edgar thought.

"We need to get going and find Joe!" As Edgar stepped by, Steve grabbed his arm.

"He's gone, Edgar. Last thing I heard were his screams, but now . . . it's been dead silent."

Edgar looked into his friend's eyes. He had never seen him like this before. He was horrified. Taking a deep breath, Edgar began limping over to the dead miner's body. He bent down and grabbed the rusty pickaxe. His arms ached as he lifted the heavy cobweb-covered weapon.

"You've got the light. Lead the way."

~

Dracula and Frankenstein, in their tattered, bloody costumes, made their way across the cave. Steve's fading flashlight illuminated the bottom of the steep hill that they had fallen down. "You think there's an easier way to get back up there?" Steve asked. Edgar glanced around the cave for any other paths.

"I don't think—" A large object crashed down next to them. Blood erupted in the air, soaking the boys, as it tumbled along the ground. It was a body. It was Joe.

The wide-eyed boys looked down in horror at their friend's soggy corpse. His throat was slashed open with his head bent so far back that it was almost torn off completely. His suit and bandages were drenched with dark red blood. Joe's body still pulsed and contorted. *Was he still alive?*

The boys, still frozen from shock, turned to look up in unison to see where Joe had come from. Steve lifted his flashlight, illuminating a dark figure above them. Edgar, once again, saw those same glowing cat eyes in the dark, looming over him. The light revealed an enormous bat creature hanging from above. Its eyes were pale white like a corpse. It had crooked clawed feet, patchy gray fur, and a trail of Joe's blood dripping from its fangs.

It let out an ear-piercing screech. Edgar staggered back as he covered his ears. The unholy creature let go of the cave ceiling, extended its large bat wings, and descended down toward the two trembling boys. Edgar began to run away, and looked back to see Steve still frozen in place—his eyes almost transfixed to the dead eyes of the vampire. The large creature swooped down and grabbed him with its claw-like feet. Edgar was blown over by the force of the wings as they flapped, rolling across the ground. Pain shot through his body as he crashed into a boulder. He looked across the cavern to see his screaming friend rise up into the air. "No!" Edgar cried as he rose to his feet. The vampire ascended farther, disappearing into the darkness. He chased after them, pickaxe in hand, unable to see anything. He was not ready to lose another friend tonight.

Steve fought back, hitting the creature's feet with his fists and attempting to pull himself free. Its claws dug deeper into the boy's shoulders. He screamed and bit down on the vampire's foot until he drew blood. It was black and thick like tar. It tasted like battery acid and smelled even worse. He didn't stop. He kept biting deeper. The monster's skin was cold and dense. Its icy black blood was freezing his teeth. Steve continued screaming, now gargling on the demon's blood. He kept biting down until finally its grip began to loosen. It roared as it released the boy. The vampire continued to fly away as Steve descended into the black abyss.

Grinding his teeth, Edgar fought through the pain. He staggered over rocky grounds and bounced off jagged walls. Up ahead he could see a light, a tiny beacon in this black hellscape. He slowed to a stop, breathing heavily, and bent down to grab the light. It was Steve's flashlight.

"Steve?" he whispered.

A gurgling burst came from the dark. Edgar stepped forward, lifting up the light to reveal his friend. Steve lay sprawled out, impaled by a large stalagmite. Blood was everywhere. His head shook as he spewed more blood from his mouth. He was choking while his hands felt around his stomach. The boy was attempting to push his intestines back inside to no avail. Steve's bloodshot eyes turned to look over at his horrified friend. Edgar stood there, unsure of what he could possibly do, as his friend spat up black blood. He cried and squirmed before finally going limp. His friend was dead. His red eyes still glaring back at him.

The world was silent. All Edgar could hear was the *thud* of his own heart beating, "I'm sorr—"

Once more, the vampire let out a blood-curdling scream that boomed off the walls like fireworks. Edgar turned and ran for cover. He could hear the loud swoosh of the bat wings over head. His muscles burned as he sprinted, feeling the weight of the pickaxe that was slow-ing him down. Up ahead, he could spot the entrance of another tunnel hidden between the rocky walls. As he pushed himself harder, the monster was gaining speed and closing in on its prey. Edgar could smell its rancid breath behind him. Reaching the tunnel, he lunged forward, pushing off the walls and propelling himself farther inside. His knees were scraped and shoulders beaten, but he was still alive.

The vampire crashed into the narrow tunnel entrance. Its wings flapped wildly as it tried to squeeze inside. Inches away from the boy, it chomped at his feet. Specks of blood and drool splattered across Edgar as he kicked back at the demon's face. Gore and entrails dripped from its black tongue as its eyes stayed locked onto him, eager for its next meal.

Huffing, Edgar raised his pickaxe and charged at the vampire, swinging the blade down into its neck. The beast cried out in pain. Black-tar blood spewed from its veins and dripped from its mouth. The piercing screech burst Edgar's eardrums. As Edgar pulled back at the ax, the vampire swung its winged arm, backhanding Edgar and sending the boy crashing into the wall. Hearing something crack, he looked down, fearing a bone was broken, only to find the handle of the ax had broken off. The head of the ax remained lodged into the starggering vampire's neck.

With the broken ax handle and the nearly dead flashlight in hand, Edgar crawled away from the demon. It bit at the ax before tugging it loose from the pulsating wound. It tossed the bloody chunk of metal away, rattling off the walls like gunshots. The cat-like eyes glowed in the distance watching as the boy ran farther down the dark corridor. Edgar sprinted across the darkness, spotting the way out just ahead. He began his attempt to climb up the steep cavern wall. Desperate to escape, Edgar dug his bleeding fingers into the cavern wall. He heard the thunderous flapping sounds of the creature's wings closing in on him. He was so close. If only he had more time. In an instant, the claws grabbed the boy and he felt the talons pierce his shoulders. His feet dangled, kicking for any surface to latch onto.

Edgar fought with the monster, beating at its claws with his broken ax handle. As the bat soared through the underground, the freezing air sent chills down the boy's spine. All he could hear was the deafening screams of the monster and its thunderous wings flapping again and again. The vampire was struggling to fly. Blood continued to run down the hideous figure. Edgar finally raised his broken handle and stabbed the jagged wood into the vampire's clawed foot. It screamed, tightening its grip on him. Edgar cried out as he continued stabbing at the bat's leg. Losing control, the monster crashed into a cavern wall, sending it and the boy tumbling down into the darkness below.

Edgar spat out blood and teeth onto the rocky ground. His broken body struggled to rise up. Pain surged through his limbs as he reached out for his dying light. The boy's stomach churned as he took in the putrid air. It reeked, as if the earth itself was rotting. Pointing the light down, he discovered a sea of bones and dried blood coating shredded clothes, shoes, wallets, and backpacks from dozens—maybe hundreds—of victims. Bodies of men, women and even children. Skulls, some still coated with bits of rotting skin and hair, littered the cave. They stared back at Edgar as if to welcome him to his final resting place. These corpses wore t-shirts, sports jerseys, torn jeans, suits, and dresses. Some outfits even looked as if they came from another century.

How long has this thing lived down here? How many people have died here?

Edgar didn't have answers, but he prayed that these victims did not suffer long. Behind him lay more bodies of the lost miners. Cobweb-coated skeletons were rotting against the walls, their jaws dropped in eternal screams. Next to these dead men were stacks of wooden crates. Edgar peered inside to see several sticks of dynamite. "Jesus . . ." the boy whispered, as he backed up, nearly tripping over a small duffle bag. He bent down and opened it, revealing emergency flares inside. "I hope these still work . . . " he whispered as he reached inside. His flashlight flickered once more before dying. The world was black.

The cave was silent.

The flare erupted into a blazing red fire. The flickering light illuminated only a portion of this massive space. His head spun as he looked all around him, desperately trying to find any way out. As the light sizzled in his ear, his eyes spotted strange formations hanging from above. These objects were not made of earth or ice, but of flesh. Vampires. Dozens of these creatures hung sleeping throughout the cave. They were all smaller than the beast he had fought off. *Children?*

Edgar's heart was pounding and his lungs were wheezing as he struggled to breathe. The blood-soaked boy glanced back over at the miners' wooden crates.

The creatures all remained enveloped in their wings above. Edgar knew he had only so much time before they were all awakened. He rushed over to the crates, counting three—possibly more—filled with ancient dynamite. Edgar cautiously held his blazing flare away from the explosives. Before he could reach into the box, the vampire soared across the hall, tackling Edgar. He kicked and swung his fists at the beast. It was slower and weaker now. Its pale skin and fur were coated in its dark blood. The demon's white eyes glowed with hatred and hunger. Edgar grabbed the monster's bloody neck, jamming his fingers into the wound. The vampire cried and twitched. It clenched the boy's bruised arm and flung him across the cave.

Edgar's vision was starting to blur. The crimson flare lay burning on the cavern floor, and near it was the jagged wooden handle. Edgar's nerves jolted, scattering pain throughout his body, as he crawled across the icy ground. Muscles in his arms and legs trembled. Dried blood pulled at his skin. The monster let out a chilling war cry that rattled the walls of the demon's dark den. Edgar cover his ears to no avail as the sound echoed in his brain.

The monsters that coated the red ceiling of this hellscape began to awaken.

Their ears twitched, wings unfolded, and their fangs flickered in the violent light. The vampire charged at Edgar for one final strike. Its claws scraped along the stone floor as it scrambled his way. Edgar rolled over on his back as the devil came down over him. The vampire's fangs and tongue lashed out inches from his face. The putrid smell of death and copper flooded the boy's senses. Its pale eyes blinked in a look of surprise. The bat tilted its head down to discover that Edgar had impaled the monster's chest with his wooden stake.

The vampire squealed as it began to twitch and transform. Its bones cracked and shifted under its skin that tightened and stretched. The creature was shedding its fur and its claws became hands and feet. Edgar noticed that the skin began to rot and peel away. He was aging rapidly as he became more human. It was as if the years were finally catching up to this ancient being. Teeth and fingernails fell out as his skin melted off his bones. His eyes, now a faded green, oozed from his skull. The gooey remains cascaded onto the boy until all that was left were bones that had scattered across the ground.

The vampire was no more.

The blood-soaked vampire killer turned and crawled toward his fading flare. His breathing was heavy and uneven. His body was shaking and his head pounding. The fire sparked in his hand like burgundy fireworks in a cloudy night sky. His tired eyes watched as demons crawled along the ancient walls above him. Some had begun to take flight. Dozens of these monsters began charging toward him. They would devour the killer of their father, or perhaps, he was just another nightly meal to them. A smile grew on Edgar's face as he tossed the flare into the crate of dynamite.

~

A broken, bloody figure crawled across the rocky floor. Shredded fabric lingered behind him, dragging along the ground like broken fingers. As midnight grew near, he finally made his way back up to where this nightmare began. Edgar laid back amongst the cold rock and gazed up at the moonlight. Faint beams of light shone down through the open wound of earth above him. The moonlight illuminated the dust that danced through the air like fireflies.

His skin was layered with cuts, gashes, bruises, and blood. He could feel his muscles torn, teeth chipped, fingernails jagged, and bones broken. Black blood dripped from his mouth. A tar-like substance covered his body. Specks of dust and rubble coated the tired trick-or-treater. After losing his two friends, he was ready to take out every creature down there, hoping that no one else would have to suffer the same fate. His heart ached, knowing there was nothing else he could have done, but his soul could rest easy knowing that those monsters were banished to the darkness for eternity. His breathing grew faint, his eyes fluttered slowly, as he took one last glance at this Halloween night. For a moment the world was still.

Silence echoed through the cave.

~

Edgar's eyes flashed open. They were pale and empty, glowing like the moon. His body twitched and convulsed as it began its metamorphosis. Bones in his face shifted and hardened, grinding under his skin. His brow sharpened and his eyes sunk in. His mouth sprang open, revealing ever-growing fangs that descended from under his now flattening nose. The boy was gone and all that remained was monster. Its lungs screamed out into the night sky, rising higher and higher until it sounded human no more. The corpse of Edgar trembled and snapped. Wings formed from skin along the creature's pale arms. Its veins pumped darkness through its black heart.

A vampire was born on Halloween night.

Children laughed as they ran from house to house. Orange and purple lights flickered and fog engulfed lawns. Candy bowls rattled as kids searched for their favorite chocolate bars. The night was bliss, as were the people, unaware of the horrors that lived just below. The door to this horrid home creaked open from a cold October breeze once more, welcoming the world in — or perhaps — letting the darkness out.

MOTHER
Kimberly Pinzon

MAYBE NEXT YEAR YOU CAN dress up as something . . . nicer? How does that sound, honey?"

Dad's keys jingled as Kelly jumped from foot to foot, her bulging pillowcase crackled with the sound of all the candy she'd collected. There were a few apples in there — *garbage* — and someone had even tossed in an orange. An orange? Who did that? But she was delighted with all of her candy and the scattering of quarters some of the elderly had tossed into her sack. They weren't edible, but she could buy more candy with them.

"I *like* Freddy Krueger, Dad." Kelly pulled her plastic mask off and waved it in the air. The mask smelled gross, and even though she loved the melty pockmarked face, she was glad to be taking it off. *"Slash, slash, slash!"* She dropped the mask in her pillowcase and swiped her plastic knife claws at her dad. Freddy Krueger was so cool! He killed stupid teenagers in their dreams, which they all deserved. Teenagers were dumb, and Kelly couldn't wait for the VHS to come out for Freddy's second movie so she could watch him kill more of them.

He pushed the door open and sighed. He wasn't even sure how his daughter had seen the first Freddy movie. He certainly hadn't taken her. Kelly sped off into the house for the kitchen and dumped her pillowcase out on the kitchen table. "I know, Kelly, but, is Freddy Krueger really for little girls? What about Jem? Or a Care Bear next year?" He looked hopeful as he watched his daughter sort through her candy, separating them out according to some internal system he didn't understand.

Kelly paused her sorting and looked up at him. Her eyes, usually a mild and dull brown, seemed to hold a green, glowing sheen to them.

A trick of the light, he reminded himself. *Only a trick of the light.*

"Mommy likes the costume. She told me."

He bit his tongue to stop himself from arguing with her. The child psychiatrist had told him it was better to allow her to have these moments than to fight with her about it. He thought it was a load of bullshit, but he was trying for Kelly's sake.

"Hey, hey, hey! You know the rules!" He snatched the open Snickers bar out of her hand. For a moment, the glow in Kelly's eyes intensified and the air around her shimmered. He held firm, reminding himself that this was only his imagination, stress over dealing with his daughter. "There could be razor blades in these. I need to check all the candy, and once I do, you can eat five pieces."

"Ten," she demanded, crossing her arms.

"Five," he enunciated, looking over the Snickers. "Here, this one's fine." He handed it back to her and she chomped a big bite out of it.

The doorbell rang. Kelly stiffened, her wide eyes darting to the door.

"Well, go on then," her father said, gesturing toward the front door.

She dropped the Snickers bar and took off, her green and red striped sweater billowing behind her, pillowcase clutched in her fist.

He dropped his head in his hands, reminding himself again that the psychiatrist said this was just a phase, things would get better. He was pretty sure the psychiatrist didn't have any kids of his own, otherwise, how could he say that? Did he not know how girls got when they became *teenagers?* What was he going to do then?

That would have to be a problem for another day, another year. For now, with Kelly occupied at the door, he could check her candy without her scrutinizing every candy he discarded. You couldn't be too safe nowadays. Psychos putting razor blades and poison and who knew what else into candy. Those Satanists were getting into everything these days . . . candy, Tylenol, schools. They could even live in the neighborhoods, creepy old men hanging around in their yards, pretending to stare at the sky while they were probably waiting to snatch a wandering child. One just couldn't be too safe.

He stuffed a Hershey's bar into his mouth. Dad Tax.

~

Kelly grabbed a large bowl full of candy from near the front door, her fist with the pillowcase tucked underneath it. She pulled the door open and was greeted by four children who shrieked "Trick or treat!" Four plastic faces—a Care Bear, a Cabbage Patch Kid, Bat Girl, and another Care Bear—stared blankly back at her. The contrast from the darkness outside and the light inside made it difficult to see their eyes other than brief flashes through the eye holes. Cold air drifted in, swirling around her legs clad in black leggings.

The four waited expectantly, their buckets and pillowcases held out.

"Lemme see what ya got," Kelly leaned forward, sheltering her bowl of candy against her body so no grabby hands could snatch any.

"What?" Cabbage Patch kid asked, his voice muffled behind his mask. "You're supposed to give us candy." Kelly peered into his purple bucket with Frankenstein on it first. Her hand darted in, grabbing his full-sized Snickers. Batgirl squeaked, and Kelly's hand dunked into her pillowcase before she could pull it away, coming out with a handful of candy like a claw machine game.

Kelly grabbed another handful of candy out of the blue

Care Bear's sack, depositing it into her own, and reached for the pink Care Bear's green bucket. The Care Bear pulled the bucket away and grabbed her wrist, almost tight enough to hurt. "Give us our candy back! You're being mean!" The girl pulled her mask up so her voice could be heard clearly. "Give. It. Back."

Kelly looked from her wrist to the girl's face and back. "Let go of me." Her voice was calm, firm, not at all betraying that Kelly wanted to tear the girl's hand off.

The other child glared, squeezing her fist tighter, until her eyes shifted to the space behind and above Kelly. The hardness in her face melted and her lips wobbled open. Kelly pulled her wrist out of the girl's loosened grip with a smirk as the other children whimpered and stepped back.

"Give me your whole bucket. Now!" Kelly demanded. The pink Care Bear looked away from the shimmering spaces around Kelly and met her eyes, glowing an unnatural green. She screamed, dropped her bucket and took off, shoving between her friends and knocking Cabbage Patch Kid to the ground. The other two chased after their friend, leaving Cabbage Patch Kid to scramble backward, his mask askew and exposing chubby, tear-stained cheeks.

Looming over him, Kelly whispered, "Boo." He shrieked and rolled over, scrabbling away on hands and knees, his purple bucket forgotten, candy spilled all over the ground.

"Hey!" Kelly looked over her shoulder at her father, interrupting her scooping up the candy into the bowl. She picked out a few crunchy brown leaves from the bowl and let them flutter to the ground. "What happened here?" He surveyed the bucket spilling out its candy guts, Kelly hunched over and scooping them up. His daughter stared at him, and he told himself that it was the old porch lights making her eye's glow that eerie green again.

"The boy got scared because his friend pushed him. They all ran away, and he left his candy, and so did the girl." Kelly finished scooping up the candy, annoyed that the boy had screamed, and her father had come to investigate. He was dressed in a shiny spandex shirt and shorts that *she* could probably fit in: his workout gear for his fluffy-haired workout god, Richard Simmons. She liked his sunshine personality and that he kept her father occupied for long periods of time.

Unfortunately, Richard Simmons hadn't been occupying her father in this moment and here he was, staring down at her, trying to figure out what to do with her.

"Well," he began, rubbing his chin between his fingers, "bring the buckets inside and if the kids come back, you'll give it back to them. And their candy. You've got plenty. Make sure you give each kid two handfuls." He shivered, goosebumps prickling over his skin. "Come inside, it's cold. I've got your candy sorted and your coloring books out."

Kelly didn't feel cold, wrapped up in the warm Freddy Krueger sweater, but there was candy and coloring inside.

At the kitchen table, Kelly eyed the pile of candy left by her father. The infamous Dad Tax had been enacted upon her stockpile, but she would more than make up for that with the kids wandering around hoping for candy.

"I'll be in the den if you need me, honey," he called out. She didn't bother responding, instead stuffing a Three Musketeers bar in her mouth and sorting through her crayons. From the den, the voice of Richard Simmons told his followers to breathe in and breathe out and lift their arms into the air.

"Mom? Why don't you let daddy see you?" Kelly asked the question absently, delicately pressing her crayon to the page and shading in a ladybug. "I don't want to go to the psychiatrist anymore." She scribbled the red crayon over the rest of the ladybug. The air around her sighed and grew heavy, wrapping around her. "Yes, but he has pictures of some other lady around the house. That lady is a *lie*, mom."

The air shimmered and started to take on a dark color. It growled and Kelly felt herself bristle, preparing for her mother's reprimand.

The doorbell rang and the shape dissipated.

Kelly jumped up from the table. Richard Simmons, who had been drowned out by her mother's voice, flooded back in, imploring his followers to lift higher and step faster. Kelly followed his advice and ran to the front door. She grabbed the candy bowl and checked behind her for her mother before opening the door.

Two excited children with their bored-looking parents stood there, candy buckets extended. She couldn't see their faces behind their plastic Hulk Hogan and Princess Leia masks, but she could just tell they had huge smiles on their faces.

Kelly felt her mother withdraw from behind her and knew that she wouldn't be getting candy from these kids. Parents were a no-go for Mother; they caused problems when she appeared and scared their kids. Even these parents, distracted by their conversations and not paying an ounce of attention to their kids at a stranger's door, would certainly notice if their kids started screaming and crying.

"Here's your candy," Kelly said cheerily, depositing two handfuls of candy into each of their bags. The kids squealed and wheeled around back to their parents. Kelly watched them go, meeting up with their parents who guided them past the tall hedges and back onto the street. A small Dracula walked past, looking around, and she thought he would come to the house for candy — a perfect victim — but he passed. She sighed and tilted her head to the side.

In the den, her father was doing lunges, a sheen of sweat covering his brow.

"Maybe you should get a little headband like the people on the show," she suggested.

"What?" He looked startled to see her and missed one of his steps, stumbling. "What are you talking about, Kelly?"

"You're sweating," she shrugged. Hands on his hips, her father looked at her, breathing heavily. "A headband would help."

"Right, yes, you're right," he said. His brow furrowed for a moment, his eyes wandering to the space over her shoulder. It looked like there was something there, like a shimmer in the air usually reserved for heat rising from asphalt. "Have you, uh," he rubbed his eyes to clear the sweat and the weird image over his daughter's shoulder. "Have you handed out a lot of candy?"

Kelly tilted her head and shrugged noncommittally. "There haven't been too many other kids since you started your video."

"Oh, okay, well . . . " Richard Simmons drew his eyes back to the television. "Let me finish this video and then I'll come color with you, okay?"

Kelly smiled and wiggled. "Okay! Mommy will like to spend time with you, too."

Her father smiled awkwardly at her as she skipped away, back to the kitchen.

She barely had time to sit in her seat and pick up a crayon before the doorbell rang again. Kelly hopped up, her mother's presence whisking away to the door.

When Kelly pulled the door open to reveal the trick-or-treaters on the other side, she narrowed her eyes at the two boys. She knew them, vaguely, from the stories other kids told. They were in high school, though she couldn't remember what grade. They weren't dressed up in costumes, instead wearing flannels against the chilly air. The blond one, pulling a comb through his wavy hair, smiled at her. She thought his smile made him look like Freddy Krueger, but a way less cool version. The other one, standing two steps closer to Kelly and the door, had brown hair teased into a poofy mullet. Kelly wrinkled her nose at both of them.

"You're too old to be trick-or-treating. Go home."

"Well, see, that's the thing, kid." Mullet boy leaned closer toward her, showing her his teeth. "We're not here for treats, only tricks. You upset my little brother, and I got a problem with that." Behind Kelly, she could feel her mother getting agitated.

"I don't know you or your little brother. So, take a hike, narbo." Kelly glared at them.

The blond guy chuckled and stuffed his comb and his hands into the pockets of his windbreaker. Mullet boy took his hands out of the pockets of his leather jacket, something shiny flashing in his hand. "Now, I know you look like a spaz, but you understand this, don't you?" He flipped out a butterfly knife like the ones she saw in those kung-fu movies. "That's my brother's candy bucket there," he gestured with the knife, "and you're gonna give it to me, and all of your candy as well."

"You should leave," Kelly growled. She put the bowl of candy on the ground next to her and squeezed her hands into fists. "Or you'll be sorry."

He grinned at her, tilting his head to the side. Her eyes seemed to glow, and her hair fluttered in the breeze. "You think you're a tough guy, huh?"

"Hey man," the blond one interrupted, "she's just a little kid. You're not gonna, you know . . . "

"Not gonna what, maggot? What?" The boy with the mullet whipped around. "She took Bennie's candy and I'm getting it back. She's just a snot-nosed kid." He turned back toward Kelly, no longer smiling. "Give me the candy."

Kelly smiled, though her eyes remained hard and were nearly a toxic neon green. "No."

Mullet boy shrugged. "If that's the way you want it." He lunged at her.

And abruptly stopped, straining against an invisible force holding him back.

Holding up her hand, his knife an inch from her palm, Kelly squeezed her thumb and forefinger together. "Like that, mother?"

The boy's eyes darted around, his knife hand starting to compress as if in a vice. He grunted and struggled, trying to pull his hand away.

"Hey, hey, stop that," the blonde boy said, his voice a pitch higher than it had been. "What the fuck, what are you doing?" Kelly turned toward him, continuing to squeeze her thumb and finger together.

"Shut up and I won't hurt you, too."

The bones in mullet boy's hand snapped. He opened his mouth to scream. With her other hand, Kelly mimed zipping her own mouth shut, and the boy's lips slammed together. He scrabbled at them, tearing strips of skin from around his mouth. Blood oozed out of the wounds and down his neck, soaking into his white shirt. More of the bones in his hand snapped, some of them tearing through his skin. The knife dropped from his grip, clattering to the ground where blood rained down on it.

From behind his sealed and bloodied lips, mullet boy's screams were muffled. His friend whimpered behind him, on the verge of wetting himself. Kelly looked over her shoulder at her mother.

"Am I doing good, Mommy?" The air around her keened with pleasure. Kelly smiled and then turned back to the boys. "You're not going to tell anyone what happened. You had an accident."

Tears coursed down the face of the boy with the mullet, mixing with his blood and creating watery red streaks. He reached out with his unbroken hand and Kelly grabbed it in her fist.

"How are we going to explain this as an *accident?* Are you crazy or stupid?"

Kelly looked at the blond boy. "I'm not crazy or stupid, but you are." She clenched her fist around the wrist of the boy with the mullet and the bones snapped, leaving his hand flopping uselessly. She released him and pointed at the blond boy's knee. Something snapped, something important, and his leg became like a rubber band, folding beneath him. He yelped as he fell, grabbing his leg.

"You little bitch," he wailed.

Smirking, Kelly released the boy with the broken hands, his fingers sticking out at weird angles. His lips burst apart with a gasp of breath.

At the house next door, beyond the hedges, children squealed a delighted "Trick or treat!"

"It's time for you to go now." Kelly wiggled her fingers

at the two boys, and they slid down the walkway, their clothes and skin tearing on the concrete as she propelled them away. "Children with candy are coming. Bye bye!" Mullet boy stumbled to his feet, whimpering, holding his ruined hands against his chest. The blond one hopped up and leaned against his friend. From behind them, children trotted down the walkway, bumping into them, oblivious to the two older boys, bleeding and injured.

As the two teenagers watched, Kelly demanded candy from the children. Instead of her hurting them, though, something manifested behind her, something dark with claws and spikes and jaws that opened around a flickering tongue. The thing didn't hold a shape, so much as shift between shades of shadow or light. It didn't leave the space above Kelly's head, but it scared the children and it scared the boys Kelly had injured.

The kids sped down the walkway, trying to get away as fast as they could.

Kelly watched them part around the two older boys like water around a rock.

"Mom, I'm going to get so much candy." She listened as her mother's voice swarmed around her. "I *knooooooow*, I know. I have to practice other things so that I can go live with you. Just, candy for tonight, okay?"

"Hey, kid!" Kelly's dad grabbed her shoulder and squeezed. "You're letting the cold air in!" He paused, looking at the two boys standing in his yard. Their make-up was spot on, and he shouted that out to them. Their eyes widened, their lips wobbling, and they turned around, stumbling out of his yard. "Well, that was weird. Come on, kiddo. In the house we go."

He stepped back, leaving Kelly at the door.

Looking out at the dark yard, leaves swirling in the breeze, Kelly smiled. Soon. Soon she'd be back in the woods, with her mother, where she belonged.

Until then, she'd play with the humans and have some fun.

Kelly stepped back into the house, letting the door shut behind her on Pike Street.

TUNNEL RAT
John FreelyKirk

MILES LEANED AGAINST A LAMP POST as he watched the first wave of trick-or-treaters begin their pilgrimage down Pike Street. He couldn't help but feel a bit of resentment wash over him as he saw them making what would surely be some of their best memories. Of course, it wouldn't be until many years from now that they would actually realize that, but that was the beauty of retrospect. Having just turned sixteen himself, Miles knew his time of trick-or-treating had all but come to an end. Hearing *"aren't you a little old for this?"* from nearly every home in the neighborhood really seemed to drive that point home. It was only a matter of time before he was blacklisted from Halloween completely, and Miles knew this must have been the universe's cruel way of reminding him that he too was growing up.

"Miles!" a muffled voice called out.

Turning his head, Miles saw a large figure waving at him from across the street. Sporting a latex skeleton mask and an appropriately paired rib cage t-shirt, Rodney approached, twirling an old pocket knife between his fingers. Unlike many of the other costumes out on display, this one practically screamed *minimal effort.*

"Where's your costume?" sneered Rodney as he rested

one leg on the curb. Miles slowly held up the plastic clown mask he stole from the lost and found bin at school.

"Way to half-ass it, dude!" laughed Rodney, his voice muffled by a mask clearly too tight for his large head.

"Look who's talking, jackass!" scoffed Miles as he slid the mask down to cover his face. Walking off the sidewalk and into the middle of the street, the duo was surprised by just how packed the neighborhood was this year. There had to be at least three dozen kids aimlessly running amok. Maybe it was due to Miss Shaw being one of the few folks in the area to hand out king-sized candy bars? Maybe it was the lack of anything to actually do around the area? Regardless of the reason, the neighborhood was much more alive than usual.

"So, are we actually doing this?" Miles asked, looking left and right as they made their way deeper into the neighborhood.

Rodney turned his head and looked directly at Miles. Not even his mask was able to conceal the large grin across his face. Rodney swung his large, tattered backpack off one shoulder and over his chest. Opening the front zipper, he dropped his pocket knife into a large mound of candy (surely stolen from some of the neighborhood kids) and pointed to a large carton of expired eggs.

"Fuck yeah, we're doing this!" chimed Rodney.

As the duo continued down the street, they got closer and closer to their target; the infamous 16 Pike St. Being their last Halloween, the two friends agreed that the only way to properly end their tradition of yearly mischief was by going out with a *bang*. Growing up near the neighborhood, Miles had heard nearly every campfire story imaginable about the creepy old house. Some told stories about vampires, some of cannibals, and others of witches who performed rituals on the young trick-or-treaters, foolish enough to step foot on the property. Miles knew ninety-nine percent of them were bullshit, but the story of Alan and Rebecca Brecker felt *different*.

While not much was actually known about the Breckers, it was public knowledge that the couple had a miscarriage in the mid-1950's culminating in the complete collapse of their marriage and shortly after, Rebecca went missing. Many blamed her husband for her disappearance, but there was never any incriminating evidence found.

Although the disappearance of Rebecca caused 16 Pike St. to pick up notoriety, it was the disappearance of several children that truly sent the neighborhood into a frenzy. Within the span of thirty years, over a dozen children had vanished without a trace, their last seen location being—you guessed it—the Brecker household. Enough angry parents hounding the police finally led the authorities to obtain a warrant to search the home. Although they never found anything substantial, the state of the house and the overall condition of Alan Brecker was enough to keep everyone suspicious. Today, the house remains in a complete state of disarray. As for Alan Brecker himself, he had only been seen outside his house a handful of times in the past thirty years. Those who saw him claimed he would exit his house late at night (often covered head to toe in dirt), look up at the sky for long periods of time, and then quietly walk back inside his home. Regardless of what was actually true or not, everyone knew something was up and as a result, the house had become a target for vandals and mischievous teenagers.

As Miles and Rodney approached the house, the sun had already set behind the dense treeline, leaving a cold, starless sky in its wake. 16 Pike St. sat sandwiched between two (nicer) houses, as cold and uninviting as ever. Practically falling apart, the house's windows were shattered, wood rotted to the core and paint completely chipped away. If there was ever to be a perfect place to shoot a horror film, this was surely it.

"I swear, this dump looks worse and worse every year!" laughed Rodney as he stopped in front of the lawn.

Waist-high weeds greeted them, dancing in the autumn breeze. As he stared at the house, Miles felt a cold drizzle of sweat travel down his brow and soak into the cheap foam padding inside his mask. While Miles never considered himself a superstitious person, this house really did make him uneasy.

Rodney eagerly opened his bag and pulled out the carton of eggs. The splatting sounds of rotten eggs echoed throughout the neighborhood as they slammed against the splintered wood and broken glass. Rodney couldn't help but chuckle as he admired the complete and utter mess he was making. Although the act of vandalism was also enough to make Miles grin like the Cheshire Cat, he couldn't help but feel like they were being watched. Just as quickly as Miles joined in, they had run out of eggs. With the job done, Miles was ready to sneak away and never return.

"Okay, dude, let's go!"

"Not so fast!" laughed Rodney, his voice still muffled by the tight plastic mask.

Kneeling down, he reached deep inside his backpack, reemerging moments later with a roll of toilet paper in each hand. He tossed one into Miles' open hand before throwing his roll at the house as hard as possible. Landing on the center ridge of the roof, the roll evenly draped itself as it tumbled down toward the back of the house.

"You're up!" Rodney said, hitting his friend on the back.

Still feeling uneasy, Miles reluctantly chucked the roll toward the large oak tree. It soared through the air, snapping several brittle branches on its descent, before unrolling on top of the house.

"Someone is going to see us, dude!" Miles barked, nervously looking around.

Dramatically, Rodney dropped his arms to his sides and turned around. This side of the neighborhood lay still, without a single soul in sight. The only thing catching their eyes was a faded yellow station wagon parked across the street. Rodney raised his arms as if to say *"What the fuck are you on about?"* before once more, rummaging through his endless bag of tricks.

"I know I brought it . . . " Rodney remarked under

his breath.

It was at this moment that the light on the front porch came to life.

"Shit! Get down!" Miles whispered, dropping to the ground.

In a matter of seconds, the duo were sprawled out on the ground, like soldiers attempting to avoid shrapnel from a hand grenade. For as long as Miles could remember, he had personally never seen any sign of life at the house and the mere illumination of the porch light was enough to make every ounce of blood in his body run cold.

"Did anyone see us?" Rodney asked, attempting to hold back a snickering fit.

"I don't know!" replied Miles, attempting to peer through the dense weeds without being seen.

Creaking hinges echoed throughout the night as the front door opened. A tall man exited the house, stopping in place on the front porch. From his position, Miles could only make out minimal details. Old and sickly, the man began to pace back and forth, his large footsteps causing the wooden floorboards to cry out with each step.

"Who's out here?" the low and raspy voice called out from the porch.

Although this was enough to shake Miles to his core, Rodney only struggled to hold in his laughter.

"Holy shit, it's Alan —*fucking*— Brecker!" he snickered.

"*Shhh!*" Miles hissed, hitting Rodney on the arm.

"I KNOW YER OUT HERE!" Alan shouted from the porch, his tone much more aggressive than before.

"LEAVE US BE, OR THERE'LL BE FUCKIN' HELL TO PAY!"

Rodney slowly began rolling side to side, using every ounce of willpower not to burst out in laughter. After scanning the property for what felt like an eternity, Alan turned around and walked back into his dilapidated home, the rusty hinges crying out once more as the front door violently slammed shut. Rodney was the first to peek his head above the tall weeds.

"Stay down for a second!"

"Holy shit," Miles scoffed, trying to slow his heartbeat.

"Leave us be!" mocked Rodney as he began to rummage around in his backpack frantically.

"That's enough, dude!" Miles exclaimed, clearly frustrated.

"Oh come on Miles, it's just some grumpy old geezer!" Rodney protested. Rolling his eyes, Miles stood up and began to walk away.

"Alright, alright!" scoffed Rodney as he stood. Miles turned back around to face his friend.

"One last thing!"

"For Christ's sake man!"

Rodney slid his mask up to the top of his head, revealing his red, sweaty face.

"Last thing, I promise!"

Miles interlocked his fingers above his head and groaned. A shit-eating grin spread across Rodney's face from ear to ear as he reached into his pocket. After sifting around for a moment, he extended his closed fist toward Miles.

"Heads or tails?"

"What?"

"Heads or tails?"

"I don't know . . . "

"Come on, don't be a bitch!"

"Fucking hell, dude! Fine! Heads?"

Rodney quickly flipped the quarter into the air. It spun multiple times before landing in the center of Rodney's sweaty palm. He quickly slammed it down onto the backside of his left hand and looked up at Miles . . .

"That makes me tails." Rodney said as he turned around and looked at the house.

"Alright, loser has to go ding-dong-ditch that crabby old sonuvabitch!"

"Are you kidding me?" said Miles.

"Nope! Now remember, the coin flip is sacred!"

Rodney confidently looked Miles in the eye as he lifted his hand revealing: *heads*. The color in Rodney's face quickly drained as he looked back up toward the house in disbelief.

"Best two out of three?"

"No, sir!" Miles chuckled, feeling a rush of relief wash over him.

"That's bullshit!" shouted Rodney.

"Like you said man, coin flips are sacred," Miles said sarcastically, raising his hands up in front of him.

Rodney bit his lip as he looked at the empty porch. Like an angry child not getting their way, he scowled at Miles before running full speed toward the house. Despite his large stature, Miles was surprised by just how fast he was. Clearing the front lawn in a matter of seconds, he was already face-to-face with the front door. Stopping in place, he turned back toward Miles. They locked eyes for a moment as Rodney slowly rose up his middle finger and smiled at him. As he turned back around to face the front door, he felt a drip of sweat travel down the back of his neck. He would never admit it to Miles, but he too was nervous. Rodney raised his hand and inched it toward the doorbell. After a brief moment of hesitation, he pressed the small button and hightailed it off the porch, dropping into the weeds out of sight. Miles following suit.

The chime of the doorbell rang like a church bell throughout the entire yard. Not even a second after their bodies made contact with the ground, the rusted hinges of the front door cried out again and the front door aggressively swung open. Like a charging bull, Alan Brecker barged down the steps and onto the front lawn. Attempting to stay as still as possible, Miles held his breath.

"I WARNED YA!" Alan shouted.

Miles scanned the horizon as best he could, but no matter how hard he tried, he couldn't see Rodney. Trying to see through the dense weeds proved nigh impossible. It was at this moment that Miles heard the most ungodly yell imaginable. Sounding like a deranged Spartan warrior, Alan Brecker began jumping up and down, pointing at the ground beneath him.

"I FOUND YA! I FOUND YA!" he screamed over and over.

"We were just messing around, sir!" Rodney's voice shouted back in a much higher pitch than Miles had ever heard before.

"YER DONE!" shouted Alan.

"MILES!" Rodney yelled.

Frozen in fear, all Miles could do was lay there and watch. His body felt like lead, weighing him down into the ground. Alan quickly raised his foot into the air and slammed it down on what Miles could only assume was Rodney's head. Rodney briefly whimpered in pain as an unsettling crunching sound echoed throughout the yard. The violent, senseless act caused Miles' heart to drop into his stomach. Eyes wide, he lay still, completely silent. Alan looked around slowly, ensuring the coast was clear, before kneeling down to pick Rodney up. Despite his scrawny arms and sickly appearance, he was very strong, effortlessly throwing Rodney over his shoulder like a bag of mulch. Blood poured from Rodney's head and onto the lawn as Alan began his way back toward the porch. Rodney's unconscious body flailed about, bleeding onto his shoulders as Alan once again violently slammed the front door shut behind him.

Struggling to comprehend what the hell had just happened, Miles continued to lie in the weeds, on the verge of a panic attack. Despite his mind being a million lightyears away, his body began to rise as if in complete auto-pilot and began making its way toward the front porch. Looking down at the large pool of blood where Rodney once lay, Miles felt queasy. No matter how hard he tried to concentrate, a million thoughts raced through his mind. Every fiber of his being told him to go inside and save his friend, but with a head stomp like that was he even still alive? He could run home and call the cops, right? Surely, they would be better equipped to help? Then again, what if they didn't believe him? Would they arrest him? They had just spent the better part of the night vandalizing the house after all. *Fuck, fuck, fuck.*

Staring at the pool of blood on the ground, Miles raked his fingers through his hair, before throwing the cheap clown mask off his head and onto the ground. No matter how scared he was, no matter how badly he wanted to leave, he knew he couldn't. As if a spectator watching his own body from a distance, he found himself racing up the stairs toward the front door. As he came face to face with the splintered wooden door, he could feel his heartbeat pulsating through his ears. Holding his breath, he grabbed the door handle and turned it, which to his surprise was unlocked. The cry of rusted hinges sent a cold shiver down his spine and caused every hair on his neck to stand up. Immediately, the smell of rotting meat assaulted his nostrils, like a punch to the face. Fighting the urge to vomit, he observed through teary eyes a small lamp illuminating a long, dark hallway. The floor of the home was hidden by mounds of trash, leaves, and fresh spots of crimson blood.

Slipping inside as quietly as possible, Miles followed the trail of blood beneath him. The house was mostly silent, apart from the faint echo of what sounded like wind howling through an open window. Somehow, the inside of the home was even worse than the outside. As he made his way deeper inside the house, the floorboards beneath him began to cry out with each footstep, making him tenser than he had ever been in his entire life. Yet before he knew it, Miles was at the end of the hallway, nothing more than peeling wallpaper there to greet him. The trail of blood ended abruptly without any indication of where it could have gone next.

Kneeling down, Miles began sifting his hand around on the floor until he felt something familiar—Rodney's backpack. He felt his heart skip a beat, knowing his friend was close by. Continuing to sift his hands around on the ground, he felt a ring-like loop catch around his finger. As he lifted up, a cold breeze and dark tunnel greeted him. As his adrenaline rush began to wane, Miles felt his body tensing up yet again. Turning his head around, he looked at the front door. It practically shined like a beacon in this sea of darkness. Taunting him from a distance, practically calling his name, he used every ounce of willpower to ignore it and descend downward.

As his eyes began to adjust to the darkness, he found himself in a narrow, hand-dug tunnel. Dirt walls faded into a dirt ceiling which stretched on for a hundred feet. Moving forward into the unknown, he felt like a tunnel rat during the Vietnam war—death lurking around every corner. By the time Miles reached the end of the tunnel, the ceiling hung so low, he was crawling on his stomach and in front of him, was a small, blue door. Inching up to the door, he turned his head and placed his ear against it. After listening for a few moments, there was nothing but silence on the other end. Slowly, he pushed on the door, which squeaked open, blowing more frigid air and nauseating smells into his face.

Unlike the dark tunnel he had just crawled through, this room was bright and vast. The walls were painted in a bright baby-blue color and had several candles mounted on it, providing some much needed illumination. In every corner of the room, large mounds of children's toys sat, each stacked several feet high; teddy bears, wooden blocks, and dolls were some of the few he could make out among the hundreds, maybe thousands, of toys sprung about the room. Rising to his feet, Miles began to walk toward the center of the room, where an unusually large rocking chair sat.

Upright with its legs crossed, as if elegantly propped, a brittle skeleton sat, sporting a large diamond necklace. Although Miles had never seen a real skeleton, he could immediately differentiate between this and a prop from the local Halloween store.

"Rodney?" Miles whispered as quietly as he could, his voice trembling.

Silence greeted him yet again as he continued to pace around the large room. Miles approached a small dresser in the far corner of the room which had various picture frames sitting atop. The first black and white photo featured a man holding hands with a beautiful woman, which he assumed to be Rebecca Brecker. Luscious blonde hair, a bright white smile and wearing a very familiar diamond necklace around her neck, she stood, practically lighting up the frame. Upon deeper inspection, Miles realized the man in the photo was none other than Alan Brecker. Except here he was quite handsome, with thick wavy hair, muscular physique, and cunning smile. They looked as normal as any couple you might pass on the street—hell, maybe even nicer.

In the next photo, a very pregnant Rebecca stood, front and center. Holding her from behind was Alan, a large smile across his face. As Miles turned his gaze to the last photo, he did not expect it to be one of the most disturbing things he had ever seen in his life, yet that's exactly what it was. Rebecca sat in the rocking chair, Alan was not in the photo, but she was not alone. Rebecca was holding *something*. Extremely elongated and sporting multiple contusions along its frail body, a disfigured child sat draped across its mother's arms like a wet towel. It had no eyes, snake-like slits where a nose should be, and absolutely zero distinguishing facial features. They both faced the camera, emotionless. Its elongated limbs were flaccid and hung down to its side like soggy noodles. The longer Miles stared at the photo, the more unsettling features he noticed. Yet, no matter how hard he tried to look away, he couldn't help but stare. After what felt like an eternity, a faint rustling sound across the room finally broke his gaze.

"Miles?" a faint voice cried out from the corner of the room.

Cautiously, Miles made his way toward the voice. As he looked down, he noticed another faint blood trail, leading into the large pile of toys. The closer he got, the more he realized this was the source of the putrid smell.

"Rodney?" Miles choked, holding his breath,

"Help me . . . "

Although every fiber of his being told him not to, Miles reached into the mountain of toys. Sifting through various soft, slimy, and rigid things alike, he felt an ankle.

"I've got you, man!" Miles exclaimed.

As he pulled back, he was surprised by just how light Rodney was. Now standing a couple feet away from the pile, Miles opened his eyes. His mouth dropped open in horror. A mangled, decomposing leg of a child sat in his hand. Although it had fought a good fight, this was his stomach's official breaking point. Throwing the leg as far away from him as possible, Miles hurled onto the stained carpet. After taking a moment to collect himself, he continued to viciously pull apart at the mountain of toys. After sifting through what felt like an endless supply of blood-stained toys, feces, and severed body parts in various stages of decomposition, he finally saw his friend.

Feeling a rush of relief wash over him, Miles began throwing mounds of junk to the side, finally revealing Rodney's bloody arm. Grabbing it, he pulled Rodney out of the pile as fast as possible. Rodney moaned weakly as he collapsed to the ground, clearly fatigued from the loss of blood due to the large gash on his forehead. Miles knelt down and placed his arm on Rodney's shoulder.

"Rodney, can you hear—"

Quickly grabbing Miles' arm, Rodney shook like a scared dog.

"Keep your voice down . . . " he whispered, raising a shaky finger toward one of the toy piles across the room.

"What are you—"

A loud voice echoed throughout the room, cutting Miles off.

"JUNIOR!" Alan Brecker's gravely voice shouted. Although he was not in the room with them, he sounded close—close enough for Miles' fight or flight reflexes to kick in.

Grabbing Rodney under his shoulders, Miles pulled as hard as he could, back-peddling across the room toward the blue door. As Alan's footsteps grew louder, Miles realized they would easily be spotted out in the open. Without many places to hide, Miles pushed Rodney behind the closest toy pile and quickly hid behind him.

Across the room, a hidden door slid open and Alan Brecker entered the room.

"Ya finish yer supper, boy?"

The room was silent.

"JUNIOR?" Alan screamed, scanning the room. As Miles followed his gaze, it landed on the pile of toys Rodney had pointed to mere moments ago. He felt his blood run cold as the mound of toys began to shift and something slithered out. The child from the photo revealed itself. While it was now much larger than the photo, there was no denying it was the same one. It slowly made its way toward Alan, like a slug, its slimy skin leaving a mucus-like residue behind it. Utterly disgusted and completely terrified, Miles watched on in horror.

"Ya need to stop playing with ya food, boy!" Alan chuckled, watching his son slowly slither by him toward the large toy pile where Rodney once was.

Unable to use its deformed hands, the creature resorted to using its large head to slowly sift through the junk. Alan crossed his arms and watched like a proud parent marveling at their child's accomplishments. After sifting through the pile for a moment, the creature stopped, looked down, and began to whimper.

"What's wrong, Junior?" Alan asked, slowly kneeling down in front of the pile.

"Isn't that where ya left him?"

The creature continued to make guttural noises as Alan began to sift through the pile himself. He began to dig faster.

"DAMN IT!" Alan shouted as he jumped up, darting his eyes around the room.

"ASK YER MOTHER WHERE HE WENT!" Alan shouted, pointing at the rocking chair.

Even without eyes, the creature looked directly at the chair in the center of the room. It stared for a few moments before diverting its attention back toward its father.

"He's here, Junior. We'll find him!" Alan shouted.

Slowly, the creature began to slither toward its father.

"I said we'll find him, boy!"

As he began backing away, it wasn't long before Alan's back was flat against the wall, leaving him nowhere to go.

"Back away, Junior!" Alan shouted as the creature continued to advance. Alan grabbed a baseball bat from the toy pile next to him and raised it high, ready to defend himself. The creature began to arch its back, rising high like a viper ready to strike.

"I SAID BACK AWAY, JUNIOR!" Alan shouted once more, his voice echoing throughout the room.

Realizing it was now or never, Miles reached under Rodney's shoulders, squatted down, and began to back-pedal toward the exit.

As the creature lunged forward to strike its father, Alan hit it square across the face with the bat, causing it to turn its head and whimper.

"I TOLD YA, JUNIOR! YA ONLY EAT WHAT I BRING!"

Pulling the blue door open as quietly as possible, Miles couldn't help but turn his head to watch the chaos unfolding across the room. The creature turned its head back toward its father and, without a moment of hesitation, lunged at him, enclosing its large mouth around his head. Alan Brecker's muffled screams echoed throughout the room as the creature effortlessly lifted Alan into the air and began to slam him down onto the ground over and over. The sound of Alan's bones cracking repeatedly echoed throughout the room as he writhed in pain. Unable to even gasp, Miles helped Rodney squeeze through the narrow doorway. As Miles pulled the door shut, the hinges whined.

Looking up, Miles noticed the creature no longer had its back turned to them, but was instead facing them directly. Although unable to see them, it was still aware of their presence. It continued to stare in their direction, its face covered in blood and Alan's lifeless body hanging out of its mouth like a rotten banana peel. As slowly as he could, Miles grabbed the handle and began to pull the door toward him. Right as the door was halfway closed, the hinges let out a faint whine. *Of fucking course.* Biting his tongue, Miles closed his eyes for a moment, hoping it hadn't noticed. Immediately, the creature tilted its large head to the side like a curious dog. The severed muscles and tendons that once held Alan Brecker's head to his frail body began to snap one by one and, like a wet sponge, Alan's lifeless husk splattered onto the ground. Letting out a loud screech, the creature slithered across the room toward Miles. Despite its odd appearance and many deformities, it moved faster than anything Miles had ever seen.

"RODNEY, GO!" Miles shouted, slamming the door shut and bracing it with his leg.

With blood still pouring from his head and fighting to stay conscious, Rodney began to crawl down the tunnel. The door violently shook as the creature let out visceral screams. Pulling with all his might, Miles looked behind him. To his surprise, Rodney was almost to the end of the tunnel and was waving him to follow.

"COME ON!" Rodney's shaky voice echoed.

Miles knew he had to let go of the handle. He closed his eyes and braced himself.

One . . .

Two . . .

THREE!

As he let go, the frail door ripped open with such force that the walls shook. Miles spun around and began to crawl forward as fast as he could, not daring to look back. Screeching as it slithered behind him, the creature grew louder and louder. Like a rat in a snake's den, Miles gave it everything he had. He knew if he stopped he was dead. Pushing through both physical and mental exhaustion, Miles began to crawl up the wooden staircase.

"The door!" Miles shouted as he turned around, pointing at the trapdoor leaning against the wall.

Grabbing each corner, Miles and Rodney slammed the trapdoor down. Before it could latch, however, the creature's head stuck up between the trapdoor and the floorboards.

"SHIT!" Rodney shouted, practically collapsing onto the trapdoor in an attempt to weigh it down. Miles joined him, hoping their combined weight would shut the door or decapitate the abomination—or both. No dice. The creature continued to screech as it wiggled up and down, causing the trapdoor to slam up and down like a mechanical bull. They both knew it was only a matter of time before the creature overpowered them.

"Miles, I need you to hold the door down!" Rodney slurred, evidently fighting to stay awake.

"What?"

Rodney crawled off the trapdoor toward his backpack, laying a few feet away. Despite giving it all he could, Miles was losing the battle and the creature was moments from escaping. Closing his eyes and bracing for the worst, Miles continued to push down with all of his might. Not a moment too soon, Rodney staggered back next to him, kneeled forward and began stabbing the creature in the face with his pocket knife repeatedly. Blood gushed out and was flung about as the small blade slid in and out of the creature's face. Howling in pain, the creature quickly began to slither backward. The duo's combined weight caused the trapdoor to violently slam shut.

As Miles slid the thick deadbolt shut, the two friends collapsed in exhaustion with their backs against the wall. Sitting in silence, neither of them knew what to say or how to comprehend what the hell had just happened.

As they sat there, trying to catch their breath, they looked at each other. Although they were alive, the look in both of their eyes all but confirmed that they would never forget this nightmare. At least one positive thing came to light as Miles sat lost in thought—Halloween had officially outstayed its welcome and he was finally at peace with the idea of growing up.

ECHOES OF TERROR
Nadine Stewart

HELP! HELP!" I CRIED OUT, pounding my fists against the window of my family's yellow station wagon as my chest heaved with panic.

Tears streamed down my face as I frantically searched for any sign of my parents and siblings . . . anyone for that matter. I had found myself lost and alone in the wide-open field, home to the overflow parking lot for the amusement park. Hundreds of cars lay still with not another soul in sight. The park was closing, the music and rides were winding down, and I could hear the lyrics to Tiffany's "I Think We're Alone Now" drifting out from the fairway, but where was everyone?

"Mom? Dad?" I yelled into the warm breeze of the starry summer night. The smell of sugary treats and popcorn lingered in the air. "Help! Please! Anyone?" I whimpered as I watched the monsters crest the hill in the distance under the silver light from the full moon.

This can't be happening again . . . this isn't real.

But it was happening and they were getting closer. All of them. They were all here. The Wolfman, Frankenstein's Monster, the Mummy, the Creature from the Black Lagoon, and every single cartoon villain from Scooby-Doo. Leading the charge was Count Dracula himself, larger than life and growing in size as the hoard stampeded down the hillside. Even his fangs, dripping with blood, seemed to lengthen as the moonlight glinted off them. Sweat was beading across my forehead as I stood frozen and trembling with my back pressed up against the side of the car, the metal—still hot from the relentless heat earlier in the day—now burning my exposed shoulders. Gaining ground, the creatures were getting closer . . . almost upon me now. I opened my mouth to scream, but I suddenly had no voice. Throwing my arms over my face, I cowered as I waited for what would come next . . .

~

Jenny's eyes snapped open as she gasped for breath. She lay there paralyzed and disoriented; the light from the day had turned to dusk and her room was flooded with shadows making it difficult to tell what time it was. Her body was wracked with sweat, she could feel her acid-washed jeans sticking to her thighs, and her Bon Jovi concert tee was drenched, clinging to her sticky back. Her heart was racing, and it felt like someone had reached their hand into her chest and was squeezing her heart with an iron grip. Unable to move her limbs, Jenny lay staring at her ceiling. The fresh-faced images from the posters above her bed started to come into focus. The New Kids on the Block eventually calmed her till she was finally able to pull herself up to the edge of the bed. A wave of nauseating dizziness washed over her, threatening to make her dry heave.

Even after all the times she had suffered the same nightmare, it still amazed Jenny that each time was just as terrifying as the first.

She must have fallen asleep while trying to get her homework done after school. The red glowing numbers from her alarm clock indicated it was 5:05 p.m. Tonight was Halloween and her mom was adamant she wouldn't be allowed to go out with her friends if her room wasn't clean and her homework finished. Jenny, still weak from the waning adrenaline rush, struggled to remove her sweaty clothes. She stumbled out of them, trying to untangle her pant legs as she made her way to the Jack and Jill bathroom she shared with Andrea, her younger sister. She could hear her sister and her friends giggling on the other side of the door and yelled for them to get out because she was coming in whether they liked it or not. As Jenny opened her sliding door, she caught sight of Andrea's shadow passing through at the other end of the bathroom.

"Aren't you going to shut your door?" she yelled at her sister.

With no answer, Jenny peeked her head around the door ready to voice her frustrations. But there was no one there. She could have sworn she heard half a dozen girls in here just moments before. Everything was still and eerily quiet. So quiet you could hear a pin drop. The silence was broken by a ringing in her ears; a quiet humming that intensified into an ear-splitting white noise. She clasped her hands over her ears and shut her eyes tightly as she sunk down the wall onto the cold floor tiles.

~

My mouth formed the words, but no sound escaped my lips.

"Mom? Aunty?" I mimed, my hands pawing at my throat desperate to get their attention.

I was standing in our living room looking down the hall. Illuminated like a light at the end of a tunnel, I watched my mom and aunt sitting at the small 1950s-style kitchen table gabbing away to each other as usual. Looking over my shoulder, I watched as a black, leather-gloved hand slowly emerged from behind Dad's medieval wall tapestry.

Oh no, not again.

Trembling, I turned to call out for my mom once more as the gloved hand wrapped itself around the handle of Dad's replica spiked ball and chain flail also hanging on the wall. (You'd think we lived in a decrepit old castle and it was Halloween every day with all of Dad's theatrical hobbies . . . instead they just gave me nightmares).

As the hand reached toward me, I turned back to the doorway leading to the hall. I started running. I ran faster than I ever thought was possible but there was only one problem, I wasn't moving. No matter how fast I tried to run, I wasn't gaining any ground, I was running in place as if stuck on a treadmill. Stuck with a giant menacing hand and arm extending toward me. Unable to speak or scream and stuck in the same spot, I looked back once more; it was closing in on me now, stretching open its hand ready to grab me. At that very moment, as if time unfroze and sped up, I reached the kitchen table just as I felt the gloved hand graze the back of my neck, and just as . . . the doorbell rang . . .

~

The doorbell was ringing. Jenny could hear its muffled tones echoing through the house as she swung her legs over the side of the bed and let out a pained moan. Why did her legs ache as if she had just finished running ten laps of the track in P.E. class? The scars on her legs weren't as visible in this light but she knew they were there, the pain reminding her of what she and her family had gone through last Halloween, how hard her injuries had been for everyone to deal with.

Ding-dong . . . Ding-dong . . .

Jenny's eyes fixed upon the clock on her nightstand. 6:06 p.m. Trick-or-treaters? But how did she end up back in her bed? The last thing she remembered was peeling off her sweat-drenched clothes and cussing out her sister but here she was waking up from another recurring nightmare in the same clothes she was wearing earlier. Jenny stumbled to her feet, letting out a painful moan as she tried to will her aching legs to move and wiping the sleep from her eyes. She felt groggy and lethargic like she had when she had woken up from her surgery after the accident.

Ding-dong . . . Ding-dong . . . the doorbell chimed again.

Where is everyone? Jenny wondered to herself as she made her way down the hall, but something about the doorbell chime seemed off. It sounded like it was far away or warbled how her baby brother's Teddy Ruxpin doll sounded when the batteries started to die.

From the top of the landing, Jenny heard the big, old front door creak open and made out the sound of brief, indistinct chatter before the solid wooden door thudded closed again as she made her way downstairs. When she reached the foyer, she smelled her mother's Dior Poison perfume lingering in the air and saw the kitchen saloon-style doors swinging on their hinges. A large bowl of candy with a fake severed hand poking out of it sat on the console table next to the door. Just as Jenny was about to swipe a pack of candy cigarettes from the bowl the doorbell rang again. She grabbed a handful of candy, prepared to drop it in the pillowcase of some little ghost or witch, but when Jenny opened the door, no one was there. She stuck her head out onto the porch, but the night was still and silent and not a person was in sight. The only thing she could hear was some loud music buzzing through the night air from somewhere in the neighborhood.

Well, that's weird, she thought as she deposited the handful of candy in the pocket of her jeans rather than back in the bowl.

"Mom?" Jenny called as she turned back to the kitchen door. "Mom, can I go meet up with my friends now?" She pushed through the swinging doors expecting to see her mom pulling the mummy dogs out of the oven that she made for dinner every Halloween. But other than some dirty dishes soaking in the sink, there was no sign of her mom.

Ding-dong . . .

"I got it!" Jenny yelled. Within seconds, she was at the door, opening it quickly. She looked out at the empty porch, confused.

What the?

"Hello?" she called out. She could hear faint shuffling coming from the driveway but nobody was there.

"I know someone's out here! Stop messing around!" she yelled into the empty night.

Something wasn't right. Pike Street should be packed with trick-or-treaters by this time of the night, but the neighborhood was dead quiet. The only sounds were the low eerie whistle of the wind gently blowing and rustling the dry leaves in the oak trees lining the edge of their property and the gentle, distant bass of music still filling the air. Maybe her clock was wrong, maybe she had slept later than she thought and now it was just the dumb teenage boys from school playing Ding-Dong Ditch while egging the rundown, creepy house across the street. She closed the front door . . .

Ding-dong . . .

Mad now, Jenny whipped open the door only to be confronted with an empty porch once again.

Impossible!

Now she was starting to freak out. Closing and locking the door as fast as she could, Jenny backed up slowly, fear starting to grip her senses. Her white slouch socks caught on the edge of the rug covering the hardwood floors and she fell back landing on her butt.

Ding-dong . . . Ding-dong . . . Ding-dong . . . Ding-dong . . . Ding-dong . . . Ding-dong . . .

"Go away!" Jenny yelled as she shoved her hands over her ears.

Ding-dong . . . Ding-dong . . . Ding-dong . . .

Her ears started to ring, and the foyer started to spin before . . .

Ding-dong . . .

~

I loved to play hide and seek in the clothing aisles at Kmart while my mom took forever to pick through the sales racks. We didn't have a Kmart near where we lived so we had to drive about two hours across state lines and always made a day trip out of it. Not much had changed as I got older, except now I just hid in the magazine aisle flipping through the latest issues of Tiger Beat, YM, or Super Teen to see which ones had the best celebrity posters. But today was different. The store was dark, and I was outside standing in the middle of the parking lot looking in. I could see myself inside the store. I was younger, maybe five or six, my hair in pigtails, and my face and little hands were pressed up against the department store window with tears streaming down my face. I looked to my left and watched as my parents loaded my sister into the back of our big, yellow, station wagon and started to drive away.

"Wait," I called, waving my arms, trying to get their attention, but they were already leaving the parking lot.

Turning back, I was now standing at the doors to the store yanking and wrenching on them but they were locked up tight. I tried to get the attention of the employees walking to their cars, but no one could see or hear me. The younger me just stood staring back at me with big tear-filled, sad eyes.

"It's okay, they'll come back for you," I whispered, placing my hand against the cold glass of the window.

The scene before me started to fade as I was sucked backward away from the store, my hand still reaching out toward the younger me.

~

Why would they forget me?

Ding-dong . . .

Jenny woke once again in her bed, this time with silent tears trailing her cheeks. Wiping her eyes on her shirt she read the clock, 7:07 p.m.

Ding-dong . . .

She heard a stampede of little feet run past her door and down the stairs with a *thud, thud, thud, thud, thud.* Her brothers sounded like a herd of elephants running through the house. How two young boys could make so much noise she'd never understand. She also didn't understand why she was waking up over and over from the recurring nightmares that had haunted her for as long as she could remember. Or how she ended up back in her bed time and time again.

Jenny took a step toward her bedroom door, she floated across the floor as if being pushed forward by an unseen force. She felt like she was standing still and the house was moving around her. The hallway zipped past on either side of her like going eighty miles an hour on the freeway. The stairs carried her down like the escalator at the mall, depositing her at the front door.

Ding-dong . . .

A rush of cold air washed over Jenny and sent shivers up her spine as the front door opened on its own. She could swear she heard people talking—a quiet, mumbling, chitter-chatter—but the porch and driveway remained empty. She could still faintly hear the thrumming bass of music reminding her of the party she was supposed to be at with her friends.

"Mom? Dad? Where is everyone?"

Out of the corner of her eye, she caught two small shadows running past as they ducked into the family room before she heard the familiar giggles of her brothers as they rough-housed with each other.

Jenny followed after them.

"Hey guys, where is Mom and Da—", she shook her head and spun on her heel as she entered the room taking in her surroundings. Her brothers were nowhere to be seen.

That's weird, she thought.

Looking around, she noticed the clock on the mantle read 8:08 p.m. Approaching the fireplace to get a better look, Jenny found things were out of place. There were always family photos and various knick-knacks her mother collected lining the mantle on either side of the brass clock. But now on the left side of the clock was one family photo that had been taken at the local Sears with her aunts, uncles, and cousins a few years back, and next to that was a smaller framed photo of her family standing in the driveway of their house. At least it looked like their house . . . only it had a fresh coat of bright yellow paint. Mom and Dad had been arguing for the last two years about repainting the house but they either couldn't find the time or settle on a color so they had never gotten around to it.

Confused, Jenny scrutinized the photo further. The

large cast-iron address number 17 were prominently displayed on the siding that framed the garage door and were visible over her mother's left shoulder. Jenny felt the hair on the back of her neck prick up as her eyes wandered to the rest of the photo. There was her mom and dad, who looked tired but the same. Dad may have had a few more gray hairs than Jenny remembered, but she admitted to herself she hadn't paid much attention to her family recently other than to ask to borrow the car or hurry through meals to get back to homework and talking on the phone to her friends. Andrea's hair was cut into a short bob, and she had bangs that Jenny had never seen her sister have before. Her brothers were a bit taller than they should be. Come to think of it, everyone looked older than they should be. And where was she? Jenny was noticeably absent from this family photo.

Goosebumps rose on her arms, and a heavy weight settled in her chest. Jenny took a step back as her eyes settled on the large brass urn on the other side of the clock. Reading the inscription, she gasped and felt her stomach turn as the room began to spin . . .

"In Loving Memory of our beautiful daughter Jenny."

Smaller font at the bottom read: *"If tears could build a stairway and memories a lane. I'd walk right up to heaven and bring you home again."*

The date etched on the front was one year ago, the night of her accident.

Jenny felt bile rising in her throat as she wrapped her arms around herself and slowly stepped back from the fireplace in a daze.

Vroom-vroom . . .

A loud, steady rumble broke through the fog that froze Jenny in place. Her waking nightmare was interrupted by the sound of the family station wagon's engine roaring to life. Running to the garage door, still hoping this was all an elaborate Halloween prank, Jenny tried without success to turn the knob. She used both hands to tug, twist, and pull at the door with no luck. Screaming and crying in a panic, Jenny yelled out for her family.

"Mom? Dad? Anybody!"

She slapped the door over and over with one hand as she continued to jiggle and jostle the doorknob.

"Please, wait!" she cried, starting to hyperventilate.

She could hear car doors opening and closing and the engine revving. Jenny braced her foot against the wall to use as leverage as she wrenched on the door one more time; at last, it flew open, nearly knocking her to the ground. She tried to catch a glimpse of her family and get their attention but was immediately blinded as the station wagon's headlights flicked on. Shielding her eyes with her hands, Jenny tried to reach the car, to get in, to go with them, but her feet had become cemented to the garage floor. She reached out toward the car, crying and begging for them to wait. Her ears started to ring as the station wagon was enveloped in a shroud of exhaust, illuminated from the headlights and the outside flood lights on the front of the garage.

"Please don't leave me behind!" she wailed.

The faded yellow station wagon was gone, sucked back out into the night leaving only a swirling fog of exhaust in its path.

~

Jenny's eyes snapped open as she gasped for breath. She lay there in her bed, paralyzed and disoriented as the light from the day waned. She felt sticky and sweaty; she could feel her acid-washed jeans sticking to her legs and her Bon Jovi concert tee clinging to her back. Her heart was racing, and it felt like it would burst out of her chest.

Just another nightmare, she thought to herself. The clock on her dresser read 5:05 p.m.

Ding-dong . . . Ding-dong . . .

OLD MAN JACOBS AND
THE KITCHEN CABINET

Jason A. Jones

OLD MAN JACOBS SAT ON his porch at the 18th house on Pike St., a dangling bulb flickering in and out next to a strip of fly paper, covered from top to bottom with lifeless forms of small, flying insects, did little to allow passersby to notice him. His fingers fiddled with a lit cigarette, taking a drag every few seconds. He knew that soon there would be a swarm of brats from the other houses in the neighborhood choking the life out of the peace he was enjoying, rocking back and forth in his chair. It was Halloween night and he trembled in his red and black flannel as he looked out at the street, knowing damn well he wouldn't be giving away any candy, the same as the last twenty years. He eyeballed two kids, suspiciously, as they walked by, a gnarled hand tightly gripping the armrest of his rocking chair. Directly across the street, behind the big, iron gate, was what sounded like a party going on. He couldn't be sure because of the huge bushes surrounding the house, but it sure as hell sounded like it.

"Damn kids. Two full hours of this Halloween shit," he mouthed silently under his breath which erupted into a coughing fit. After stomping out the cigarette under his boot, he got up and went back inside. He flipped off the outside porch light, wandered over to the fridge, and pulled out a can of beer. He popped the tab and sent some suds down his gullet while walking to his red recliner in the living room. Danny Jacobs sat down and turned on the lamp beside him. He picked up the TV Guide and thumbed through a few pages trying to find something good to watch. He ended up settling on an episode of *Magnum P.I.* after flipping through the four or five channels he had to choose from on his twenty inch black and white television.

During a commercial break, Danny grabbed himself another beer and happened to look out the kitchen window, noticing red and orange leaves spinning about at the feet of the trick-or-treaters trudging along the sidewalk. He shivered and thought about the coming winter and was glad he'd collected enough wood for his fireplace when—

There was a small rapping sound at his front door.

He stood still, his feet planted firmly to the floor, hoping whoever was at the door would go away. After a few minutes, he slowly approached the door and peered out from the blinds. He noticed a faint orange glow on his porch and knew instantly what it was.

A jack-o'-lantern. A rotting one at that.

What the hell?

"Nope, not in the mood," he hissed through his teeth. He opened the door and looked down. The jack-o'-lantern had the classic face carved into it: the triangle eyes, nose, and sharp teeth on the mouth of it. Splotches of mold covered most of the pumpkin and as he continued to gaze at the orange orb, the grin seemed to widen. With one swift move, he kicked it from the porch, out onto the sidewalk where it exploded into pieces, the small flame on the candle fading out.

"Hey! Watch what you're doing, old man!" a pimply-faced teenager roared as he dodged the oncoming assault. He continued walking as Old Man Jacobs slammed the door, flipping his middle finger. He walked back to his chair and sat down, beer in hand. On the TV screen, Thomas Magnum was running away from two Dobermans, Zeus and Apollo, while Jonathan Higgins' laughed maniacally.

Thirty minutes later, with trick-or-treating in full swing, Old Man Jacobs, again, heard a small tapping sound on his door. He tried desperately to ignore it but it kept getting louder and louder, the tapping, violently pulsating in his ears. Finally, he blew out the remaining smoke in his lungs, smashed a cigarette in the ashtray, and mumbled obscenities as he walked toward his front door.

He opened it to a small boy, carrying a large pillowcase, blood seeping from the bottom of it; Danny didn't pay any attention.

The child was dressed as Frankenstein's Monster, complete with plastic mask and vinyl smock tied around his back and neck. On the front of the costume was a cartoonish image of the monster, arms and hands extended outward. The boy's head was tilted to one side. He stood there, hands down at his side, the pillowcase still in hand.

"Can't you see my light's out, boy? I don't have nothin' for ya. Get off my porch!" Danny demanded as he looked down on the child, one hand beginning to ball into a fist. The trick-or-treater said nothing.

"Are you deaf, son? Where's your mom and dad?" Behind the mask, the boy's eyes were sunken in and bloodshot. A sudden chill went up Danny's spine and settled into his neck. He lifted his balled hand and rubbed the coldness out of it.

"If I getcha something, will you skedaddle?" Danny asked, his voice slightly quavering.

The kid continued to stand there, head tilted, giving Old Man Jacobs the creeps.

"Hold on, I'll be right back."

Danny stepped inside and frantically looked around the kitchen. He was tired of asking questions, tired of the disruption, and tired of all the rotten kids in his neighborhood. He needed to get something and get it quick so the little shit would leave. After rummaging through a few drawers and looking in his cabinets and staying clear of the padlocked cabinet, Danny found a bruised apple in a bowl on his countertop. He snagged it quickly, opened the door and stopped dead in his tracks.

The boy was sitting on his knees, head bent down, staring at the orange gore splattered in front of him.

A sickening feeling came over Danny when he looked at the back of the boy's head. The fruit fell from his hand and rolled near the edge of the porch.

The child's head was caved in, maggots writhing around the bleeding flesh.

"You didn't like my gift?" he whispered into nothing. Muffled sobs emanated from behind the Frankenstein mask as the small boy smashed seeds and pulp. His hands slammed into the concrete, hot red liquid spilling from his knuckles.

Danny cursed and shut the door with a *thud* and locked it. The boy could be heard beyond the door, sobs turning to laughter. A few moments went by and Danny peered through the blinds again with frightened eyes. Frankenstein's Monster was gone.

Nervously, Danny sat back down in his recliner, opening up a fresh pack of cigarettes. He grabbed the remote and turned up the TV in order to drown out the eerie silence. Although he could hear the horrible caterwauling outside in the street, he could hear himself thinking and *thinking* was something he did not want to do. He glanced in the kitchen at the locked cabinet, left of the sink, and shuddered.

Ten minutes later, above the noise of the TV, he could hear scratching sounds and small cat-like whines coming from his front door.

"Not this shit again," he said, rubbing his temples in circular motions. He didn't want to open the door again but his curiosity got the best of him. He slowly reached for the door knob, turned, and opened.

The bloody pillowcase was lying on his rocking chair, fresh blood dripping onto the rotted wooden planks of his porch. He gagged and immediately held a hand up to his mouth. He stepped back inside and heard a small giggle coming from upstairs. Danny knew that little fucker was up there, but how in the hell did he get *inside?* As he ventured toward the staircase, his left foot fell upon something soft and wet. He looked down and, in his horror, saw the decaying remains of a stray cat. It has been opened up, its entrails wrapped around its small body like duct tape. Its head was open, brain matter oozing through a crack in its skull.

Quickly, he dodged and stepped over it with his other foot and reached for his shotgun from the gun rack on the wall and began to climb the staircase. He was taunting whatever was up there.

"I know you're up there . . . I've got a loaded gun and I'm not afraid to use it. You wanna see what this motherfucker can do? Just stay where you are . . . just . . . stay . . . where you are cause you're about to find out." He made an immediate inspection of the gun to see if it had a live round in it. It did. As soon as he reached the second-story landing, his heart began leaping inside of his chest.

He had to pass by the bedroom he had shared with his dead wife.

And that was where Frankenstein's Monster was hiding. He just knew it.

I don't want to go in there. Please God don't make me!

He gripped the shotgun tighter as he gently put an ear up to the door.

Silence.

And then he could hear the springs from the queen-sized bed creak as if someone was jumping on the bed. *His bed . . . their bed.* He quickly opened the bedroom door, the hammer on the shotgun sliding back as he entered. He raised the gun to eye level and stopped.

There was no one there.

No one was jumping on the bed, no one had made a mess of things. Everything was neat and tidy, just as he'd left it when his wife died.

But then he heard a commotion downstairs in the kitchen. He ran as fast as he could, nearly falling in the process. As soon as he reached the doorway to the kitchen, Old Man Jacobs could feel a lump beginning to form in his throat. The recurring nightmare he'd had for the past few years had come true.

The padlocked cabinet was open and it was empty.

He turned and immediately fell to the floor and backed up as far as he could to the nearest wall, his eyes enlarging, taking in the scene before him.

The boy in the Halloween costume had the dried, matted, blood clotted hair of Danny's dead wife in his small hand. He was slowly dragging the carcass toward the living room, making small grunts beneath his plastic mask. He kept dragging and dragging until he reached the sofa which sat adjacent to Old Man Jacobs recliner. The child spoke in a muffled, gravelly voice, sending waves of cold up and down Danny's body.

"Can you sit Mommy up, Daddy?"

"Get the hell out of my house!" Danny screamed, his lungs on fire. He began to cough and wheeze. He fell beside the recliner, one hand reaching for the armrest. It slipped and he fell completely to the floor, his eyes staring at the ceiling as something suddenly loomed over him. It was the boy. The front of his vinyl costume was now covered in blood.

"Is Mommy sleeping? I can't get her to wake up." The trick-or-treater walked back toward the couch, his little hands began to pull on the decaying, skeletal remains. Whatever little flesh was left started to tear away from the bone. Old Man Jacobs pulled himself up and sat in his recliner. He stared at the boy as he kept tugging on his wife's corpse. Danny could still see the bullet hole in her skull and he thought about when he had shot her upstairs in their bedroom as she held on tightly to their dead, little boy, the back of his head bashed in by a baseball bat.

Old Man Jacobs finally got up from his recliner and lifted the rotting woman onto the sofa and adjusted her accordingly . . . lovingly. The small boy climbed up beside her.

"I don't want to trick or treat anymore, Daddy. Can I take

my mask off?"

"Sure, son . . . sure," Danny said, exhausted, tears falling from his eyes. He knew he couldn't escape this time. He knew he needed to face the past once and for all. The boy placed his mask beside him as he reached for the TV Guide. He handed it to Danny.

"Can we watch a scary movie?" The boy asked through his horrid toothless mouth, his face a mangled piece of meat.

Old Man Jacobs lit another cigarette, flipped through the TV Guide with trembling hands and found the movie, *Deadly Blessing* on Channel 4. The child nestled into his mother's side and laid his head upon her exposed shoulder bone. Outside, trick-or-treaters roamed from house to house, jack-o'-lanterns lighting their way.

MOMMY, IS THAT YOU?
Don Tucker

ON THAT COOL OCTOBER MORNING, all of Henry Hoffman's friends told him that he was crazy. They sat around the rectangular cafeteria table and told him that he was bonkers, out of his mind, just plain nuts.

"If you go over there, you'll end up as fertilizer for his garden," said Prez as he blew the wrapper from his straw into Henry's face and dropped it in his milk carton. Prez's real name was Roosevelt Donovan, but years of being teased forced his hand to adopt the much snappier nickname in honor of the 26th president.

"Ya. Or end up in his freezer or something," chimed in Sid Ramsey.

"Or you'll end up like Mrs. Fletcher and accidentally fall down the stairs," said Molly Price, who added quotation fingers to the word *accidentally*.

"What do you have to do anyways?" Prez asked as he catapulted a ball of mashed potatoes and corn from his plastic spoon. Henry avoided it at the last second.

"He wants me to rake his lawn, feed the cat, water his plants, stuff like that."

"Tell that old creep to do it himself," Molly suggested.

"He'll be in Florida for a month to visit his brother. He's giving me forty bucks a week."

"Looks like my next twenty rounds of Pac-Man are on you," Prez mumbled as he shoveled mashed potatoes in his face.

"I have an even better idea," Henry smirked. "Halloween party at the Fletcher house!"

Even though it was announced two weeks ago, and most of their parents had told them as well, they were reminded right before lunch that they had no school on Thursday. Remembering details adults have told them was not a strength of high school students. Mrs. Glendenning, their English teacher, told them over the deafening cheers.

"Profess . . . *huh?* What's that?" Prez asked.

"Professional development, Mr. Donovan." She saw that a blank stare remained on his face, so she continued. "Teacher meetings, Mr. Donovan. No school on Thursday. Why the school board voted on giving you no school on Halloween is beyond me, but that's above my paygrade."

Their little group defied all high school norms, they were an amalgam of all the cliques put together. The tight-knit group had been inseparable since Mrs. Walsh's second-grade class. They were equally composed of the jocks, the band geeks, the stoners, and the freaks. Their unique makeup gave them an in with everyone at school.

Prez, the starting center for the football team, licked a napkin and tried to dab spilled gravy from his jersey.

"Party at Fletcher's? But he lives on *Pike Street.*"

"What's the matter Prez? Too chickenshit?"

"Eat me, Molly. You guys know I'm in. It's just that house. That big iron gate and giant bushes surrounding it, just gives me the creeps, that's all."

"Not as much as it creeps me out," added Henry. No one asked what he meant by that.

Molly tossed her jet-black bangs from her eyes and turned to Henry. "I suppose I need to get the beer." Molly's brother had graduated a few years ago and had no problem buying beer for the high school kids, as long as he got something out of it.

Henry Hoffman's house was a modest ranch with a two-car garage and a basketball hoop in the driveway. Mr. Hoffman worked at Sears in the mall selling refrigerators and washing machines, and Mrs. Hoffman worked part-time at the Savings & Loan on Main Street. Henry occasionally fought with his younger sister, got mostly Bs and Cs in school, and from any onlooker's point of view, lived a perfectly normal life.

In Henry's backyard there was a tiny fire pit dotted with wrinkled Miller cans, covered in black soot. On a nice evening, you could find Mr. Hoffman sitting in his backyard with a cigar, enjoying himself. Much to the dismay of Mrs. Hoffman, on nights when he was enjoying it a little too much, he would stop going all the way to the garage to toss his cans and opt for the fire pit instead. He would piss behind the shed so he wouldn't wake her going in and out of the house, but she didn't know about that part. He almost got caught a few summers ago when she noticed an odd patch of bleached, dead grass behind the shed that refused to grow. Beyond the shed and the piss-soaked grass was thick forest. So thick you could throw a broken branch into the woods and it wouldn't hit the ground. It would absorb into the canopy, fortifying it that much more. There was a trail which had been beaten in slowly for fifty years, snaking through tributaries of roots and shallow, rock-filled streams. A mile or so later you would emerge, most likely covered in sap and mosquito bites, at the backyards of Pike Street. If you walked behind Henry's house, you would eventually arrive at 19 Pike St. The address of Cyrus and the late Marguerite Fletcher.

Three years ago, at the beginning of summer break, Mr. Hoffman walked into Henry's room after a long day of work and was in a foul mood. The room was a mess, and he was sitting amongst dirty clothes and dishes playing *Metroid* on Nintendo. The sight rubbed him the wrong way. Mr. Hoffman ripped the plug from the wall, sending the Nintendo crashing to the floor.

"Get off that damn thing and get outside. I don't want

to see you in this house until those street lights are on."

Prez and Sid were next door neighbors, and the quickest way for Henry to get there was down the trail and then through the yards of Pike Street. Sneak past the Fletcher house, avoid being seen by Old Man Jacobs across the street who never turned down an opportunity to yell at trespassers, run through another short patch of trees, and you would be home free on Lindell Avenue. That was where Prez and Sid lived, and where there was a working Nintendo.

That morning the air was thick, humid, and seemed to be weighing down upon him. After inspecting his Nintendo to make sure there was no permanent damage, he listened to his dad and got the hell out of there. The walk through the woods left splotches of blood on his neck and forearms as he slapped the incessant mobs of mosquitoes. Pricker bushes scraped and poked his legs, and his Black Sabbath shirt stuck to him with sweat. He reached the clearing and spotted the steep, gabled roof and rounded towers of 19 Pike St. Henry always paused before he made the run to Lindell Avenue, most kids in town tried to avoid being seen by these ornery residents at all costs.

Stories of Pike Street were so well known, most kids could recite them by heart. Like any game of telephone, the story would differ depending on who was reciting it. Embellished details and outright fabrications were added, but sometimes the stories were all too true. More than once, someone would tell a story with all sincerity that they heard from their older brother or uncle. Someone would overhear it and say, *Bullshit! My grandfather told me that one when I was a kid*. Henry could tell which ones were true based on the facial reactions of his parents. When he asked about some stories, they would laugh it off and remark how kids have been spinning that yarn since Eisenhower was in office. Other stories he asked about resulted in his parents sharing a silent glance across the dinner table. Mr. Hoffman would ask for another slice of meatloaf, leaving the question to die on the table.

There was the story of Hank Brunansky, who returned from World War II a changed man. Hank came home from Okinawa with one less eye than he had before he left. That eye was good enough to see that his wife was eight months pregnant even though he hadn't seen her in over a year. When she ran off with her old flame, and he couldn't bear to be in that house for one more moment, he bought a small ranch on Pike. Once jovial and friendly, he evolved into a cranky hermit who would blast his shotgun in the air when kids cut through his lawn. The mailman found him one morning, still swaying with the morning breeze in his rocking chair. He was missing most of his head and his beloved shotgun lay at his feet.

Then there was the story of twin sisters Melanie and Melody Bingham. They were last seen leaving their house to help an old woman with her garden, who also lived on Pike. They never returned home on that summer day in 1975. As her sunflowers reached gargantuan heights, rumors swirled around school that Melanie and Melody were now fertilizer.

Henry Hoffman had his own personal story about Pike Street, one that he didn't need to verify with his parents because he saw it with his own eyes that summer morning his dad kicked him outside. A few years back, tragedy struck the Fletcher household. When Cyrus and Marguerite Fletcher moved to 19 Pike St., they appeared to be the only normal couple on the street. *Just wait,* people said. *They will end up freaks, just like the rest of them. It's something about that street.* They had moved all the way from Oklahoma, and the low real estate prices of the quiet neighborhood caught their eye.

Being one of the youngest couples on Pike, Cyrus and Marguerite had one of the youngest children in the neighborhood, three-year old Zachary. They had just left Hooper's, the town's only grocery store, when they began arguing about what many couples argue about in a small town struck by hard times: money. They approached a hairpin turn by Moosehorn Lake, and when Marguerite reached in the back seat to pick up the pacifier that Zachary dropped, her body jerked the steering wheel to the left, sending their 1973 Buick Regal flying over the short guard rail. The murky water ate the car quickly, and after a lengthy struggle, only Cyrus and Marguerite's heads emerged. Countless trips back under were fruitless, they couldn't find the sunken car in the pitch-black waters, and even if they did, it was too late. Firefighters held back a soaked, shrieking Marguerite as she attempted to jump back in the water for Zachary.

The loss of a child led to inevitable struggles in the marriage. On Monday, they could find themselves silently accepting what had happened as a lesson from God. By Tuesday morning, they could be near suicide with their thoughts, damning each other all the way to hell. Their beautiful Victorian home showed as much grief as they did. The forgotten lawn crawled over the iron gate. The porch slowly bowed as if it was frowning, and the bright coat of green paint faded into a drab olive hue. Cyrus held on as long as he could, watching his wife slowly descend into madness. In a small town, word spreads fast about vans that show up with men in white jackets to whisk someone away to Hemlock Hills Treatment Facility. The townsfolk didn't know what to say to him so they stopped saying anything altogether. People would avoid him at Hooper's, steering their carriages away from him like he had a contagious disease. Cyrus worked at the local hardware store where customers would often exit with the wrong kind of screws because they didn't want to make small talk. The rumors swirled the longer Marguerite was at Hemlock Hills. She was in and out several times over the next few years. She would return, and he would tell people at the hardware store that she was feeling much better—whatever that meant. Like clockwork, she would have some sort of meltdown at the park or in the post office, and the white jackets would return. On the final time he brought her home, Henry Hoffman happened to be wandering through the woods in their backyard, on his way to play Nintendo. Still heavily medicated upon her return, Cyrus laid her down in the bedroom and went downstairs to watch a baseball game in his recliner.

Cyrus was awoken by something he prayed was in his dreams. The wails of a toddler were what he thought he heard, followed by a crash of glass. At the top of the stairs stood Marguerite in a nightgown, blood steadily dripping to the floor. She was holding a dripping shard of glass in her hand and only looked at her husband, ignoring his cries.

The story that circulated around town was that in a struggle to get the glass from her hand, Marguerite was thrown over the banister, crashing to the floor. Word never got out if she died from the fall or from the cuts on her wrist, but she died all the same. And Henry Hoffman saw the whole thing from the massive veranda windows in the back of the house. After heavy questioning from police, Cyrus Fletcher was freed from any wrongdoing, but that did nothing against the unstoppable force of small-town gossip. It spread through the town faster than any disease would and those who wanted to harbor their suspicions did so.

By the time Wednesday rolled around, everyone in the school knew about the party at 19 Pike St. on Halloween night. They sat at their normal table while people they didn't even know came to get the details.

"Molly, tell me you got the beer?" Henry asked.

"Sure did, the keg is sitting under a tarp in my garage as we speak."

"And Sid, I assume you got the weed?"

Sid, whose eyes were so bloodshot he looked ill, was preoccupied with his feet moving from side to side on his skateboard under the table. "Huh?"

"I'll take that as a yes. And Prez, you made sure that everyone knows to cut through the woods behind my house? Tell them to park at the church at the end of the road. If cops see all those cars on Pike, they will know something is up."

"Have no fear boss, I'm on it! And Henry, you followed my request and made sure there will be some babes there?"

"Yes Prez, there will be girls. Last I heard, some girls from Mountview High are coming."

"Mountview?" Molly interjected. "Make sure you wrap it up twice, Prez."

"He would need to find a girl willing to sleep with him first," Henry said.

"Good point," Molly laughed as Prez punched Henry square in the shoulder.

~

On the evening of October 31st, Cyrus Fletcher was 1,500 miles away in Fort Lauderdale and the only thing the kids had to worry about was trick-or-treaters strolling through once it got dark. They worried amongst themselves about a possible nosy parent parading around trick-or-treaters, looking to end their night of fun. That's why Sid, much to his chagrin, was not at the Fletcher house with Prez, Molly, and Henry. As much as he tried to avoid it, he was roped into taking his little sister trick-or-treating. When he was done, he would cut through the woods behind Henry's house and join the rest.

"Make sure you don't smoke all the weed before I get there," he warned Henry earlier in the day.

"Sid. You're the one bringing the dope, remember?"

"Oh ya."

They told everyone the party was a go once it was dark, but the three of them were there around four in the afternoon, making sure everything was good to go. They were able to get most supplies through the woods, but the keg required a discreet delivery from Molly's brother. More than one curtain moved to the side to peer at the strange vehicle on the forlorn street. As Molly's brother tapped the keg in the living room, Henry couldn't help but glance at the top of the stairs. His eyes followed the trajectory that Marguerite took that day. She would have landed where the keg sat now.

"And she's ready!" Jimmy, Molly's brother, shouted as foam shot from the tiny hose into his plastic cup. Henry tried to fill his cup, but a solid stream of sudsy foam came shooting out, soaking his shirt.

"I remember my first beer!" Prez yelled as he added batteries to his boombox and began blasting a Van Halen cassette.

Henry, now soaked in beer, went upstairs to use the bathroom that was attached to the master bedroom. In a cabinet next to the sink, he found a towel and began to dry himself. The foam got in his hair as well, and when he ran the towel over his shaggy mop of a hairdo, he thought he heard something. Some sort of muffled speech. The rings of the shower curtain scraped against the metal rod like nails on a chalkboard. The steady drip of water permeated the small, tiled room. It wasn't from a faucet. It was dripping from something. No, it was dripping from *someone*. An impossibly pale, bony hand reached around and gripped the curtain.

"Zachary . . . have you seen Zachary?" the voice gurgled.

The curtain flung open, and standing in the clawfoot tub was a soaking wet Mrs. Fletcher. Entire patches of skin were missing and the ones that remained were decayed and flopped around as she spoke. "Are you Zachary? You've gotten so big," she said as she reached out one arm toward Henry. He felt her hot decaying breath against his face and shuddered before he sprinted out the door.

"Henry? Are you okay?" Molly asked from the bottom of the stairs. He could smell the stale scent of beer and cigarette smoke already wafting through the house.

"Ya. I'm good."

"Are you sure?" Prez asked right before he belched. "You don't look so hot. You're whiter than Molly's Irish ass."

"Now how the hell would you know what my ass looks like you perv?"

Henry suppressed what he's almost positive he saw with his own eyes, and drank a few beers with his friends to calm his nerves. At one point, he had to put a hand in his pocket to hide how much he was shaking.

"It's freezing in here," Molly complained, rubbing her fishnet adorned legs. "Which one of you Einsteins opened a window?"

They all looked at each other and shrugged. Molly changed the cassette from Van Halen to The Cure.

"This ain't party music!" Prez whined. "Turn off this crybaby shit!"

The conversation about the window morphed into a heated musical debate. In the kitchen, the curtains of a singular window flapped in the breeze. Henry looked at his watch. It was 5:30, twilight had arrived and so had the exuberant yelling of children, sweating into plastic masks as they paraded around their plastic pumpkins and pillowcases. Henry glanced out the window and saw a group of trick-or-treaters, one adorned with the timeless costume of the white bedsheet ghost, another in a strange white gown with what looked like some sort of makeshift beak. Others tripped over their own shoelaces, daring their friends to race them to the next house. In between songs on the boombox, they heard the doorbells up and down the street, followed by *TRICK OR TREAT.* Not a single person had approached the creaky deck of 19 Pike St. The bucket of candy that Molly kindly brought sat untouched.

An hour had passed, and Sid still hadn't arrived with the dope. As a matter of fact, no one had arrived. People should be here by now. *Anyone* should be here by now. Henry turned the kitchen light off so he could see onto the back deck. Wet, muddy footprints led a trail across the deck and down the stairs. Henry followed the trail through the Fletcher's backyard until he got to the tree line and stared at the seemingly endless black chasm that could bring him home. As if being pulled by something greater than himself, like he was watching footage of a dream, he ventured in. *I know this path better than anyone,* he thought to himself. Henry had been running through those woods since he could walk, and could probably jog home with his eyes closed if he had to.

Henry was navigating the path without issue, trying

his best to avoid sticks and leaves, when he tripped over something that shouldn't have been there. He was so close to home he could see the faint glow of his television, most likely with his father asleep in front of it. It did not make a sound that belongs to anything in nature. Crawling back to it as he rubbed his shin, he made out the word "Budweiser" printed on the box. The light from his own street made things slightly visible, and as his eyes adjusted, he spotted cases of beer, backpacks, and a boombox that was still playing "Hungry Like the Wolf." The speakers were face down in the dirt, gurgling the sounds of Duran Duran into the muddy soil. The sloshing of feet caused Henry to drop where he stood and hide behind a large oak tree. There was a small pond close by, really a large puddle more than anything. The stagnant water smelled something awful and was a breeding ground for mosquitoes. A few more sloshes, then the crunching of dry leaves. Someone was coming into view from the shadows. Henry heard coughing and labored breathing, and when the moonlight hit him just right, he saw that it was Sid. His reddish hair was the first thing he noticed, and the fact that it looked wet.

"Sid! Are you okay? We need to get everyone the hell out of the Fletcher house, now!"

Sid took a step toward Henry and then fell face first onto the forest floor, too weak to even brace his fall. Sid did nothing except gurgle up foul-smelling pond water. A whispered voice followed his gasping in the darkness. Marguerite walked right in front of Henry, close enough to again smell her rotten breath and feel the flowy, lacy fabric of her nightgown. She paid him no attention. Her soaked nightgown clung to her rotted flesh as she glided right by him and knelt before Sid.

"Oh Zachary, my poor baby. Zachary, please wake up. Mommy loves you very much." She lovingly cradled Sid's limp head, brushing his blood-soaked hair out of his face.

"There, there, my love, mommy is going to make it all better. Hush now, Zachary."

She began to hum a lullaby only mere feet away from

a frozen Henry. Her melodic voice was almost inaudible over the monotonous drone of the crickets and the occasional distant car clunking over potholes. The first step he attempted toward home cracked a large branch on the ground. Her voice immediately changed from a soothing lullaby to a raspy groan as she let Sid's head slam back to the dirt.

"This isn't my baby! This isn't my Zachary!" Her nightmarish voice bellowed through the still air. Like she was pulling weeds from her garden, she snatched a handful of his hair and pulled upward, severing Sid's head from his body.

"You!" she screamed, pointing a bony, dead finger in Henry's direction. Sid's lifeless, empty eyes were facing him. A clod of dirt and a worm inching its way along clung to her index finger. Her voice returned to its sing-song pitch.

"You, are you my Zachary? You've gotten so big, baby. I always knew you would grow up to be so handsome. Come here, my sweet baby, mommy wants to hold you."

When she attempted to grab a handful of Henry's shirt, he pulled away in defense. He was left holding a lacy sleeve and an arm; it came off clean like a wishbone. Henry threw the arm at the steadily approaching Marguerite, and sprinted back toward the Fletcher house. His chest burned by the time he reached the backyard and he vomited into the shrubs he was supposed to be taking care of. He fell like a brick and screamed for his friends. Van Halen was still blasting inside. They couldn't hear a thing. Henry's fumbling hand reached for the doorknob and the music abruptly stopped. *They heard me, thank God*, he thought.

When Henry sprinted in, no one asked where he was or why he was covered in dirt. In fact, they said nothing at all and stared at the front door. The doorknob jiggled.

"Maybe it's our first trick-or-treater," said Molly.

"Who cares? It better be Sid with the weed," retorted Jimmy, impatiently waiting on the payment he was promised for supplying the keg.

A small hand with dirt caked underneath its fingernails pushed open the door. There stood a young boy, no older than four, soaking wet and sobbing. His unkempt hair looked as if it could break the teeth on a comb. Various twigs and leaves were fused into the knotted mess.

"Holy shit! Excellent costume, little man. Help yourself to some candy. You forgot to say 'Trick or Treat,' though." Prez proclaimed, tossing a cigarette butt into a beer can.

"I . . . I . . . I miss my mommy! I want my mommy!"

His sobs erupted into full blown wails. Molly, with her budding maternal instincts, snatched him up and held him tight. Before she could offer any words of consolation, the child lifted a shard of glass from his hand and buried it into Molly's shoulder. She shrieked and let him fall to the floor with a *thud*.

"You're not my mommy! I want my mommy!"

They rushed to Molly's side. Prez ripped the shard from her shoulder, and removed his football jersey to apply pressure to the gushing wound. Jimmy scrambled to find the phone. Before he finished dialing 9-1-1, the back door opened with a long, deliberate creak and a rush of cool air flooded in. The house shook as the door slammed shut. A picture in the living room fell from the wall and shattered. A steady drip of water echoed throughout the now silent house. The boy, whose hand slowly dripped from the bloody glass, shut the door behind him.

"Mommy, is that you?"

ROGER AND THE GHOST
Paul Lonardo

S HE HEARD THE LAUGHTER OF the trespassers as they made their way across the lawn. The three boys who mounted the steps to the front porch were not wearing costumes, but she knew instantly that it was Halloween. She strongly disliked the holiday and avoided it at all costs, but it caught her by surprise this year.

"Let's go inside and divide up the take," said the boy carrying two pillowcases filled with candy.

"Just as long as you divide it equally this time," another boy spoke up.

"I'll decide what's even," the first boy shot back.

A sudden pounding on the door rattled the walls and ceiling, dislodging a layer of standing dust inside, which drifted down around her like dirty snow.

"Trick or treat, Dead Girl."

She quickly ducked behind the couch when a shadow appeared in the window across the living room.

"I think I saw her," the third boy screamed.

"Where, where?"

"I don't see anything."

The window filled with silhouettes.

There was a tapping on the glass as their meager hand-held flashlights partially penetrated the pitch-black interior. This was the only window in the entire house that wasn't broken. Because it was completely concealed by overgrown hedges, it was protected from the stones that the local teens frequently hurled at the old house. She had plugged up the other windows with cardboard, though it was more for privacy than as any sort of hindrance.

The rambling two-story Victorian had a turret and oversized porch that was not at all welcoming. It was mired in perpetual shadow, even in the daytime, and the floorboards were loose and creaky. Because the lot was larger, the property was farther away from the adjacent homes, as if the other houses didn't want to be next to it. Nobody had lived in the old Crenshaw place since a young girl died there and the family moved out ten years ago. The children in the neighborhood, believing the abandoned house at 20 Pike St. was haunted, were typically afraid to set foot anywhere near it, except on Halloween. This night had a way of making some kids brave, or at least daring enough to act on things that otherwise scared them. Mischievous children would wander closer to the house than usual, walk around the grounds, and occasionally knock on the door. They wanted to see a ghost. However, if any of them had ever found themselves in the presence of an actual ghost, she couldn't be sure how they might react to her, so she would always spend Halloween night locked in the basement. That's why she hated Halloween.

"Over there. Behind the couch, near the fireplace."

"I see her! Come on! Let's get her."

Now, she felt trapped. She would already have been in the safety of the cellar behind the steel-reinforced door if she had realized that it was October 31st. Her only hope was to make a run for it before the teens got inside. There was a large open space between her and the door in the kitchen that led to the basement. She was sure to be seen, but she had no choice. She dashed toward the kitchen, hoping the shadows would conceal her movement.

As she entered the kitchen, the back door started to

open.

Oh, no, she thought, remembering that she'd left the door unlocked after coming in from the backyard that afternoon. She stopped and quickly dove under the kitchen table as someone entered the house.

"Is anyone here?" The soft whisper was followed by the sound of the door closing and the *click* of the deadbolt.

She crawled on her hands and knees across the floor to the far end of the table as the intruder came further inside. The legs of the boy stopped directly in front of her, between her and the cellar door.

"It's okay. You can come out." The boy's voice was kind. "I don't mean you any harm. I just want to meet you."

She didn't move for a moment, then she slowly crawled out from under the table and stood facing the boy.

"Hi," said the tall boy with a gentle smile. He had on a white robe with a separate oversized hood that was pulled down behind his head.

"Hello."

"My name is Roger. What's your name?"

"I don't remember."

The house was dark, but she was glowing with a low, throbbing luminescence. "You don't seem surprised that I can see you."

"This is the only night of the year that just about everyone can see me," she said. "I'm not really sure why. I think it's because people expect to see ghosts on Halloween, and their minds are open to it."

"I see you all the time," Roger told her.

"You do?"

"Yeah. Out on the back porch. Sometimes in the backyard."

"There used to be an old tire tied to the branch of a giant sycamore tree that I used to like swinging on," she said. "It's gone now, but I still like to go outside and try to remember what it was like then."

"What else did you like to do?" Roger asked.

"I don't know."

"You don't look like a ghost," he told her. "You seem

like a regular girl."

He smiled at her and she averted her eyes.

"What's it like to be . . . " he began. "You know?"

"It's not bad," she said.

"Aren't you lonely? Do you miss being with your friends?"

"I never had any friends when I was alive," she said.

"I don't have any friends, either."

"What about those boys outside?"

"Oh, that's Dennis, my older brother, and his friends, Jaden and Alex. I was out trick-or-treating with Dylan. He's my little cousin, so I don't think that even counts as a friend. Those big boys came along and took our bags of candy. Dylan ran home crying and I came here to get our candy back from them. I thought maybe you could help me."

"Me, help you?"

"Sure."

"What do I have to do?" she asked.

"Do you ever scare people?"

"I try not to scare anybody."

"But you could? I mean, if you wanted."

"I guess so." Roger smiled at her, and she couldn't help but smile back. "And you'll be my friend if I help you?"

"We're already friends," Roger told her. "Besides Dylan, you're the only other kid that will talk to me."

"What do you want me to do?" she asked.

When he finished telling her his plan, the sound of shattering glass from the living room caused them to look up.

"Okay," Roger said. "It's time. Let's go." He paused briefly and looked her in the eyes. "Thanks."

A moment later, they disappeared into the basement together as the three teens entered the house through the broken window.

"Whoa!" Dennis exclaimed, shining his flashlight around the vast living room. The sparse furnishings were festooned with cobwebs and covered in a half inch of dust which rendered the room colorless, reminding him of one of those black and white TV programs he used to watch when he was little.

"This place gives me the creeps," Jaden said. "I say we get out of here."

"Let's see what we got first," Dennis said as he opened one of the bags and reached a hand inside. "Give me some light."

The other boys fixed their flashlights on Dennis, whose eyes widened with fright as something attached itself to his hand. Their beams revealed the lower part of his arm swarming with cockroaches.

"What the . . . " he began as he withdrew his arm from the sack and shook it vigorously to dislodge the vile insects before they made it above his elbow.

Dennis dropped the pillowcase and the roaches spilled out, disappearing under the sofa and into the nearby walls.

Just then, a small figure in a white robe appeared out of the gloom and stopped near the boys. The hood was pulled up, concealing the identity of the wearer, but Dennis recognized the homemade costume as the same one that his younger brother had been wearing.

"Roger?" Dennis stepped closer to the hooded figure. "What are you doing here?" He reached down and pulled the hood back. When it dropped down, there was no face, no head, nothing at all inside the costume. Then the robe fell to the floor and there was nobody inside.

"What's going on here?" Alex asked.

Dennis was too shaken by what he had witnessed to respond.

"Can we get out of here now?" Jaden begged.

Something moved inside the other pillowcase Dennis was holding and he released it from his grasp. It struck the floor with a heavy *thud* and out rolled a jack-o'-lantern with a carved scowling grin. But what Dennis saw was a severed head belonging to his brother. He took a step back and yelped. "Let's go," he said breathlessly and set out quickly in the opposite direction. The other boys followed.

"Where's the window?" Jaden asked, his voice shrill and full of panic.

"It's got to be here," Dennis said, more of a demand than a statement. But as they continued along, there was only an endless dark wall.

"We must be going in the wrong direction," Alex suggested. "Let's double back."

They headed back the other way, but there was still no window to be found. Their frantic movement released clouds of dust particles into the air, which swirled all around them, diminishing their vision even further.

"We're trapped," Jaden bellowed. "We never should have come in here."

"You better shut up," Dennis warned him.

All at once, their flashlights went out at the same time and it became as black as a tomb inside the old house.

"My batteries just died," Alex said.

"Mine too," Jaden said, panicked. He shook the plastic case feverishly, then struck it with his other hand to try to get it to work. "What are we gonna do?"

"We're gonna stay calm," Dennis said evenly. "This house isn't that big. There are other ways out."

A loud *bang*, like the tailgate of a dump truck opening, was followed by the sound of a heavy granular substance being emptied. All around them damp soil began to pile up rapidly. It ran over the tops of their feet and continued pouring in.

"We're being buried alive," Jaden croaked.

They maintained their position atop the rising tide of earth, riding it like a semi-solid wave. Higher and higher they went, well beyond where the ceiling should have been. Completely blind and terrified, their pleas and cries for help did not resonate. It was as if they were underground, and no one could hear their anguished screams. Soon, they were at the peak of a high mountain of dirt, where they were no longer able to maintain their balance. One by one they fell, tumbling down the steep slope. In an uncontrolled descent, their faces impacted the dirt as chunks of soil lodged in their ears, noses, and mouths.

Sputtering and coughing to keep from suffocating, the boys thought they would continue to fall forever. Then, without warning, they rolled to a stop, their bodies collecting in a heap. It took a moment for them to get their bearings, and to their collective astonishment they found themselves lying on the ground in front of the old house. No one said a word as they surveyed one another's faces, which were caked with mud and blood.

Dennis was first to get to his feet. "We tell no one about this," he warned his friends.

Alex and Jaden nodded and then all three boys quickly strode away from the house at a brisk pace, almost running.

Watching from the broken window, she and Roger laughed.

"That was awesome!" Roger said. "You're pretty good at that. Especially for never having scared anyone before." He looked down at the pumpkin lying on the floor and nudged it with his foot. "I really liked that trick. Did you see the look on my brother's face when he thought it was my head?"

"It was nothing," she said.

"Nothing? It was nothing short of spectacular."

She blushed.

"Thanks again," he said.

"I should thank *you,*" she said. "That was fun. I probably used to like Halloween a lot. I do now, at least."

"I meant, thank you for being my friend," Roger said. He stepped close to her and gave her a hug, and even though she did not have a physical body, she felt his embrace.

№ 21

THINGS THAT GROW IN THE DARK
Austin Hinderliter

S HE ALWAYS HATED THIS TIME of year. Beds of Black-eyed Susan and Zinnia were replaced with dead, wet leaves that crunched underfoot, making her already unsteady feet even more wobbly. And don't get her started on the poor Gaillardias—their bountiful orange and red blooms replaced with the dull colors of late-autumn gloom.

You're all doom and gloom. That's what her Richard used to say.

But after her double knee replacement three years ago, getting around the garden wasn't as easy as it used to be. Age had stolen the spring in her step. Like her flowers, her brightest days were a thing of the past.

Bled of color, she was wilting and, in another winter or so, would be resting among the decaying flowers.

Such thoughts were morbid, she knew. Richard, until the day of his death, forbade her from talking about those thoughts. Carol, the hospice nurse, always complimented her bouquets, though. And she had to admit the arrangements had brought color to the room as the life drained from her husband, but not even their fragrance could mask the stench of death.

Cut flowers rest at Richard's grave from the first to

last blooms. Each year, she shakes her head as she walks across Rose Hill Cemetery at the lack of flowers on the graves. Even the artificial arrangements are becoming rarer, not counting the ones that have seen several summers and have been chopped up by the mowers. Moss now covers most of the epitaphs. But not her Richards. She sees to that, carefully tending to his plot with even more care than her garden. Her Richard deserves only the best.

"Hey lady, what's your drive?" The voice pulled her from her thoughts.

Her cloudy eyes squinted. It was hard for her to see dark shapes against dark backgrounds, and dusk was quickly approaching, which meant it would soon be time to retire to her comfy living room.

"Do you have a problem or something?" It was a girl's voice, or more specifically, an unruly teenager from the sound of it.

"I beg your pardon?"

"I said, what's your problem? Sitting here staring straight through me."

This girl has a lot of nerve, she thought. "I apologize for staring. I can't see too well, especially at night. You see, I have cataracts and night blindness and —"

"Do you have any candy or not?"

Candy? Oh, was it the thirty-first already?

"I'm afraid I don't."

"Eat crow, you old witch!" Squinting, she could barely make out the girl descending the porch steps before being swallowed by the night's maw.

Another youngin with no respect. What is happening to this country?

She refused to believe this was the same nation her Richard fought so hard for. All the sacrifices she had made, only to be cursed at. And on her own property no less! People should respect their elders. She always had been taught to do so. Schools became too busy teaching liberal studies and women's rights and forgot to teach common decency.

Not that her neighbors were any better. That Shaw woman across the street was dating a man at least half her age. Could you imagine? Then there was that yapping Jack Russell of hers that pooped in her yard and dug up her tulips. But look at the owner, cosseting that dog as if it were a child!

You're all doom and gloom.

"You're right, Richard." She stood from the rocker, glancing at the empty chair beside hers. "Let's call it a night." But as she headed for the front door, something caught her eye. She squinted. Three kids stood under a streetlight, their backs to her, staring at number 22. Unmoving, they did not break their stare as she demanded them to get off her lawn.

"Shoo! Shoo!" she yelled, but their unmoving stance did not falter. A car turned the corner and pulled up in front of the house across the street, its headlights cutting through the night and illuminating trick-or-treaters winding along the curved sidewalk. That Shaw woman and the half-her-age boyfriend. Good, let them handle this!

I'm far too old to deal with the little hassles.

Flickering light from the television illuminated the vines of the William Morris wallpaper, giving the subtle yet apparent illusion of growth as if the vines and evenly dispersed lilies were alive and crawling along the navy background. They had hung the wallpaper shortly after moving in. She cut while Richard pasted, and except for a medially dissected hummingbird, the different pieces of the pattern aligned beautifully. The bird, which Richard nicknamed Alfred after Alfred Hitchcock—they had gone to see *The Birds* at the Great American Theater, which terrified her but filled Richard with glee—initially annoyed her. How could everything else be a perfect match except for a single bird? But now it reminded her of Richard and had become one of her favorite things in the house after his passing.

At times, when listening to the television—it was becoming harder and harder to see, especially on their old, static-filled set—she would talk to Alfred. Telling him stories about the good old days, when they first met, their date nights, working in the garden together—her tending to the flowers, Richard to his vegetables.

On bad days, she would tell Alfred about the low points in their marriage. The miscarriage. She never tried again. The basement flooded in the summer of '73. The cracks in the foundation that had reopened since Richard's passing.

On other days, they would rest in the living room in silence. Those were the days she liked the most. When there were no good memories, there were no bad ones to take them away.

She shuffled across the room and sank into her wing-back chair. The upholstery, while not exact, closely matched the wallpaper motif. And like the wallpaper, it too had seen better days.

Channel 4 News was midway through a Halloween broadcast. Walter Ryan was giving viewers tips on trick-or-treating safety. Always go in pairs. Always check your candy.

Nothing but old-fashioned horse sense, she thought.

"We have some breaking news at the top of the hour: A macabre discovery in a local graveyard. Several graves have been disturbed at Rose Hill Cemetery. Authorities are investigating the situation and are urging anyone with information to come forward."

"Was that Rose Hill Cemetery, he said?" It was so hard to tell over the static. She reached for the end table, found the remote, and turned up the volume.

"The community is shocked and saddened by this unsettling news. We will update this story as authorities work on trying to understand who would commit such a heinous act. In other news—"

"Oh, please don't let it be Richard! Not my Richard," she sobbed. The remote fell to the floor. Alfred remained silent as Iiana crawled around him.

She pulled a handkerchief from her pocket and dabbed her eyes. "Please tell me my Richard is safe," she begged, drying her tear-streaked cheeks. She had to do something, but what? If Richard's grave were disturbed surely the police would have called by now. Still, she had to be sure. Had she kept Carol's number? After Richard died, she said to call morning or night if she needed anything.

Bam, bam, bam!

She jumped, startled by the sudden noise at the front door. Who on earth could it be at this ungodly hour?

Bam, bam!

There were two more knocks. Then silence. Walter Ryan was talking about the Halloween Parade. She wished there would be a new development on the Rose Hill Cemetery story. She had to know her Richard was safe.

Maybe it was Carol at the door! *Yes.* She had seen the story on the news and came over to check-in. There were three more knocks as she pulled herself up from the chair, leaning on the walker next to the side table even though it frustrated her to do so. *Bam. Bam. Bam.* Was a knit cardigan over a nightgown appropriate to wear to the cemetery? She knew the answer was no, but this was urgent. Besides, the hoodlums traipsing through her neighborhood were dressed far worse, she imagined.

"I'm coming, Carol!" She unlocked the door and pulled it open. "Carol?" She flicked a switch and turned on the porchlight. A dark figure stood at the bottom step. "Carol? Is that you?" she asked, squinting through the darkness. "What are you doing?"

The silhouette moved, winding up their arm as if throwing a baseball. Why, they were throwing a baseball! Right at her! Before she had time to react, the white shape flew through the air and smashed into her hip.

"Oh!" she yelped as it shattered on impact. She leaned against the doorframe for support. Her hand reached for her hip, touching something hard. And crunchy. And wet.

An egg.

Carol had thrown an egg at her!

"Got you!" Cruel laughter followed. Then another higher-pitched laugh joined in. "Tricked you, tricked you, we really tricked you!" the voices chanted.

"You little bastards!" she screamed, wiping yolk on her sweater. She stepped onto the wooden-floored porch. There was a crunch beneath her slippers. Eggs. More eggs! It hadn't been Carol knocking on the door, after all, but two little hoodlums egging her house.

"Get off my property!" she yelled, leaning against the doorjamb to steady her balance.

"Tricked you, tricked you, we really tricked you!" They continued to chant, one voice coming from her left, one from the right. She squinted, but by this point, her entire yard was darkened by the night's cloak.

She wiped her slipper back and forth on the welcome mat — not that it did much welcoming these days, as she seldom had visitors — while trying to catch a glimpse of the little demons on her lawn, disturbing her garden, dead as it may be.

"I said get off my lawn, you little bastards!"

Bam!

Bam!

~

"Nice throw, Sanok!" Kyle boomed, throwing another egg at the plate-glass window. "That was a direct hit! Like, direct-direct! Right in the kisser!"

"Thanks," Shawn muttered, the excitement of their Halloween Night hijinks having worn off. He could never say no to Kyle. So, when Kyle wanted to TP the Donald's over on Plum, he said yes. When Kyle asked to take candy quite literally from a baby (okay, maybe the kid was like five, but still) he had done it. When Kyle asked for him to climb that dogwood over on 14th to snap a picture of Sally Hutton changing into her costume, he did it — ending up with a broken Polaroid that slipped from his grasp and a cock harder than a Jolly Rancher.

Sally had looked so hot in that maid's outfit.

Bam! Another egg smashed against the wooden siding.

"Aww, shit, that was the last egg!" Kyle sighed. He tossed the empty carton to the ground among the dead leaves and brown shrubbery. "Now what are we supposed to do?"

"I dunno, man. Maybe we should call it a night."

"Don't be a spaz! It's Halloween. This is like, the one night a year it's acceptable to play tricks." Kyle smashed the egg carton into the wet earth with the toe of his shoe, splattering mud up the side of his jeans.

Playing tricks. Is that what they were doing? Shawn wasn't so sure. Hitting an old woman with an egg? That just made him feel like an asshole.

"I dunno. I mean, I already broke my camera, and besides, it's —"

"Totally worth it though, huh Sanok?" Kyle winked and nudged him in the ribs.

"Yeah, I guess," Shawn said, shrugging. "So, what do you want to do?" He pulled on the sleeves of his down coat to cover his hands. The wind scattered leaves across the yard, and it was getting colder. Kyle had more meat on his bones though and he didn't seem bothered by the temperature drop. Shawn Sanok was a stick. He knew because that's what the boys in the locker room always called him.

Well, that was one of the nicer things they called him, anyway.

"We could stop at my house to get more toilet paper, then head back over to Sally's."

Shawn wouldn't mind seeing Sally again, but that would take them over forty minutes on foot, and he knew his old man would have a cow if he came in any later than eleven thirty.

"Why don't we just walk over to Line Street? Ding Dong Ditch a few houses and scare a few girls. Keep it simple."

"Or . . . " Kyle flashed a cavity-ridden grin. He pointed behind Shawn's shoulder. The open gate banged against the wooden privacy fence. Pickets and posts were mostly rotted, and there was a hole under the kickboard, probably from an animal that had burrowed beneath. "We could go in there."

"Yeah, and do what?" Looking through the gate was like looking into an abyss. Total, scared-shitless darkness awaited those who were brave enough to enter. Shawn knew that wasn't him. Sixteen years old, and he couldn't go to sleep without his nightlight.

"You're not scared, are you Sanok?" Kyle was howling.

"No!" Shit, he had to play it cool. He didn't want Kyle to think he was a wuss. "You just didn't strike me as someone who liked to watch old ladies undress."

"Sure, Sanok. Whatever you say. If you're not afraid, prove it." Kyle motioned to the gate. To the shadows beyond . . .

"Fine. But I'm going home after this."

"Whatever you say, Sanok," Kyle said. He was only a few feet behind, but Shawn had difficulty hearing him over the hollering wind.

The gate's metal hinges clanged against the fence as they approached.

Shawn gulped. His hand trembled as he pushed the gate open, hesitating momentarily on the threshold. Strange things happened on Pike Street. At least, that's what he'd heard. It was a street he mostly avoided his entire life. But Kyle persisted they egg the old witch's house. Rumor had it she killed kids who trespassed on her lawn, then planted flowers to mark their graves. Kyle even claimed he saw her several times wandering through the old cemetery on the hill.

Kyle also alleged that's what happened to Jenny Roberts. That she had wandered down Pike and the old witch on the corner killed her. Shawn heard she moved with her family to Chattanooga. But now, on Pike Street itself, in the old witch's garden, he wasn't so sure.

"Dude, go!" Kyle shoved him forward, pushing him into the backyard. He stumbled and struggled to regain his footing. Something was wrapped around his ankle!

"Get it off me! Get it off me!" he shrieked. "Kyle, please get it off me! Something has my foot!" Shawn flailed in the air, trying to yield off whatever had him in its hold. His eyes were starting to adjust in the darkness, but he still could not see what had him in its clutches.

Kyle was gasping. It had him too!

"Nothing's got you, Sanok!" Kyle chortled at his friend's fear. "Whoa! Watch it, will ya? You almost got me in the face!"

"It's grabbed my arm!" Shawn was in sheer panic.

"Yeah, I know. That's me!"

Shawn quit flailing and kicking. He pulled loose from Kyle's grip and bent to feel through the darkness that seemed to whirl around him. His hand touched something rough. He recoiled, then reached down again. It was soft. A lobed leaf that was attached to a vine. Then he felt the rubber toe of his Chuck Taylor beneath the vine. He was snared by a plant.

Kyle slapped both thighs. He doubled over, practically wheezing. "Oh man, oh man. I can't breathe. I can't breathe."

Shawn pulled his foot free, sending him tumbling backward and landing on his ass.

"Oh, man! It keeps getting better!" Kyle wiped away tears streaming down his large cheeks.

A twig snapped.

Shawn sat still; his backside splattered in mud. He could feel it seep around his jeans and the band of his underwear. Like the muddy water, a chill ran down his spine.

Creak.

Had he heard that? It was hard to tell over the wind and Kyle's incessant, pig-like snorts.

Creak.

Yes, he hadn't imagined the sound. He remained in the muddy puddle, his legs stretched out before him. He squinted through the blackness, struggling to see much beyond the toes of his shoes.

"You kill me, you know that? You really kill me." Kyle extended an arm.

"Something had my foot," Shawn cried, taking Kyle's hand and pulling himself from the mud.

"It's just a pumpkin patch, man! And look at the size of these pumpkins! Have you ever seen anything like em?"

Shawn couldn't see much of anything. But as he looked

closer, large gourd-like shapes materialized from the night's depths. The pumpkin rinds glistened as if covered in a thin layer of yellow-orange slime. But that wasn't the weirdest thing about this patch. As Kyle had said, these pumpkins were massive.

"Imagine the mess these could make!" Kyle stepped through the knee-high vines and smacked one of the gourds. "What are you waiting for, Sanok? Let's go!"

Shawn stood on the edge of the patch. He shivered from the cold. His shoes and socks were soaking wet, and muddy water continued to drip down his legs.

Creak.

His scrotum crawled.

Creak.

What was that noise? And why didn't Kyle seem to notice?

"Come on, man! I can't move it by myself. Let's take this one." Kyle thumped the pumpkin on the patch's edge. "We can roll it through the gate and smash it on the old witch's front porch!"

Something moved.

"What are you waiting for? Let's go!"

"I think there's something in here . . . " Shawn looked at the thick pumpkin vines running along the damp ground. Was it his imagination or were they moving? No. Not just moving.

Slithering.

"Are you gonna help me, or not?"

"No." The defiance in his voice came as a surprise.

"Huh?"

"I said no! You have dragged me all over town tonight. We did everything you wanted to do, and I didn't complain once. And look at me now, Kyle. I'm covered in mud and freezing, but I'm done. I said I was going home, and I meant it. I'm out of here!" Shawn only took several squishy steps before he heard the scream. He didn't even reach the gate.

"Shawn, help! Somethings got me!" Kyle yelled.

By the time Shawn turned around his friend was gone,

and the backyard had fallen into silence. Even the wind had stilled.

"Kyle?" Shawn took a tentative step around the puddle he had fallen in. "Kyle?" He took another step. "Come on, man. This isn't funny."

He treaded over one of the trailing plants and approached the pumpkin Kyle had stood next to. Four parallel marks cut through the pumpkin's ridges. They were jagged and became less pronounced as they clawed down the gourd's side. Shawn placed his shaking hand on the surface, matching the marks to his fingers. It was obvious a human hand had made these markings.

Creak.

"Dude, cut it out!" Shawn spun around, expecting to come face to face with his toothy friend and the pieces of gummy worms that had been stuck in the crevices of his mouth for half the night. But Kyle wasn't there. Only the gloom. Still, something had made that noise, and Shawn was certain he had seen one of the pickets move to the side as if something had wriggled through the fence and the board had fallen back in place.

This has to be a joke. Right?

When Kyle wasn't telling a joke he was playing one. Scaring your best friend—the ultimate Halloween night capstone.

"Ha, ha. Very funny, Kyle," Shawn deadpanned. He had finally stood up for himself and this was Kyle's way of evening the score.

As he took a few steps farther into the pumpkin patch, the clouds parted and a sliver of moonlight snuck through the billows, bathing the backyard in blue light. For the first time, Shawn could see the size of the garden. Were the yards on Pike Street all so big? He didn't remember them being so long, but the expanse before him stretched far into the distance. Pumpkins and vines snaked all the way to the fence, which was the only thing stopping the creeping plants.

Five fence pickets were missing at the far end of the yard. Diffused light from neighboring houses shone through the gaps and illuminated the tops of several pumpkins.

"Give it up, man," Shawn said as he stepped further into the garden.

Something moved at his feet.

Shawn stopped; his breath caught in his throat.

A few leaves shook to his immediate left as if something beneath the green inferno had just disturbed them.

"Kyle?" Shawn's voice quivered. "Kyle, knock it off. You'll be sorry . . . " He took a few more steps, careful to not get his foot caught on a vine again. The leaves brushed against his legs as he walked farther into the patch.

That's when he saw the corpse.

At first, he didn't think it was real. Kyle was playing one of his tricks. Or a few neighborhood kids also got it in their minds to scare the old witch on the corner. But then it moved. And when he saw the vines, he knew it wasn't a joke.

The man emerged from the leaves. Whisps of white hair still clung to the scalp stretched over bone. Black maws and uneven teeth filled the center of his face. His lips were gone, receded by death.

Shawn staggered backward, nearly tripping over one of the pumpkins.

Dirt clung to his black suit. And the vines. The vines were like tendrils, circling his midsection, coming out of the jacket cuffs before wrapping around his skeletal hands.

Shawn fell backward. He jumped to his feet. Eyes wide, nearly frozen in fear.

The gnarled teeth of the corpse parted. One of the tendrils snaked out of his mouth. The voice was a creak, like the sound a long-sealed casket lid would make upon opening.

"Get . . . "

Shawn felt a vine curl around his ankle.

"off . . . "

It tightened.

"my . . ."

It pulled him under.

"lawn . . ."

~

Knock. Knock. Knock.

Channel 4 was finishing its coverage of the Halloween festivities when the three consecutive raps came from the front door. Perhaps Carol had finally received the voicemails she had left. Or maybe, just maybe, it was a police officer. The department had all but dismissed her concerns, saying they would have an officer check Richard's grave in the morning and get back to her, but she knew it was all hogwash.

Oh! What if it were those little demons again? Throwing eggs at her and her house! The nerve! She would have to see if that Wilkinson boy on Line Street could clean her windows. Hopefully, he wouldn't charge her an arm and a leg.

Begrudgingly, she used her walker to shuffle to the front door. She unlatched the chain and pulled it open. She squinted, expecting an egg to pelt her in the face. But the street was silent. Trick-or-treaters had long retired to their houses to sort through their pillage.

"Hello? Is anybody there?" Only a dark haze lay before her. The little vandals must have also called it a night. Good riddance!

As she turned to close the door, she noticed the bright spot of color on the welcome mat. Her old bones creaked as she bent down.

A single red rose had been left on her doorstep.

THE CANDY SNATCHERS
Reece G. Donnell

S HARON SHAW ROUNDED THE CORNER and saw the house approaching rapidly to her right.

"Thank God," she muttered, bringing the car to a screeching halt.

With a glance in her rear-view mirror, she was assured her poker-straight blonde hair and make-up were still impeccable. She didn't look as frantic as she felt. Exiting, Sharon only briefly glimpsed costumed kids on the street. She'd forgotten entirely that today was Halloween. She retrieved two sacks of groceries from her back seat before kicking the door shut and teetering on spiked heels up the porch steps.

"Goddamn it!" Sharon hissed as she fumbled in her pantsuit pocket for her keys. "Why bother?"

With a click and the rustling of paper, Sharon was inside. Closing the door, the tip-tap of paws on the hard-wood greeted her.

"Teddy!" Sharon exclaimed as she rested the groceries on the side table. "Teddy, baby! Come to mama!"

She knelt with open arms and the ginger Jack Russell dog leapt at her ample chest. As Teddy began to lick her face, Sharon Shaw remembered her immaculately applied make-up.

"No, no, baby," she chided. "Not right now, Mama's in a rush!"

Sharon stood, retrieved her groceries again, and wobbled down the hall and into the kitchen. Teddy followed, his head bobbing as if he agreed with her every word.

"Mama has to drop these groceries off," she began breathlessly. "Then, we're gonna get you something to eat! And then I need to go get Daddy Jamie from work."

Sharon stopped at the kitchen counter and looked at her watch. It was eight o'clock.

"Shit," she whispered. "Why the hell did I say I'd pick him up when I knew I had to shop? Surely, he can go one night without getting laid? I'm too old for his libido."

~

"No, no, baby," Sharon chided once more, trying to close the front door. "You stay there! Mama will be right back with Daddy Jamie."

The door finally closed without the intrusion of a wet nose and Sharon decided to forgo the lock, there was no time. Quickly, she turned.

"Oh, *Jesus!*" She shrieked as she came face-to-face with a chalky white visage.

Catching her breath, Sharon took in the sight before her and smirked.

"It's Halloween, right?" She muttered.

Standing on her porch, Sharon saw three macabre figures, each one with their own flash of color. The tallest brandished a scythe, adorned in a black robe, and wearing a deathly-white skeleton mask. Next to that, a shorter figure, clad in a Day-Glo orange jumpsuit, wearing a similarly garish jack-o'-lantern mask. Finally, there was a witch, her pointed hat sitting atop a neon-green mask surrounded with black netting and tattered clothes. In their hands, the masked phantoms held orange paper bags adorned with the phrase: *"HALLOWEEN LOOT!"* Seeing Sharon acknowledge this, all three held their bags open and tipped their heads in unison. The action made Sharon smirk once more.

"Cute," she whispered, throwing her hair back. "Sorry,

kids, I'm in *such* a rush tonight. I didn't even remember about this stupid holiday, so . . . "

Sharon sailed down the steps and pulled the car door open.

"Got no candy for you," she shrugged. "Try again next year, maybe I'll remember."

Ducking into her car, Sharon spotted the old woman across the way in her rear-view mirror and paused. Her hand was raised—was she waving at *her?* Sharon waved back, but quickly realized the old crone was shoeing trick-or-treaters away from her precious flowers. She wouldn't see anyway; the old bitch couldn't see beyond her nose.

That dog-kickin' bitch, she thought as she closed her door.

As Sharon reversed away, the masked figures remained on her porch, watching her.

"Those little shits better be gone when I get back," she muttered.

~

"I just don't get it!" Jamie O'Neill cried with a shrug. "I mean, why go to the trouble of buying groceries, and not cooking? Instead, I get *this.*"

He held up a paper bag and the scent of fast food wafted to Sharon's side of the car. Jamie threw himself backward and folded his arms, eyeing Sharon from beneath his floppy hair.

"Now, now, mister," Sharon began with a knowing smile. "Don't sulk, you're showing your age."

"*Pffft,*" Jamie waved away. "You sound like my god-damn mom."

Sharon laughed.

"I'm certainly old enough to be," she agreed. "But . . . Your mom could never do what I'm going to do to you later. And if you're *good* . . . I'll take you out for dinner this weekend."

Jamie gave Sharon a side long glance, but couldn't suppress a smile.

"Yes, mommy," he conceded meekly.

"That's what I thought," Sharon nodded.

Inwardly, Sharon cursed herself, knowing that he'd be all over her tonight, when all she wanted to do was relax. As she turned onto Pike Street, Sharon steeled herself for another night of rabbit-like eagerness from her young lover.

~

"What the hell is that?" Jamie asked, peering into his side mirror.

Sharon spotted the three masked figures across the street with a glance behind her.

"Oh," she dismissed with a smile, "just some kids I ran into earlier . . . I think they're sore that I had no candy to give them."

"Oh, right . . . " Jamie began thoughtfully. "It's Halloween."

Sharon stepped out of the car, eyeing the silent children across the street. They stood completely still, their gaze never wavering from her car.

"Hey," Jamie nudged as he passed by, "I think they left us something."

Turning away and following her lover, Sharon spotted the large jack-o'-lantern sitting by her front door.

"What the . . . " was all she could manage. "You think *they* left this?"

Jamie kneeled, lifting the sizable pumpkin as its flame danced before his face.

"Well, it wasn't here before, was it?" he asked.

Without waiting for an answer, Jamie stood and moved to the edge of the porch, lifting the pumpkin over his head.

"Hey!" he called to the figures across the street.

Sharon considered intervening but ultimately remained silent.

"Thanks for the token!" Jamie continued. "But you still aren't getting any sweets, losers!"

As the words left his mouth, Jamie brought the pumpkin down, letting it splatter on the concrete below. A mess of seeds and goo exploded as the smoldering candle rolled down the driveway.

"Jamie!" Sharon cried. "You didn't need to do *that!*"

"Balls…" her lover grumbled. "Now come on inside, Daddy Jamie is hungry."

Without a word, Sharon followed him. The last thing she saw through a crack in the door was the three masked figures, still silently watching across the street.

~

This was what Sharon wanted, some downtime. She was lying atop her bed in a white silk robe, a glass of wine in one hand. Jamie had come to her and they had made love. He was unusually gentle, choosing to take her atop the covers and allowing her to cradle him afterward. Then he'd disappeared downstairs, instructing Sharon to "relax."

"Hmmm . . . " she moaned lazily. "Halloween isn't so bad after all."

Sharon closed her eyes, preparing to drift off in her contented haze. That's when she heard it.

THWACK!

Sharon's eyes shot open.

THWACK!

She sat up with a frown. *What was that?* Listening closely, Sharon waited for the sound to come again.

THWACK!

Her head shot toward the bedroom window, that's where the noise came from. Sharon watched, a strange tingling seizing her gut, waiting…

THWACK!

Something bounced off the window; she'd seen it. Rising, Sharon gingerly approached the window.

THWACK!

The latest was punctuated by a *crunch* as it lodged between the glass and the frame, causing a small section to splinter.

"What the *fuck?*" Sharon whispered, running one manicured finger over the broken spot.

It was rocks from her own backyard that someone threw at her bedroom window. Then the howling started; a high-pitched, guttural howl from somewhere in the darkness. Sharon's blood ran cold as realization dawned.

"Teddy . . . " She whispered.

~

Jamie was reaching to the fridge for a beer when he heard it. Sick, unnatural howling. He froze in dumbstruck fear. Then came a knock at the back door.

"The hell . . . " He whispered, closing the fridge.

The howling continued as his hand seized the doorknob and he unlocked the door. *Is someone out there?* Pulling the door open, Jamie was greeted with a cold waft of air. The porch was empty, and as he stepped outside, the howling went on. "Hey!" He cried when he saw a silhouette.

Illuminated by the pale moonlight, Jamie saw a cloaked shadow running from the backyard. As they rounded the side of the house and onto the street, the howling faded, growing fainter and fainter with each step they took toward their escape.

"Now, just what in the hell was *that* all about?" he pondered as he stepped back inside. "I bet it's those little bastards again."

Smirking, shaking his head, Jamie padded his bare feet back to the fridge and procured his beer. Pulling the tab, he flopped down lazily on the couch and turned his attention to the television.

"Uh-oh," he smiled, taking a sip.

A teenager banged and screamed for someone to open the front door as a man in a white mask drew closer. The music intensified and Jamie felt his heart begin to pound, condensation on his beer began to mix with sweat from his palms.

BANG! BANG! BANG!

The sudden rattling at the window made Jamie leap from the couch and splatter beer all over his tank top.

"Fuck!" he cried.

BANG! BANG! BANG!

Glancing at the living room window, Jamie could see a silhouette beyond the curtains.

"Damn little *shits*," he hissed before storming from the room.

Three more bangs at the window covered the sound of Sharon's footsteps and Jamie ran into her rounding the bottom of the stairs.

"*Sharon!*" he cried, taking her by the shoulders.

Stepping back, the sight of his lover stunned Jamie into silence. Sharon was ashen-faced and trembling.

"Jamie," was all she managed.

"Shar, what is it?" Jamie asked.

"My baby! Have you seen my baby?!" Sharon cried. "I haven't seen him since we got back! I didn't even think!"

Jamie ran a hand through her long blonde hair and looked into Sharon's terrified eyes.

"Now, just slow down, babe," he soothed. "I'm sure Teddy's *fine*, just got into a cardboard box or chasing the toilet paper again."

Sharon shook her head emphatically.

"No," she began, pointing toward the kitchen. "I heard the howling outside, and someone threw stones at my bedroom window! Something's happened to my baby, Jamie."

Jamie shook his head as his face darkened with rage.

"Yeah, I heard it too, and I caught the little shit making the noise."

"Wha—" Sharon frowned.

"It's those *kids*, Sharon," Jamie growled. "Those little bastards in the masks. They've been knocking on the windows, and I saw one running out of the backyard. You said they threw stones?"

Relief washed over Sharon as she blew out a sigh and shook her hair.

"Yeah," she managed, shaking in response. "Broke one of the panes."

Just as the words left Sharon's mouth, another loud knock rattled the front door. Sharon leapt toward her lover.

"Goddamn it, anyway," Jamie whispered. "Those little rats! I'm not putting up with this all night. Halloween is over."

In one swift motion, Jamie unlocked the front door,

swept it open, and was already screaming before he knew what he was saying.

"Hey, you little *bastards!*" He bellowed. "Knock it *off* before I call the goddamn police. We'll see how much they care about your fucking candy!"

He scanned the street and could see nothing except discarded tissue paper and dead leaves.

"I bet those pussies are in the shadows," he muttered to Sharon before shouting at them once more. "Stop scaring my girl!"

As he turned, what Jamie saw made him freeze in his tracks. The wall next to the front door was smeared with a crudely drawn *X*. The huge symbol was crafted from something Jamie couldn't see in the poor light, but it covered most of the wall, including the number 22. The substance dripped onto the wood below, forming a small pool that moved toward Jamie's feet. He reached hesitantly and rubbed a finger against the symbol, finding the substance to be wet with no real scent other than a coppery tang.

"Fuckers," he snarled. "Committing vandalism now, huh?"

Wiping his hand on his tank top, Jamie stepped back inside and locked the door. Sharon waited for him; her hands anxiously clasped together.

"Well?" she questioned.

Jamie shrugged.

"No one's out there," he explained. "Look, it's just a kid's prank. They've painted a big old thing out there and broken some glass. If it stops now, we'll let it go and I'll clean up tomorrow."

Sharon didn't respond, her face was once again ashen, staring dumbfounded at her lover.

"Sharon?" Jamie prodded.

"What *happened* to you?" Sharon whispered. "You're *bleeding*, Jamie!"

Jamie looked down at himself, finally seeing the mysterious liquid clearly in the hallway light, it was a deep red.

"It's . . . " he began. "It's just paint . . . Their stupid

prank."

"It's *blood!*" Sharon snapped.

As if to compliment her words, three more bangs rattled the front door. Sharon recoiled as Jamie pressed a finger to his lips.

"Hey!" He bellowed once again. "We've called the police, y'know?"

In an instant all was silent, the only thing audible was Sharon's tremulous breathing. Then a sound came from beyond the door, softly at first, but quickly growing in volume and intensity.

"*Woof woof... Woof woof... WOOF... WOOF... WOOF!!*"

"Aw no!" Sharon groaned. "They've got him! They've got my dog!"

Frantically, she moved to unlock the door.

"Sharon, wait!" Jamie yelled as she tore the door open.

The unusually still Halloween night was suddenly filled with shrieking, a sound that came from the very depths of Sharon's soul. She had screamed three times in succession before Jamie made it over the threshold and saw what she wailed over.

"God in heaven . . . " he whispered at the sight.

Hanging from one of the porch rafters was Teddy. His leash formed a noose around his neck and his tongue hung limply from one corner of his mouth. His torso and stomach were a mess of hanging entrails that dangled between his hind legs like spaghetti from a fork. Blood ran down the porch steps in a thin, macabre river.

"Oh *god!*" Sharon wailed before making a run for the porch railing and retching violently.

"Sharon . . . " was all Jamie could manage as he spotted the three masked figures across the street.

"Teddy!" Sharon shrieked.

As Jamie watched, the small figure in the pumpkin mask pulled a gun from their waistband and took aim.

"Sharon!" Jamie cried.

Jamie saw Sharon's eyes widen in pain. Something had hissed through the air and landed with a quick, wet *thud.*

"*OW,*" Sharon yelped as she pinwheeled up against

Jamie's chest.

"Shit!" He hissed, quickly righting her. "Sharon, look at me!"

"Something . . . something *shot* me!" Sharon squeaked, dumbfounded.

There was a *pop* from across the street and something whizzed through the air. This time it culminated in a faint wooden *crack*. Jamie saw the sharp metal dart protruding from the porch wall.

"Jesus *Christ*," he said.

The words had barely escaped him before the pop and hiss came again. Pain flared from Jamie's bare shoulder as a dart embedded itself in his flesh. Blood began to trickle down his arm.

"FUCK!" he cried, quickly seizing Sharon. "Come on, we've got to get back inside!"

Confused, Sharon hurried through the front door, another dart erect in her upper back. Jamie quickly followed, and to his horror, he saw two figures racing across the street toward the house, as the Pumpkin-clad form took aim again. He slammed the door, turned the deadbolt, and fixed the chain. Jamie searched the hallway for something . . . anything, before jamming a chair under the knob.

"Okay," he whispered. "Alright . . . "

"What?!" Sharon screeched. "None of this is alright!"

Jamie approached her slowly.

"Turn around!" he said.

Sharon eyed him suspiciously, beginning to back away. *"No! You're not pulling this thing out of me!"*

Jamie cast a glance at his wounded shoulder.

"Shar . . . " he began softly. "We don't really have time to argue. Look, it doesn't hurt."

Jamie pulled the dart from his arm. He gritted his teeth through the searing pain, keeping his face stoic. Slowly, Sharon approached him.

"Just hurry," she grumbled.

Jamie pinched the dart in her upper back and pulled.

"FUCK!" Sharon screamed as it came free.

Jamie let the dart clatter to the floor as he turned her around and looked into Sharon's terrified eyes.

"Never mind that," he said firmly. "We have to decide what we're going to do."

Sharon only shook her head.

"Are you slow? We're going to call the fucking *police,* right now!"

With a shove, Sharon moved Jamie out of the way and hurried to the living room. On the television, the babysitter cowered in a closet. Sharon swiped the phone from its cradle and relief began to flow through her body, only to be quickly replaced with unbridled terror, anew.

"Oh no . . . " she whispered tremulously.

"What?" Jamie asked from the doorway.

"Aw, *noooooo!*" Sharon howled as the tears began again.

Jamie rushed to her and took the phone she held aloft. Holding it to his ear, he heard nothing.

As if to compound the growing terror in his gut, everything suddenly went dark. Jamie looked around frantically as Sharon, stunned, remained silent.

"Shit . . . " he whispered in the darkness. "They've cut the power."

"And . . . the phone," Sharon added.

The momentary silence was broken by the crunching of glass. Both looked toward the living room window.

"The glass . . . " Jamie uttered. "They're trying to shoot through the glass."

"*Can* they?" Sharon asked as she gripped his arm.

Sharon watched as he pulled open the living room curtains and brought the interior shutters over the window. Watching him do so, she was sure the glass would shatter and he'd be impaled by a hail of darts.

"On the floor," Jamie ordered. "Just in case."

Sharon hunkered down in front of the sofa as Jamie kneeled with an arm around her.

"What are we going to *do?*" she whispered.

"*Your gun!*" Sharon cried as she shot to her feet.

Quickly, Jamie pulled her back down again.

"Great idea," he hissed. "Of course, I have the gun I

use to protect *my* apartment here at *your* house."

"You don't keep it on you?!"

Jamie didn't answer.

"This is my fault," Sharon said softly, after a long pause. "I . . . should've been nicer to them, given them some treats."

Jamie scoffed in the darkness.

"Can you hear yourself?" he asked, quickly standing. "I mean, can we see ourselves? Treats? Candy? They're goddamn kids! I'm going out there."

Immediately Sharon was at his arm.

"*No,*" she implored. "We don't know what else they've got . . . Besides, the bigger fella, in the skull mask . . . "

" —is thirteen at most, and won't stand up to my fist in his face," Jamie interrupted.

Before Sharon could say another word, Jamie was making his way to the kitchen. Both were careful to duck in front of the window looking onto the backyard. From that position, Jamie reached to the counter and pulled two knives from the butcher's block. He handed one to Sharon and wrapped a hand tightly around the other. Still crouching, he made it to the back door, unlocked it, and turned the knob.

"Now, you lock this behind me," he whispered.

"Jamie . . . " Sharon began to plead.

"Hey, hey," he began with a smile. "I'll be right back."

With that, Jamie disappeared around a crack in the door and Sharon leapt for the knob. Hearing the satisfactory click, she stopped holding her breath.

~

Jamie stood in the shadows of the back porch, keeping his chef's knife raised in a striking position. Scanning the backyard, all seemed calm. He could hear nothing but the light breeze and the occasional cricket chirping. After descending the porch steps, Jamie began to sidestep along the house, keeping to the shadows offered by the rain gutters above. With every step he looked left, right, up, and down. Still, he saw nothing. Approaching the front yard, Jamie could hear his heart pounding in his ears. He was inches away from running out of cover, and would likely be shot down by darts any second.

"They're kids . . . " he breathed. "Just kids. Be nice . . . be reasonable."

Mustering all the courage he had, Jamie slipped the knife behind his back and walked out into the dim light.

"Hey . . . " he began shakily. "Hey, kids? Where are you? I'm sure we can reach an understanding."

Jamie took a step forward as he spoke.

"We could stop all this mess —"

The pain was so sudden and extreme that Jamie did little more than squeak. Crumpling to the ground, he began to draw deep, guttural breaths, but sound evaded him. His thoughts raced as his left leg seemed to burn, but somewhere in all the confusion, Jamie managed to look down.

"*Oh . . . Sweet Jesus!*" he cried.

A bear trap was clamped around his left ankle. It had bitten completely through the flesh and driven half the bone out through his foot. There were just centimeters of intact tissue leaving the appendage attached to his body. Trying to breathe through the pain, Jamie began to reach toward the mangled limb. A sneaker-clad foot stopped him as it crashed down on his injury, making Jamie howl in pain. As he did, he saw that they'd surrounded him. The jack-o'-lantern had his gun trained on Jamie, the witch stood by his head, and the cloaked, Death-like figure continued to keep the unbearable pressure on Jamie's ankle.

"Oh god!" he screamed, a tear rolling down his cheek.

Each figure cast a glance at the other, the Skull nodded toward The Witch and she removed the head of her broomstick, revealing a gleaming spear. They all had their weapons trained now: a gun, a spear, and a scythe.

"Please . . . no," Jamie said weakly.

~

Sharon's gut continued to churn. Jamie had been gone so long, but she hadn't heard a sound. Should she go out there? She was crouched by the front door with one hand around the knob. Jamie's words echoed in her head and gave her a modicum of comfort.

"They're just kids," she whispered, aloud.

With the surge of adrenaline, Sharon rose and unlocked the door. The night air hit her pallid face as she quickly turned it away from her beloved, butchered Teddy. As she navigated the porch, she kept the knife tight in her grasp.

"Jamie?" She dared as she reached the lawn.

"Sharon!"

The voice was nondescript, a loud whisper, but it was close by. Sharon sped up her step.

"Jamie?!" She called. "Kids? Hey, look, I'm sure we can . . . *Oooft!"*

Her words were cut off as Sharon collided with something solid and fell to the ground. Taking a moment, she felt a bead roll down her forehead, onto the bridge of her nose, before dripping off.

Blood.

Reaching up, she rubbed her forehead and, upon retracting her hand, she noticed it stained red. With a gasp, she glanced upward and saw what she had collided with. For the second time that night, her shriek shattered the silence.

"Nooooooooooooooooo!"

What she'd run into was Jamie, strung from the oak tree on her lawn. Sharon's face had met the exposed entrails hanging from his stomach. Looking at his contorted death stare, Sharon feared she might vomit again, until she heard that sound once more.

"Sharooooooooooon!"

Looking toward the backyard, Sharon saw all three of them standing there, weapons raised, and slowly coming toward her.

"No!" she cried before leaping to her feet.

At speed, she made it across the lawn, up the steps, and back inside. However, as Sharon locked herself behind the door once again, she realized she was completely alone now.

"Leave me alone!" she sobbed.

~

"Mommy?"

The calls drew Sharon from her stunned stupor, she wasn't sure how much time had passed.

"Mommy!?"

This time it was punctuated by sobbing.

"Where are you, mommy? I can't find you!"

Rising slowly, Sharon undid the deadbolt but kept the chain in place. Letting the door slide open and peering through the crack, Sharon saw a flash of pink in the street. A little girl in a glimmering fairy costume and a matching set of wings was slowly making her way down Pike Street.

"Mommy!?" She shrieked. "I want to go *home*, Mommy!"

"Shit . . . " Sharon whispered.

Quickly she undid the chain and threw the door wide.

"Hey!" She cried as she lurched down the porch steps. "Hey, kid."

Sharon looked down at her tear-stained face, knowing that she couldn't let this angelic princess fall victim to her tormentors.

"Can you help me find my Mommy?" the little girl asked between sniffles. "We were trick-or-treating and I . . . I lost her when I went off with a big group of kids."

Sharon knelt and took the child by the shoulders.

"No, I can't," she began, quickly. "But listen to me, it's not safe out here. There are bad people out tonight and you need to run, okay?"

Suddenly, the child raised her right arm and brought a hand across Sharon's face in a painful glancing blow. Realization hit Sharon like a gut punch as the fairy-clad child began to smile.

"Oh lady," she began sweetly. "All you had to do was give us some candy. Now, *you* need to run."

"No!" Sharon cried as she shoved the child away and made another dash back to the safety of her home.

Trying to keep an eye in every direction, she couldn't spot any masked figures. With a leap, Sharon made it back through her front door and to locked-in safety.

Resting against the door, she panted wildly.

"Sharoooooon!"

As if stabbed by an icy knife, Sharon's blood ran cold. Not wanting to, but having little other choice, she turned and followed the voice. Slowly, she inched down the hallway, wishing she had her knife now. Rounding the living room doorway, Sharon saw them: two figures in silhouette standing before her fireplace. Pumpkin and Witch had made it inside. A gasp escaped Sharon's lips as she tried to speak. No words came, but the creaking of the stairs filled the silence. Turning her head, Sharon saw Death's skull-faced visage round the banister. He pointedly blocked her path to the front door, before beginning to unlock it.

"What do you *want?*" Sharon finally managed.

The fairy stood upon the porch and made a confident entrance when the door was opened. As she strode in, the little girl acknowledged the larger masked figure graciously.

"Oh, lady," the fairy mused as she shook her head. "Just give us the *fucking* candy."

Hysterical shrieks escaped Sharon as she ran in a clumsy tableau to the kitchen, the figures followed. Slamming against the back door, Sharon shook the knob wildly, trying to open it.

It wouldn't budge.

"Nooooo!" she whined.

Turning, Sharon saw the little girl enter the kitchen, her costume sparkling in the darkness. Behind her came Death, his scythe drawn, and then Witch and Pumpkin. They stood in a line, barring Sharon from leaving the kitchen. She was trapped.

"Wait!" she cried.

She began to fumble along the kitchen counters as she sobbed nonsensically.

"Wait!" was the only word that came out clearly.

With one last, far away bolt of realization, Sharon pulled open her large pantry cupboard and began to rifle through long-forgotten snacks. Items hit her in the face and bounced along the floor, but pure adrenaline drove her on. Finally, a flash of orange reached to her out of the darkness and her hand seized around the box.

"HERE!" Sharon screamed as she thrust a packet of Terry's Big Cup Peanut Butter Swirls before her like a weapon.

Sharon watched as the little girl took the box from her before smiling sweetly.

"That's all you had to do," she said in a voice that belied her young age.

With a look to her cohorts, each child turned and began to walk away. Sharon felt relief wash over her and let out a long, tremulous sigh. Just as she did, The Fairy paused in the doorway.

"The box says six," she frowned.

"What?" Sharon snapped through a vibrating jaw.

"The box says six," the little girl repeated. "But . . . there's only three in here . . . and well, there are four of us."

To amplify her point, The Fairy slammed the box to the ground. As she did, her masked allies turned back to Sharon and the little girl stood aside.

"Oh god, *please!?"* Sharon pleaded as her legs buckled and she sank to the floor.

With weapons drawn, the three masked youngsters formed a circle around Sharon Shaw as she found her voice for the last time and began to scream.

TRICKS
Billie Karras

THE NEEDLE SLID EASILY IN THROUGH the wrapper, through chocolate and nougat and caramel and sweet-salty peanuts. Sam licked his lips, tasting the chalky smack of makeup there, liking it. The syringe's glass reservoir glittered bluely through its hash-marks in the dim basement lights, and all at once it struck him that it looked very much like something plucked out of some '70s science fiction film; colors saturated, its lines fuzzy, twin chrome flanges twinkling with mad antiquity, and really . . . could he be sure he *wasn't* in a movie?

He considered this. It would be something *old* if it were anything. He loved old movies. And poorly acted, oh yes. But most of all, if he was in a movie, it would be this: crass, so crass — so *violent* — you'd think its very *reels* would be splattered with tacky stageblood. And oh, how he loved blood. Bright and hot and sticky and *orange* and —

Sam blinked. The sound his pancake makeup made, a kind of cracking in the otherwise silent air of the basement, was very loud indeed. *Shhhhhhh,* he thought. He was mildly alarmed to find that he was shaking a little. What was going *on* with him?

The clown laughed down there in the moldering belly

of his old house. His voice was the long, slow creak of hinges swung open in the dead of night. He knew *exactly* what was going on with him, and the J&B he'd been so thirstily sucking down was only part of it. It was the task at hand, of course: at once almost cartoonishly evil and, moreover, such an over-fucked bitch of an old cliché that it was, well . . .

Almost *comforting* in its candy-corn classicality.

HALLOWEEN TREATS POISONED, the headlines tomorrow would blare, and you could really cozy up on a tufty plaid sofa to the thought of *that* baby, couldn't you? Oh, fire crackling, shadows dancing, wind outside blowing red autumn leaves up and down child-haunted streets . . . Sam could, anyway, oh yes. Sam's morbid little heart just about fucking *swooned*. And yet, all the same —

He was beginning to feel nauseous.

Using his free hand, Sam reached for his glass and found it empty, save for a little whiskey-stained slush. He snatched up the bottle. Drinking like that, he couldn't help but see himself as Kurt Russell in *The Thing* — his smooth cheeks bearded, his short hair grown long and big and wavy, his droopy, hooded eyes suddenly piercing and blue. Fire stung the back of his throat — wincing, he imagined it was gasoline. *I'm a* reeeeal *light sleeper,* he thought giddily and, at last, the film grain in the air began to sharpen back into the high definition of good old reality.

He set the bottle back down and got back to work. Depressing the plunger with practiced grace, he pumped four cc's of pale liquid blue straight into the candy bar's center like black tar heroin into a junkie's last remaining uncollapsed vein. It was pentobarbital, a fast-acting barbiturate. The good stuff. The sort of thing vets used when the family dog got rabies, or cancer, or ran over by the mailman's jolly white truck. It worked, of course, on people, too.

Sam plucked the needle out of the candy at last. It was a miniature Snickers bar. He held it up, squinting. It looked good, just as clean as the rest. He parted the flap to see the seam and couldn't even see the hole. Piece of cake. He shuddered to recall what he'd done last year, the way a man might shudder upon recollection of a long day of July yardwork, but boy—

Had it been *rewarding*.

It'd been razor blades then, and they had been a royal pain in his ass. Pulling the wrappers apart, planting the steel, gluing the flaps back together again, carefully, carefully, oh so fucking carefully—it'd been fun, though, the way cooking can sometimes be if you didn't have to. But the best part? That hadn't come until the following morning, at the hospital. He'd been a nurse there for, oh, the last six or seven years, give or take, and he liked it okay. Pay was good. Food was alright. Sometimes, he got to see people in such states of agony it made his belly bloom with giddy warmth, and all in all—yes, he liked it just fine. But that November 1st last year had been, bar none, the single greatest shift he had ever worked in his life.

All day he'd stood there watching as the doc sewed up little lips and slitted cheeks and sliced-to-the-bone gums. At least two children had had to have pieces of their tongues reattached, and for a third, a normally quite bubbly and witty little girl named Lindsey Turner, this hadn't even been possible. In her surprised, hurt, and panicky terror—one second eagerly biting into a Reese's Peanut Butter Cup and the next drooling blood and spit and melty bits of half-chewed chocolate—she had swallowed it.

Hearing this, seeing it as he stood off to the side in his scrubs and his nitrile gloves while the doc sewed her up with grim sorrow glittering dully in his eyes like snowy headlights in a funeral procession, Sam had needed to bite his *own* tongue just to keep from spraying laughter all over the room and thereby blowing the whole happy trick right then and there. And he had bit until it bled.

No one had died that night and, although secretly disappointed, Sam had pretty much known that they wouldn't from the very beginning. Last year had been more of a trial run, an experiment, to see just how much he could get away with. Skittish parents had cried *check your candy!* since time immemorial, and he'd suspected he would need to be very careful indeed if he didn't want to open his Christmas presents that year in the electric chair. Upon researching the subject, however, Sam had been amazed to find out that, in fact, there had only been two recorded cases *ever* of children being murdered via Halloween candy. And in both of them, the murderers had been not Old Chet Fester the Child Molester, nor the Boogeyman, nor Jack the Ripper—the crimes had, in *fact,* been perpetrated by none other than the children's parents themselves.

Sam had been deliciously tickled by this. And more, he had been *emboldened.* He'd all but skipped his way home from the dusty guts of the old town library, dreaming of what he would, could, *dared* do come Halloween. And afterward, sitting in his bedroom carving fun faces into his thighs with a leftover razorblade, listening halfheart- edly as the snowy television set on his dresser announced the arrival of the new year, Sam had decided that when *next* October rolled around, well . . .

It would be time for a little escalation.

And now, as he stood in his basement room, just a drunken son of a bitch in a dimestore clown suit, the antique needle staring up at him from the table all the while, its hollow tip beading with azure poison, oh, so like the fang of a pissed-off rattlesnake, *yes,* oh *yes* at *last*—

The time had come.

Upstairs, he heard the faint, hollow *ding!* of the bell at the front door. He could have screamed. Instead, he grinned. Under the dim light of the old incandescents, his lips grease-painted sloppily red, it wasn't a smile so much as it was an ax-wound with teeth up the middle. It widened as he tossed the candy into a large plastic bowl. It landed in a bed of a hundred others. *All the good stuff, kiddies,* Sam mused with a chuckle. *Not an apple in sight.*

Then he grabbed the bottle, the bowl, and headed upstairs. The feeling of retro, horror-movie unreality had returned now, making his vision glow, his spine straighten. His very flesh seemed to prickle and crawl with the snowy arcs of television electricity. This time, he decided to let it stay. This time, he decided he liked it.

Just as he reached the top of the stairs, the doorbell rang again.

It was 6:41.

~

The sky over Pike Street was a calm one, purple as bruised flesh, and not a contrail nor a cloud in sight. The crescent moon, still a ghost in its translucence by the dying light of day, hung crookedly, as if the very night itself were tipping the world a sly little wink before making its grand entrance.

The child, also alone, walked aimlessly along the cracked, weedy sidewalk. He was in no particular hurry; it was still too early to do any meaningful trick-or-treating. All the same, he didn't want to be home. His father was at work — an evening shift stocking shelves at the Shop Smart uptown — and that meant Terry would be there alone. And if she was alone, that meant she would be drinking. The child would just as soon not be around for that. His father's girlfriend had never exactly been a country peach at even the best of times, and she had a way of getting especially unpleasant when she was drunk.

And so he walked, plastic pumpkin bucket bumping lightly against his thigh with each aimless, with each wandering, restless step. Leaves rustled in the breeze. The pale-pink sheet he had over him swished. It had been white just last week — he'd spent better than an hour cutting holes out for eyes, sewing circles of black mesh into the holes, and the costume had been perfect. But then Terry (drunk, of course) had thrown it into the wash along with some socks and the knitted red sweater his father had gotten her for her birthday. She'd returned it later that evening without even so much as a shrug in apology. The child supposed it was alright, though. A pink ghost could haunt just as well as any other, couldn't it?

The streetlights flickered on. The child shivered in a sudden gust of wind and, as he did, looked up into the sky again. The moon had grown brighter. The purple had darkened to black. A smattering of stars glittered softly, but that was all. Not even so much as a plane. Except . . .

The child's mouth fell open with a hollow little *plop* that was audible only to himself. *What . . . ?* he thought, and hadn't the slightest idea.

The sky was empty no longer.

A comet, or a shooting star, or something, but it was *weird.* Neon fire swirled around a point of light so dazzling it almost hurt to look. The thing slashed across the sky, beneath the base of the moon. Then, suddenly, it zagged up above it. It was the strangest thing he had ever seen in his life, and although he had never hallucinated before, he wondered if perhaps he was now. It was just too freaky. All the same . . . he felt a smile crawl across his face. He couldn't help it; the thing was just too beautiful. And best of all —

It was *pink.*

Across the street, a babbling pair of children — a mummy and a vampire — were making their way up the sidewalk. The child noted them with mild interest and, grounded now by their presence, decided that he *wasn't* imagining things — it really *was* a shooting star. And why not? He remembered something he'd heard on television, from that kind-eyed science man he'd always thought looked a little like Mr. Rogers: *We live in a grand universe, full of mystery.* To the child, who'd had few friends that weren't characters in books, this had felt exactly right. To him it *was* grand, it *was* full of mystery. In spite of all its loneliness.

The child, whose name did not matter, closed his eyes behind the eyeholes he'd so carefully crafted and made a wish. The shooting star zagged again, flared, and then was out like a spent sparkler, as if it had heard the child's beseechment somehow and was now off to grant it. It had been a pure wish, a sweet one; just the sort of thing one might expect from the precocious heart of a motherless boy as he wandered costumed and alone on this chilly October night. But it was a wish that wouldn't come true.

The child would be dead by morning.

The clown's house was dark, lit only by flickering jack-o'-lantern candlelight and a single bell-shaded lamp on a table in the front room. The wood-paneled walls there were pictureless, grimy with dust and yellowed with the nicotine of a thousand dead cigarettes. The floor was bare, the furniture sparse, and the television, an old Zenith color model with rabbit ears and a missing volume knob, sat opposite a lumpy red EasyChair. Year-round, these latter two were the room's main features. Tonight, however, there were the pumpkins—here by the door, there on the steps, and everywhere in between. They grinned with gleeful eyes and crooked teeth; mad faces, bathing the room in their dusky, Samhain glow. But the clown—pickled in whiskey, caked in makeup, clutching his big orange bowl of death hard enough to put stress marks on the sloping curve of its candy-corn painted sides—wasn't grinning at all anymore.

He had royally fucked up.

The first hour or so had been *perfect.* His first trick-or-treaters of the night, a pimply group of uncostumed teenagers, had each received their candy in turn, dropped into grocery bags, one by one and off they went. Likewise with the next ones, and the next. They'd go home, Sam's poisoned pieces lost in a sea of a hundred others, perhaps eating them tonight, perhaps not. Either way, who would be able to say where they'd come from—what was one Twix from another? It would be difficult to narrow down in any suburban neighborhood; on Pike Street, most folks took Halloween *seriously*—at least, that was how it seemed. Even now, after his previous years' razor-bladed festivities, every bowl was stocked, nearly every window was wisped with spiderwebs and splattered with fake blood. You could stay out past midnight and still not hit every house, at least as far as Sam knew or could tell.

But then it happened—those *kids,* those *kids,* those

goddamned silent spooky weirdo *kids.*

It'd begun normal enough: they'd rung the bell, stood patiently for the door. There were three of them: one, a vampire with a red-lined cape and plastic teeth, another a mummy wrapped in Ace bandages and smudged around the eyes with her mother's cheapest eyeshadow; the third, centered between the other two, was a ghost. Draped in a sheet with holes cut out at the eyes and a pair of blue-and-white Keds poking out from below, this one was the smallest — probably their kid brother. Or *sister,* Sam had thought to himself in spite of the boyish shoes. Because the sheet's color (despite its status as the traditional choice for any self-respecting specter) hadn't been white.

It had been pink.

Sam grinned down at them, candy bowl in hand, waiting for that wonderful, not-quite-unison chorus of *trick or treat!* It didn't come. Instead, they'd just *stood* there, the vampire's face slack, the mummy's blank, and the ghost's nothing but an outline; the bump of a nose and two black, empty eyes.

"Er . . . Happy Halloween!" Sam clucked, giving his best clown voice, trying to cut through the odd tension that seemed to thrum between them. He dropped a piece of candy each into their buckets, and the children made no move, did not speak. Sam shifted, feeling awkward and . . . nervous? But why should he be nervous? His hand itched for his bottle. He began to turn. "Alrighty, well. Stay safe out there, k —"

But then something terrible happened, something he couldn't believe he'd never thought of, something he couldn't believe he'd never in his whole life even seen occur until right this very moment:

A tiny hand, snaking out from beneath the pink sheet, reaching into the bucket for the candy — to *eat* it, good sweet Christ *to eat it right here* . . .

Sam's eyes bulged, but what could he do? Say — *hey, don't eat that, it's poison* — ? Oh, but what would happen in ten minutes, when the impolite little cumstain dropped dead? They'd be able to point to *his* house, to *him,* and what then? All at once his bowels were very hot, very full. He ignored them, trying to think, trying to —

But it was already too late. Then there was a crinkling sound beneath the sheet, followed by chewing, wet and smackful. And then . . .

Silence.

Sam tried desperately to keep the storm off his face. Seconds passed; no one moved. Then at last, one by one, they turned, walked down the porch steps . . .

And were gone.

That had been less than sixty seconds ago, and now here he was — pacing his front room, needing that drink more than ever — shuddering with fear and naked, pulsing fury. Would it hurt when they shot his head through with enough electricity to put down a small elephant? Would his scalp burn? Would his eyeballs burst? He thought it would; thought they might. But what could he do? Sam put the bowl down, snatched his J&B and took a long, painful pull. Coughing, he realized that he already knew. There was only one thing.

He would have to go get them.

Sam put the bottle back down, snatched his keys off the television. He breathed, willing his reality back to celluloid, and the world obliged. It was going to be okay. He was going to be okay. And why?

Because —

"*I'm* the monster," he said, and *that* brought his grin back, sure it did, bet your *fur*. Because no matter *what* happened, no matter how bad things might get, no matter how they stabbed you, or shot you, or burned you, or maimed you — they could blast you off in a rocketship to outer fuckin *space* if they wanted to . . . there was always a sequel. And the monster *always* came back.

So Sam was out the door again. He was going to hop in the car, cruise down the street, find that trio of freaks . . . and then he'd stop them. They couldn't have gotten far, and he was a big man. He'd stuff them into his old Buick like sacks of straw, ripe and ready to fill out a scarecrow's burlap flesh, and then he'd fix them. But he only got as far as the welcome mat before he had to stop again, his scream stopped only by the grinding grace of his own clenched teeth. It sat sharp in his throat, painful, like a sliver of swallowed fishbone.

On the stoop were three small, skinless skulls. They grinned, and baby teeth glittered between their jaws like pearls in the sleepy light of the moon. Seated in each small, eyeless socket were candles. Wax dripped off bone like tears, and the flicker of their flames bathed Sam's clown-shoed feet in dancing shades of burning yellow. He backed away, confused, helpless, and nearly tripped over the sill. He searched the street before him, not knowing what he was looking for, seeing nothing but lined blacktop and old trees and the houses across the way—

Then he saw them.

The mummy, the vampire, and the little pink ghost, just . . . standing there, between his car and the cracked edge of his driveway, just . . . *standing* there, watching him. And he was *afraid*. And how could this be? He was the monster—*him, him, HIM.*

Suddenly a wind kicked up, bitter and howling, biting Sam like cold razors. The candles went out in a chuffing *poof*, sending six wisps of smoke lazily up from their sockets. Then that, too, blew away, and he was staring at nothing but dead, empty blackness, like the clouded midnight sky, like the sheeted face of the pink ghost, like the blazing eyes of demons gone dreamlessly off to sleep.

And the monster, at last, began to scream.

～

The sidewalks of Pike Street were teeming now with ghouls, goblins, and all manner of things that go bump in the night. Here was a Michael Myers, his cheap rubber mask too big for his head, the knife in his hand plastic and splattered with fake blood. Here was a werewolf, torn flannel poked through with plastic fur and looking more like a puppy in a grunge band than Lon Chaney in the moors. Here was a zombie, a princess, a corpse bride; they giggled, all of them, running from house to house, pillow-sacks and pumpkin buckets bumping their knobby knees and filled with Butterfingers and Tootsie Rolls and Mars Bars and small, rattling boxes of blackly festive Willy Wonka Nerds.

Here, coming up the cracked, weedy sidewalk, was another group. Silent, these. They did not run, they did not laugh, and there were three of them: one dressed as a mummy, another dressed as a vampire, the third dressed as a ghost. Its pink sheet fluttered in the breeze behind it like an ectoplasmic tail, and its face was featureless, just two black holes for eyes and the bump of a nose.

Trailing behind them—perhaps their father—was a man in a cheap clownsuit. He walked much as they did, with that strange, plodding step—as if, perhaps, his costume was uncomfortable. Lifting a hand to his face (his free hand, for the other held a big orange bowl of candy), he felt the skin there, probing, preening, as if to make sure it was still there. Satisfied, the clown walked on, drinking in the sights, the decorations, thinking of the fun to be had and the tricks to be played. He stole a glance at the starry sky above and grinned. So pretty, Earth's moon.

The house they ended up choosing was a shoddy old thing. Its decorations were cheap, its paint cracked and sun-washed into a color that was impossible to discern by the dusky throw of the arc-sodium streetlights. Inside, a sullen little girl sat on the couch, staring at the television, barely watching whatever drecky horrorshow her father had put on. He was in the kitchen, fussing over his famous caramel apples. Her mother was out, God knew where, and the girl sighed. In her mouth, the scarred lump of tongue in the back of her throat sat like a throbbing rock. It still pained her sometimes. In her lap, her hands made shapes absently. ASL was still a struggle for her.

Suddenly, there was a knock at the door—they did not have a bell.

"Hon," her father called. "Can you get that?"

Lindsey Turner went.

The first thing she saw was the clown. He loomed behind the children like a monolith, some Barnum & Bailey monstrosity, and she had to stifle a gasp at the very sight of him. His face, made-up in greasepaint and smudged with sweat, was *wrong*. His nose hung crookedly. His eyes drooped. His cheeks bulged. At his neck, a flap of skin hung over his ruffled collar, and beneath it, she could see something else, something gray, but it was flesh. She could tell because there were veins swimming in it.

Fighting the urge to slam the door in their faces, she began to dole out the treats — some for the mummy, some for the vampire, some for the ghost — but then, from the corner of her eye, she caught a flash of something in the clown's ratty, rust-stained glove, something metallic, something, perhaps, like a razor —

"Honey?"

She had yelped, of course — in surprise just as much as out of fear — and her father was coming now, thank God. Lindsey got ready to slam the door after all, got ready to run into his arms, got ready to hear his gentle reproachments about the progress she'd been making with the child therapist she saw each Thursday *(remember what Dr. Martin said, sweetie, it's called exposure, and it's good for you, and you have got to face your fear)* —

But it hadn't been a razor at all. Lindsey Turner almost laughed. A Snickers bar, that was all, just one of those miniature squares they sold at Shop Smart for the holiday, and how could she have been so silly?

But then the clown — still staring at her with those horrible dead eyes, still holding his tiny bit of foil filled with chocolate and nougat and caramel and sweet-salty peanuts — *smelling* now, like a black, gangrenous wound and she could almost see it as it festered, oozing pus and crawling with flies and the fat, writhing worms that were their children.

The clown began to grin, and that grin chilled Lindsay to the bone like nothing she'd ever seen in her life. It wasn't so much a grin, she decided, as it was an ax-wound with teeth up the middle. His cheeks cracked, and lipstick dripped down his chin, and Lindsey realized with renewed horror that it wasn't lipstick at all. It was blood, and she couldn't move, couldn't breathe, all she could do was watch—watch as he lifted his free hand up to his face, watch as he brushed over that horrible leaking smile, watch as he went past his nose, past his cheeks, toward his eyes—

"What's wrong?" Her father was at her side now, his hands on her shoulders in an empty show of protection. He might as well have been miles away. *"Hey,"* he said, addressing the things on the porch now. "Just what the hell is going on here?"

But then he, too, had to stop and watch as the clown hooked his long, dirty fingernails into his eyelids, working them beneath the skin, pulling. Blood gouted, splashing Lindsey's cheeks in fluid that was far too cold, far too thick. There were two tiny, wet crushing noises, the sound sparrow's eggs might make when crushed between sweaty palms, and she watched as the white jelly that had been the clown's eyes oozed down his stretching cheeks like curdled, rotten tears. There was another sound, like the sound sinew makes when it's ripped from the side of a cheap steak, and finally . . .

The clown was a clown no longer.

It clutched its mask of dead flesh between fingers that were suddenly much too long. The white gloves it wore had, at some point, burst open at the tips and its claws, curving like scythes in a late autumn harvest, abruptly opened, dropping the crumpled scrap of clownface onto the stoop with a sickening *splat.* Lindsey's scalp prickled with sour fearsweat. Far away, urine began to trickle down her legs. It was warm, at first. Then it was cold.

The thing's visage was a primordial nightmare come alive; the basal, primitive sort of horror that sets upon the deepest corners of the brain with a needlelike point and a razorfine edge and *twists.* It had big black eyes, wide and tilted. Beneath them were twin slits, a pale perversion of the nasal cavity in a human skull. They whistled lightly as it respirated. Its face was gray, swimming with veins, and its skin was slick, slick, so slick, like the flesh of a dead salamander that's only just now begun to putrefy. And with a mouth that drooled black slime, with a voice clicking and chittering and yet utterly *devoid*, as if inside it lived the very blackest part of space where no stars shined, where no planets spun, where the night was forever, where the dark was *alive* —

The thing from the sky spoke at last.

"Trick or treat."

And as its hellish children finally moved forward, as the girl with no tongue and her father tried to shut the door in vain even as the walls inside began to bleed; as a strange sort of shooting star lit up the empty night air with pink fire once more, the thing from the sky put the candy in its mouth at last and chewed, slowly, savoring it wrapper, chocolate, poison, and all. And oh . . .

How it wished Halloween could come *every* night.

$N^{\underline{o}} 24$

MISCHIEF NIGHT
Brad Acevedo

WHEN THE WIND BLOWS AND CASTS about the shifting of the seasons, so too do the echoes of a world beyond our very own. Through leaf-strewn sidewalks and lamp-lit streets, we find ourselves embroiled in the crisp air of a time brimming with death, life, and frolic. It is a time when those who seek a single night of a new identity can emerge into the streets and cast their inhibitions aside.

A night for more than just candy and costumes. A night for more than just spirit-warding lanterns and devious deeds.

This night, Halloween night, is for the children.

The residents of Pike Street knew that their neighborhood was a popular jaunt — for the good or the bad — for the little ones. One homeowner in particular answered the summons of a chiming doorbell to be greeted with a most unusual sight, even for this magical night.

The little girl on his doorstep wore a mask of shiny porcelain. It arched forward, a beak-like protuberance with stark white feathers branching out from either side, resembling an odd confluence of a masquerade mask and an 18th-century plague doctor. A crack scarred down the left side of the beak and tied to either side with black ribbons were things that glinted in the porch light.

The homeowner reached behind himself into the dark recesses of the unlit home interior and fumbled around for a moment, grasping for his empty candy bowl.

He turned back toward the girl and stumbled back with a slight gasp. There were more trick-or-treaters. He hadn't even heard their approach, and he surveyed his new visitors with curiosity and confusion.

There were three more children, each in unusual costumes. One clad in a furry suit bedecked with claws and fangs; a beast of indiscriminate origin. Another in a full black bodysuit with painted bones, a traditional skeleton guise, although the skull perched on and over the kid's head like a helmet. The third little one was clad in a comparatively boring, plain white sheet with eyeholes. Your basic bedsheet ghost. Beyond the cavalcade, at the apex of the walk stood an adult clad in jeans and a dark hooded coat. No doubt the kids' chaperone, an older sibling or cousin, perhaps.

The homeowner raised a tentative hand in greeting to the older one on the sidewalk. No response. He shrugged and knitted his brows in apology, showcasing the lack of candy in the bowl.

The little girl in the bird mask turned back to the Chaperone as if to seek approval. Then she reached up alongside her mask, pulled something shiny off the porcelain visage, and lashed forward, snipping off one of the homeowner's fingers in the process.

The girl giggled musically, a sound the man would find delightful in other circumstances, were it not blotted and obscured by his own wail of shock and pain. The other children followed suit, tackling the man to the ground. The hairy monster and skeleton children pinned him down as the bird girl unveiled her twin apparatuses of torture: silver and gleaming scissors, now stained red and wet.

The girl withdrew a latex mask from the darkness and stretched it over the man's head. Had he been able to witness his own assault, the homeowner would see that he now possessed the guise of an exaggerated cartoon clown, all garish white paint and a bulbous red nose. The ghost child hurried forth and passed its comrade a small, nozzled device. The little girl pressed it into the nose slits of the clown mask and squeezed the device. Wet, hot agony ripped into the man as something liquid and searing flooded the confines of the guise, adhering vinyl to his flesh. His screams were muffled and then subsided to a groan as his lips melted together into a morass of molded skin.

The children stood back to behold their handiwork. The flesh continued to bubble as the man in the clown mask succumbed to the pain, and melted skin began to pool out to stain the amber-hued walkways of Pike Street.

The children shrugged at the lack of candy, but the child in the hairy monster outfit found one treat: the severed finger of the man in the clown mask. He scarfed it down noisily and joined the bloodstained, cherubic procession as they made their way back toward the sidewalk. They left the house quiet, dark, and open—an abyss of silence.

Gazing left to right, the bird girl chose a direction and pointed onward. Five figures traipsed through the crackling leaves, the sidewalk freshly damp from a mid-afternoon shower. Here, amongst the lanterns in the warmly lit windows and amongst other (more innocent) frolicking children, they ventured forth in search of more treats and tricks.

~

"Goddammit, I hate Halloween."

Samantha Castle sighed in her home, located at 24 Pike St. At the present time, despite her claim, she was busy putting the finishing touches on her costume.

Her guise consisted solely of a pair of cat ears and six stripes of eyebrow pencil-applied whiskers that she just couldn't seem to get right. She leaned closer toward the mirror, carefully applying the makeup.

"Shit!" she cursed, dashing a line across her nose, startled out of concentration by the insistent ringing of her phone. She stumbled into the kitchen and scooped up the receiver in frustration. "What?!"

"Well, good evening to you too," said a lilting voice on the other end.

"Oh yeah, Dani, sorry," Samantha apologized to her good friend for the outburst. The costume was, in essence, naught but a favor owed to her longtime friend and confidant. Danielle had been there to help Sam through the past couple of years after her parents' passing, and she owed it to her to play designated driver at the Owens' Halloween Bash. Costumes required, but maximum effort certainly not, hence the half-effort that Sam was currently struggling with.

"I'll decide later if I want to accept that apology or not," Dani teased. Sam rolled her eyes. "Are you almost ready or what? How long does it take to draw a couple of stripes on your face?"

"Longer than you'd think," Sam replied. Her hands were shaking as she rubbed at her nose, fumbling the receiver with her other hand. The streak wouldn't come off, dammit. To make matters worse, it zagged across and obscured the tiny three brown dots that stood on the mocha skin of her right cheek.

"Well, hurry up. I'm getting hungry." The sound of mock snarling echoed over the phone. Danielle had informed her friend of her plan to go as Amanda Bearse's character from *Fright Night,* and it seemed she was practicing for the role.

"Go nibble on Kevin's ass or something until I'm ready," Sam chuckled.

"That's not a bad idea. He's looking rather tasty tonight now that you mention it." Dani yelled into the background, "Hey, babe, come here a minute!"

Sam chuckled and shook her head. She loved the feistiness Dani introduced into her life, the life that sparkled from her bright blue eyes. Maybe tonight wouldn't be so bad. She could use it, God knew.

"You sure you'll be all right to drive?" Dani asked.

"Yeah, I'll . . . I'll be fine. I promise."

"Okay, well, just call me soon," Dani informed. "And Sam, don't forget the tail. It completes the whole damn ensemble."

"For you, hon, only for you," Sam smirked.

"That's my girl," Dani replied. "Tonight's going to be fun, I promise."

"Yeah, I know," Sam replied. "See you soon."

"Bye."

Sam hung up the phone and concentrated. One more attempt at her makeup. So far, so good. Almost done. *Annnnd* . . .

~

The doorbell rang.

Sam's hand skidded. "Damn!" Another streak. She abandoned the futile task and approached the front door. She really should have put up a sign to ward off all the kids.

Samantha flung open the door to reveal a quartet of children flanked by an adult. Each child held out burlap sacks in unnerving unison while their guardian remained stoic and silent at the foot of her porch.

"Sorry guys, no candy," she explained. "Go, uh, try the place next door."

The children didn't respond. Strange costumes, too. There was a little blonde girl that looked like a little white bird, a boy in a skeleton outfit, a little boy in a hairy   . . . what was that, a bear? A wolf? He was slathered in bits of red, matting his fur and giving a look that seemed too macabre for such a young kid. In the back of the group, a fourth child lingered, obscured entirely in a classic ghost sheet with cut-out eyes. The sheet seemed like it should have been a pristine white, but it was smeared with specks of red that glistened wetly under the porch light. The adult remained back, clad simply in dark jeans and a hooded coat. Quite the odd collection.

"No candy, guys. Sorry."

The children did not deliver the polite response she had expected. They simply stood, silent and motionless.

The boy in the beast-bear-wolf outfit broke the moment by picking something out of his plastic fangs and flicking it off into the dark.

"No guys, I just said, no candy. Go check down the street. I heard that the older Shaw lady is handing out king-sized peanut butter cups." There was no response from the silent quintet. "Okay, I'm going to close the door now."

The door closed almost all the way but stopped inches from sealing her in the quiet tranquility of her own home. She glanced down at a tiny white slipper wedged in between the door and the frame. The little girl in the beaked mask opened the door boldly and held out her sack again.

Samantha Castle had had enough. If these kids had been polite, she might have rustled up some loose change for them or cans of New Coke. Something to appease them, at least. But this brash act crossed her personal line. She opened the door wide and gave the little girl a light shove. The child staggered back into the hairy arms of the beast boy. Sam regretted the physical contact but maintained her firm composure.

"No, kid, that's not the kind of thing you do to a stranger," she said sternly. She turned her gaze toward The Chaperone. "Hey pal, what are you teaching your kids? Whatever it is, it isn't working. Now get out of here!" She slammed the door boldly shut and took a deep breath. She really hated this night. And despite all this, she had to work up the gall to get behind the wheel of a car.

She turned to head back into the house. A *thud* sounded from the large bay window in the living room.

"What the hell?" She walked into the darkened room and inspected the glass portal. A brownish smear coated the exterior of the glass. As she bent forward and peered at it closer, another smear appeared with a sudden *thunk*, startling her backward.

Sam took a step back and watched as more and more brown lumps began to smack against the glass. She hoped to God it wasn't . . . she took a step forward, comforted that the glass would protect her. She squinted her eyes to gaze closer at the material. It didn't look like shit; that was a relief.

One of the lumps began to slowly slide down, leaving behind a streak of—*hair? And . . . was that a tooth?*

Sam opened the door carefully and looked outside. Beyond the shadows of her front walk, small forms flitted amongst the shade of the night. She opened the door wider, and one of the nasty brown objects smacked into the side of the house right alongside her. It left a greasy brown and red splat. Sam dodged to the side as another lump smashed into the walkway before her.

"You little shits!" Samantha yelled, her face scrunched in fury. "Get off my property before I call the cops!"

The bird girl stepped forward and cast one more lump in her direction before the kids scattered off.

Sam scoffed . . . and took a direct shot to the face. The bird girl cocked her head in mocking triumph, disappearing into the shadows once more. Sam gasped in shock and disgust, spitting out a wad of brown, black, red, and pink. It tasted as oily as expected and, curiously, kind of sweet.

She swiped the muck off her face, smearing one of her fresh cat whiskers, frantically wiping it away. She snarled and paced back into the house, lifting the phone with a huff.

"Hello? Yes, I need to report a vandalism. A bunch of kids just threw something at my house and . . . "

Silence.

"Hello?"

A sound. The phone emitted a low drone, not unlike a swarm of bees. She held the receiver away from her head even as the noise descended into an obscene crackling noise. Now, a hissing noise. The sound of raw meat cooking over a spit until supple and juicy. Was that . . . ? Children giggling.

She hung up and staggered backward. The doorbell rang, a shrill peal in the chaos of the night. Oh God, what now?

She knew better. She wasn't answering that door. Even with the light that blazed forth through the inset glass, promising to hold the nightmares at bay, like her mom always said it would. Even with the light growing brighter, stronger, hotter. Dangerously so.

She wrenched open the door. A fire leaped forth, yet rather anticlimactically. A single lit jack-o'-lantern adorned her front walk.

Part of Samantha was relieved at the image of such a traditional standard of this particular night, despite her feelings toward the holiday. In light of the bizarre events that had transpired, the cheerful grin and light blaze comforted her, and established a feeling of normalcy and familiarity.

Like most good things, however, this would not last. The candle within the gourd flickered and extinguished. From within, something stirred. She stood, shell-shocked and frozen, as the leering face of the jack-o'-lantern exploded forth. A gamut of seeds and chunky globs of innards spewed forth, followed by something . . . moving. It lashed forth with serpent swiftness, lashing into the hem of her jeans with scissor blades. Sam screamed and leaped back, even as a tiny form burst out of the mess. Homunculi arms groped through the pumpkin guts, and a fetal form braced on tiny arms, pushing itself off of the front walk where it dripped with orange goo in a bastardized, embryonic parody. Birdie, the little girl in the beaked mask, stood there before her. Sam was frozen still, even as blood dripped from her cut ankle and from the knife in her hand. Birdie cocked her head silently. She thrust out her trick-or-treat sack once more, and Samantha Castle slammed the door shut with a sob.

Her mind was blank, her face covered in grime, gore, and smeared makeup. She staggered through the living room and briefly caught her reflection in the blank stare of the TV. Amidst all this, her birthmark still stood out, and she briefly remembered her mother telling her about the "angel kisses" and how each little ethereal peck would gift her with three special spots, right on her cheek. She felt it briefly and wiped some of the grime off.

The phone shrieked, and Sam quickly ran to answer, raising it tentatively. "Hello?" A voice that quivered with trauma.

"Sam?" A familiar cadence, a welcoming one at that.

"Oh Dani, thank God," Sam breathed in relief. "Listen, there's something going on here. I don't—I don't . . . Where are you now? Are you home? Is Kevin with you?"

"Don't worry about that. Listen, Angel, it's getting kind of late."

Angel?

"Dani, call the police and send them to my place, please. I can't . . . I can't get through . . . "

"The police? Did you start a party without me?"

"No, Dani, I'm serious! There's something going on—"

"Sounds like you're having fun over there, Sam."

"I—"

"But listen to me: if you *really* want to have a good time . . . just get them some treats. It's as simple as that."

"What . . . " Sam was at a loss.

"It's "Trick-or-Treat" Samantha, seriously, it's not that complex. Treats for them or tricks on you. They only get one night a year to sample our wares, and they're not going to waste it. Every other night . . . food, candy, treats . . . It turns to ash in their mouths, Sam. Can you imagine an existence like that?"

"Wait, who?"

"The children, you dumb bitch!" Dani exploded on the other end, although Sam suspected she was not speaking to her good friend, and shuddered at the thought of where the girl might actually be. "This is a special night, a wonderful night. It started differently, long ago. But now it belongs to the children. They're just having fun. They came to visit me earlier . . . "

"Whoever the fuck this is, I am *not* having fun," Sam snarled, anger replacing fear. "I want this to end; I did *nothing*."

"Maybe next year, turn off your porch light, and they

won't stop by," the voice suggested.

"These are *not* children."

"Well, maybe not the kind you're used to seeing."

Sam seethed. "So, if I give them what they want . . . they'll all just go away?"

"That's how it works, isn't it?" the voice said. *"But . . .* you need to get them what they really want. And be nice to them too; they're just little ones after all."

"How do I know what they want?"

"Just follow the children, Sam. They're the lions. You're the calf. A little child will lead them, and all that. You know how it goes. Or maybe you don't," the voice teased.

"What happened to Danielle? Where is my friend?"

"Act fast, Angel. Little tummies are rumbling, and they're not very patient."

Click.

Sam dropped the receiver, sobbing. Tears streaked through the caked substances on her face, cutting a swath through the mess. She bent down to pick up the phone and was caught off guard by another *thump* on the window. She stood her ground yet leaned forward to spy past the newest lump of matter on the window and into the yard.

Samantha had always liked the wide oak tree in their front yard. She remembered the swing her father had built and tied to the lowest limb, and bless his heart, it hadn't been a very sturdy construction. It had collapsed one spring day, and little Angel Sam had tumbled to the ground in a heap of tears. Her father picked her up, comforted her, and then he and her mother fixed her ham and peanut butter sandwiches, her favorite. It was a mighty and old tree, and she had promised to never have it removed, knowing it wasn't the tree's fault she had been hurt.

But the tree wasn't itself. The old oak was being defaced, corrupted. The mockery of arboreal affection taking place outside steamed her soul and curdled her heart unlike anything else. There was that damn skeletal child, prancing about gaily without a care in the world. He hurled back and chucked a string of material into the air, where it sailed freely, before draping over the very branch where her swing had once barely clung to. The little shit was actually TP-ing her home. And yet the material unfurled and tossed into the branches was not the traditional 2-ply one might pick up at a Market Basket. As Boney continued to hurl the cords, the light caught it perfectly, and Samantha noted the red and gray gristle clinging to what she knew —*knew*—were the innards of some poor fool who had crossed the children's path.

Sam sniffed and then screamed a raw scream of rage and fear. She had no further time to process as she swiftly realized that Boney's vandalism had been but a distraction. The large bay window suddenly shattered, and she backpedaled swiftly with a shriek. Beastie shook his dazed little furry head and shook off shards of glass from the hole where he had been hurled in like a living battering ram. The rest of the children quickly piled in. The Other One in the ghost outfit hopped up and down manically and stepped directly on the broken glass with bare feet. Meanwhile, The Chaperone simply observed from beneath the gore-bedecked oak tree.

Sam dashed away and hurled herself down the hall, passing by the near empty room that had once belonged to her parents and slamming her own door shut.

She stood there in the dark, in the quiet, breathing heavily and listening for any motion out in the hall. She brushed off more of the grime coating her face and wiped it on the bed nearby. In the process, more of the muck wisped across her lips, and she shuddered again at the sweet and distressingly pleasant taste.

It didn't take long for the children to reach her door. The first slam rattled the simple wooden door on its hinges. The second slam jostled it further. The third resulted in an audible, rending *crack*.

"WHAT DO YOU WANT?!" Sam screamed. "Leave me alone!"

The slamming and commotion in the hall abruptly ceased. A rustling and chattering of high-pitched, unknown voices permeated the quiet night. Sam realized this was the first time she had heard the children speak, but she couldn't make out any words. A slip of paper, yellowed and tattered, suddenly appeared from beneath the door.

Sam snatched it up quickly. She flicked on the overhead light (no bother hiding; they already knew where she was) and inspected it.

GIVE US SOMETHING GOOD TO EAT

The door smashed open with a thunderous crack. Birdie and Beastie dropped their skeletal cohort, his hard skull having been used as an effective battering ram. As before, The Other One and The Chaperone remained passive in the dark of the hallway beyond.

The three aggressors advanced quietly and slowly, taking their time. Sam's knees collided with the edge of the bed, and she dropped backward, sitting on top of the comforter.

"Raid the kitchen," she said, quietly. "Take anything you want. Anything. Just leave me alone."

Birdie snuffled softly beneath her mask and jerked one small, pink hand backward over her shoulder—a motion to move. Sam shook her head wildly. Birdie reached out to Samantha gently. Quick as a honed predator, the little girl reached down, grasped Sam's ankle, and squeezed. Sam gasped and withdrew, scuttling up farther on the bed. Birdie gestured for her to look.

Sam reached down and lifted the hem of her pants. The slash wound from before was now covered in thin, black fibrous membranes. Before her startled, make-up-bedecked eyes, the fibers wove into the cut and sealed it shut.

She knew better. She knew they weren't about to simply shift gears and be kind and gentle. They wanted something, and a simple act of kindness was just the way to go about coercing her to their will. She weighed her options. Cower here in the bedroom and be viciously massacred, or follow the children and see what they wanted. Maybe look for an opening once she was out of the confined space. It was an easy decision.

Birdie reached out her hand, and Sam took it cautiously. "I don't have much of a choice, do I?"

Beastie shrugged and toddled along out of the room, impatiently motioning for his cohorts to follow. The arcane parade made their way out toward the living room, amidst the crunching of broken glass, scattered bone, and blots of spilled blood. As Birdie led her along, Sam stole a glance at the carnage that had fouled her home.

"This has been an exciting night, huh?" she said to nobody in particular.

She giggled in spite of everything. God, she was losing her mind. Maybe none of this was really happening. Maybe . . . maybe she had never left her place beside her mom in the ambulance and had been carted off to a facility with friendly nurses and nice, soft, gentle padded walls. Something soft and gentle just sounded good right now. Something . . . sweet.

She wiped off another piece of muck from her face and sucked it off her own finger, gently and longingly. She liked it.

The children led her outside; she stole a glance toward the car. HER car, not her parents' car. No, that one was gone. Much like her parents themselves, lost in a scream of mangled steel on this very night a year prior. Charred and claimed by (hell)fire not unlike the old Stoddard Manor that used to reside in the field next door.

Samantha held back a sob as The Other One, the little child in the stained sheet, pressed an empty burlap sack harshly into her trembling hands. The child reached out and pointed down Pike Street toward the next house down the street, the little one's arm covered in oozing, festering pustules. Her gaze followed the rotting appendage. Beyond the pools of festering amber lamplight, another contingent of trick-or-treaters walked in the opposite direction. Three children (a pink sheet-ghost?) and an adult in a clown outfit. She sighed, wistful for nights when such a parade of guises would present itself as the most unusual sight of the evening. Days long gone, perhaps tarnished memories to never be recovered. Not tonight, not ever.

Samantha nodded to the child, took a single step, and then decided that she would not become the latest soul claimed on this night. She threw the bag over the top of the child's head and shoved the little one back into its brethren.

Her feet carried her faster than an autumn wind down the yard, aiming to run to a salvation that didn't seem to exist in the surreal hellscape of this cold night. The chill settled into her heaving lungs, her bones, and her very soul. The cold coalesced into the small of her back in a sudden bodily *thud*, and she pitched forward. Her fall was broken by the oak tree, that stately sentinel. She fell; a pair of scissors plunged into her back from a perfectly executed throw, yet she found herself held upright.

Sam gasped in pain and clutched frantically at the handhold. It felt greasy, warm, and wet. And then she realized this was the tree the children had vandalized earlier, and in her panic, she fell further into a spider's snare of warm and steaming entrails. She became entangled in the web of innards of untold prior victims, and finally, the cold overwhelmed her against the warm ropes, and it all became . . .

Too much.

She slumped amidst the innards, swaying gently in the motions. Samantha was all but dead weight, her many wounds festering even as she swayed there, wrapped in a blighted embrace. The children grasped The Other One and ushered the child forward. It reached up and grasped Sam's gore-addled face with a small hand and lifted her upward gently. Sam, resigned to her fate, allowed herself to look. The sheet had torn further, and a single crystal blue eye peeked outward.

The other children whispered excitedly. The beast boy grinned at her with a bleeding shark's grin, and she saw for the first time that his mouth played host to all matters of fester, rot, and decay. Brown, cracked teeth and skittering fat, oil-black beetles scurried hurriedly even as he crunched down upon his own tenants and licked his lips with a sticky-wet tongue.

The Other One spoke, "Angel."

She planted three soft kisses on Sam's cheek, sticky residue remaining as she pulled away from the Angel Kiss birthmark. Then, with a flash of cold steel and amber moonlight, carved a strip of flesh from Sam's face. The tiny fiend tilted her head back and swallowed the morsel whole.

Samantha Castle sobbed: "Why?"

The child beneath the sheet spoke again, in a familiar voice that caused the girl to wail in further degradation of sanity. Dani's voice echoed from the child: "It's really quite simple. They wanted something sweet. And now they have it."

"I'll give them what they want," Sam replied weakly.

"Candy?" The foul thing laughed. "It was never about candy. They wanted something sweet, and what more saccharine than the little angel herself? These little ones, they only spend one day amongst us, and all they want to do is have fun. And what, pray tell, could be more fun than the corruption of the innocent? Especially those who don't appreciate the spirit of this special night. But you'll learn; they'll teach you, Angel."

"I don't understand . . . "

"You will."

She thrashed against the slick, visceral ropes that restrained her. And she knew. Samantha knew that even in this small body before her, this corruption and unholy transmogrification, Samantha felt the closeness that could only come from someone she loved, like a sister . . .

Sam opened her mouth to declare what she accepted as a malignant truth, a manic grin lighting her bleeding visage: "Dani? What happened to *Fright Night?*"

Birdie cut off further retorts by shoving The Other One aside and snipping off Samantha's nose with her scissors.

Sam fell back into shock as the blood mingled with the

black, brown, and gray coating amidst her once pristine face. The children parted as one more figure approached. The Chaperone marched up and stood. Silent and still, always so silent and still. For what hurry could one possibly have when their chosen one is so subdued, so accepting of their fate?

The Chaperone reached up with gloved hands and peeled back his hood. Samantha Castle glanced up from her prison, bleeding and entangled in the strewn guts of untold and unknown victims, weary and resigned.

What lurked beneath the hood of the adult-sized figure might be better left unsaid, unheard, and unseen. Yet on this night of the dead, when foul things frolic unseen amidst excited children, Samantha Castle experienced the unknown. There in her old stately oak near the cul-de-sac at 24 Pike St., sprawled amidst the corrupted form of a dear friend, she succumbed and allowed herself to be lost within the abyss beneath the hood.

The entrails began to move. They snaked over the prone body of the young woman and began to squeeze and intertwine. They enveloped her like an obscene cocoon, a motion spurred on by the formless, unknown contents of that shadowed orifice beneath the hood.

Sam heard it.

The buzzing, the low drone. The buildup of something approaching in her head.

She felt it.

Her limbs beginning to contort and shrink.

And before she fell into blackness, The Other One reached forward and shoved a wad of melted candy and brownish-black matter into her gasping mouth.

She tasted it.

It tasted sweet. Oh, so sweet.

~

Sometime later, where Pike Street and Line Street converged, another house was paid a visit on this most unusual, magical, and arcane evening.

There were six on this night — five children and their young adult companion. The boldest of the group stepped forward and rang the doorbell. It was answered swiftly by a young man.

The man surveyed his visitors swiftly. Two little boys: one in a skeleton outfit, one as a—what was that? A bear? A werewolf? Three little girls—one looked like a classic bed sheet ghost, save for an unruly tear and a few stains. The one up front wore a white gown, and a creepy-looking beaked mask (heavily cracked and taped) framed her blond hair. The third little girl kept her halo bedecked head down, her chin pressed against her frilly white dress.

He nodded in approval and presented a purple plastic bowl heaped with candy. The man kept an eye on the hoodie wearing teen standing at the foot of the walk.

"Hi there, kids!" He spoke with a transplanted Canadian accent. "You guys know the magic words if you want some candy, right?"

Silence.

"You guys don't talk much, do you?" he asked.

The kids held out smudged burlap sacks in silence. The act was beginning to unnerve the man even further, and he wanted them off his porch. "If you're going to be rude, then guess what?" the man said. "No candy!"

The children began to whisper, the first sound he had heard them make. The little ones finished conferring and pushed the little girl in the frilly dress forward. The child raised her eyes, her halo sparkling in the orange streetlight. She had dark hair, a chubby and cherubic face tinged with what looked like soot or ash. Five jagged streaks of face paint cut across her face in an asymmetrical display. Her nose was but a misshapen smudge of flesh. An unfortunate scar cleaved across one cheek, supplanted over a trio of small, beige dots. Were it not for the morass of scar tissue, it might have been a cute birthmark.

He never saw the boy in the skeleton costume moving. He didn't see the child heft up a plump jack-o'-lantern and smash it downward. But he did feel the weight of the gourd as it collided with his head. He felt the *thud* of wood against flesh as the two boys grasped his ankles and dragged him down the front porch steps.

He felt it all. Through tear-addled eyes, the man gazed upward at the children. The one in the bird mask was calling the shots, the teen hovering in the background. The girl in the ghost sheet accepted something shiny from the beak-faced child, and the man felt the tear in his abdomen and the sharp tug as his guts began to unspool. He felt the squelching and the white-hot pain as the others began to collect the shards of shattered pumpkin and globs of seeded orange pulp and shove them into his increasingly hollow cavity.

The little angel with the cat whiskers hovered over him, seemingly lost in the act. A gesture from the others, and she lowered her hands down, inserted a set of too-sharp fingernails, and ripped away the face of the man. He didn't see what happened next—the skeleton boy draping the freshly skinned face over his skull and making a sarcastic pantomime.

Their night had just begun. The children had collected their bounty of sour and salt, and one more taste eluded them on this night. Yet the group and their new addition knew that there was still much to see. They would find the sweets that they craved. The treats on this night of tricks existed just beyond the pale fringes of worlds unseen and unspoken. And so, until the sun rose on this night, this would be their playground.

The children grasped the ankles of the dead man and began to drag him away. After sampling a few more nibbles, they, with the help of The Chaperone, hoisted him onto the picket fence surrounding the man's property. A perfectly ghoulish tableau to greet further visitors, although they would find the home empty and devoid of any candy peddlers.

They made their way down the street, empty sacks swinging gaily as they walked. The little girl in the angel outfit hesitated for just a moment. The ghost-sheeted girl returned, paused, and held out her hand, blue eyes twinkling in the harvest moonlight. The angel accepted the invite and, hands held, the two forever friends joined their new circle as they skipped happily down the street, eager to see what tricks and treats this night might have in store for all of them.

~

The night is awash in the shrieks of children, the blaring of spooky sound mix cassettes, and the crunch of desiccated autumn leaves. This world seems different. No more barren and quiet streets; no more impish, bloodthirsty rogues. But then . . . such events tend to carry with them an aura of inevitability.

Such it was, and such it shall be. On this night, children only want to hold on to what is sweet and fun, but who's to say that they can't slake their thirst with a little bit of sour and salt?

Blood and corruption, the very essence that runs silent yet always present on the rain-slick streets of Pike Street.

MISS SHAW'S SPECIAL BOY
Todd Condit

Halloween 1986

KENNY'S BLACK CONVERSE HI-TOPS crunched down on an orange leaf as he led his group of friends on their annual Halloween mission: to get as much candy as possible and eat it until they felt like throwing up. It was one of, if not *the* best nights of the year for kids their age. Thirteen-year-olds with the freedom to stay out late, play pranks, and beg for candy in that electric time of fall. Leaves were in the process of falling, the air had a chill in it that smelled like sweet earth, and best of all, they were with their friends.

So far, the night had been a success. Kenny, Susan, Mark, and Tommy, all dressed in various characters, each had bags weighted down by large amounts of candies.

"I think it's time to call it quits, guys," said Mark as he shifted his candy-filled pillowcase from hand to hand. Like his other 7th-grade friends, he was strong, but was still at that sweet spot between pre-high school stamina and middle-school lethargic tendencies. They were all still in that zone of being comfortable cuddling with Mom under a warm blanket while a scary movie played on the screen. Soon, they wouldn't be. At least, not openly, without feeling ridiculed by their friends for doing something as *disgusting* as openly loving their mothers. So the night's adventure was wearing them all down.

Kenny stopped and whipped around on the sidewalk. His Indiana Jones hat cocked to one side as he sized up his friends.

"So you're saying it's not the years, honey, it's the mileage?" Kenny said with his best Harrison Ford smirk and swagger. Susan, Mark, and Tommy looked at him, dumbfounded.

"*Raiders*, guys," Kenny pleaded to no avail. "*Raiders of the Lost Ark!* Oh, you've got to be kidding me! Look who I'm dressed as, put two and two together for crying out loud!" Kenny plucked a Snickers bar out of his bag, quickly unwrapped it, and stuck it in his mouth while motioning to his Indiana Jones costume, complete with whip tethered at his side.

"Ohhhh . . . yeahhh . . . right. *Raiders*," Tommy said with a fake sound of knowing in his voice, which was slightly muffled by a white sheet draped over his head. His mother had carefully cut out the eye holes that night before he headed out for the evening to haunt the streets looking for sweets.

Kenny shook his head in disgust. "I swear, sometimes I feel like you don't even like movies. I mean here I am quoting *Dr. Jones*," he said with his best Short Round impression from *Temple of Doom*, "and you don't even catch the reference."

His friends groaned in unison at the upcoming movie-based rant that was common from young Kenny. They all loved *Star Wars*, *Day of the Dead*, and *Back to the Future* like every other kid their age, but Kenny took it to the next level. His room was adorned with Universal Monster models, *Fangoria Magazine* cutouts, and every other piece of movie memorabilia he could get his hands on.

"Oh, here we go again," teased Susan as she adjusted her orange and pink plastic Uzi machine gun that she thought matched well to her favorite character, Sarah from *Day of the Dead*, who she was dressed as for the night.

The kids didn't notice that their group had resumed

walking. Kenny's plan of distracting them with movie quotes to keep the trick-or-treat train running had worked. They continued walking down the street looking for a house that had its light on or lit jack-o'-lanterns on the doorstep, indicating that the house was indeed accepting candy beggars.

The group turned into a driveway and walked up to the front door of a house. The porch had a family of jack-o'-lanterns, each with a flickering candle illuminating the insides of the smiling pumpkin faces. Two other kids, one in a skeleton and the other in a clown mask, surveyed the new candy in their bags as they left the house in search of more.

"My turn!" Mark shouted as he pushed his way through Indiana Jones, Sarah, and ghost Tommy and up to the front door. He rapidly pushed the doorbell button and didn't stop until he heard a man's annoyed voice from inside the house.

"Ok okay, I'm coming *Jesus H. Christ!*" the muffled voice said.

Mark took a few steps back as the door opened, revealing a man in a cheap Jason Voorhees mask holding a big bowl of candy.

"Trick or *treatttttt!*" the group shouted in unison as the man looked at each of them.

"Okay, what do we have here? Indiana Jones, a ghost . . . a girl with a gun, and a zombie. Very cool," the man said as he grabbed a fistful of candy and held it out for whoever stepped up first to open their pillowcases.

Mark stepped forward and accepted the candy. "I'm Bub, actually," he said, sheepishly. Mark had rubbed some gray makeup on his face in an attempt to not only look like Bub the Zombie from *Day of the Dead*, but to also hopefully impress Susan. He figured Bub and Sarah would work well together since they were from the same movie.

"Alright cool, Bub the Zombie," the man said, clearly not knowing, or caring. He quickly filled the kid's bags and retreated back into the comfort of his home.

They surveyed their newest additions to their haul and turned and began moving up the street.

"Ok Kenny, seriously. My feet hurt and it's getting cold," Susan said and stopped. Mark bumped into her and turned bright red under his gray Bub makeup. Susan didn't notice.

"Ahh man, just a couple more. Please?" No one spoke. "Let's at least hit up Pike Street."

"Ugh, what for?" said Tommy with visible disgust. "That's way the hell out there and there's nothing worth it, plus that old creeper that chain smokes on his porch is definitely going to ogle Susan if we go that way."

"Man, screw that old dude! And Georgie Miller said that 25 Pike St. is giving away king-sized Reese's Peanut Butter Cups," Kenny said. His eyes were wide and hopeful.

Susan sighed. "First of all, Georgie's an *idiot*. Didn't he claim a house was made of candy too at some point? Plus when did you even see him tonight?"

"Well . . . he said that last Halloween the old lady who lived there was giving them away. So it's *probably* the same," Kenny said with a defeated tone.

"Let's just go home guys," Susan said as she turned to head back the way they had come, toward the street that the four friends lived on. Defeated, Kenny snatched an M&M out of his bag and poured the contents into his mouth.

"I'm going to keep going guys, I for one, am not letting king-sized candy bars go unclaimed. Besides, what would Indy do?" Kenny smirked as he adjusted his hat and started walking backward.

"Sorry man," Mark said. "See you tomorrow?"

"Yeah, Kenny, let's meet at my house tomorrow and all trade candy, okay?" said Susan as Mark and Tommy nodded in unison at her suggestion.

"Yeah, okay. I'll see you guys tomorrow. Oh, and guys. Happy *Halloweeeeennnn,*" Kenny said with a ghostly quiver in his voice. He turned and walked toward Pike Street and Susan, Tommy, and Mark walked home. No one looked back.

~

Kenny whistled the theme song to Indiana Jones as he turned the corner onto Pike Street. The temperature had dipped and a wind started whipping the dead leaves around the cracked sidewalk. The moon played hide and seek behind ghostly white clouds and made the shadows of normal things look like monstrous creatures in its wake.

Kenny continued down the sidewalk in search of a house with signs of candy-giving life. He was about to give up when he turned down a bend in the road and saw a well-lit, decorated house at the end of a cul-de-sac. An old, overgrown dirt path cut its way through the tall weeds alongside the house at number 25, retreating back into the woods.

"Bingo," Kenny said, quickening his pace toward the home. A colorful witch blow mold with a purple hat decoration sparkled as he walked up the cement pathway toward the front door. From the door, a paper black cat hung by a single square of tape. A large jack-o-lantern smiled at him with one big buck tooth and triangle-shaped eyes, its little candle flickering inside the empty cavity.

Kenny noticed the light behind the door's peephole shift as if someone had been standing on the other end, waiting for kids. He reached out a hand and knocked hard before taking a tentative step back. He heard shuffling feet and the rattling of candy in a glass dish as someone approached and opened the door. Kenny was bathed in warm light and the smell of fresh sugar cookies assaulted his nostrils. He breathed in deeply and smiled.

"Trick or treat!" Kenny shouted to the sweet-looking old lady standing in the doorway across from him. She wore a well-worn pink bathrobe, an equally worn, grey slip that used to be white. She held the glass dish he'd heard in her kind hands, and it was indeed filled with candy.

"Oh my, my, my! Look at you! Professor Indiana

Jones himself, at my door of all places!" she said in a not unpleasant high-pitched and at the same time soft older lady voice.

Kenny smiled for a few reasons. Not only did she know *exactly* who he was dressed as, but her bowl of candy was *also* filled with king-sized candy bars of all types.

His friends, he thought, were going to shit themselves when he showed up with a bag of king-sized bars to Susan's house tomorrow.

"Yes ma'am," Kenny said, smiling, as he grabbed the edge of his hat and tipped it toward her. She laughed and continued standing there, taking it all in.

"What's this nonsense about calling me ma'am? Call me Miss Shaw, darling!" She pulled out a Hershey's bar, just as oversized as the rest, and held it out to Kenny.

"Thank you, ma'am . . . I mean, Miss Shaw, have a good night," Kenny said as he turned to head back down the street.

"Now wait just a second, dear. You're the first trick-or-treater I've had all night, and I happen to know for a *fact* that nobody else on this block is giving out *anything* this good this evening. I can't just let you leave with one measly candy bar and no fresh cookies!"

Kenny smiled wide at the word *cookies* and breathed in another lungful of the buttery, sugary smell wafting from the house.

"Come on little Indy, let's get you some. And a glass of milk? Gosh, maybe a nice glass of hot cocoa to keep that chill out of those little bones of yours. Like your mother probably makes, right?"

Kenny grimaced inwardly at the mention of his mom. She wasn't exactly the milk, cookies, and hot cocoa type of person. She was more of a slap, punch, and send you to bed without a meal kind. He gratefully stepped inside and into the parlor of an old but well-kept home. The door shut behind him as he took in the cozy home.

The walls were covered in framed black and white photos of various people that he assumed were her family members. Old-style, brightly colored furniture filled the rooms and felt like a snapshot from the 1960s.

"Come into the kitchen dear," Miss Shaw said as she walked by, her slippered feet making shuffling noises across the old shaggy carpet. He followed her into a modest kitchen and sat at a wooden table. She opened the oven and pulled out a steaming sheet of fresh cookies and began placing them on a plate.

"Thanks for inviting me in Miss Shaw, I really appreciate it," Kenny said as he looked around the kitchen. Miss Shaw placed a fresh glass of milk in front of Kenny followed by the plate of cookies.

"Don't mention it, honey, I'm just happy to have a *healthy*, young boy in our home," she said with a warm smile. "Now let me get that hot cocoa on the stove so your mother doesn't worry about you being out so long.

"Oh, she won't care," Kenny said through a mouth full of cookies. "I could stay out all night trick-or-treating and she wouldn't even notice." He took a big swig of milk and let out a slight burp.

"Interesting," Miss Shaw said. She stood behind him, staring down as he ate and drank. Her posture was stiff and her face drooped and darkened. "Well shoot," she said. Still standing as still as a statue while she looked down at Kenny. "It looks like I'm all out of cocoa, but don't you worry, I have some in the basement." She didn't even pretend to look in the pantry, but Kenny failed to notice. "Back in a second," she said as she disappeared down the basement steps.

Kenny continued munching away and was startled as he heard a loud *bang* followed by a muffled shout from the basement.

He stood up and walked to the closed basement door.

"Miss Shaw? Are you ok?"

He opened the door and heard Miss Shaw whimpering in the basement. "Please, help me dear! I fell," cried Miss Shaw.

Kenny hurried down the steps into the dark basement in the direction of Miss Shaw's voice. He stepped off the last step and the lights went out, plunging the dirt-floored basement into total darkness.

Kenny stepped forward, arms outstretched searching for a wall to cling to.

"Miss Shaw?" he called out but was met with silence. He heard shuffling across the dirt floor and headed toward it, fearing that Miss Shaw had passed out, or worse.

He heard wood creaking as if someone was walking back up the steps. Suddenly the lights turned back on. He shielded his eyes from the shock of the light and saw Miss Shaw standing at the top of the steps by the basement door, peering down at him with a warm smile.

"Oh dear. Oh dear, dear, dear." She slowly shook her head from side to side as if something deeply saddened her.

"Happy Halloween honey, don't eat too fast," she said, peering over Kenny's shoulder into a dark corner of the basement.

Kenny whirled around and looked in the direction she was speaking to. Warm urine ran down his pants as he took in the deformed, humanlike creature that sat on its haunches like a dog in the corner of the room. The thing stood up, its bones creaking as the monstrosity unfolded itself to its full, abnormal height. Open sores, runny with pus drained from various areas on its nude body. Its inflamed, diseased penis dangled, a drop of greenish fluid dripped from it and landed on a broken toe-nailed foot that hadn't been trimmed in about 25 years.

The thing lumbered toward a frozen-in-place Kenny. It ran a plump tongue across its cracked lips in anticipation of the meal to be had.

"Thank you, Mommy," it said with a raspy, wheeze-filled voice.

Miss Shaw smiled down as her boy, Little Petey—who wasn't so little or young—took his time eating this child who had the unfortunate luck of visiting her home. Kenny's cries of pain as he was ripped apart and eaten brought a smile to the deformed creature's mother's lips.

~

1 Year Later

Susan watched TV as a newscaster spoke in muted tones about her missing friend, Kenny.

"It's been one year since Kenny Johnson was last seen on Halloween night. Law enforcement continues to pursue all relevant leads and asks the public still to please come forward with any and all information . . . "

She walked across to the TV in disgust and turned the dial, cutting off the newsman's voice in mid-sentence. Susan's friend group had come together the first few nights after Kenny's disappearance. Searching the woods from top to bottom, interviewing neighbors and other trick-or-treaters, searching for any clue of what could have happened to the young boy. But like with anything, Kenny's memory faded with time as the kids continued on with their normal lives. They just assumed that he had run away to get away from his deadbeat mother. Especially since she didn't seem to give a shit about her son's whereabouts.

But Susan didn't. She felt like she was the only one, even out of her now smaller friend group, who still cared about Kenny. She had her theories of what happened, of which she had investigated herself and slowly marked these off her list of possibilities. That Kenny had gotten lost in the woods, snatched by a passing car, or killed by his mother, were a few of her theories that she scratched off the list for one reason or another. But one remained on it.

Pike Street.

Kenny had been on his way to Pike in search of candy. Could he have disappeared there? Maybe. The cops had interviewed everyone on that street and were satisfied with the results. But she wasn't. Something was seriously fucked up about that *entire* street. She figured tonight, Halloween, would be the perfect time to check it out again. She'd go down tonight and try to retrace the steps that Kenny probably took, and would kick both Tommy and Mark's asses if they refused to help.

It was 10 p.m. when Susan, Tommy, and Mark arrived on their bikes at the entrance to Pike Street. Mark and Tommy had reluctantly agreed to this by a combination of peer pressure and feeling guilty when she said Kenny would still be looking for either of them if the roles were swapped and they were the ones missing.

"Okay, so we're here. Now what?" Tommy said as he pushed the kickstand down on his bike and got off the seat. Nobody had bothered to dress up this year, the magic was gone now that Kenny wasn't here plus they were all fourteen now. The urge to do *kiddy* things like trick-or-treating was rapidly leaving them.

Susan tightened the straps on her backpack and peered down the street at the various homes. "Well, we go down and look around. I figure we start with homes that Kenny would have visited last year," Susan said as she started walking, the boys quickly shuffled after her.

"How the hell are we going to do that Susan?" Mark asked.

"Yeah, we've already looked here and found jackshit!" Tommy finished for Mark.

Susan whirled around, pissed off at the tone of the boys. "Yeah, we did. In the fucking summer. We have to match what Kenny did, it's the key to all of this," she said as she continued walking.

The boys looked at each other with apprehension. Tommy tentatively spoke up.

"Key to what, Susan? Do you hear yourself? Kenny left! That's it!"

They had walked the street shortly after Kenny's disappearance but saw nothing out of the ordinary.

"No! Wrong! Everyone is fucking wrong! Kenny did not just run away. Something happened to him. And I cannot believe that you, two of his best friends, are complaining about looking for him."

Her eyes glistened with tears as she peered into each of their faces.

"Just fucking go, I'll take care of this myself," she snorted as she walked away. The boys looked at each other briefly before their shoulders sagged in defeat and embarrassment before turning and following Susan up the street.

Susan wiped tears away as the group walked. Nothing stood out. Just houses on a shitty street until they turned at a bend and saw a house lit up for the holiday. They glanced at one another and proceeded toward it.

Miss Shaw's house looked exactly like it did last year when it swallowed Kenny up. The colorful witch blow mold twinkled at them, the black cat cardboard cutout stuck to the door just a bit more faded than last year, and a fresh jack-o'-lantern smirked up at them. Classical music could be heard from inside the home as the group arrived on the porch. Susan held out a fist to knock but as her hand fell toward the wood, the door quickly opened, causing Susan to stumble inside into the arms of Miss Shaw.

"Oh my!" Miss Shaw shouted in surprise as Susan fell into her arms. "I did not expect a group of young people to be on my doorstep at this hour!"

Susan peeled herself away from the woman and choked back a gag at the sour smell of her. She smelled like warm milk left out in the sun.

"Sorry ma'am, we were just trick-or-treating," Mark said to the woman.

"Oh, is that so? Then where are your costumes?" Miss Shaw asked, crossing her pink-robed arms.

"Oh, we're dressed as *teenagers*," Tommy said with a smile and a smart-assed tone.

Miss Shaw stared at each of them, her features a blank mask as her vision seemed to glaze over like she wasn't there anymore.

Her focus snapped back at the sound of something falling in the house.

"Oh, that must be Little Petey, that cat gets into everything!" Well children, please step inside, I left the bowl of candy in the parlor. Blasted me and my old age, you forget important things like a candy bowl on Halloween!" Miss Shaw said as she stepped aside for the kids.

The boys hesitated but Susan confidently strode into the room and deeper into the house. Susan took it all in, looking for anything that could point to Kenny having been there.

Miss Shaw closed the door and turned the key on the lock, removing it and placing it in a pocket of her pink robe in the process. She glanced at the basement door, a blank expression on her face before she turned on her pleasant old lady persona.

"Come children! The candy awaits you all!" she sang as she waddled toward the kitchen. The boys scrunched their noses at the smell of her.

Susan walked into the kitchen and deflated when she didn't see anything that could have belonged to Kenny. Lit scented candles were placed at random intervals along the counter, doing their best to hold back the sour stitching of not only the old woman but the house in general. A rotting, sour smell mixed with the various scents created a gross combination of odors.

A rustling of chains and a low moan crept up through the floorboards.

"Dang, how big is that cat?!" Mark said at the sound.

Miss Shaw ignored the boy and walked over to a cabinet, she opened the door and an Indiana Jones hat tumbled out of it. Susan's eyes went wide.

"Where did you get that hat?" Susan asked as she stood up and walked over to Miss Shaw.

"Oh, this old thing? This belongs to Little Petey, my son," Miss Shaw said as she walked backward into the kitchen. She stepped to the backdoor and removed a key in the lock.

"I thought Petey was a cat?" Susan said.

Shaw placed the key in her pocket and sighed deeply.

"I'm not sure he'll have room enough for three. But I suppose I could always save the leftovers. Little Petey is a special boy, after all, he needs his protein. You see, he was born . . . different. And, well . . . if you were a mother you'd understand," she said.

"What the fuck are you talking about, lady?!" Mark

said, voice cracking.

Miss Shaw walked toward a metal electrical panel near the back door, opened the panel door with a screech, and flipped off the master switch, plunging the house into near-total darkness save for the flickering candles.

Miss Shaw shuffled to the basement door and yanked it open. She took out a bundle of keys and inserted one into an old padlock that held a long chain secured around the stair handrail. She let the chain drop and briefly watched as it rumbled down the basement steps, which were lightly illuminated by more scented candles.

"Dinner's here, son. Come on up and help momma out," she shouted into the flickering darkness before turning and heading up the stairs to her room.

Little Petey stretched his body out and began running up the basement steps. The chain that had held him in place fell onto the floor in a heap.

"Oh fuck, where did that crazy bitch go?!" yelled Mark as he stumbled over an unseen chair and ran in the direction of the front door. He didn't get far before viciously colliding face-first into a wall and falling back like a bag of bricks.

"Oh my God!" Tommy said as he began to cry.

"Don't panic, guys!" Susan shouted as she dropped to a knee and flung the backpack off her shoulders. She reached inside and clutched a flashlight. She turned it on and tossed it to a wide-eyed Tommy followed by a small pocket knife that she had taken from her father's desk.

"Here Tommy!" Susan yelled as the flashlight soared through the air toward her terrified friend. The flashlight hit him in the chest and dropped to the floor, rolling away. The knife fell uselessly to the floor. Susan reached in and grabbed another flashlight as Little Petey thundered up the basement steps, growling like a rabid dog.

The flashlight rolled and stopped when it came in contact with Mark's unconscious body. The beam of light pierced the darkness and illuminated the half-open basement door. Tommy reached for the flashlight and froze in terror at the site from the door.

The beast known as Little Petey stared out through the opening. Its mouth dropped, drool made its yellowed, jagged teeth gleam as its eyes lit up in eager anticipation of the meal to come.

Three things happened at once: Little Petey stretched out a grotesque hand, grabbed Mark by his hair, and began dragging him toward it; Susan grabbed her flashlight and sprinted to the front door, jumping over Mark in the process; and, Tommy shit his pants in fear.

Susan arrived at the door and cursed when she was unable to open it, she looked around and sprinted up the stairs as the creature in the basement pulled Mark toward it as it crawled over his body, saliva dripping down on the boy's face caused him to wake up in a panic.

Mark screamed as the thing's open maw came down on his nose, ripping it off in one shake of its head. Blood gushed and filled Mark's mouth causing him to gag and choke. He turned to the side and vomited as the thing chewed on his nose, the cartilage snapping as it greedily chomped.

Little Petey shuddered as it swallowed Mark's nose. Then, it smiled. "You," it said with a rasp, "taste like chicken."

Mark screamed, tried to push himself away, but the monster above him placed one hand on his chest and pushed him down onto the floor. With another hand, it thrusted a finger into Mark's eye socket and plucked out an eyeball, the stem of which stretched taut before severing and snapping back into the ruined socket. Little Petey flicked the orb into his mouth and crushed it like a fruit-filled fruit snack, jellied sclera swirling around its mouth.

Tommy finally grabbed the flashlight and got up. He grabbed a blender off the counter and smashed it across the back of Little Petey's head. The blender exploded into glass splinters and Petey roared, turning and striking a fist into Tommy's jaw, separating the lower part of his face from the boy's head. Tommy tried to speak but his jaw just flopped open. The monster clutched the jaw and yanked it off with one quick motion, showering the kitchen with fresh gore.

Tommy took a few shuffling steps and then collapsed to the floor. The creature picked up a bare, jagged toe-nailed foot and drove it into the back of the boy's head. Mark looked at his friend through his remaining eyeball as the creature stomped down at him. The vision of Tommy's exploding head reminded him of the time he and his friends had thrown a watermelon off Kenny's roof. The explosion of watermelon guts had thrown themselves in a wide arc on the driveway. Tommy's head did the same.

Little Petey ran a finger through the puddle of gooey brains and brought it up to its deformed lips. It sucked greedily at the substance and shuddered with pleasure while Tommy's body twitched below it.

It turned and peered at the remaining boy, the sight of his ruined eye leaking white fluid made its stomach grumble. Little Petey stood to its full height, the moon-light seeping through the windows casting an eerie glow on its blood-covered body as the candlelight danced over the spreading pool of fluids. Mark shuddered at the sight of the creature standing in the blood of his friend's body. Tears leaked out of his good eye as the creature scooped gore from the kitchen floor and started stroking it on its engorged penis. The creature smiled at him as it continued stroking. It walked toward him.

"Mommy usually doesn't let me have dessert before dinner, but I don't see her right now. Do you?" It said with a smirk as it continued stroking itself as it walked toward the boy.

Mark saw the glint of the small pocket knife and lunged for it. Little Petey paused and laughed, then suddenly sprang forward. Mark fell to his knees in the warm blood and slashed the knife across Little Petey's groin. The blade cut through the diseased penis like a knife through rotten butter, severing it mid-shaft. Little Petey howled in pain as its severed penis spiraled through the air, hitting the wall with a meaty *thud*.

Mark lurched to his feet and ran toward the front door

as the creature screamed in pain and rage behind him. Mark found the door locked and then crawled up the stairs, his wounds throbbing in pain. Just as he arrived at the top landing, Miss Shaw appeared out of nowhere with a wooden baseball bat and brought it viciously down on the crown of Mark's head. The bat painfully reverberated up Miss Shaw's hands as the boy's head cracked open, splashing bits of brain against the wall. Mark's body spasmed once as the life left his remaining eye and fell back down the stairs in a dead heap.

"Whoopsies," Miss Shaw said at the dead boy's body. "That little bitch is somewhere up here, Petey!"

Susan hid in a closet as she listened to the fight downstairs. Tears slid down her face as she listened to her friends die. She was committed to killing the old bitch and that monster or die trying. Miss Shaw came into the room and sat on the edge of the bed. She was lightly humming to herself without a care in the world.

Susan reached into her bag and pulled out a long kitchen knife, clutched it in one hand as she gently opened the closet door, and slipped into the darkness. She crept behind Miss Shaw and in one quick motion grabbed her by the hair and dragged the knife across her throat. The woman's skin parted and a sheet of blood spilled down her chest. She gargled and turned around wide-eyed as she peered into her killer's face.

"You fucking stupid bitch, now he's going to get out," she sputtered as life drained out of the wound. She dropped to the bed and rolled over onto her back.

"This is for Kenny you psycho bitch!"

Susan clutched the knife in two hands and raised it above her head and drove the blade into her face repeatedly, punching through meat and bone. In her rage, she didn't hear Little Petey come in behind her. The creature let out a cry at the sight of his mother and ripped Susan off of her, throwing her into the wall with a loud *thud*.

Little Petey scooped up its mother in his arms and began crying, rocking her gently back and forth.

Susan shook the daze out of her head and slowly backed out of the room. She tiptoed down the stairs and began crying at the sight of Mark's body. She shuddered as she took in the scene of the bloody kitchen. She headed for the only door open to her and walked down into the basement. She flicked on her flashlight and showed it around the dirty floor. She let out a whimper at a ripped pile of an Indiana Jones costume. Gnawed bones stuck out at various tears in the fabric.

Kenny.

A roar from upstairs shuddered through the house as Little Petey resumed the search for Susan.

Susan left her friend's bones and ran to a workbench, looking desperately for a weapon among the flickering candles. She noticed a rusted metal gas can and let out a sigh of relief when she shook the can and gas swished back and forth. She grabbed one of the candles, careful not to put the flame out, and began pouring the gas in a line toward the stairs to burn the house down from the basement up.

"You killed my mother!" Little Petey whined as it appeared behind her. It slapped Susan across the face. Stars danced in her vision as she tumbled down the stairs. She landed with a huff as the air exploded out of her lungs. Petey stooped so it didn't hit its head on the ceiling and lumbered after her, holding one deformed hand to its bleeding, ruined crotch.

Susan pushed herself to her feet and grimaced at the smell of her gasoline-soaked clothing. She looked at the bones of her long-dead friend and back up to the lumbering beast coming toward her. She sighed in acceptance and clutched the fallen candle off the ground that had managed to stay lit.

She backed up as Little Petey shuffled toward her, hatred and rage in its eyes.

She threw the gas can at the monster, the remaining contents flying through the air as the can tumbled, bathing the creature in its deadly liquid. Susan closed her eyes and held the flame to her gas-filled clothing, she lit up with a sudden whoosh and ran toward the creature, dripping flames as she went and embraced the thing, engulfing them both. Susan laughed as the deformed creature screamed and they both burned alive.

$$\text{N\underline{o}}\,26$$

THE SORTING
Jane Nightshade

GROWING UP, THE KIDS IN my neighborhood always had our age-old Halloween rituals. We didn't know where they came from or who devised them or how long they'd been around. We just followed them and never thought much about it, like millions of other kids all across the country on Halloween.

My favorite ritual was the sorting of the candy. When it was time to sort, most of us kids would usually gather at a house belonging to this kid named Hector Hernandez. Hector's parents had converted their garage into a rumpus room, and we would file into it with our bulging pillow sacks or pumpkin-shaped buckets of candy. Then Hector would give the signal and we'd sit cross-legged on the green shag rug and dump all our goodies out in piles before us.

Each kid had their own way of sorting. I preferred to sort by type of candy. Chocolate bars in one pile, gummy fruit things in another pile, hard candy in a third pile, a fourth pile for miscellaneous stuff like Sweet Tarts and Necco Wafers. And then a fifth pile for stuff nobody wanted, like mini-boxes of raisins, new toothbrushes, religious tracts, and other things given out by people who didn't like Halloween. I usually tried to trade that junk away. I knew I could always dump off the toothbrushes on this super-nerdy girl, Brandy, who brushed her teeth four times a day. The raisin boxes and religious tracts were, sadly, a hard sell.

The year I turned thirteen was my last year of trick-or-treating. It was also the year that Hector's grandma died right before Halloween, and the whole family left town for two weeks. Which meant we had to find a new place in which to do our traditional candy sorting.

My own tiny house was out—there was no real place to sort but the living room, and I couldn't see my friends doing that while my parents sat on the couch and stared at them like they were bugs under a magnifying glass. Proper sorting required freedom from adult eyes—that was one of our unwritten, ancient Halloween rules. The ones that we always, *always* honored.

Most of my friends were in the same boat, vis-à-vis the housing situation. Puffy, who lived two doors down from me, offered his screened-in back porch, but it wasn't heated, and it was little better than sorting in an open field. Then the new kid, Beans, stepped forward, and offered his house.

No one knew what kind of house Beans lived in; we'd only been hanging out with him for a couple of months. He wasn't technically a part of our neighborhood, but he showed up a lot in all of our usual hangouts, and we just sort of adopted him. Beans told us that his dad was a doctor, and their house had a family room, a recreation room, *and* a study, in addition to the usual rooms everybody else had.

Puffy was enthusiastic about Beans' offer. Puff was our *de facto* leader. The kid who made most of the decisions, the one who thought up the best games for us to play, and the guy who made sure everyone got along, more or less. Nobody resented him for it; he was just a natural leader, fitting into the role like a hand in a well-worn pitcher's mitt.

We met later behind our school's softball backstop (without Beans, of course) to vote on the vitally important matter of finding a new sorting place. Puff put it succinctly to the crew: "The way I see it, we've got no choice but to use Beans' house. It's either that, or we each go home without sorting after trick-or-treating."

Various cries of protest immediately rose up: "No sorting? That's barbaric!" and "If we don't sort, how do we elect the King of Candy?"

The King (or Queen) of Candy was the kid who collected the most/best candy from trick-or-treating. We all went to the same houses and shops, so it often came down to whoever was best at convincing adults to slip them a bigger or extra piece on the sly. There was a complicated scoring system that nobody knew the origin of, but which we all followed without question. If you won King of Candy you'd get bragging rights and your choice of one treat from each kid's pile. It was a very sweet ride for the winner who, of course, would always pick everyone's best—a full-sized Snickers or a jumbo box of Sugar Babies—you get the idea. Puffy always won. He was the champ of subtly charming grownups into giving him more than anybody else. We all tried hard to get the prize on the off-chance that he would have a bad night, however.

"I vote for Beans," said Brandy the Nerd, shocking everybody with her unaccustomed forthrightness. "He doesn't seem like a bad kid, even if his dad is rich. And we can go back to Hector's next year if we don't like Beans' place."

In the end, everyone voted for the Beans option except for one hold-out, Arnold Zwissig, a disagreeable kid who always took a contrarian position whenever possible.

Beans' face lit up when he heard the news; I guess he felt he was now really one of us. "We can use the recreation room. It's got a pool table and a TV. We can watch scary movies after the sorting, if you'd like."

It sounded like a grand plan. When Halloween came, we all showed up at 6:30 p.m. near the big oak tree next to an open field that was our main neighborhood gathering place. I had decided that my costume that year would be a giant playing card, the ten of diamonds. The Puffmeister helped me make it. We took two large rectangles of cardboard and painted them, then hooked them together with twine into a sandwich board, with an opening at the top for my neck and head. Puffy told me, "you look ultra-cool for a girl, Kath," when I tried on the finished product for him. I blushed all over from the approval.

Puff went as a riverboat gambler. He'd managed to find an old brocade waistcoat at a rummage sale and a fedora he'd decorated with an ace of spades in the hatband. He looked super-sharp. Brandy came as a sorry-looking dragonfly with crepe-paper wings that kept falling off, and Arnold was a crook in prison stripes drawn with black markers on a pair of old white pajamas.

Beans came as Jesse James, in a store-bought costume that outclassed everyone else's gear. But he was gracious about it and said nice things about our home-made Halloween get-ups. Finishing out our group were the twins, Markie and Lou, who came predictably as Tweedle Dee and Tweedle Dum, and Dawn, our dark-haired glamor girl, who wore a spy costume.

As usual, we split up into twos and threes and ran from house to house, yelling "trick or treat" at each door, holding out our bags and pillowcases for goodies. If an amiable-looking lady or man answered the door, I flashed my best Eddie Haskell smile, hoping to get an extra piece. Sometimes it worked, and I mentally patted myself on the back, thinking I had a good chance of winning Queen of Candy this year. Then again, that's what I thought every year. So far, it hadn't panned out.

The night wore on. We were scarcely aware of the passing of time. We mingled with kids from other neighborhoods, yelling as we ran by with our pillowcases, buckets, and grocery sacks, trading information about which were the most generous houses for treats or which had the scariest yard display.

Our complete group then met at the oak tree at the appointed hour of eight, when most houses were starting to turn off their porch lights, signaling they were out of candy.

Beans arrived with a girl of about nine in tow; she shadowed him like a wraith. The girl was wearing a blue Cinderella dress with bouffant sleeves and a long full skirt. A very pale girl who didn't say anything, with silvery hair and colorless eyes. She was not sporting a sweater or a jacket but didn't seem bothered by the late October cold.

"Who's the kid?" Puffy said to Beans, pulling him aside. "She's a bit young for our crew." We didn't usually go out with much younger kids, unless somebody's parents forced us to drag along a kid brother or sister.

"Kid?" replied Beans, confused. "Oh, you mean *her?* She's my . . . *cousin.* Her name is Adela."

Puffy snickered. "Adela? That's a grandma's name, Beans. Weird."

"She won't get in your way. She mostly just likes to watch," said Beans. "Always watching."

We all grudgingly tolerated the presence of Adela as we trudged to Beans' house, which turned out to be a huge old two-story hulk with pillars in front and a balcony off the top front window. It was on Pike Street; one of our town's so-called "historical homes" at 26, and Beans' family had certainly gussied it up.

Every surface inside was either exotic wood, or marble, or crystal, or patterned silk. I was afraid to touch anything, even the lead-crystal doorknobs.

Beans' mom was pretty, blonde, and fashionable, not a hair out of place. She was dressed in a cute witch costume with a puffy skirt and a shiny conical hat. She offered us hot chocolate, warm apple cider, and lemonade, accompanied by sugar cookies, frosted to look like either black cats or pumpkins. We also met Beans' doctor dad, who wore a mad scientist costume. He greeted us in a jovial manner that belied his sober profession.

The recreation room was in the basement, and it put Hector's "rumpus room" to shame. It not only had a pool table, but another table set aside for ping pong, next to a very large TV.

"This is wild," Puffy cried, cramming his mouth with a pumpkin cookie.

"I've never seen a room this cool," he continued, spraying orange crumbs everywhere as he tried to talk and chew simultaneously. Everybody else in our crew was just as impressed. I could see the wheels turning in their minds and realized that Hector's green-shag-carpeted rumpus room wouldn't be needed next year.

After about a half-hour of candy-eating and libation-swilling, someone said, "It's time!" and we sat down on the carpet—a thick, tasteful brown plush—and waited for the signal.

Puff had to remind Beans that, as our gracious host, he was the official sorting starter; Beans was just that much of a newbie. I felt kind of sorry for him because he always appeared to be so eager to be accepted by us.

Beans took off his cowboy hat and tossed it into the air. "Okay everybody—ready, set, go! It's sorting time," he yelled gleefully.

I dumped my pillowcase on the carpet and started picking out the chocolate bars, which usually rated the highest on the King of Candy scale.

"One, two, three . . ." I began counting.

We were sitting in a circle, with me perched between Arnold and Brandy. Puff and Beans were directly opposite me, with the twins and Dawn on either side of them.

I glanced over at Brandy's pile and saw her hand make a beeline toward the toothbrushes. God, she was weird. But not as weird as Adela, who had collected no candy and just hovered slightly outside of our circle, watching. Always watching—with that pale face that never smiled or changed expression. I caught her looking at me and it was as if she was sizing me up somehow, weighing me like I was a piece of Halloween candy myself. I also saw her at another time moving her bony forefinger around the circle, counting us.

I was unnerved by Adela; her watching us while we sorted was almost as bad as having parents do it. But then

I thought, what harm was she doing? She said and did nothing. I returned to counting my candy bars, craning my neck every few minutes to assess the competition for King of Candy. I felt special and happy. All of my friends were radiating the excitement—the sheer joy—of being a kid on Halloween. A kid with a full pile of treats and a gang of friends that would last forever—or so we thought.

"Four, five, six . . ." I counted seventeen chocolate bars, some of them full-sized—Maybe I would win after all.

But then Puff gave out a yelp of glee and held up a small dark toy. "I got a Darth Vader mini-action figure!" he crowed with triumph. "Brand new—still in the box!"

I was crushed. I was pretty sure that a brand-new Darth Vader action figure scored way higher on the King of Candy scale than my seventeen chocolate bars. Where had he gotten it? I'd gone to the same houses and stores, and nobody gave me any kind of action figure, let alone a Darth Vader one. Well, that was another year gone—there was always next Halloween, I thought.

The scoring for King of Candy ended around 9:30. Puff won. Again. He not only had the Darth Vader action figure, but he'd also managed to somehow accrue twenty-six chocolate bars, eleven of which were full-sized.

Nobody was surprised. I had to give him my premium double-thick Hershey's bar, and Arnold had to cough up a six-pack of Bubble Yum. "Nice doing business with you, folks," he gloated good-naturedly, a wicked eye gleaming out from under the brim of his riverboat gambler's fedora. "King of Candy, totally undefeated!"

We all laughed and talked after that, and opened up our second-best piece of candy to eat, and everything was as it should be on Halloween: maniacal sugar rushes, uncomfortable costumes, the twins doing bad imitations of Boris Karloff as Frankenstein's monster.

Until the strange moment when Adela stood up from just outside the circle and pointed to Puffy. "That one! That's the one I want!" she shrieked like a crow. "Aunt Caroleen and Uncle Bedford—he's the one I choose."

There was some uncomfortable giggling, and then an

even more uncomfortable silence in the circle, as we all started to realize that Adela wasn't joking. Whatever she had chosen Puffy for, we all apparently knew it wasn't necessarily a good thing.

Dawn's face was frozen in a voiceless scream; Arnold gripped my arm like he had a pincer claw instead of a hand. Jaws dropped all around our circle—except for Beans' jaw, I noticed. He was the only one of our gang who didn't look shocked or confused or disturbed. In fact, he flashed me an oddly satisfied smile, and then his face started to turn as pale, still, and hollow-looking as Adela's. His fancy Jesse James costume somehow wasn't new anymore, but tattered and covered with gross spots of something that looked like mold.

Dawn finally screamed aloud and Brandy cried out, "surely it's a trick," in a nervous way. The boys started looking wildly around, as if trying to find an escape route.

"Who . . . who are Aunt Caroleen and . . ." Arnold muttered to himself, and I looked around and saw that Beans' parents had crept quietly down the basement stairs and into the recreation room while we weren't noticing.

They stood next to Adela, who was floating slightly above ground, her bare feet hanging straight down from the now-bedraggled hem of her Cinderella dress.

Beans' parents had changed, too, just like Beans—his pretty blonde mom was no longer quite so pretty, and the only hair she had were a few wisps of gray cobwebs attached to a brutally stark skull. Her body had shrunk almost to its skeleton and the now-ancient witch costume hung on her like a moldering potato sack. Beans' dad still looked like a mad scientist—but in a bad way, not a funny way. Spiders and worms were crawling all over his blackened lab coat.

The room, too, had suddenly changed. The furniture and pool table were covered with dust and spiderwebs, and the TV was replaced with one of those big wooden radios that people had in the early broadcasting era, the kind that looked like a church.

Beans got up from our circle and stood next to Adela and his parents. "Umm," he said, in a somewhat apologetic manner, "I kind of forgot to tell everybody that we in this house have our own Halloween sorting ritual that we cherish and love and practice every year." He patted the floating Adela's shoulder and smiled at her fondly.

"We love our traditions, but of course, to each his own. You guys sort candy . . . and we sort *people!*" He smiled and his teeth were cracked and rotten. "This year, it's Adela's turn to sort and she's done a fab job! It's been a great Halloween — maybe we'll see you all next year!"

Then Beans and Adela and his parents and the whole house began to fade away, and we watched in horror as Puffy, too, began to disappear. He reached out for a hand to hold onto, and I jumped up and tried to grab his, but it was already ether, thin air, nothing solid I could touch or grasp.

"Puff," I cried. "Don't let them take you! You can't go — you're the King of Candy! The best King of Candy ever."

"I — can't . . . " his voice weakly protested, and then he was gone, and we were all standing in an open field, amongst our now-pathetic-looking Halloween loot and the charred ruins of a crumbling old house. All of us except Puff, whom we would never see again, ever.

Arnold and Dawn were crying, and one of the twins threw up orange-colored vomit.

I had a dark epiphany the next miserable day. The field was where the Bedford Stoddard Manor once stood, owned in the 1930s by a doctor's family who had all died when their house caught fire and burned to the ground — on Halloween. Town lore said the Stoddards were a strange bunch, with a niece who "wasn't quite right in the head." I remembered the way Adela looked at me that night, as if she were sorting *me,* and I shuddered as I realized I was probably the runner-up in the Stoddard family's "sorting" game.

That night marked the end of trick-or-treating for me; I never went out again. But I kept Puff's Darth

Vader action figure, hidden away in a chest with my most beloved sentimental treasures and tokens — "still in the box."

I thought for the longest time that maybe I would see him again and I'd give it back, and we'd make cheesy costumes and go out for candy and then sort at Hector's like always . . . but it never happened.

Nowadays I always turn my porch lights out and pretend I'm not home when it gets dark on Halloween.

FINAL HALLOWEEN
Scott McGregor

SIMON INSPECTED THE SIGN AS he chewed a bite-sized licorice, pondering whether he could visit a few more houses before the thunderstorm. The alleyway formed by tall wooden fences the color of eggshell led straight to a neighborhood renowned for housing the kinds of people who were generous with their candy.

Since age four, Simon had loved candy in all its wonderful forms, so much so that when he turned seventeen — in spite of people telling him he was too old — he still partook in the tradition of dressing up and scavenging houses for sweets. He promised himself seventeen would be the final year he'd go trick-or-treating — his final, true Halloween, so he needed to make it worthwhile. Which is why, for the past three hours dressed as an eye-patch-wearing pirate, he hit up every nearby neighborhood, one house after another, filling up not one, but *two* pillowcases of candy. The one location left to plunder for snacks belonged to a place he had never visited.

Pike Street.

In previous years, he and his dad had skipped Pike Street when trick-or-treating. *The place is filled with nothing but sleazy people who're too greedy to hand out anything,* he had told Simon. But Simon figured his dad probably avoided the neighborhood out of pride, not wanting to appear like a peasant pleading for candy. But without Dad around, he could decide if he wanted to add another area to his collection of treats for his last Halloween venture. Unlike his dad, asking for candy didn't hurt Simon's self-esteem.

The clock on the nearby tower showed 10:10 p.m. According to the forecast, the downpour should commence in about twenty minutes. *Twenty minutes is surely enough time to visit a few more houses before the rain, and what Dad doesn't know won't hurt him.*

So, he went.

~

After five minutes of walking in the dark, he spotted street lights past the wooden fences and a ginormous oak tree shaped like a mushroom. The walk took longer than he expected, and a line of sweat ran down his face. Hauling forty pounds of candy for hours was the most exercise he'd engaged in all year. But he put his back into it and continued onward, for he felt it'd be worth the haul once he arrived in the suburb.

Finally, he reached the end of the path and entered a cul-de-sac formed by three houses. At the center of the street, the oak tree overlooked the lavish neighborhood, twice as high as any of the houses. From across the street where Simon stood, he noticed another alleyway between two houses.

Between the three houses, two kept their lights off. On Halloween, the absence of lights typically served as a code for *We're not giving you candy, so get lost.* So, he focused solely on the one house welcoming trick-or-treaters: House 27. He heard it calling to him.

Come get your candy, Simon.

As he walked, the faint, wet taps on his head and shoulders distracted him. He extended his hand, feeling the raindrops dampen his palm. He dashed across the street, hoping to get home before the rain drenched him.

He moved up the porch and saw five jack-o'-lanterns sitting atop a wooden stand, none lit. He paid no mind to the designs carved into the pumpkins and rang the doorbell. A woman pushing forty opened the door, dressed in a red and black dress—a witch costume, Simon guessed—and a towel wrapped around her hair. Simon spotted faint specks of makeup along her neck, washed away. When he noticed she held a silver bowl filled with full-sized candy bars, he knew he'd hit the jackpot.

"Trick or treat!" he cried gleefully.

She glared at Simon with one of her eyebrows raised, confused. "You again? Was one coffee crisp not enough?"

First, Simon paused, his smile loosening, and then said, "I don't know what you mean."

"Are you still lost? I could write down the directions if that's easier for you?"

"Um, no? I'm not lost. I'm just here trick-or-treating."

"Ah, back for more? I see you fixed your costume. That was quite the tear on your sleeve, but now it looks brand new. Also, how'd you dry off so fast? You were sopping wet."

During Simon's previous Halloweens, he fell victim to a fair share of houses pulling pranks on whoever strolled up, most of which involved someone sneaking up from behind and scaring the pants off him. Based on the woman's bizarre greeting, he figured this was such a house. So he looked over his shoulder, cautious of his surroundings. But he saw no one. When he looked back at her, he asked, "Is this some sort of Halloween skit?"

"Skit? You're the one who keeps showing up at my door."

"I don't know what you mean. This is my first time in this neighborhood."

"Enough with this. Do you need directions or not?"

"No? I'm here for candy like every other kid."

"You know what, here you go." She held out a full-sized Kit-Kat. "I doubt I'll get more kids, so you can have a second helping, but that's it. I'd appreciate it if you stopped coming here."

"Uh, thanks?" Simon said, reluctantly accepting the

candy.

The woman produced an irksome glare before she slammed the door. He stepped back onto the road, noticing the rain hastened. The lights of the woman's house switched off, which Simon took as her saying: *Leave me alone.*

"That was weird." He unwrapped the Kit-Kat and left the same way he'd entered, enjoying a late-night snack as the storm crept in.

~

The thunder cracked above, frightening Simon.

The mild drizzle shifted into a relentless shower. His skin shivered, his pirate costume was soaked. Despite the added weight from his stuffed pillowcases, he jogged onward, eager to return home and out of the storm.

Was the path really this long before?

After trotting down the path for what must've been ten minutes, he saw another oak tree and house lights in the distance. He set free a heavy sigh, relieved. But, when he saw the giant tree, he noticed it looked awfully similar to the one on Pike Street.

That can't possibly be the same tree? I've been walking straight for ten minutes.

The flash of lightning startled him.

He fell backward, feeling his costume stretch and rip as he hit the ground. Thunder roared, and he saw the oak tree collapse. A loud *thud* followed in the distance, followed by a woman's scream.

"Holy shit!" When he lifted himself off the ground, he saw the tear in his sleeve. "Great, just great."

Simon jumped, trying to spot where the tree landed, but the fences stood too tall. He darted forward, powering through the rainfall, wanting to see the aftermath of the lightning strike.

At the end of the path, he dropped his candy bags and clasped onto his knees, panting. Once he caught his breath, he saw a cul-de-sac formed by three houses. An enormous oak tree towered over the neighborhood. After walking straight down the path he left from, he somehow ended up back here?

Blinking, he wiped his eyes, making sure they weren't playing tricks on him. As he eyed the tree on Pike Street, he remembered the tree that collapsed from the lightning strike mere moments ago. Must've been a different tree in a different neighborhood nearby.

All three houses in the cul-de-sac kept their lights on. But why now and not earlier? Maybe they'd now be open for trick-or-treaters, and he debated whether he wanted to knock on a few more doors.

I can't, my costume is wrecked, and it's late, plus the rain . . . The rain.

Simon needed to pause and think about it to realize it wasn't raining anymore. Not only that, but the roads and driveways looked dry, as if a drop had never even hit the ground. He remembered the forecast stating the storm wouldn't let up until morning, so why had it suddenly stopped?

He fixated on House 27, home to the woman who had handed him the Kit-Kat, lights back on. Observing more closely, he spotted the dimly lit jack-o'-lanterns on her porch, each with a face more terrifying than the last. So, after he'd walked away from the woman's house, she turned off her lights, waited until he left, then switched them back on and lit her jack-o'-lanterns? Why? Did he really leave such an awful impression?

Standing in front of the house, he heard the woman's voice in his head: *Please stop coming here.* He still couldn't fathom what he'd done to upset her so much. But Simon also remembered something else she'd told him: *I could write down the directions if that's easier for you?* He didn't understand why she'd said that before, but now it was too fitting of an offer to decline. So, he walked up the steps and rang the doorbell again.

The woman opened the door, wearing the same dress from earlier, but this time, various coatings of black-and-white makeup canvassed her face. She redid her makeup? *What's wrong with this woman?*

They stared awkwardly at each other until she said,

"Most people say trick or treat once the door opens."

"Sorry to barge in again, but I think I'm lost. I was wondering if I could get those directions you talked about before?"

The woman raised an eyebrow. "Pardon?"

"After I left the cul-de-sac, I somehow ended up back here. Bit odd."

"You were here before? Nah, couldn't have been. I would remember a kid dressed like you. That's quite the costume. I like the idea of a pirate, but did you swim on your way here? You're soaked. That's also quite a rip on your sleeve."

"Yeah, I fell on my way back here, plus I got drenched by the rain."

"Rain?"

"Yeah, from earlier? What about the lightning strike? That was pretty scary, huh?"

"Don't know what you mean. I don't recall any lightning, and it hasn't rained all night—not yet, anyway. It's supposed to start any second now."

"I'm so confused."

"You and me both, kid."

"Do you seriously not remember me? I was here like fifteen minutes ago."

"Can't say I do. The last kid I handed out candy to was here an hour ago. I was just about to wash up for the night, but then you showed up at my door. But if you're lost, I can tell you how to get out of here."

"Yeah, sure, that'd be awesome." Simon didn't enjoy whatever mind games the woman played, but the sooner he found his way back home, the better.

"If you follow the road out of here, it should take you down to Line Street and then onto Barlow Street."

"Perfect, that's where I live. Thank you."

"Oh, and here you go." She held out a coffee crisp.

"Another one? That's so kind of you."

"Not sure what you mean? Handing out candy is what you do on Halloween."

Simon didn't bother replying to her comment and

snatched the coffee crisp.

"Have a nice night," she said, closing the door.

He proceeded down the road and left the cul-de-sac for the second time.

~

He walked down the sidewalk for ten minutes, exhausted. He looked for any sign that read Barlow Street but to no avail. Step after step, house after house, the road felt endless. His grip around his candy bags loosened, hands sore after carrying loads of snacks for hours.

God, I can't wait to get home.

He shut his eyes and lifted his head, taking long, deep breaths. The rain running down his face calmed his nerves. The rain rinsed away his sweat. The rain . . .

He opened his eyes and saw the rainfall, drenching his costume with a second wave. When had it returned? And how hadn't he noticed?

By now, the rain had likely seeped through his pillowcases, and he feared his candy might be watered down, spoiling his favorite aspect of the holiday. The hairs on his skin shot up from the cold, and a harsh swell of goosebumps crept. If he stayed out in the storm for much longer, he risked catching hypothermia.

Seriously, how much longer to the end of this street?

A few minutes later, he received his answer. He power-walked, eager to enter Barlow Street and for the night to conclude. But moving closer, he realized wasn't Barlow Street.

Once again, he arrived at the cul-de-sac, but one significant difference caught his eye this time: the giant, knocked-down oak tree. A group of residents huddled around beneath their umbrellas to inspect the scene. Simon hesitated, wanting nothing more than to return home and feast on his sweets. But curiosity overtook him, and he moved to the collapsed tree.

Simon approached the closest person, a greasy-looking man dressed in a bowler's shirt. Simon tapped on his shoulder and asked, "Excuse me, what happened?"

"Oh man, craziest thing I've ever seen. Lightning

knocked down the tree."

Lightning. "How long ago?"

"Fifteen, maybe twenty minutes?"

Simon tried to recall precisely when he saw the lightning from earlier, and fifteen to twenty minutes ago sounded about right. But it couldn't be the same lightning strike, for he saw the oak tree standing perfectly tall within Pike Street afterward.

Confused, he scratched his head and said, "This is crazy."

"It came out of nowhere. Poor guy."

"Poor guy?"

"I thought dissecting frogs in high school was gross, but what the ambulance stretchered away, I'll have nightmares for years. I could've sworn he pointed right at me before it happened too."

"I'm sorry, I don't understand what you—"

"No!"

The shout—which caught the crowd and Simon's attention—roared from a woman dressed in a bathrobe stained with red smears beneath the cotton. The same woman Simon had interacted with two times already.

Her mouth hung open in a wide *O,* and her eyes fixated directly on Simon. She lifted her finger and pointed toward him. "It's him. He's back. How can he possibly be back?!"

Everyone stared at Simon, looking as confused as him. He shrugged his shoulders and raised his hands, unsure how to respond. "Is this a joke or something?"

When he spoke, the woman jolted back to her house, shutting the door and switching off the lights.

"What's her problem?" Simon asked the bowler shirt man.

"She's just spooked is all. Between you and me, she's always been a bit of a nut."

"Tell me about it. I talked to her before, and she gave me directions that led me back here. Speaking of which, do you know a quick way to Barlow from here?"

"Take the path over there."

Simon glanced over where the man pointed and spotted the second alleyway — the one path he hadn't left from yet. "Ah, thank you. I've been walking around in circles for what feels like forever. Have a nice night."

For the third time, Simon left Pike Street.

~

He hurried down the path with haste, feet sore and palms clammy. He considered abandoning his candy bags to make his trip home easier. But after everything he endured, he deserved to treat himself. With all the wandering and exhaustion, he couldn't let his last Halloween be for nothing. And so, he tightened his grip around his pillowcases and walked onward.

Five minutes later, Simon spotted another mushroom-shaped tree past the fences, and a swift rush of panic overtook him. When he reached the end of the path, he saw a cul-de-sac and an oak tree towering over the neighborhood.

"What the hell? This has to be a different neighborhood."

"No. No, no, no." He ran over to the tree, inspecting how it possibly stood again — no marks, no crack in the base. "This can't be happening? There's just no way."

Only one logical explanation: It was all a prank, a Halloween skit the neighborhood played on trick-or-treaters. He didn't understand how they pulled off the on-and-off rain shower, the lightning storm, or taking down the tree and putting it back up, but he knew a Halloween trick when he saw one.

"Alright, this has gone on long enough." Simon reverted his attention to the house he had received candy from twice, lights off. He trotted up the stairs of House 27, jack-o'-lanterns unlit again, and knocked on the door with three heavy *thuds*.

The woman opened her door, dressed in a clean, white cotton bathrobe. She sighed, unamused, and said, "Listen, kid, this is getting old. Are you punking me, or are you pretending you're lost to get all my candy bars?"

Simon clenched his fists. "I'm not the one pulling a

prank, you are. All of you are, and I'm pretty tired of it. Acting like you know me then don't know me, giving me directions that lead me back here three times, the huddle around the tree with your neighbors — it's an impressive act, and I'll admit I fell for it. I'm not sure how you pulled that crap with the tree, but I'm not playing anymore. The jig is up."

A vein on the woman's forehead throbbed, and her skin turned a ruby red. From her side, she grabbed her silver bowl and tossed a dozen candy bars onto Simon's feet. "There, you win. I don't have anything left to give you. Now, please, for the love of God, stop coming to my house!"

Simon dropped his candy bags. "Cut the shit. You're going to tell me how to get back to Barlow right now, or you'll regret it."

The woman lifted her hands as if a gun was pointed at her. "Buddy, relax. I don't want any trouble."

"Oh, you've got it, that's for sure."

She attempted to shut the door, but Simon nudged his foot forward to prevent her from closing it.

"I'm not leaving until you tell me how to get out of here," he said.

The woman reached for something to her side, and a moment later, Simon saw she held onto an aluminum baseball bat. She swung for Simon's foot. He reeled backward, barely escaping. Foot out of the way, she slammed the door, and Simon heard her lock it. That didn't prevent him from knocking on the door loudly and swearing off the top of his lungs, demanding directions out of Pike Street.

Lights from the other houses flickered on, and people opened their doors to inspect the commotion. Amongst the residence, Simon spotted the greasy-looking, bowler shirt-wearing man on his porch.

"Well well, look who's joined the show." Simon stomped down the stairs and stood at the center of the street near the tree, watching all the eyes fixate on him. He pointed his finger at the bowler-shirt man. "Remember me? I'm the guy you've all been messing with for the past hour. My father was right. You're all nothing but a bunch of assholes who like to poke fun at other people."

As Simon ranted, the woman emerged from her house and darted to Simon, baseball bat in hand. "This is bordering on harassment, buddy. I'm warning you, I will call the cops if you don't leave."

"Go for it. Let them come. I can't wait to tell them about the crap you've pull —"

The strike of lightning struck the oak tree. From behind, he heard a loud crack, and when he turned around, he noticed the tree shift in direction. Too late to make a move, the tree fell where Simon stood.

Whatever remained of him splattered onto the woman's robe, thus concluding Simon's final Halloween.

Caleb J. Pecue is the owner and editor for Terrorcore Publishing, which specializes in bringing back the vintage feel of the 80s. His short story, The Turning of a Card, was published in the second volume of *Horrorscope,* edited by Harriet Everend. Another of his short stories, One More Time for Old Time's Sake, is published in *Gridiron Gates of Hell* for charity. By day, he works at a university in Illinois, advising students; by night, he works to find short stories to publish and writes his own that he hopes to publish.

Briana Morgan (she/her) is an active member of the Horror Writers Association. Her work has appeared in various anthologies, and she has self-published eight books, including the Godless 666 Award-winning *The Tricker Treater and Other Stories,* and *The Reyes Incident.* When not writing, you can find her traveling, watching horror movies, playing video games, or spending time with her husband and her cat.

Elisabeth Tuttle is a lifelong fan of all things horrific and fantastic with a soft spot for nameless terrors and escapism. When she's not haunting the streets of Boston, you can find her gaming, screaming at metal shows, or dreaming up fun new ways to desecrate human flesh. Her contribution to Doors of Darkness II is her first first published work, and she has plenty of ideas to continue making people feel just a little nauseous in the future.

Louie Sullivan definitely wants to trade, but only if you've got Reese's (especially the white chocolate ghosts!) He is a graduate of Fordham University and Saint Peter's University, reads about a hundred books a year, and goes to the movies as often as humanly possible. You can also find his work in the anthology Doors of Darkness by Terrorcore Publishing, and in issues 62 - 64 of The Sirens Call.

Nick Krenn's immediate impulse, when he first started writing stories, was to make them scary. He loved horror in all its forms of entertainment. Growing up in the '80s with plenty of horror on TV, he was enamored by slashers, haunted houses, demons, and critters. Then, in the '90s, he found inspiration from the young adult horror titans, R.L. Stine and Christopher Pike, and wanted to follow in their footsteps one day. Now, he's happily married with a young son and many indoor pets and finally starting to live his dream of giving you nightmares.

Ryan Peña is the owner of Bad Soul Records, A punk rock and roll musician, filmmaker, writer, radio show host, director, producer, exterminator, US Army veteran, and most importantly a husband and father.

Kevin Higgins lives in New Jersey, where he enjoys hanging out with his wife and daughter, listening to punk rock and watching reruns of King of Queens. A video producer by trade, Kevin picked up writing in his 30s, focusing on horror and thriller short fiction. His story Last Burn of the Day was recently published by Undertaker Books. His favorite author is Richard Chizmar.

David E. Kruegger writes Horror fiction about the Upper Midwest. He lives in Minneapolis with his wife adn their collection of RPGs and cookbooks. You can see his house when you land at the airport, if you know where to look. Follow him on Substack to see what he's up to and to read exclusive essays and short fiction.

Christopher Robertson writes cinematic pulp fiction that's often described as both wholesome and gruesome, sometimes in the same sentence. He won both the Gold award for Best Novel and Silver for Best Audiobook at the 2023 Godless 666 Awards.

Alex Crandall is a parasitic brain slug from the planet Gorpulon-5, currently inhabiting a civil engineer in Indianapolis. Alex enjoys typical human activities, such as consuming sustenance for survival and discussing recent meteorological phenomena. He would be very appreciative if you could point him in the direction of your leader.

An Oregonian raised in Southern California, **Lennox Rex** has always been enamored with storytelling and the thrill of good horror. His work appears in various magazines, HorrorScope Volume 3, Doors of Darkness, and Trans Rites. To him, life is best enjoyed with music, body mods, and plenty of coffee and sweets. He lives with his husband, their three children, and nowhere near enough books.

Brady Tiel hails from small town Canada where he writes feverishly about the odd things humans might achieve if they push discovery, innovation, and their ego one step too far. Tiel writes science fiction and horror. Tiel has looked to other greats such as Michael Crichton and Alastair Reynolds for inspiration in his writing. The weirder the better!

Vanessa Leonardo is a horror writer from Staten Island, New York with an MFA in Creative Writing from the New School. She currently lives with her wife in New Jersey. The writers that have most influenced her were those she read as a young teen such as R.L. Stine, Stephen King, and V.C. Andrews. She loves anything spooky, scary or paranormal.

Matt Hickey is a writer and musician living in Texas with his wife Jes and their dog Hoagie. He's been self-publishing comics, dream diaries, and music as long as he can remember. Besides writing he spends his days as a music specialist working with children in underserved communities in Houston.

Tucker Joneson is a writer, artist, and filmmaker. He published the illustrated children's book, The Soldier Bear. He has also created several animated short films including, Hide & Shriek, Hero, and Pinhead, which have been selected and awarded in film festivals. He is currently working on publishing his own anthology books in the future. He currently lives outside of Knoxville, Tennessee.

Kimberly Pinzon escaped from New York to the beautiful and terrifying world of Appalachia with her partner and two dogs. When not struggling to write, she likes to get lost in the woods (literally, not figuratively, it's embarassing at this point), watches RuPaul's Drag Race, and tries not to kill all of the plants in the garden. Kim's first book, Final Girl Redux, is a relaxed exploration of the role of the Final Girl throughout the history of the horror movie. She's also written a YA science-fiction novel involving alternate worlds, Through the Mirror, and her collection of horror short stories, Creeping Shadows.

John FreelyKirk is a writer, actor and filmmaker from Albuquerque, New Mexico. Growing up reading the Goosebumps series by R.L. Stine, led to a complete fascination with the horror genre. Over the past few years, he has used his love for the genre to write and direct several award winning short films including Happy Anniversary, It Lurks in the Shadows and The Starlight Motel. Although new to creative writing, he deeply enjoys the medium and looks foward to writing more in the near future.

Nadine Stewart is an author, poet, and media creator. Her short fiction has been published in several anthologies including Terrorcore's Doors of Darkness v.1, Voices From the Mausoleum's That Old House the Bathroom Anthology, Autumn Tales II from Anatolian Press, Readings from Cursed Room 301 from Mad Axe Media and the charity anthology Gridiron Gates of

Hell. Just to name a few. She has also curated Curbside Curses: The Yardsale Anthology. Nadine has always been an avid reader with a wild imagination. Born into a creative family of artists, from a young age she was always "performing" for family and friends and creating poetry only ever seen by those closest to her. She was born and raised in beautiful British Columbia, Canada, and she now resides in Washington State. You can follow her on Instagram @nadine.stewart.author @house_of_the_macabre @stewartsocialcreations

Jason A. Jones is an Industrial Painter by trade and part time writer. He has several publications in various anthologies and his full length debut novella, Starving Alice will be published sometime in 2024. He lives in Indiana with his wife and 2 cats.

Don Tucker is a high school teacher from Massachusetts whose work has previously been featured in The Daily Horrors, the newest issue published by Two-Headed Press. His father, much to the dismay of his mother, let him watch The Shining when he was eight years old. After not sleeping for weeks, he has been an avid fan of anything horror ever since. He is currently working on a novel and a short story collection.

Paul Lonardo is a freelance writer and author with numerous titles of both fiction and nonfiction books. He has placed short stories and nonfiction articles in various genre magazines and ezines. He is a contributing writer for Tales from the Moonlit Path and an active HWA member.

Austin Hinderliter is a graphic designer by trade, holding a BFA and MFA in Graphic Design. His interest in 80s horror paperbacks, especially those with a skeleton on the cover, led to a vastly growing collection of vintage books. His stories take inspiration from past eras, so don't expect a cell phone in sight. His story, *The Night Hearse,* is published by Undertaker Books in the first volume of *Stories to Take to Your Grave.*

Reece G. Donnell has been a journalist of three years for Scream Magazine. Offering There's Something Wrong With Barbara to Doors of Darkness, it is his hope that The Candy Snatchers will show a sense of campery and humor, expanding his scope as an author.

Billie Karras has previously been featured in *Fish Gather to Listen, Cult Horrotica* magazine, and *Doors of Darkness.* He lives in Phoenix, Arizona.

Brad Acevedo writes from the gator-infested shores of Gulf Coast Florida. He also performs creative work for a 501C3 non-profit haunted attraction, co-writing stories on the attraction's lore with his wife. When not writing, he can be found studying local legends, documenting travelogues of the area and curating his own absurd collection of pop culture figurines. He has been previously featured in works from Quill and Crow Publishing, Jazz House Publishing and Voices From the Mausoleum as well as the E-Zine, The Crow's Quill.

Todd Condit loves all things horror, from movies and books, to games and podcasts. When hes not messing around with horror, he's hanging out with his wife and kids or standing at the helm of a sizzling BBQ grill.

Jane Nightshade, a native Californian, is a former corporate communications specialist turned horror writer. Her fiction has appeared in numerous anthologies and magazines, and has been dramatized by NoSleep Podcast and Octoberpod. She is the author or editor of four published story collections: The Drowning Game, independently published in digital form on Amazon; A Scream Full of Ghosts, from Dark Ink Publishing; Jane Nightshade's Serial Encounters from HellBound Books; and the upcoming Ghosts Never Leave from Unveiling Nightmares Publishing. Her non-fiction writing has been published by several major horror sites.

Scott McGregor is a Canadian writer based in Calgary. He graduated from Mount Royal University with degrees in English (Hons) and Sociology with a background in Creative Writing. He is the author of over 100 short stories. His fiction has appeared in various anthologies by Hellbound Books, Oddity Prodigy Productions, Crystal Lake Publishing, Eerie River Publishing, DBND Publishing, Bag of Bones Press, and many others. In 2022, he released his debut novella "Mr. Hangman" under Black Hare Press, which is a homage to detective thrillers. Scott is also the Chief Editor for January Embers Press and curated the "Writer's Retreat: Tales of Writing and Madness" anthology alongside Harriett Everend. Caffeine, board games, and movies are some of his several addictions. Sarcastically appealing and unapologetic, Scott is either drinking tea or sassing the ones he deems friends in the off time he isn't living and breathing stories.

www.ingramcontent.com/pod-product-compliance
Lightning Source LLC
Chambersburg PA
CBHW032117310726

48972CB00001B/252